M000004433

MARY E. CALVERT

DOING WHAT IS RIGHT
NEVER FELT SO WRONG

THE SECRET OF THE HOLD

THE SOULTREKKER CHRONICLES
BOOK TWO

Cover and Interior book design by One of a Kind Covers

THE SECRET OF THE HOLD
Copyright © 2019 Mary Calvert

License Notes
This book is licensed for your personal enjoyment only. This book may not be re-sold or given away to other people. If you would like to share this book with another person, please purchase an additional copy for each recipient. If you're reading this book and did not purchase it, or it was not purchased for your use only, then please purchase your own copy. Thank you for respecting the hard work of this author.

Published by Veritana Press

VERITANA PRESS

ISBN 13: 978-1793435323

Contents

DEDICATION

For Rob.
To the ends of the earth I would go to be with
you.

ACKNOWLEDGMENTS

Once again, I am forever grateful to Marjorie Vawter of The Writer's Tool Editing and Azalea Dabill of Dynamos Press for pushing my writing to a higher level, for helping me let go of my favorite overused words and prompting me to find better, and for your overall support and encouragement. This trilogy would not be a reality without you both.

To my family, thank you for your love and support. I wouldn't want to experience this adventure with anyone but you by my side.

To all my friends and fans who have continuously asked me when my second book would be out, I'm happy your wait is over. Your support means more than words can express.

And once again, I am grateful to a creative God who gave me the vision of a magical world that could be anything I wanted it to be and for giving me the words to bring it to life so others could step inside it, too.

Thanks to author Jeff LaFerney for taking time from his busy schedule to read the first two books of *The Soultrekker Chronicles*. Everything happens in God's good timing, and your review was worth the wait.

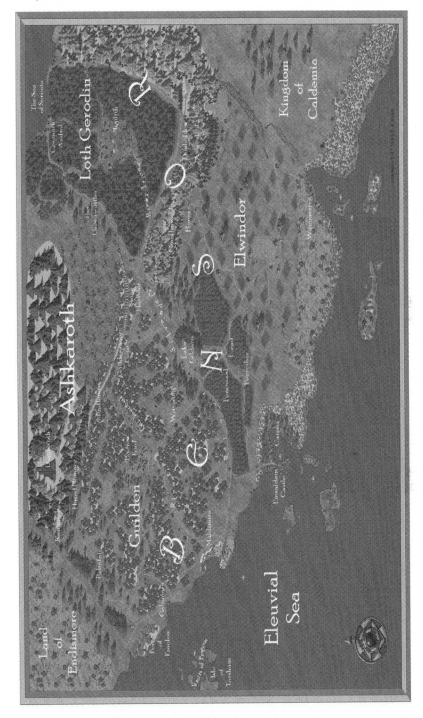

THE SECRET OF THE HOLD

THE SOULTREKKER CHRONICLES ~ BOOK TWO

Mary E. Calvert

VERITANA PRESS

"From the shadow of Arnuin's Hold
Where river bends and reeds shine gold,
Elwei's heir shall wake the light
Of Veritana's stone so bright."

CHAPTER 1

I was uncertain how much time had passed since I stepped into Dr. Susan's office. Under a hypnotic fog, I was only vaguely aware of anything happening outside my own body. The only reality were the images in my mind—memories of my *other* life—memories that retraced two and a half Bensorian years I lived in another world during a brief moment of time in this one. As for what was going through my therapist's mind, I could only imagine it wasn't every day she came across a client who "disappeared" for a night to go live another life in another body.

From a place far, far away, I heard her clear her throat. "Er, Margaret...that is, *Arwyn*, I want to make certain I understand you correctly," she began. "You suddenly appeared, having taken possession of a different body, in this land called Bensor having little recollection of the life you left behind..."

"When I first came to Bensor, recalling memories of that life was like trying to peer through a keyhole from ten feet away. Nearly three years have passed and that opening is now the size of a rabbit hole, and through it I see fleeting images of huge steel birds flying through the air without flapping their wings, boxes magically producing pictures that move, and people...familiar faces I knew once, long ago. And that hole—it grows slightly larger with every passing day."

"Er, yes, but now you have managed to make a new life for yourself with the help of your friends Fronda...Fronda..."

"Frondamein," I whispered to my therapist. The sound of her voice strangely intruded from time to time upon the visions in my head.

"And Loralon and the others," Dr. Susan continued. "And now you have met the elf, Galamir, whom you believe has led you to your purpose, your reason for having been brought to Bensor in the first place, which is to help bring about the downfall of this…er…Draigon."

My stomach tightened at the sound of his name. "It is because of him I have gone into hiding," I said, my mind recalling the small cottage of my friends—Fendred, Helice, and Rumalia—where I lived in secret for several weeks. Having had the audacity to stand up to Draigon and then to help one of his prisoners escape from the dungeons of Dungard (although I was not entirely certain he knew of *that* offense yet), no doubt put a target on my back. Through my actions, I managed to make an enemy of the most powerful man in the land—one who hinted he planned to bring about my ruination. But I could not stay in hiding forever.

"I am restless, wanting ever so much to return home, having little more to busy myself than the few books of Eliendor's I was able to bring with me. I try to make myself useful, but three women about such a small cottage is a bit much, and I do worry I am intruding." I sighed.

"Still, they are kind and quite accommodating. After all, was it not I who was instrumental in returning their long-lost daughter to them only a short while ago? Nevertheless, I am relieved at the coming of the first snow, for I know it will not be long before Kiril comes to take me home…ah, and here he is!" My mind skipped along, picturing my young friend riding down the lane atop his horse, appearing as though he had shed a few more pounds since I last saw him. "Tearfully I tell Fendred, Helice, and Rumalia farewell, with promises to visit them in the spring."

"But is it really safe for you to return to Baeren Ford?" asked Dr. Susan.

"Kiril tells me there have been fewer sightings of Draigon's soldiers with the rumor of my sudden disappearance, and Loralon has done her part to corroborate that rumor. Furthermore, with winter approaching there will be little travel on the road between Mindlemir and Maldimire for the next two months."

"But your neighbors...they were upset with you before you left."

"Yes, though I have been home but a day, I look outside the cottage window and see a line of people seeking my healing services, and it gives me a degree of satisfaction to think that during my absence they perhaps came to miss me." A triumphant smile spread upon my face. "I am glad to find the old hermit, Eliendor, well...and with the help of Kiril, the three fugitive dwarves have stashed enough supplies to get them through the winter until the day comes when I can see them safely home to their mountains. Though, 'twill be a dangerous journey to be sure..."

"And?" Dr. Susan urged.

But I could not speak. My mind recalled that distant place—the scent of lavender sachet and the crackling wood in the fireplace, the delighted squeals of little Amerigo as he played on the rug before the fire, and the way the rays from the noonday sun broke into a thousand prisms as they latched onto the snow on the eaves outside—all the small things I had come to love.

"The spring thaw comes early this year, bringing an end to what has been a blessedly mild winter, and the residents of Baeren Ford celebrate the Blizzard Feast with as much merriment as years past. Yet, oh, for Galamir to return! How I long for a new adventure, to see the fabled elven city of Isgilith! Why, I am practically giddy with anticipation, dancing about the cottage when I spy the first hint of daffodils poking up from the ground!"

***

As soon as I returned home from my self-imposed banishment, I began to prepare for the trip I would be taking in the spring. Having spent a good part of early winter helping Feyla and her three children battle a string of influenza and stomach ailments, I was able to barter with the dyer's wife for several yards of her finest fabric, the same fabric she purchased on our trip to Maldimire the previous autumn. The rest I paid for with a portion of the remaining gold coins I stashed away in the thatched ceiling above my bed.

After all, as Loralon pointed out, clothing suitable for village life would not be acceptable for my visit with the "genteel elven folk." She then set out to create two long, flowing gowns in shades of lavender and pale green for me to wear in their company.

"If these don't make ye look like an elven princess, then nothin' will," Loralon said from time to time, admiring her own skill.

And she was right. I seriously doubted any elven seamstress could have created more exquisite garments.

In the meantime, Kiril, who was employed at the tavern and knew practically everyone in the village, set to work paying the town undertaker to procure two longer-than-average coffins from the town carpenter and slipped him an extra silver piece to assure he kept quiet concerning the unusual request. He was also able to find an old broken-down cart rotting away in a farmyard north of the village. It took little convincing for the owner to let Kiril tote it away to his own stable, where he spent much of the winter repairing it in his spare time.

Then, late one evening in early spring, Kiril took the refurbished cart with the two coffins on board by moonlight to the barn of his uncle Leoric, a gruff old man who was obliging enough when it came to family but typically kept his affairs to himself. The items were stored there, along with the strongest but smallest horse he was able to buy with the few coins I gave him for the purpose.

Smuggling three dwarves to the Andain Mountains was proving to be an expensive proposition. Funding these various ventures significantly diminished my stash of gold, the original fortune I mysteriously found in my possession when I first arrived in Bensor. Yet I was determined to see my three fugitive dwarf friends back to their home. As soon as the weather allowed, I made my way to their cave to find them only a few pounds lighter, though certainly with more meat on their bones than when I first found them starving in the woods months before.

There were still two weeks remaining in the month of Second Winter when the tulips and daffodils began to emerge from the earth. Already the warmer temperature prompted the villagers to shed their heavy woolen cloaks and venture outside wearing only their long-sleeved tunics and gowns. Such an early spring was a welcome relief to the normally drab last days of winter, and the whole village came back to life as the central square resumed its daily business with as much fervor as ever.

Several more weeks passed as I waited patiently for Galamir to return. The thought of taking to the road to visit his city deep in the mysterious forest of Loth Gerodin when the air was alive with the freshness of spring made me eager to depart. Not to mention the fact that I noticed, much to my dismay, the increased presence of Draigon's lieutenants in the village. They came and went quietly, but always they tended to linger on the edge of the woods just above Frondamein's cottage. I wondered if they were still looking for me, trying to determine if I had indeed moved on. The thought of being spied upon was quite disconcerting, not to mention the ever-present fear someone could show up at any time and arrest me for the dwarf Froilin's escape from Dungard and for harboring him and his two dwarf pals in a nearby cave. Certainly a long holiday away from the village would lead them to believe I had left for good.

It became more obvious to me that there existed a tension to living beneath the ancient bastion of Arnuin's Hold standing sentinel above the village, an ever-present reminder of the unfulfilled prophecy concerning Bensor's true ruler who would emerge from its shadow. 'The Hold,' as the villagers called it, had not only put the entire village, especially the young men who came of age, under the watchful eye of Draigon, but it also drew attention to the presence of a supposed elf—me.

It was quite clear Draigon hated me. Although my neighbors did not necessarily share his low opinion of elves, there were some who had always been suspicious of me, wondering why I would recklessly choose to live in the mortal village and not with my own "kind."

The truth was, I had little choice in the matter. It was only when Galamir showed up that I suddenly found my choices expanding. He promised to come for me in the spring and take me to visit his elven home. The possibility it could help illuminate my true nature was both exciting and a little terrifying.

And then one day Galamir returned. Loralon, Amerigo, and I were walking home from the market when we looked up the road and noticed a small group of people staring curiously in the direction of the cottage. It was not long before we could see the cause of the commotion, for there on the front lawn, sitting on the edge of the well, was the elf, playing his flute as if oblivious to the curious onlookers.

Galamir looked up as we approached and gave a low bow. "Greetings, Arwyn, Miss Loralon, how happy I am to find you well."

"And it is indeed good to see you!" I exclaimed as I clasped his hand in the typical elvish manner.

Loralon smiled shyly, glancing smugly at the growing audience outside her cottage. "Ye must be tired to the bone. Come in and rest yerself while we prepare th' evenin' meal."

"Dear Loralon, 'twould take much more than a day in the saddle to tire this elf, though I well remember your fine cooking and would be glad to dine with you again," Galamir said in a slightly raised tone of voice, glancing sidelong at the crowd with a shrewd smile upon his face.

Just then little Amerigo emerged from behind his mother's skirts and walked shyly up to the tall elf.

"Ah, Amerigo, I wondered where you were hiding," Galamir said, as he picked up the little boy and tossed him into the air. Amerigo laughed gleefully as Galamir twirled him around, his little feet kicking wildly with delight.

"I trust your journey was without incident," I said, as we all stepped into the cottage.

"Yes, my dear Arwyn. It was as if there is no shadow hovering over the land. Although I did encounter a fair share of Gargalocs and men whose intent is rather questionable, they all seemed content to let me be. I passed through the land with little more than a few questions concerning the nature of my business. It bodes well for our own journey. That is, if you still intend to return with me."

I nodded eagerly. "I've been anticipating your return and will be ready to leave within the week, once I have seen to my patients a final time."

"But you must know our journey may not be without peril. And you must be prepared to spend several nights sleeping under the stars, or worse, if the weather does not hold."

"I will be ready," I promised.

"Good," Galamir smiled. "My mother and father are looking forward to having you as a guest in our home, and the high elf Valdir Velconium is particularly interested in making your acquaintance."

"Valdir Velconium?" I had heard the name before, and I knew he was an elf of utmost importance in Loth Gerodin.

"Yes, he served for ages on the Endaran Council until the days right before Draigon took control. When it was clear the tide was turning, he and his wife and two sons fled Maldimire and returned to Loth Gerodin."

"Sounds as though ye'll be treated like a queen," Loralon commented quietly, her eyes downcast.

"Aye, that she will. We've not had the pleasure of such an honored guest in Isgilith for quite some time."

I could not help but laugh. Things must be very slow

indeed in the elven city for my arrival to be so anticipated. "You do flatter me, Galamir. But it is I who should feel honored."

"Please, sit and rest yerself," Loralon interrupted. "Arwyn and I'll see to dinner."

Galamir required little persuasion to place himself onto the settee where he kept the curious Amerigo entertained until the food was on the table a while later. As we ate, he talked about all manner of subjects from the unusually mild winter to the upcoming Faerenfel. Loralon and I were no less amazed than when he first made our acquaintance. Hardly any time seemed to have passed since then, and yet I felt as though I had known the fair elf for ages.

For the next several days I made rounds about the village to see my patients one final time before our departure. There were the usual spring sniffles and sore throats that needed tending, but otherwise there was nothing more serious than a case of eczema and one young woman named Megelta who was still at least two months away from giving birth. Should her time come earlier than expected, the midwife Darya was on hand to assist.

On the day before our departure, I paid one last visit to the dwarves in their cave, leaving instructions to meet at Eliendor's cottage two hours before sunrise. They packed what few belongings they could take with them and nervously paced about their cave, anxious to get a start on what was to be a risky venture at best.

After stopping to tell Eliendor goodbye—and to receive his inevitable warning to be especially wary of all unsavory characters on the road—it seemed I had tied up all loose ends. I returned home to a little last-minute packing of my own, my heart beating rapidly as I anticipated the adventure ahead.

When I led Avencloe into the stable, I discovered Frondamein's steed, Haseloth, standing there. With all the excitement building up to the trip, I forgot it was time for Frondamein's leave. Nevertheless, I was glad for his return as it would make the house a little less lonely for Loralon following my departure and would give the couple long overdue time to themselves.

"Rest well tonight, for tomorrow we begin our journey," I said to Avencloe as I removed the saddle from his back.

I was about to enter the cottage through the stable door when I heard Loralon crying on the other side.

"Don't fret yerself, me dear," I could hear Frondamein say compassionately. "Ye knew this day would come."

"Aye, but I've grown quite fond of Arwyn. 'Ow lonely 'twill be now, with not another grown-up about." Loralon cried. "'Tis bad enough for ye to be gone all the while, but at least I had 'er company. There's not been a dull moment since she arrived."

"Aye, but ye know ye canna keep a wild bird in the cage. 'Twouldn't be fair," Frondamein said gently. "Miss Arwyn needs to be with 'er own kind, to make a life for 'erself, e'en to be married. Ye know there's no man 'ere in Baeren Ford what would court 'er. 'Er best bet to find a proper 'usband is with th' elves."

"I suppose I've not thought of Arwyn as the marryin' type, so different she is," Loralon admitted. "Though there's a warm-blooded woman in there I'll wager, one what yearns for a man. I know ye to be right, dear Frondamein, but do ye really think she'll find a husband among th' elves? I still say she's as 'uman as you and I."

There was a pause as I strained to hear Frondamein's response. "Indeed I hope so," he said at last. "Say, what o' this Galamir?"

"Tch, no!" Loralon cried.

"And why not?"

"'Tis a woman's intuition, me dear. Nay, I kin see it in 'is eyes. Though fond of 'er 'e is, 'e doesn't fancy 'er the way a man does when he's in love."

"A pity. Arwyn needs a good one what 'as the passion to match 'er own."

With tears streaming down my cheeks, I backed away from the stable door. My eavesdropping suddenly brought to light feelings that lately became more difficult to suppress. Until then, I had been fairly successful establishing a happy life for myself in Baeren Ford. However, deep in my heart I knew all along I did not really belong in the mortal village— yet I was not altogether certain I would be more at home among the elves or that I was really an elf at all. The time was soon coming when I must choose one or the other, for I could not continue to live indefinitely with Loralon, no matter how much like family she had come to be.

As for the issue of marriage—that touched even deeper yearnings within me, long since buried. There had been times, in my more lonely moments, when I secretly longed to be wrapped up in the arms of a man. But I quickly dismissed them, knowing they would not soon be fulfilled, if ever.

I took a deep breath, wiped my eyes, and cleared my throat to announce my presence. In a moment, I entered the cottage with a smile upon my face. "Frondamein, how good it is to see you!"

Frondamein and Loralon's heads jerked toward the door as I entered. "And so glad I am to be home," he said, smiling weakly. "Loralon tells me ye're to be off come the morn'."

"That I am," I replied cheerfully. "But only on holiday. I shall return well before the summer."

"'Tis good ye'll be back by summer," Frondamein said with an almost relieved sound to his voice. "And this Galamir fella, he'll keep ye protected upon the road? Ye know 'tis not safe to travel these days, 'specially for a woman, and 'specially under the saircumstances ye've placed yerself. I dunna want to hear ye've been retairned to Dungard now, or e'en wairse for that matter."

I laughed. "I know I'll be in good hands…and I promise

to be wary."

"Verra well. Seems Loralon's made ye a fine farewell meal, and for me 'tis a fine 'omecomin' dinner. I say we sit down and enjoy ourselves."

The evening meal was pleasant enough, with Loralon and I recounting the events of the winter, as Frondamein's last visit home came soon after I returned from Fendred and Helice's and before the deep snows set in.

However, it seemed to me Frondamein had more on his mind than the village gossip, as if he knew of something brewing in the land that could change our destinies forever. He hinted at it throughout the evening meal—his post at the Guildenmoor Gate could end shortly and he hoped someday soon to return to farming. Could it be Frondamein knew something about the mysterious Alliance Galamir spoke of?

Galamir had offered me the possibility of not only a grand holiday, but a chance to fulfill a greater purpose in Bensor, a chance to become part of this Alliance, an underground movement of elves and men set to rebel against Bensor's usurping, tyrannical leader, Draigon, at some undisclosed time later that year. If all went well, the rebellion would oust Draigon and his minions, ushering in a new age in Bensor.

But I also knew freedom for Bensor would not come without bloodshed, and though I did not relish the idea of combat, my bow and arrows were poised to join the fight.

Was Frondamein aware of what was brewing? Or that I, of all people, had been asked to play a part?

Of one thing I was certain—no matter what role I would play, I had been brought to Bensor to help bring about the downfall of Draigon and to help heal that broken land. Meeting Galamir simply revealed a conviction that had burned deep in my heart for a very long time.

I was impatient to begin.

CHAPTER 2

"Now that I stand at the brink of adventure, I wonder if it would be more sensible to simply return to my bed and the warmth and security of the little cottage that has become my home."

"I think it's only natural to have some misgiving when you embark on something new," Dr. Susan replied.

"'Tis dangerous to step outside one's front door and to see the world beyond, and I somehow feel I shall never be the same for it."

The bell tower in the village square chimed the fourth hour. With heart pounding, I bounded out of bed and slipped into my green riding gown and leggings. My bag was packed full of clothing, oat-and-honey wafers, two loaves of bread, a dozen apples, and several of my best all-around herbal medicines, as well as a gift of a lavendar sachet for Galamir's mother. Just as I was finishing the last of my hasty breakfast of toast and milk, I heard a horse approach out front. I peered out over the front lawn to see Galamir dismounting from his horse, his frame tall against the pale eastern sky.

Sleepily, Frondamein, Loralon, and even Amerigo accompanied me outside in their nightclothes to wish me a safe journey.

"Greetings one and all, especially to Frondamein, whom I have not yet had the pleasure of meeting," Galamir said, with a sweeping bow.

"Er, pleased to make yer acquaintance," Frondamein said, returning the bow. Had the situation been different, no doubt he would have been more in awe of the elf. However, on that particular morning Frondamein reminded me of a father sizing up the young man who had come to court his daughter. "Ye've a long road ahead, 'ave ye not?"

"Indeed we have. 'Tis a long way to Loth Gerodin from

here."

"And ye'll take good care of our Arwyn, will ye not?"

Galamir smiled chivalrously. "I give you my word. She will be in good hands, and she will return safely home."

"And what of the dwarves?" I whispered anxiously.

"Kiril arrived early this morning to escort them in darkness to his uncle's barn, where they await our arrival. From there, we shall take the deerpath to the East Road for, as rumor has it, the road south of Baeren Ford is being watched," Galamir replied.

"Dear Kiril, he has risked much to aid our cause," I commented.

"Aye, and I do think he rather wishes he was coming along as well."

"I do hope someday he shall have that chance."

I looked at Loralon and saw tears streaming down her face in the light coming from inside the window. "Oh, Arwyn, ye will be retairnin' 'ome to us, will ye not? It's just...well, ye've become as a sister to me and I shall miss ye so."

I smiled gently as tears of my own threatened to flood my cheeks. "Loralon, you, Frondamein, and Amerigo are my family, the only family I have ever known here, and I could hardly bear to leave you forever." I embraced my friend. "I cannot foresee what the future may bring, but you must trust I do not mean to ever simply abandon you after all you've done for me."

Through her tears, Loralon managed to smile. "Then 'ave yerself a grand time. I should like to hear all about th' elven city and yer adventures when ye retairn."

"Aye, Miss Arwyn, and may the road be kind to ye as well," Frondamein added.

I could no longer hold back my own tears. A flood streamed down my face as I embraced Frondamein and Loralon once more. I also picked up the yawning Amerigo and held him quietly for a moment. "I shall miss you, little one," I whispered into his ear.

Sleepily the child stuck his thumb in his mouth. I kissed his cheek and then gently placed him into his mother's arms. I turned toward the waiting Avencloe, saddled and laden with my belongings. After I mounted, Galamir handed me my bow and quiver full of arrows, and I strapped them over my shoulder.

As the first fingers of light came reaching over the eastern sky, I said the last of my farewells before turning toward the road. With a pang of regret, I urged Avencloe onward, all at once uncertain if I should simply return to the familiarity of the cottage and the warmth of my own bed, not sure if a more adventurous life was really what I wanted after all. My cheeks still moist, I resisted the urge to turn back and kept my eyes glued to the road ahead.

In silence, Galamir and I turned onto the lane leading around the south end of the lower lake. We rode over the two bridges connecting the eastern shore with the western, glad it was still too early for the bridgekeeper who lived on the small island in the middle of the lake to be out. We at last stole into the woods to the south on a narrow road that eventually led past the cottage of Kiril's Uncle Leoric. There we found the old huntsman sitting on a chair outside his front door, checking the tension in a crossbow. He looked up as we approached and grunted with a nod in the direction of his barn.

Galamir and I dismounted and opened the barn door, where we found Kiril had already seen to preparing the little horse Crumpkin and cart for our journey. Hutto, Goodren, and Froilin were already sitting in the elf-sized coffins that were to conceal them throughout our journey. Wide-eyed, their chests heaved with relief when they saw us standing there.

"Let us depart in haste," Galamir urged. "I smell rain in the air and do not fancy getting stuck in a bog in the middle of the woods, though you'd best lay low until we are well away from any prying eyes."

Kiril accompanied us as we took off into the forest on the deerpath leading past Leoric's cottage, and although the path was narrow and slightly winding, it was at least flat and clear of debris other than a tree root here and there. Only once did Galamir and Kiril have to get behind and push when we came upon a tight place between a tree and a stump, but sturdy little Crumpkin pulled with all his heart to see his load safely around all obstacles.

The going was slow, but we eventually made it to the bog that signaled our approach to the East Road. Yet between us and the road was a low muddy spot that sloped into a stagnant pool. The horses themselves had no trouble traversing the soft ground, but the cart got stuck—so stuck the dwarves were forced to climb out and help Kiril and Galamir push from behind. The whole process took precious time, and I thought I could hear the sky rumbling in the distance.

Once we came to dry ground again, it seemed a good place to bid Kiril farewell.

"I could see ye as far as Fendred's," Kiril said, with unexpected eagerness.

"Master Kiril, I am forever grateful for the aid you have given us, though I think we had best see ourselves forward for the sake of our ruse."

"Aye, I suppose I'd not pass for an elf." Kiril nodded, though in his eyes I saw a hint of disappointment.

"Master Kiril," Hutto said, "we'll ne'er forget ye and what ye've done to help us."

"'Twas an honor, sirs," Kiril said, bending over to give each dwarf an emotional bear hug. Even Goodren seemed affected by the touching display, and I thought I heard him sniff when Kiril embraced him. "Ye'll keep an eye on Miss Arwyn, ye will?"

"Aye, that we'll do," Froilin replied.

Kiril then looked me in the eye. "Ye *will* keep yerself out o' trouble, won't ye, Miss Arwyn?"

"I'll do my best," I promised with a smile.

"Have no fear," Galamir said, as he clasped Kiril's hand to his chest. "On my honor, if it is within my power, no harm shall come to her."

With the dwarves safely locked away in the coffins, we cautiously peered up and down the East Road, yet there was no one to be seen in either direction. As we made our way onto the main thoroughfare, I turned and peered back into the woods where Kiril remained, gazing after us before we disappeared around the bend. As we did I could feel my heart ache at the thought of leaving my friends in Baeren Ford forever, no matter how glorious the elven city may turn out to be. It was a comfort to think our "farewell" need not be permanent.

For a while we rode in silence, still surveying the road for signs of other travelers. Crumpkin was tethered to Galamir's horse, Calyxa, and so our going was slowed significantly. Galamir sat rigid in his saddle, his head cocked intently to the road ahead even as he glanced behind from time to time.

Once we travelled a little over a mile and left the last cottage well behind, Galamir gave a sharp whistle and the lids to the coffins opened, revealing the three dwarves inside. Fortunately, the sides of the cart were high enough to conceal their presence as long as they remained seated.

"I thought ye'd ne'er give the signal," Goodren complained. "We've gone but a short distance and already I wish to be rid of our cramped travelin' arrangements, what with Froilin kickin' me in the head every few minutes."

"If ye'd scoot yerself down a bit, then there'd be no need for me to kick ye," Froilin protested.

"The airhole is right at yer head. If I'd scoot down further, I'm likely to suffocate."

"Then suffocate and be done with it! We'd not have to hear yer mindless chatter all the way home."

"Pipe down!" Hutto warned. "We're barely out of earshot from the village."

"Easy for ye to say. Ye have to share yer coffin with our belongin's, not with an impudent and, might I add, smelly ol' dwarf," Goodren said.

"Quiet down all three of you! If I have to listen to your arguing all the way to the Andains, then Arwyn and I will have to let you find your own way," Galamir said sternly. Then he turned to face me, and I saw he wore a sly smile.

"And leave us he would, considerin' he's an elf and we're but a handful o' lowly dwarves."

"Shh, Goodren!" Hutto said. "Now, I'm sure Mr. Galamir wouldn't abandon us, but I can't say as I would blame him if we keep carryin' on as we are."

"Verra well," Goodren conceded, "but I do wish Mr. Kiril had made us larger breathin' holes."

"Ye're so full o' hot air as it is, why should it matter?" said Froilin.

Goodren's face turned red, and he was about to protest when Galamir suddenly motioned for them to be quiet. I could see him stiffen in his saddle as his eyes fixed upon the road ahead. I had heard it, too—the sound of approaching horses. Quickly the two coffin lids shut and the dwarves grew silent.

As the approaching riders came into view, we could tell by the pair of hulking bodies at least two were not human. They were Gargalocs, and the third wore the gray uniform of those in Draigon's service. There was no place to hide; we had already been spotted. With the cumbersome cart having to be pulled behind, thought of flight into the woods was pointless. I glanced over to see Galamir's hand twitching at the ready should the need arise to draw his sword. My own weapon, my bow and arrows, I had learned to nock in an instant, but I truly hoped to avoid a conflict.

As the three approached they stared coldly at the two of us. One of the Gargalocs spoke rough, incomprehensible words. The other Gargaloc grunted in response, while the man dressed in gray steered his horse between Galamir and me. Such a gesture was rude at the very least but also quite threatening. He maneuvered close enough to the cart to peer inside.

I held my breath as I looked back and watched him glancing cautiously at the two coffins lying there. He spoke to the Gargalocs in their harsh language and, with one last sinister glance toward Galamir and me, muttered something under his breath before continuing on down the road.

When the three were out of sight, Galamir and I breathed a sigh of relief. Galamir gave the "all clear" whistle, and the dwarves cautiously emerged from their hiding places.

"Who were they?" Hutto demanded.

"Whoever 'twas, they're in desperate need of a good bath," Froilin commented. "I could smell 'em e'en from inside me coffin."

"They were Gargalocs," Galamir said solemnly, "which is why the three of you must listen more and talk less." The three dwarves remained silent for several moments, as if they were three children who had been scolded. "This certainly does not bode well for our journey. I'll be much relieved when we arrive at our first destination for the night."

"Aye, I suppose we should lay low for a while," Froilin said as the blood drained from his cheeks.

By midmorning the first droplets of rain fell from above, sporadically for a while, then with greater frequency, until the sky at last let loose with a deluge. Galamir and I pulled our cloaks around us as best we could to protect ourselves from the onslaught of the pelting rain. The road was thick with mud, and we could see but a short distance ahead through the veil of water. The going was slow and precarious, and I wondered if this were simply a sign for me to abandon my plans and return to Baeren Ford.

Still, a feeling I would forever regret it if I gave into fear and discouragement urged me onward.

After a while, the rain let up a bit and began to fall at a slower, though regular pace. I looked over at Galamir, whose golden hair was plastered to his head. He was humming a tune to himself as though oblivious to the less than ideal conditions.

For a while longer we trudged through the mud and rain, glad at least we met no one along the road save a local farmer and a shepherd boy herding his flock across the road.

"It shan't be long now," Galamir commented optimistically as we entered yet another stretch of woods.

Within the hour I began to recognize my surroundings, and eventually the cottage of Fendred and Helice came into view a little off the road. It was now midafternoon, and the unexpected change in the weather had slowed our progress. By now, all we wanted was a hot meal and dry clothing, although the dwarves had managed to stay fairly dry in their coffins.

As a boom of thunder growled overhead, I rapped on the front door of the cottage. Through the small window in the door, I could see Helice peering out to see who had come to call, and with a click of the latch the door flew open.

"Arwyn! Galamir! We've been expectin' ye e'er since Mr. Galamir came through a few days ago," Helice exclaimed. "Now get yerselves in out o' the rain."

Grateful for the invitation, the five of us stepped inside. Rumalia, sitting by the fire with a pair of knitting needles in her hand, nearly bounded across the room to embrace me.

"Arwyn, 'tis so good to see ye again!" she said, not seeming to care my clothes were soaked through and through.

"My, let me take a good look at you." I examined the girl's dark locks, grown out a great deal over the winter. Her face had lost the sun-tinged appearance of those who lived to the south, and had gained a healthy, pink glow. She looked rested, and her smile attested to her newfound happiness.

"How grown up you are!"

"Aye, that I have."

"I trust all is going well."

"We're gettin' along quite well, at that," Fendred commented as he emerged from the corner where he had been working on several pelts.

"You know Galamir," I said, as the elf bowed carefully, trying not to drip on the wooden floor. "And these are our friends Hutto, Goodren, and Froilin." Each dwarf bowed politely in turn.

"Aye, we know yer story and 'ow ye mean to retairn 'ome," Fendred said. "Ye're more than welcome to take refuge 'ere for a bit, 'specially seein' as the weather's not fit for a-travelin'."

"That it isn't," Helice said. "Now get yerselves into some dry clothes afore ye catch yer death of a cold. Well, I suppose that only applies to the little uns, seein' as elves don't take ill as the rest of us do. Still, ye should change up and get comfortable. Rumalia and I will see to dinner, while Fendred tends to the hairses."

It felt good to be dry again and in front of an inviting fire while the rain continued to thump against the roof above. Despite the fact my body was not as sensitive to temperature as others, I could nevertheless appreciate the warmth around the hearth, both from its embers and from those who gathered there.

As our clothes dried on the mantel, we all crowded around the kitchen table and exchanged stories and news of our goings-on since last we were together. I was pleased to see how comfortable Rumalia was and how much she had blossomed since the fall. It was an altogether relaxing experience, one truly appreciated by travelers weary from a grueling first day on the road.

That evening Galamir and the three dwarves made themselves comfortable on the floor of the parlor, right beside the glowing fire. Having drawn straws for more comfortable arrangments, Froilin was able to sleep on the spare mattress I had used in the fall. For the dwarves it was the most luxurious sleeping arrangement they had experienced in months. I, however, shared Rumalia's bed. Nestling between the warm blankets, sleep tugged at my eyelids.

"You seem happy," I whispered in the darkness, trying to stay awake for a few minutes longer.

"Aye, they're kind folk," Rumalia answered, with a yawn. "'Twas a bit awkward at first, but now we've grown accustomed to each other. I've e'en grown to love 'em again."

"Very good." I smiled wearily as I nuzzled my face into the warm softness of the down pillow.

A glorious sunrise illuminated a fresh, green world outside, and the new day held the promise of being a better one for traveling than the one before. Galamir, the dwarves, and I rose early and made ready for our departure, thanking our hosts exorbitantly for the food and shelter they had provided. Even the horses were well rested and eager to begin the day's journey after a night in Fendred's stable. Laden with sandwiches made with leftover ham from the night before, we waved farewell and took to the road once more.

"Ah, what a glorious day 'twill be," Hutto said. He sat back in his coffin and smiled as the growing sunlight shone upon his face.

"I didn't think dwarves were so fond of the sun, preferring the darkness of your caves," Galamir commented.

"A common misconception, me Lord Galamir, a common misconception," the dwarf said cheerfully.

"Still, you'd best keep your head down," the elf warned. "We are traveling through several villages today, and who knows what foul persons could be lurking about. Gargalocs and Ashkars are becoming all too bold these days."

The day turned out to be as glorious as Hutto had predicted. Seemingly overnight the leaves on the trees had popped out, robing the world in a fine, lacy coat of green. As we traveled along, the temperature rose and soon Galamir and I shed our cloaks and enjoyed the warmth of the day.

From time to time I glanced behind me, fully expecting to see Eliendor's raven, Talthos, sitting on Avencloe's rump, sent there by the lore master to keep an eye on me. But the bird was nowhere to be seen.

The landscape changed little the farther east we traveled. The road meandered through forests, through open fields dotted with quaint stone fences that kept sheep and cattle from wandering onto the road, and across bubbling brooks overflowing from the deluge of the day before. How fresh the air smelled; it was a pleasure to be outdoors.

Toward midafternoon, we passed through the village of Wittering, almost halfway between Baeren Ford and Gildaris. Throughout the day, we had met many along the road, mostly locals going about their business or out strolling in the fields and rolling hills enjoying the spring weather. Most who glimpsed us stared as we passed. We must have been a strange sight indeed: two elves on horses, the male elf's horse tethered to a smaller horse pulling a cart along behind. But it was not until we reached Wittering we encountered a threat from anyone.

The village was a little larger than Baeren Ford, with stone buildings covered in blankets of ivy lining a series of canals that started in town and then stretched south through the countryside for the purpose of irrigation and trade, making Wittering a substantial market town. The main road through the village was a hubbub of activity, with people going to and fro, seeing to their daily business. Most stopped and stared as we passed through, and the attention made me uncomfortable.

Goodren, Hutto, and Froilin remained still and silent in

their hiding places, and we prayed none of the villagers would become too curious about what we were transporting. As we approached the eastern end of the village, both Galamir and I caught a glimpse of a Gargaloc standing in the shadows of an archway. He turned and entered the doorway of a tavern upon spotting us. I held my breath as we passed and hoped he hadn't alerted his comrades of our presence.

Galamir urged Calyxa and Crumpkin to pick up the pace, and it was not long before we cleared the easternmost buildings on the edge of the village. I was quite happy to return to a more remote area.

Still, three Gargaloc sightings in two days were quite disconcerting. Their presence was becoming all too common. What business could they possibly have in Wittering?

For a while longer we rode in silence. Galamir thought it best not to give the "all clear" signal until he was sure we were not being followed. We traveled on for as long as we could, until the light of day began to wane. While there was still some light in the sky, Galamir led us down a small lane that stretched out to the north, well clear of the East Road. There we found a safe spot in the woods to rest for the night.

After a dinner of roast rabbit, the last thing I remember as I lay upon my sleeping roll, staring into the fire as Galamir played his flute and sang elven tunes from old, was being quite glad I had not turned back the day before.

CHAPTER 3

"Yet another elf I meet. With eyes like a winter's day and hair with flecks of blazing fire, he reminds me of an angel. And although we have only just met, he seems to fancy me."

"How do you feel about his attraction?" asked Dr. Susan.

I grew silent for a moment, trying to sort through the surprisingly strong emotions this new acquaintance drew out in me. "Uncomfortable in some ways. And yet . . . I cannot deny I find him quite mesmerizing in a completely different way than Galamir."

The next morning, we were again greeted by a brilliant sunrise in the eastern sky, illuminating the world, golden beacons stretching out across the land. The five of us took to the road early and continued heading in an easterly direction. As we rode along, the land rose before us as the rolling fields gave way to small hills and the hills to small mountains. Again we made camp that night a safe distance from the road, away from the prying eyes of any fellow travelers, fair or foul.

At noon of the next day, we happened abruptly upon the River Silvendell. The river was quite wide at that point and the only way across was by ferry. From afar I saw the opposite shore, where a large flat raft floated into the middle of the river with several passengers aboard, including those of the hooved variety. The ferry captain was busy cranking a thick chain through a central shaft in the vessel. The chain spanned the width of the river, bolted to sturdy trees on both banks. However, Galamir turned Calyxa and Crumpkin north, ignoring the approaching ferry. And it was not long until we passed the southern end of Lake Gildaris, where the water spilled into the Silvendell to continue its trek to the sea.

I gasped when I first caught a glimpse of the large body

of water, nestled between lush green mountains rising up on either side.

"It is an amazing sight, Lake Gildaris," Galamir commented. "'Tis one of the most beautiful places in all of Bensor."

"I would have to agree." I stared at the shimmering blue water of the lake. I wished the dwarves were able to see the sight before us, but they locked themselves in their coffins after Galamir warned them we approached a more densely populated area.

The southern half of Lake Gildaris split into two sizeable forks. We traveled along the western shore of the western fork, but the eastern fork of the lake eventually emptied into the Lower Silvendell, a smaller but nevertheless powerful river, which flowed off into Elwindor and eventually emptied into the sea at Carona.

For some time we traveled alongside the lake, and I admired the way the mountains, clothed in green robes of early spring, framed the placid waters below. Tiny rowboats floated on the surface of the lake, filled with fishermen who waved congenially as we passed. Pretty little cottages dotted the hillsides all the way down to the shoreline, as did ancient stone fences, lined with a kaleidoscope of wildflowers. Pleasant lanes wound their way into the hills to places where waterfalls cascaded down the sides of mountains and eventually emptied into the lake. How I longed to follow those paths up into the sunlit fields above.

We passed several small villages along the way, but most of the larger villages sat on the far side of the lake. The western shore was lined with grander dwellings I could only imagine wealthy Bensorians owned, based on the sprawling manors sitting closer to the shoreline amidst acres of orchards and vineyards.

Several hours passed as we rode slowly to the north, passing estate after estate, until we rounded a promontory and spied a cone-shaped island in the middle of the lake, rising from the water like a giant snail. It sat at the tip of the long, wide peninsula that split the southern half of the lake in two, like a giant axe. As we drew closer to the tip of the peninsula, a narrow bridge connected the island to the point of land. The island itself was terraced, each level surrounded with walls at various levels all the way up to a circle of Omni at the pinnacle. How beautiful it looked, even from afar, and how sad to have fallen into a state of disuse, thanks to Draigon who made worship of the All unlawful.

The main road then veered away from the water and into a wood, and for a short while we traveled under the protection of the trees until we came to a fork in the road. Glancing around with caution to make certain no one was coming, Galamir led us away from the main road and down a long pathway along the edge of a small bay to a promontory. A large house, surrounded by terraced gardens, loomed before us. We were almost directly across from the tip of the peninsula and the grand island in the center of the lake.

"It is fortunate we have arrived before the setting of the sun, although the safe house is always open," Galamir said.

Our surroundings appeared blessedly out of the way and quite peaceful, as if life on the lake's edge came to a halt with the setting of the sun.

We rode through an iron gate and stopped before a carriage house. Galamir gave a sharp whistle and immediately a young boy of perhaps ten emerged from the stable. A puppy danced along behind him.

"Ah, Oerchli, tell your father Galamir of Loth Gerodin has arrived."

Obediently the boy ran down a stone pathway to the house and was gone for several moments. Soon a striking man with speckled gray hair and a tall, thin frame walked hastily around the side of the house.

"Ah, Galamir, we've been expecting you," he said. "And you must be the elven maiden of Guilden." He smiled at me.

"Arwyn, I would like you to meet Benedrake, friend of the elves," Galamir said.

"It is indeed a pleasure," I replied.

"No, lass, the pleasure is mine." Benedrake winked. "Now, Galamir, are you carrying the cargo we discussed earlier?"

"Aye."

"Oerchli! Come, lad, and see these weary horses and the cart into the stable. And make sure the door is shut tight behind you."

"Aye, sir." The young boy took Avencloe's reins.

"Come, we must make haste," Benedrake said, as Galamir and I dismounted. He glanced in the direction of the road, yet nothing stirred but the pine trees swaying in the gentle breeze.

I looked around in wonder as we entered the grand foyer of the manor, for such a large dwelling place easily surpassed even Ingmar's, Baeren Ford's most wealthy resident, with its grand, sweeping oak staircase, marble floors, and glowing crystal sconces. Ingmar's house, in contrast, though quite comfortable, was much more masculine and modest, even though he could certainly afford a much grander dwelling such as this.

A middle-aged woman appeared in the doorway leading to a parlor in back of the house. "Dear Galamir, we have been awaiting your return," she said, in a formal though pleasant manner.

"Etherea, it is indeed good to see you again," the elf replied.

"Miss Arwyn, I would like you to meet my wife, Etherea," Benedrake said.

"It is a pleasure to meet you."

We bowed our heads politely to one another.

"You have a beautiful home," I commented, glancing around at the oak paneling lined with numerous old portraits of the family's kin.

Etherea smiled reservedly, unable to hide her pleasure. "You are most welcome here. Now, do come and rest yourselves."

She led the way into the parlor where large windows overlooked the lake in back. I looked around at the fine furnishings, such as I had never before seen in a mortal dwelling, and I sat down carefully on a luxurious settee, amidst shelves and shelves of books.

"You notice our books," Etherea said. "Sadly, we are but a few of the mortals who still have such a collection, and most are written in the elvish language."

"Our, er, *association* with the elves has permitted us to learn their tongue," Benedrake added.

"Benedrake has been an invaluable aid in our cause," Galamir explained. "I have brought you here not only because it is a safe refuge on our journey but also to acquaint you with the inner workings of the Alliance."

"So this is the secret headquarters you mentioned?" I asked, feeling slightly disappointed it was not in a setting more mysterious and full of intrigue.

"Not exactly, yet we are very close to it. When darkness falls we shall go there."

Now *that* sounded more promising! I watched as Benedrake lit two lanterns and then disappeared through a back door. As I gazed out a window he soon appeared down on a landing next to the water, where he hung the lanterns from a grape arbor.

"My husband is signaling the others to send a boat for you," Etherea explained.

"How intriguing!" I commented, feeling privileged to be privy to something so secretive.

It was not long before the back door opened again, and Benedrake appeared in the parlor with the three dwarves by his side. "Your friends here gave young Oerchli quite a fright." He laughed. "As a young boy, he's naturally curious about such things as coffins, but never did he expect the occupants to come rising out."

"We should have warned him." Galamir laughed.

"Aye, but so intent I was on getting the two of you out of sight it slipped my mind. Poor lad"—Benedrake chuckled—"no doubt he jumped out of his shoes!"

The three dwarves huddled together, looking quite uncomfortable and out of place in the fine surroundings of the manor.

"Please, do have a seat," Etherea offered warmly, despite the dwarves' disheveled appearance. They were all in desperate need of a bath from riding in cramped quarters the previous three days. "I'll have the housekeeper make us some tea." With that, Etherea disappeared into another room.

I felt sorry to see the dwarves uncomfortably positioning themselves along the opposite settee. Everything about the house was quite refined and shipshape, and I knew they would have been happier in more earthy surroundings.

Galamir and Benedrake stood at the window of the parlor overlooking the lake and spoke in hushed voices. It seemed the dwarves were in no mood for chitchat, so I sat there and idly passed the time looking about the parlor until my gaze alighted on the ring I wore on my hand.

How long had it been since I had paid it any mind, this one token from my long-ago life of which I had little memory? Absently I removed it from my finger, admiring the rich, deep purple stone in the center. And then I noticed something I'd never seen before—or had forgotten—a curious engraving on the inside of the band: Tootie 6/17/38.

What on earth could it mean?

My thoughts were interrupted when Etherea entered the parlor, followed by a rather buxom housekeeper carrying a silver tea service on a tray, and I slipped the ring back on my finger. Politely she offered a cup first to me and then to the three dwarves. Each reluctantly took a cup and held it as though they clutched a mug of ale.

"I do hope you will forgive the unremarkable welcome

you have received here in our home." Etherea sighed as I heaped a spoonful of sugar into my teacup. "In days long past, we hosted grand events in this manor, and people from all over Bensor would attend—mortals, elves, *and* dwarves," she said, looking ruefully at the three dwarves.

"Now it is being used to host an underground movement, and it seems there are few matters more important at the moment than that," I said encouragingly, as I gave her hand a squeeze. "And perhaps it will help to bring back those happy days once more."

"Aye," she said, with tears in her eyes. "Omni willing, I should hope that will be the case."

No sooner had we finished the contents of our teacups than Benedrake spotted someone in the lamplight coming up from the landing toward the house. By then it was dark outside, for though the days were getting longer, it was still early spring and the sun had set by dinnertime.

There came a quiet knock at the back door, and Benedrake again slipped out of the room. I stood up and walked over to the place where Galamir waited. Benedrake reentered the parlor with an elf by his side. He was only the second elf I had ever seen, yet already I understood why they were considered the most noble race of all in that world. Their graceful, elegant manner and *mostly* incorruptible nature set them apart.

This elf was tall and slender and a suit of light blue adorned his body. At his side hung a mighty broadsword; its sheath was etched with intricate elven runes. Wavy light brown hair tinged with flecks of deep auburn crowned the top of his head, and he gazed at me with glistening eyes of steel gray. His cheekbones were chiseled high upon his face, his nose was fine and proud, and his lips were full and perfect. He was altogether beautiful. I had to catch my breath as he continued to gaze at me.

"Miss Arwyn, this is Callas, a member of the elven contingent here at the Alliance," Benedrake explained.

The handsome elf walked up to me and bowed low, taking my hand in his and kissing it gracefully. His lips felt chill from the cool evening air. "Greetings, Arwyn! I was not here when Galamir returned last fall and told us of your immense beauty, but I doubt even my eloquent friend here did it justice," he said as he looked into my eyes with a slightly impish smile.

Galamir, with cheeks tinted red, cleared his throat and took a step toward me. "Callas is the son of Lord Valdir Velconium, elven lord of Isgilith. We have long been acquainted with one another."

Callas cut his gaze over at Galamir. "Indeed, though you are all the more acquainted with my brother, Vandaril, he who has chosen to remain close to the safety of the forest. I, however, have left the secure borders of Loth Gerodin in my desire to serve our just and worthy cause."

"And this is certainly a noble cause; though whatever role we play, whether at home or abroad, is no less noble than any other," I said, feeling slightly uncomfortable.

I remembered hearing Galamir mention the name of Callas. I also remembered he had chuckled slightly and used the words "puffed up" in the same breath. I laughed to myself, as I now stood face-to-face with the brazen elf.

Now I felt tension between the two. Galamir surveyed his friend warily. Was it jealousy? Or was he simply being protective of me as an older brother would?

Callas laughed and offered me his arm, turning toward the back door. "Then come, and I shall show you the noble inner workings of our sanctuary."

"And what of the dwarves?" I said, stopping cold in my tracks. Callas had yet to acknowledge their presence. "They will be accompanying us, will they not?"

Galamir shifted his weight uneasily.

Callas glanced over at the dwarves on the settee. "Ah, fine gentlemen, do forgive me for being distracted by your charming companion. I know a little of your troubles and will ask you no questions, though I sympathize with your plight and consider any enemy of Draigon's to be a friend. However"—his face showed the remorse I heard in his voice—"I regret I cannot take you into the inner workings of the Alliance."

"Doggone elves, all the same," Goodren muttered. "So high and mighty ye think ye are."

"I am afraid he is right," Galamir said, "though I had hoped it would not have to be so. Yet, in truth, it is of utmost importance only those directly involved in our mission know of our secret location."

"Not to worry," Callas said, addressing the dwarves. "Benedrake and Etherea will likely provide you with more comfortable lodging and better food even than we can. But please understand it is not our intent to offend."

"Well, ye did," Goodren muttered.

"Goodren!" Hutto said, jabbing him in the ribs. "Ye'll mind yer manners. They're only doin' what they must!"

"But will they be safe here?" I asked.

"We've a special chamber already prepared," Benedrake said as he went to the bookcase and, after removing a secret wooden panel in the rear, he pulled a lever. The bookcase swung open, revealing a set of stairs disappearing into the cellar. "You needn't worry as you can lock it from the inside as you wish. Down below it is spacious and clean."

"And we'll have a hot bath prepared for you soon, and plenty of food," Etherea offered.

The dwarves' eyes brightened at the mention of food, and for a moment I wished I were staying in the lovely home as well. But if I was to be privy to the Alliance, I had best do that which I had come to do.

Benedrake and Oerchli had brought our personal belongings in from the stable and laid them on the floor of the parlor. As we gathered them, Galamir spoke lightheartedly to Callas. "To what do we owe this pleasure, Callas? You do not usually transport guests across the lake, as busy as you are with other matters."

"Ah, but I knew to expect you," Callas replied. "And I wanted to be the one to accompany Arwyn to our hideaway." Callas winked as he offered me his arm once more. "Come, Arwyn, I shall help you down to the water. The footholds can be treacherous in the darkness."

I relented and slipped my hand into the crook of his arm, though I found such familiarity so soon after meeting him slightly unnerving.

"From this point onward we must remain quiet until we enter the sanctuary," Callas said in a hushed tone. "Secrecy has been our greatest defense, and at worst we must appear as a fishing party out on the lake for the evening. Yet let us hope in the darkness we will arouse no suspicion."

"We shall expect your return by sunrise?" Benedrake asked.

"Yes," Callas answered. "If our new friends wait until after daybreak to depart, then they must either delay their exit or slip out the *other* way that leads into the village. Such would not be prudent." He then turned to me. "You see, Arwyn, the enemy has infiltrated even the fair villages at the lake's edge, and so we must be wary as it is not always obvious who is friend and who is foe."

I nodded understanding, grateful for the extra caution.

Quietly, he led the way out the back door and down a set of stairs to a landing at the water's edge. Gingerly he stepped into the waiting rowboat and with a dramatic, sweeping movement, chivalrously held out his hand for me, leaving Galamir to place our belongings in the stern. "Your royal barge, milady."

I took Callas's hand and maneuvered to my seat. In a matter of moments, Callas untied the boat from a piling, and we headed out over the placid water. Up ahead, in the light of the pale crescent moon, we could just make out the silhouette of the island in the middle of the lake.

Tiny lights burned inside the island dwellings of people

who had already turned in for the evening, and the village remained quiet other than the occasional sound of a barking dog coming from somewhere within its walls. As the black mass loomed up ahead, I could see the boat was heading directly for it until the village that spiraled up toward the sky was at last right above us.

By some fortunate event, a passing cloud temporarily blocked the moonlight just as the boat approached the bottom of the island and drifted silently beneath a stand of trees hanging over the water. It then slipped in a small cleft in the rocky shoreline and into the inky black of total darkness. I realized we had entered a cave at the base of the island, and I wondered how large a place it was. What secrets would I possibly find within?

CHAPTER 4

"What an honor it is to be privy to the Alliance. Knowing of what will soon come about in this land is both exciting and frightening. I wonder what aid I can possibly give to this cause. Perhaps my bow will someday be of use for a greater good," I said. "And then there is Callas. I find his flirtations quite amusing, although I imagine such is his nature. And yet, when he looks at me with his luminous gray eyes, I can feel blood rush to my face. 'Tis rather disconcerting to have such conflicting feelings stir in me from one I have only just met."

Callas gave a low whistle like that of a nightingale, and all at once a dim light appeared several feet away. A young elf carrying a lantern appeared at the top of a narrow pathway leading down to the water. Callas and Galamir rowed over to him and cast a line in his direction. The elf grabbed the rope and tied it tightly around a boulder at the water's edge. Carefully we disembarked onto the rocky landing and were guided up a narrow pathway along a lantern-lined tunnel that sloped gently upward for approximately seventy feet.

I thought of Froilin, for being in such a place again brought back all-too-vivid memories of another underground place where we had been not too long before— Dungard. And yet already I could sense this underground bastion did not have the same malevolence as the dungeons below Maldimire.

Finally the tunnel opened up, and we walked out onto a landing in the midst of a cavernous room. Three large iron candelabra illuminated people, both mortal and elvish, men and a few women, going to and fro. They seemed to be preparing several long tables sitting in the middle of the room for the evening meal.

The air inside was surprisingly warm for such a huge

subterranean room, and I looked up in wonder at the high walls of the cavern where we could see yet others going about their business through large openings that looked down upon the activity below. There must have been numerous honeycombed passageways and chambers throughout the whole underground system. To think so much activity was happening in secrecy right below the noses of the people who lived in the village above was almost amusing.

"Ah, Galamir, I see you've returned," came a voice from the room below.

I looked down to see a tall, burly man with an air of authority walking up the steps to the platform. He wore a tunic and boots made of fur, and two shaggy sideburns on either side of his face. Galamir greeted the mortal man warmly in the fashion of elves and turned toward me.

"And this must be the elven maiden who dares live in the midst of humans," the man said as he approached.

"Arwyn, I would like you to meet Thenodar, the leader of our endeavor."

"My lord," I said politely, and I bowed my head slightly.

"Galamir has told us of your friendship with the lore master, and though I've not had the pleasure of meeting him, I know he is much revered by the Lord Valdir."

"Indeed there is much more to him than meets the eye, it seems," I commented, as much to myself as anyone, still wondering about the nature and importance of Eliendor's association with the elven lord.

"Any friend of Master Eliendor's is a friend of the Alliance, and we hope you will join our cause," Thenodar said.

"A worthy cause it is, though how I can be of use remains to be seen," I replied.

"When the time arrives, Thenodar will lead us against the forces of Draigon," Galamir explained. "He has much skill in the art of battle, and years ago he fought with Caldemean forces against their enemies to the east."

"But no mercenary he is," Callas added. "Thenodar rose to the rank of colonel in their army and has proven himself many times on the field of battle."

"But a Bensorian I am at heart," Thenodar said. "For you see, my mother was Bensorian and my father, Caldemean. Following the wars, I returned here to my mother's homeland in a quest for a more peaceful existence, only to be dismayed by the growing insidious threat to the south. It was several years ago I realized Draigon must be stopped, though his grip on our land had grown so I knew it must be done in secrecy. That is when I called upon my elven friend, Valdir Velconium, to join us in this movement."

"It appears you run a tight ship," I commented, as I looked down upon the happenings below.

"I beg your pardon," Thenodar said.

"I mean, you have a very organized system, here."

"Aye, that we do, and that I shall show you later this eve, but first we dine," Thenodar said.

With that, he led us down a flight of stairs to the floor of the cavern. All about the room people were glancing at us. Galamir apparently frequented the secret headquarters, for there were several who walked over to greet him warmly. It was obvious he was well respected, even liked, by many. But that was hardly a surprise.

Callas stepped up beside me as we descended the staircase. "I do apologize that your friends were not allowed to accompany us, but we must be extremely careful whom we allow into our inner sanctums. After all, there could be spies about."

"I certainly understand your caution, though I can assure you the dwarves harbor their own grievances against the powers that be and would happily contribute to Draigon's downfall."

Callas laughed. "Of what little I know of them, I would not doubt it!"

Thenodar led us to a long table laden with platters of meats, potatoes, and other vegetables, as well as dried fruits. Those who dwelt at the Alliance certainly were not in want of nourishment.

Thenodar took a seat at the end of the table and gestured for me to sit next to him with Galamir at my side and Callas directly across from us. It was not long before almost everyone was seated at the three long tables, and the platters of food made the rounds. The sound of goblets clinking together and of subdued merriment around the tables filled the air. But for the gravity of their mission, the inhabitants of this secret existence still managed to live a pleasant life.

"If I may ask," I said to Thenodar, "who funds this operation, for surely it is costly?"

"We have well-to-do friends throughout Bensor," he replied. "You must know a man in Baeren Ford by the name of Ingmar."

"Ingmar knows of the Alliance?" I exclaimed. "I had no idea!"

"And that is as he would want it. A skittish man, he is, who wishes to maintain the illusion that his primary concern is the workings of his mill. If you'd ask him, he would deny any knowledge of our presence or anything that happens beyond the borders of Baeren Ford."

"Bless the man! For all his riches, he does have a care beyond his own coffers." I thoughtfully took a sip of water as I glanced around the walls of the cavern. "Tell me, how were these caves discovered, and how have they remained hidden from the enemy for so long?"

Thenodar took a bite of roasted fowl. "'Tis an interesting story, that," he began. "A man by the name of Robard, who lived up in the village above, took a mind one day to go digging himself a wine cellar. But as he dug deeper the back wall of the cellar crumbled, revealing the underground fortress beneath. Seems it once housed an ancient dwarf colony, long-since abandoned. Robard kept it a secret, in the event he would need a place to hide from Draigon someday, but it otherwise held very little use.

"Years later, when he died, his son Mithgar inherited his house, and thus the cavern." Thenodar gestured to the next table where a young man with light skin and wavy red hair sat. I supposed he was Mithgar. "He's a fine young man, sympathetic to our cause, and once he heard of the existence of this movement, he offered the cavern as a safe haven for its headquarters."

"How brave he is, to risk so much," I commented.

"Aye, though you'll find there are many in this city who are involved with the Alliance, and since its inception as our headquarters, other outlets into those homes have been dug."

"So there are more than two ways to get in and out."

"Yes, which helps lessen the suspicion surrounding any one dwelling," Thenodar continued. "Still, we like to use the lake entrance and the house of Benedrake as much as possible. The mere presence of elves inside the village would raise questions. His house is a little less in the thick of things."

"I understand." Quickly I glanced across the table where Callas sat, sipping from his goblet, his luminescent eyes peering at me with such intensity I blushed. With eyes so mesmerizing, it was difficult to use the Gifts of Omni to see beyond the cool gray to the soul within. I had discovered it was much more difficult to see into an elf's soul than a human's. "Tell me," I said, turning quickly to Thenodar, "do all of these people actually live here?"

"Most do," he replied. "Although some live above in the village and enter daily through the safe houses. There are also those who hold other jobs and descend into the cavern after their work is done. Most are ready at a moment's notice to mount one of the horses we keep in Benedrake's stable and ride throughout Bensor to deliver messages and to coordinate plans with our associates at the other locations. But rest assured," Thenodar said, his gaze narrowing with solemnity, "every person who enters this place does so having proven their utmost loyalty to Bensor, and even fewer are privy to *all* our secrets."

"Yet who am I that you let me in?" I asked curiously. After all, I was the newcomer to Bensor, unlike the majority of people at the headquarters, who had been tried and true Bensorians their entire lives.

Thenodar let out a hearty laugh "Believe me, miss, anyone who would stand up to Draigon as you have is worthy of a place at this table."

"Has my reputation as a troublemaker preceded me?" I glanced accusingly at Galamir, who grinned with guilt.

"Already you are quite the legend around here," Callas broke in with a wink.

I felt the blood rush to my face at the sight of his beguiling smile.

"Er, this brings to mind a matter of utmost importance," Thenodar said, with an air of gravity. "A conversation you overheard while inside the palace of Draigon."

"Yes, I know the one you refer to," I said quietly, uncomfortable at the memory. Callas stopped eating and looked to Thenodar quizzically.

"Please apprise me, my lord, for this is the first I have heard…"

Thenodar pointed at Galamir with a large knife that had a substantial piece of meat skewered to it. "You were not here when Galamir returned to us last fall and told of this brazen elven maiden who had stood up to Draigon. Or of her serendipitous discovery."

"Nay, I'd been at my duties in Hared Nomnor all autumn. Why, I've not even journeyed home to Isgilith these past months. The first I heard of Arwyn was only days ago when I returned…but I seem to have missed an important piece of information." Callas took a quick swig from his goblet.

"Aye. It seems when Arwyn was taken prisoner in the Palace of Lords, she overheard a conversation between

Draigon and a sinister old man, who we believe may be Draigon's liaison to Dar Magreth."

I watched as the blood drained from Callas's face.

"Did…did you get a look at this old man?" Callas asked of me.

I shook my head. "Not a good one. He was bent over and his cloak concealed him."

"Callas, is anything the matter?" said Thenodar.

"Nay…well, yes…I do remember seeing such a man in the vicinity of the Gate, on the road to Mindlemir, I believe…back before winter, it was. He seemed a suspicious sort to me at the time, and yet…and yet I had no reason to question him." He then looked up, brow creasing as alarm gave way to indignation. "Why was I not informed? Had I only known, I surely would have detained him!"

"You had already left for the winter, and though we sent someone to Hared Nomnor to alert you, we could not find you before the snows set in, and we were forced to turn back."

"I was on the far end of Hared Nomnor, in Kemmich for the winter, watching the river for secret shipments of iron from Endismere. I did travel down to Peltafair on occasion. So 'tis possible they missed me."

"But now that you *are* aware, you can alert your subordinates to detain him, should he show himself again," Galamir said.

"Yes, *Galamir*, as a matter of fact, I shall set out on the morrow to do so."

Callas was polite enough, but there was a tension between the two elves Thenodar could have easily sliced with the big knife he held in his hand.

After a moment of awkward silence, I spoke up, keeping my eyes on Callas. "And what, if I may ask, are the plans to stop Draigon?"

Galamir leaned in. "I have confided to Arwyn how we have begun to stockpile weapons in secret locations around

Bensor, but she knows not of our plans for them," he commented.

"This summer is the time for action," Thenodar said, "though the exact day of our rebellion is not disclosed as of yet. By then we will have procured a secret army of men and women willing and able to fight, from all over Bensor south of the Andains, to take up arms against the enemy within each of the major villages of Guilden. Cutting off every route across the Silvendell, we shall march to the south, where we will come together to storm upon the palace at Maldimire. And we will attack Draigon's other strongholds. From there, we will take back Elwindor, the Andains, and the Greenwaithe."

"And if this plan fails?" I asked.

"Then we enlist the aid of Caldemia," Thenodar continued. "Though Draigon has not made it easy to cross the border. Still, King Hobarth knows of our plight and has pledged his support if all else fails."

The mood of my three dining companions was now very grave, and I stared solemnly at my empty plate. "Many will lose their lives," I said quietly.

"Aye," Thenodar replied. "Such is the risk when freedom is at stake."

"Tell me, Thenodar," I said, after a few moments, "what role might I play in this grand scheme?"

Thenodar gave me a sidelong glance, as if he were sizing me up. "Galamir informs me you have certain...*talents.*"

I glanced around at the three gentlemen. Callas had remained quiet those past moments, but he now leaned in with curiosity.

"She is a highly respected healer in Baeren Ford," Galamir said. "She can hit a rabbit with an arrow from a quarter mile away..."

"And I can fight!" I chimed in.

I glanced at Callas, who stared at me with a raised eyebrow as if he seriously questioned my martial prowess.

"Fight? I'd not considered *that* possibility," Thenodar replied pensively.

"My lord, surely you would not put her into the battle!" Callas protested.

"And why not?"

"'Twould not be safe," the young elf replied. "And quite a shame it would be for you to be damaged."

I could feel my blood pressure rise. But when Callas smiled a smile so captivating, I at once relented.

"And you are much too valuable to risk."

"But what value can I possibly be?" The question still remained—I needed a *purpose*.

Thenodar leaned over to me and took my hand in his. "Arwyn, your value shall come *after* all this unfortunate fighting is behind us and we seek to rebuild our country and bring reconciliation between elves and mortals."

"It was twenty-five years ago that Draigon came to power." Callas had a faraway look in his eyes as he spoke. "I was but a young lad when my father was forced to flee from Maldimire back to Loth Gerodin. There were thousands who saw the threat Draigon posed and determined to leave their ancestral homes in places such as Emelon and Fernwood, and even pockets of Guildenwood, for the security of the northern forest. And I have often wondered why we did not stand up to him." I detected a bitter sound to Callas's words. "The elves of Bensor showed their weakness, and to this day I am shamed by it."

"Callas, 'twould have been folly to stand against Draigon then!" Galamir argued. "We had no scheme in place, no organization; our leadership was splintered, and to have resisted would have been to our detriment."

"And yet once Draigon had corralled us to a faraway corner of Bensor, we were content to remain there, complacent, as his hatred of our kind spread like contagion in the weak-minded." Callas's voice steadily rose with emotion.

"Gentlemen," Thenodar interrupted, "resurrecting the errors of the past is futile. The only time we have is the present, and we must do with it what we are now called to do. Though the wait has been long, the time to act will soon be upon us. Now," he said, turning to me, "Callas *has* hinted at the purpose for which you have been brought into our midst."

"Oh?" I said, curiously.

"Galamir, here, seems to believe that, because of your familiarity with mortal ways, you would make an excellent ambassador between elves and men in the age that is to come in Bensor, after the success of our rebellion."

"'Tis true," Galamir replied. "Our years apart have bred a certain degree of mistrust and suspicion on *both* sides of the Andains. I am afraid there are some elves who have grown to think of mortals as too easily corruptible, especially after living in Draigon's shadow for so long. Having lived with mortals these past years, we hope you can help dispel those notions."

"But most of the mortals I have known only desire to live their lives in peace, out from under the rule of a tyrant. Most grieve the flight of elves from Guilden."

"Ah, but are there not some who believe we have abandoned the south these past years? Those who believe we care little of your plight?" Callas asked.

"I suppose there are a few," I conceded.

"And that is why we need you, Arwyn," Galamir said, "to help bring our two races together once again."

"And what of the dwarves?"

"Aye, but those wounds will no doubt require stronger medicine to heal," my friend said, eyes laced with remorse. "Yet again, the association you have with your three friends may be a start."

I remained silent for a moment, pondering the solemn duty being asked of me. "I would be most honored to help renew the bonds between the races of Bensor," I said at last.

"Though…I am not certain my opinion will hold much sway among your people."

"You need not fear," Callas said with a playful smile. "Already I can tell it would take little for you to win their hearts."

Galamir looked quickly away as if to conceal a look of displeasure, and I thought I heard him huff impatiently. Never before had I seen my congenial friend react so to anyone else.

After a moment of silent deliberation, I leaned forward and looked Thenodar in the eye. "My lord, if it would bring honor to this worthy cause, then you have my word—I will aid it in any way I am able."

"We are most indebted," he replied with all sincerity.

"Arwyn, the hour grows late and we must depart early come the morning," Galamir said with some urgency.

"I was rather hoping to show her our operations here." Callas pushed himself away from the table then walked over and stood between Galamir and me, placing his hands on our shoulders. "Would you mind terribly if I show her around a bit?"

"It is for Arwyn to choose," Galamir said, suddenly rubbing the back of his head with annoyance.

"It would be a pleasure," I replied politely, glancing at Galamir, whose lips were pursed.

"Callas will show you around well, and glad I am of it as I must now tend to other business," Thenodar said.

"Yes, my lord, though I am glad you have indulged me for a time," I said.

Callas offered his arm to me. I looked behind to see Galamir staring at us dubiously, and I smiled at him as if to say I had not completely relinquished myself to Callas's charms. "Would you care to join us?" I asked of Galamir.

"I believe I shall retire to the guest quarters. We could all use a good night's sleep," Galamir said, staring directly at me.

"I will not be long to bed myself," I commented, "unless these caves are much larger than I imagine."

Callas guided me down a short flight of steps into a large chamber. I could feel a blast of heat coming from inside even before I could see the smithies below. As we stepped into the room, we were greeted by an intense glow coming from several stone furnaces, thus explaining the warmth in the room above. There were iron tools lying about as well as weapons and pieces of armor in various phases of construction. They were quiet now as the smiths had quit their work for the evening, enjoying dinner around the large tables.

After explaining to me the inner workings of the smithies, Callas led me into an adjacent room. Breastplates, helmets, and gauntlets lined the walls, and on racks in the center of the room hung dozens of swords, shields, spears, and daggers.

"You have an impressive collection of weaponry here." I gazed upon a large broadsword and wondered what it would be like to brandish such a weapon.

"Yes, and more armor is made every day and shipped out by cart under cloak of night to the various storehouses across Bensor."

"And so far they have escaped detection?"

"We have indeed been fortunate," said Callas, who stared with his intense eyes. "Tell me, why would a lovely elven maiden as yourself choose to live in a mortal village and not with your own kind?" he asked pointedly.

I shrank back a little at the boldness of his question. "And yet *you* live with mortals," I replied.

Callas's features softened into a smile. "Please, forgive my rather forthright manner," he said, laughing. "My straightforward ways, I admit, are a bit brusque at times, though I do not mean to offend. Most elven maidens prefer the comforts of our cities to a more, er, simple life among humans."

"The comforts of your cities are something I have yet to see, but I must admit my loyalties lie with the good people of Baeren Ford whom I have grown to love. Even the richest of surroundings could not replace them in my heart."

"Ah, the tender affections of a female." Callas positioned himself directly in front of me, now staring indulgently. He placed his hand upon my left arm. "All the more reason why you musn't involve yourself in the battle to come. I would hate for you to be hurt."

I didn't know whether to feel flattered or highly insulted! *Puffed up*, eh? There was something about Callas that reminded me of my old acquaintance, the taverner, Hamloc, an oaf of a man with a grating personality. Yet Callas was charming, with aspirations beyond the doors of the local tavern, and it seemed his ego would be able to withstand a small lesson on my martial prowess.

"Would you please turn your head to the side?"

Callas looked at me quizzically.

"I would hate to mess your pretty face." With that, I placed my right hand upon his, trapping his hand as I levered my forearm, forcing him to bend over. With a swift kick, Callas found himself on the floor with my foot upon his chest. "I do hope I didn't hurt you."

"Madam, I can see you are indeed not one to trifle with," Callas said with a groan. I removed my foot and he stood, brushed himself off, and glanced at me sidelong. "So, you think I am 'pretty'?" he added with a mischievous gleam in his eyes.

"Pretty forward," I muttered.

"Well, perhaps you will render me the opportunity to set things right after your scathing correction of my rather, shall we say, *spirited* behavior?"

"Perhaps." I smiled, not exactly sure of what to make of his disarming smile. "Is there anything else you wish to show me?"

"Indeed there is," he replied slowly, "though you are not

allowed entrance."

"Where?"

"The map room—*the* most secret of all chambers here at the Alliance. It is the place where the details of the coming revolt are laid out, and only a select few have been granted passage."

"Oh," I said, feeling slightly disappointed.

"However," Callas said, rubbing his chin and glancing at me with a mischievous gleam, "you certainly do not seem the kind of person who would easily hand over our secrets under duress, now do you?"

"I would never do such a thing. But still, I will honor the rules…"

"There is a way," my companion broke in, "though it will involve a bit of a disguise."

"Galamir would not be pleased…"

"No, such would make him quite cross, especially were he to discover it is *he* you will mimic." Callas reached into the pocket of his tunic and withdrew a strand of golden hair, which he held up before me.

"What is that?"

"A strand of Galamir's fair hair," Callas explained with a grin, and it suddenly dawned on me why I had seen Galamir rubbing his head before. "Now, blow on it three times while I say the magic words."

I glanced at my companion dubiously but after a moment decided to indulge him. The strand of hair quivered each time I let my breath out, all the while wondering what on earth such a strange thing would achieve. Callas proceeded to say several elvish words I was not familiar with, and then I saw his eyes grow wide with a look of wonder. As far as I could tell, nothing had happened.

"What is it?"

"Look for yourself," Callas said, leading me to a shiny coat of mail. I leaned over to look at my reflection in the metal and could see Galamir's face staring back at me.

"What have you done?" I shrieked.

"Not to worry—your unfortunate state will not last for long—so we must hurry."

Callas grabbed me by the hand and we hurried down a long passageway, careful to stop and glance around each corner before proceeding. "You mustn't say a word until we reach the chamber, or surely we will be discovered," Callas explained in a hushed tone.

Breathlessly I followed along behind until we reached a doorway guarded by a robust man wearing a broadsword. As we approached, the guard's face broke into a smile. "Ah, Master Galamir, I heard rumors you'd returned. Good it is to see you!"

Callas shot me a warning glance as I bowed my head to the man.

"Er, I hate to trouble you, Kaegir, but we are in a bit of a rush. I must apprise Galamir of our latest developments before he turns in."

"Aye," the guard said. He then produced a set of keys with which he unlocked the door. Once inside, we walked down yet another short tunnel to a small room where a rectangular table sat in the very center. On the table lay a large map of Bensor, and on it were dozens of multicolored stones, placed in strategic positions. Immediately I bent over to survey the map.

"On the map we have identified, based on the color of the stone, the location of safe houses, weapons, storehouses, and the like."

I studied the map carefully. Most of the stones seemed to be concentrated in Guilden and Elwindor, though there were a few sprinkled along the borders of Loth Gerodin and in the southernmost Andains where mortals lived. The region to the south, close to Emraldein and Carona, appeared void of any activity. But most surprising was the small cluster of stones on the sleepy village of Baeren Ford, of all places!

"I see you fancy maps, by the way you study them,"

Callas observed.

I looked up from the table. "Yes, they hold some sort of fascination for me. I always like to know where I am in relation to everything else." And it seemed Alliance activity had been going on right under my nose without my ever knowing it!

"The map of Bensor has long been the same. Little ever changes."

"And would you change it if you could?"

"Indeed. The southern forests would flourish again, and the elves would return to their ancient homelands," he said, with a touch of bitterness, "rather than hiding like timid rabbits in Loth Gerodin."

I remained silent for a moment. "We all hope for that day."

"Do you see this area?" Callas said, pointing to the region between the Guildenmoor Gate and the town of Kemmich on the western border of Bensor and then sliding his finger south to the village of Peltafair. "It is my charge in this operation. I oversee all that happens there concerning the Alliance."

"Do you travel there often?" I asked curiously.

"Aye, as necessity would have it, though a rather barren territory it is, especially in the most northwestern corner of Guilden past the point where the wall ends. The cliffs there are too high and craggy for anyone to possibly traverse…and too eerily close to the lair of our enemy as well," he added. "Kemmich is a rather unsavory outpost, though an important one in our mission. I find it bearable when I must go there." Callas leaned back against the wall, crossed his arms before him, and let out a chuckle. "My goodness, you look positively hideous."

I was taken aback for a moment, until I remembered I did not exactly look like myself to others, even though to look at myself, it seemed I still wore my flowing maiden's garment and long, dark brown tresses.

"And do *you* do this often? Suddenly turn yourself into someone else?"

Callas bowed his head to the ground and laughed heartily. "Alas, not all who possess the power to transform others can do so themselves. Although," he added thoughtfully, "the children of Isgilith do find me quite amusing. Their parents, however, stuffy and respectable as they are, think my antics confounding at best and at worst, quite ill-behaved."

"And if you could transform yourself, who would you become?"

Callas grew silent for a moment and surprisingly serious. "I would become a bird," he answered at last. "I would fly over the wall, over the impenetrable cliffs of Hared Nomnor and into the lair of the enemy…"

"You mean, Bensor's ultimate enemy—Dar Magreth—the one we believe uses Draigon as a puppet."

"I would spy on her, discover her weakness—and then I would return to Bensor with this knowledge and use it to defeat her." Callas had a faraway look in his eyes.

"That would make you quite the hero."

He looked at me as though he had forgotten I was still standing there, and his expression turned to one of slight alarm. "The spell is breaking. We must leave now."

Callas took me by the arm and led me out of the room, hurrying past the guard and back down the tunnel, both giggling as we turned the corner and were no longer in danger of detection. Our escapade had succeeded!

My heart still thumped wildly when Callas turned back to me. "Ah, I am glad to see you back to normal." He gave me a wink. "And I much prefer you this way."

I could feel the heat rush to my face, and not only from our hasty getaway.

"I trust this will remain our secret?"

I smiled and nodded. I'd not had so much fun in a long, long while. "Please, the hour grows late and I am weary from our travels. Would you see me to my quarters now?"

Callas bowed cordially and again offered me his arm. He had apparently forgiven my chastening behavior earlier. It seemed we could both be a bit reckless, and that was something I rather liked.

Together we walked back up the stairs and through the great room, now empty save for a small group who remained sitting on one end of a table laughing quietly and drinking ale. At the other end of the cavern we ascended yet another winding staircase leading to the chambers above.

"Though it is modest, it is at least warm and dry," Callas said as we approached a wooden door positioned into an archway carved into the stone.

He opened the door to reveal a small, well-lit room. My knapsack, bow, and arrows had been placed upon a single bed against the far wall, and hot water steamed in a waiting tub close to the door.

"I'm sure it will be fine. Thank you for a most memorable evening. And I do beg your forgiveness for earlier," I said sheepishly.

"There is nothing to forgive," he said with a smile. "Should you need him, Galamir is in the chamber next to yours. I will be nearby as well, and I would prefer you call on me should you require anything."

"Thank you," I said as I quickly bowed my head with gratitude and entered the chamber.

I latched the door behind me and slipped off my gown. I then climbed into the hot water, indulging in its warmth and the aroma of my lavender soap as I mused over my meeting with Callas. He obviously had a knowledge of the Gifts. And even though his boldness reminded me of Hamloc, he was so intense and polished in his manner I caught myself feeling amused, annoyed, and charmed all at once.

Whether it was the bath, being completely exhausted from our journey, or the memory of gallivanting around as Galamir with a new acquaintance who made me giggle like a schoolgirl every time I thought on our little adventure together, I felt far too relaxed for one who so recently pledged herself to a rebellion that could very well fail and cause Bensor—or herself—great misery. Nevertheless, I looked Thenodar in the eye and gave him my word. To that word I would be true.

I could only hope I would not live to regret it.

CHAPTER 5

*"Glad I am to be on the road once more and out from
under the intense gaze of Callas."*

"He makes you feel uncomfortable?" asked Dr. Susan.

*"Yes, not only for his brazen behavior, but for the fact
there is a part of me, albeit a very small, secret part, that
wishes to see him again. But perhaps I shouldn't."*

"What makes you say that?"

*"Because if I fancy Callas, I do not think it would please
Galamir."*

"Does Galamir fancy you?"

*"No, nothing like that," I explained in my hypnotic state.
"Galamir is my friend and nothing more...At least, he has
never given me reason to think otherwise."*

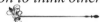

The knock on my chamber door came much too early the
next morning, and yet I knew Galamir and I must return to
Benedrake's house before the sun rose. Quickly I dressed
and splashed my face with water left over from my bath the
evening before. I then gathered my belongings and walked
out onto the landing. Already there was much activity going
on down below as the Alliance workers began their daily
business.

I found my way to the staircase and walked down to the
floor of the cavern where Thenodar and Galamir waited.

"Good morning," Galamir greeted me cheerfully. "I trust
you had a good rest."

"Indeed I did," I replied.

"Please forgive me for taking my leave of you last night,
but my duties called," Thenodar said. "However, it was a
pleasure to make your acquaintance, Miss Arwyn, and I am
pleased you will join our cause."

"I will help in whatever way I can." I promised. Callas
appeared around the corner, looking quite debonair in a suit
of green and gold. "Even if it means I must join the fight."

"And I am well convinced the lady can indeed fight," Callas said with a knowing glance, one that raised the eyebrows of both Galamir and Thenodar. "In fact, I pity the man who opposes you."

I smiled inwardly and, with our final farewells said, accompanied Galamir and Callas back through the tunnel and down to the water. The short night had come to an end, and I could barely make out the faint light of dawn seeping into the cave from beyond the opening. A young man waited in the boat, ready to take us across the lake. He could have easily passed for a common fisherman, yet he remained silent as we climbed aboard.

It was still mostly dark when we emerged from the cave into the middle of the lake. By some fortunate occurrence, a thin layer of fog blanketed the surface of the water, providing even more cover for our hasty getaway. The village above remained sleepy and quiet except for the occasional sound of a crowing rooster. Like fireflies glowing in the darkness, the light of a dozen or so lanterns glowed in the distance as village fishermen prepared their lines and dropped their boats into the water for a day of fishing. No one seemed to notice our lone skiff gliding by silently.

Up ahead we could barely make out the flickering of two lanterns in the parlor windows of Benedrake's house. The light from the lanterns loomed closer, and it was not long before the small boat ran aground. Quickly and quietly we gathered our belongings and disembarked, hurrying toward the house before the first rays of sunlight filtered over the hills to the east. Benedrake greeted us at the door and motioned for us to enter.

The three dwarves waited in the parlor, looking rested and more at ease. And clean. I assumed Etherea had made good on her promise of a bath.

"My friends, it appears you fared well last night," I greeted.

"Aye, the lady let us sleep in the guest room upstairs," said Hutto with a satisfied smile.

"We felt like princes, 'specially considerin' our accommodations o' late," Froilin added.

"Decent, it was," Goodren conceded. "A bit stuffy, but decent."

I had to stifle a smile as the other two dwarves shook their heads and rolled their eyes at their cantankerous friend.

"The poor dears, I couldn't bear to send them to the damp cellar, especially after hearing of their troubles," Etherea said as she entered the parlor, carrying a tray of crumb cakes and cups filled with steaming tea. "Though Benedrake kept a look out all night." She set the tray on a side table and offered us the items on the tray.

"Thank you," I said, as I took one of the cakes, along with a teacup.

"I remembered you like your tea with sugar, and so I took the liberty of adding some," Etherea explained. "I fear 'tis not much, though it should hold you through the morning. I had the housekeeper pack you dried beef, cheese, and apples for later, as well as a sack of honey wafers."

"We are indebted to your hospitality," Galamir said, as he lifted a pastry off the tray.

"If you will allow me," Callas said, "I must take my leave of you now."

"You are leaving us, as well, Lord Callas? You only just returned," Etherea said. "Please, take some food with you."

"I would be grateful." Callas turned to me as Etherea exited the parlor. "Arwyn, it has been a most enchanting meeting." He stared intently into my eyes. "After I have seen to my duties in Hared Nomnor, I shall perhaps make it a point to return home for the Faerenfel this year. It has been far too long since I attended, and...I find it holds even greater interest to me this year."

"I understand it is worth a trip to Loth Gerodin to experience it," I said, glancing at Galamir, who shifted his weight uneasily as he cleared his throat.

"Until then," Callas added with a bow.

Etherea returned to the parlor with a sack she handed to Callas before he disappeared out the front door of the manor. I watched as he left and then consumed the last of our hasty breakfast.

For a few moments we chatted quietly in the parlor until Benedrake's anxiety peaked, as if he were concerned about the growing daylight and the need for us to be on our way.

We took his cue and walked to the stable where we found our horses saddled, well fed, and ready to continue the journey. Oerchli stood inside the stable door, more concerned with entertaining the puppy he held in his arms than with the guests who were leaving his father's home.

"It should be a fine day for traveling," Benedrake commented as he glanced at the blue sky beginning to emerge through the mist above. "But you'd best be on your way, for a storm can come up over the hills at any time, especially this time of year."

"Indeed. We must make much progress toward Stone Harbour by the evening," Galamir said.

Benedrake frowned. "I'd keep to the south by nightfall tomorrow. The town's full of the 'other' sort, and you'd do well not to pass through until the morning, so you can be well clear of it and hopefully into the forest by the time you lay your heads to rest the next evening."

"Yes, I had considered that possibility," Galamir commented.

"I do hope you have enjoyed your stay here in Gildaris," Benedrake added as he glanced at the dwarves and me.

The dwarves bowed low to the ground.

"It has indeed been enlightening," I said. "I do thank you for aiding us on our journey."

"It was a pleasure, miss," said Benedrake. "You, Galamir, and the three gentlemen are always welcome."

Quickly the dwarves climbed onto the cart and positioned

themselves in their caskets, careful to latch them securely, especially in light of the populated area we would travel through.

Galamir and I mounted our horses, said our final goodbyes and rode back to the main road. Turning north, we continued along the beautiful Gildaris lakeshore throughout the morning. I glanced back from time to time as the island in the middle grew more distant, and I marveled to think it harbored such secrets within. And after a time, I was able to see far down the eastern branch of the lake where it curved sharply to the east around a bend. From there the lake funneled into the Lower Silvendell River and began its trek down to the sea at Carona, emptying at the darkness-engulfed Emraldein Castle, sitting alone on its island in the middle of the bay. From my vantage point, the castle could just as well have been a million miles away, so far it seemed from the land of the living.

With every twist and turn of the road snaking along the curves of the shoreline, we met friendly people in the villages and hamlets harboring quaint and hospitable-looking cottages along the way. As we rode along, I enjoyed the beauty and vastness of Lake Gildaris and basked in the sunlight as it crept over the mountains to the east. Once we had traveled well out of earshot of anyone, I turned to Galamir with a look of curiosity. "Tell me of Callas," I said.

Galamir glanced at me uncomfortably. "Why do you ask?"

"You seem, well...uneasy around him. Is there a reason, aside from his prideful attitude?"

"Aye," he admitted. "Callas carries a grievance against me that began years ago. Callas is quite an intense fellow. You are quite perceptive of his pride, but he is also ambitious. He and his brother, Vandaril, have long been rivals, although more in the mind of Callas than the elder of the two. Vandaril is more like their father, quiet and reflective yet strong and able, for he knows someday he will take his father's place and lead the elves of Isgilith. Callas has tried to be a leader in his own right, even leaving the protection of Loth Gerodin several years ago to restart the abandoned elvish colony of Fenrother farther south in Fernwood."

"Yes, he mentioned his desire for the elves to return to their ancestral homes in the south."

"Indeed, he was able to convince a number of elves to join him," my companion explained. "I, however, refused, for my loyalties are with his father and brother, and I would not abandon them. He still resents the fact I did not go."

Galamir became pensive as he stared at the road ahead. "The colony eventually failed, and all the elves returned to Loth Gerodin," he continued. "Callas returned with them, though bitter and shamed. His father tried to console him, yet I believe he has never let go of his failure."

"You would never guess it by his manner." But what had caused the colony to fail? Was it Callas's leadership, or some other force? I thought it best not to ask.

"Nay," Galamir smiled. "He is quite the charmer, is he not? That is his way, and good at it he is. 'Tis how he has risen to such ranks in the Alliance…although he does have other valuable talents as well."

"And they are?"

"He is good with a bow and arrow, and I've never seen anyone scale a mighty elderhorn tree as quickly and nimbly as he."

I laughed. "The next time I need someone to climb to the top of a tree for me, I will know who to call upon."

My comment elicited a laugh from Galamir, for which I was grateful. I much preferred to see my friend relaxed and in a pleasant mood than anxious and uncomfortable. After the many hours we had spent together on the road, hearing his tales, his songs, his merry laughter, seeing the way his care and concern for me and others went far beyond mere politeness, I had grown quite fond of Galamir. And I remembered what I had overheard of Loralon and Frondamein's conversation back in Baeren Ford about whether or not he could ever become more than my friend. Galamir was certainly dashing, chivalrous, and honorable, and he likewise seemed quite fond of me.

Yet the thought of him *courting* me had not crossed my mind. Perhaps it was because he reminded me of someone else in my distant past, someone I remembered only enough to know romantic attraction would be...creepy. Perhaps Galamir was destined to remain a friend and nothing more.

Still...sometimes the best of friends could become the most passionate of lovers.

"Your parents," I began, hoping he wouldn't notice the redness spread across my cheeks. "Are they anything like you?"

Galamir grinned. "I should hope if I told you they were, it would please you."

"Galamir, I can only imagine your parents will be as delightful as their son."

"Why then, yes, you shall be quite pleased!" he teased. Galamir then grew quiet, as if he were in deep thought. "Like a lake on a cold winter's day, the tranquility they display on the surface hides the depth of their feeling for that which they love. It is this love, this sense of service and loyalty, they instilled in me most of all. What we choose to love is what defines us."

"So...what is it that defines you? What is it that elicits such passion?" Indeed, I had never heard him speak with such emotion before.

"Bensor," he replied with a twinkle in his eyes. "She alone is my mistress. I would do anything for her."

My heart sank ever so slightly. Never could I compete for the affections of a man whose heart was so tethered.

If there had been any inkling of a romance with Galamir, it had just been dashed.

The miles crept by slowly, yet by midday we finally came to the northern end of Lake Gildaris. From there, the mountains surrounding the lake farther south melted into rolling fields through which the road followed along the River Silvendell. After leaving behind the northernmost village along the lake, the dwarves cautiously emerged from their hiding place, though they remained low in the cart in the wide-open spaces.

Occasionally we passed farmers out in their fields or barges at full-sail on the river, pushed upriver by winds from the south. Most only went as far as Stone Harbour, where they would unload their goods and then load again before beginning the long trek back to Maldimire with the current. But, by and large, we were by ourselves.

That night we camped in an abandoned farmhouse before pressing onward the next morning to the north through open, rolling hills splattered with clumps of trees and a small lake or two. It was not long after we passed the road leading west to the Guildenmoor Gate we caught our first glimpse of the southernmost Andain Mountains.

The dwarves shouted with glee upon seeing the snow-capped peaks, for they knew their home was now not so far away. Their whole manner became more relaxed and jovial—that is, until Galamir reminded them the most dangerous leg of the journey was yet before us.

It was late in the day when Galamir led us off the road and down into a field behind a grove of trees to camp for the night. The mountains loomed closer and more majestic even than before, yet it would be the next morning before we reached the gateway to Loth Gerodin.

After a less-than-peaceful night of huddling together under the cart when a rainstorm interrupted our sleep, we welcomed the morning sun as it came peering over the mountaintops early the next day. Yet it was with great trepidation we departed as quickly as possible, hoping to get well beyond Stone Harbour by noon. There was a price to pay for traveling with three fugitives, and I was beginning to look forward to at last reaching Galamir's home in Isgilith, where safety and a warm bed awaited.

"It will be most necessary on this day of all days for you to remain quiet in your hiding place," Galamir gravely warned the dwarves. "Stone Harbour is crawling with the enemy, and close as we are to the mountains, it is possible someone could recognize you."

The three dwarves shuddered before obediently slipping into their coffins. Knowing how suspicious those in the service of Draigon were of elves, I also felt none too easy about the day ahead. Even Galamir, normally quite cheerful and prone to humming merrily as we rode along, grew quiet.

From the time we left Gildaris two days before, the River Silvendell remained to the east of the road on which we traveled. We passed many of its tributaries, the largest tumbling down from the heart of the mountains a little south of Stone Harbour. Most barges stopped at the outpost there, for farther north the waters narrowed and began to meander widely, like a giant snake twisting through the village. The road on which we traveled led straight through town. It forced us to filter across four narrow bridges before we reached the other end of the village and safety beyond.

It was almost noon when the first bridge of Stone Harbour came into view, and on the near side stood three men in gray at the checkpoint. I gasped to see two Gargalocs in their company—out in the open. As we approached, Galamir leaned over to me and whispered, "If they question us, which they most certainly will, I will explain our business. Remain quiet, for they have little regard for the opinion of a woman. It would also be helpful for you to appear solemn, as if you have just come from a funeral of, say, our dear cousins Emelda and Thrinodar."

When they saw us coming, the three guards moved to the center of the road. The one standing in the middle held up his hand to halt our progress. "Stop where ye are and make yer business known," he commanded. Their grim faces held a cool welcome.

"If you would be so kind as to let us pass. My sister and I have been on the road for weeks, and at last we draw near to our home," Galamir said.

"And where exactly 'ave ye been to, to 'ave traveled so long?" the same guard asked. The other two were already poking their noses over the edge of the cart.

Galamir's expression remained steady. "We were traveling through Endismere on a quest to find the origin of a distant branch of our family when we were ambushed by bandits. Alas, two of our kin were killed, and so we were obliged to cut our journey short and return their bodies to our native land."

I glanced behind me casually and was horrified to see the two other guards reach over and finger the two caskets with an almost perverse curiosity. To make matters worse, the two Gargalocs ambled up to the side of the cart and pawed it with interest. My heart pounded inside my chest. Never before had I been so close to one out in the wide open, and it was all I could do to conceal my revulsion.

"There's no smell o' death comin' from these caskets," one of the guards grunted.

"We elves embalm our dead, for when an elf dies we have an extensive mourning period before they are buried," Galamir explained quite convincingly. "You may view the bodies if you wish, but it is not something I would desire to do."

Galamir and I exchanged discreet glances and held our breath. The two guards standing at the back of the cart wavered for a moment, perhaps thinking it better not to disturb the dead.

"Please, my sister is quite distraught. All we wish is to return home to mourn."

The man who appeared to be the leader of the three eyed me curiously. I lowered my gaze and summoned the most forlorn-looking face I could. "Then ye'll need to pay five quiddel, three for the hairses and two for the cart."

"A toll! Why, there's never been…" Galamir started to protest. He then sighed and dug into the pocket of his tunic. "Since when has there ever been a toll to pass from one end of Stone Harbour to the other?"

"A new policy, enacted by the governin' body o' this land." The leader greedily snatched the coins from Galamir. After counting them, he scribbled something on a piece of paper, which he handed to Galamir. "Verra well, you may pass."

With faces of stone, the guards waved us on. The Gargalocs scurried away from the wheels of the cart to let us pass, and we quickly proceeded across the bridge and into the city. The road curved around for a bit, following the river upstream until it veered off through a group of buildings on the edge of town. After a short distance, we came to the second bridge where two guards carefully surveyed the locals.

Most hurried past quickly, avoiding eye contact with the ever-present watchmen who had invaded their village. The villagers paid little notice to our passage, either because they were more accustomed to seeing elves or because they had grown hardened by the constant watchful eyes under which they lived.

As Galamir and I approached, my companion handed the watchmen the paper "pass" he had been given by the first group of guards.

The guard eyed the paper suspiciously and, without a word, handed it back to Galamir and waved him on through. Yet it seemed by the way he looked at us with malice in his eyes he would rather spit upon us.

As we passed over the second bridge, I glanced at the two coffins lying in the cart. They shook a bit as we traveled over the uneven cobblestoned street, but otherwise remained quiet. Who could have guessed the secrets they held?

We continued on our way into a more densely populated area and down a sloping lane to yet another bridge spanning the curving Silvendell. I peered in both directions as we passed over. A quay stretched along the riverbank, and quaint stone and timber buildings adorned with colorful flowerboxes spread in every direction. The gently flowing river cascaded over stone weirs built to control the water flow, yet someone in a rowboat navigated skillfully down one of the swift chutes off to the side.

Despite the cool welcome, Stone Harbour was quite charming—charming, yet dangerous. There were men in gray everywhere—and Gargalocs, more than perhaps in any other place in Bensor besides Maldimire. In fact, Stone Harbour reminded me quite a bit of Maldimire. Despite the different locales, both cities possessed an underlying sense of suspicion and despair—and of something sinister brewing.

On the other end of the bridge, we passed yet another group of guards mingling with one or two Gargalocs. Keenly aware they followed us with their eyes as we passed, I was glad only one last bridge remained.

We entered once more into a tangle of buildings with red roofs and twisting, narrow streets eventually opening onto a lively square with a bubbling fountain in the center. It was impossible to escape notice with our creaking cart, not to mention we drew more attention because we were elves. Still, I detected no animosity from the citizens of Stone Harbour themselves, some of whom stared us with a mixture of surprise and trepidation. And though they spoke no words as we passed, I could see their despair. How could we tell them hope loomed on the horizon, that there were those who worked in secret even now to remedy the scourge plaguing all of Bensor?

Galamir led the way across the square and turned onto another narrow street. At the end lay yet another bridge and freedom beyond...or so I hoped. So close we were. But then it seemed the road lengthened tenfold. Though my heart still pounded, I willed myself to appear calm lest my eyes give away our guilt.

Above the rooftops an imposing fortress came into view at the top of the cliff on the far side of the river. A single tower rose from the center of its walls, a harpy on its perch, waiting patiently to ensnare its victim as it emerged from the shelter of the buildings. I felt very exposed, a rabbit with nowhere to run.

Standing between us and the open road was a group of guards, some on foot, some on horseback. Those on horseback maneuvered to the center of the bridge, blocking all thought of a hasty escape. Forcing us to a halt, they surrounded us and peered at the two coffins lying in the cart. One of the lieutenants drew close and lifted his hand for silence as he lowered his ear to the cart.

"Is there a problem?" Galamir asked nonchalantly.

"Quiet!" he demanded, still listening intently. He then reached over the side of the cart and pulled at one of the lids, to no avail. "Open them!"

"For what purpose would you need to view the bodies of the deceased?"

"Ye elves, ye are a sly bunch, and who knows what ye may be smugglin'."

"Very well, you may open them," Galamir said, "but as you can tell, they are sealed shut. Do so at your own peril."

The lieutenant stopped.

"Your peril, and of all those gathered here," Galamir continued, eyeing each of the guards threateningly. "To disturb the body of a deceased elf is to invite calamity such as would make the strongest among you go mad with terror. And no one here…not one of you will be without blame. You will have this man to thank for your misery," he added, pointing at the lieutenant.

"Let 'em be!"

"Aye, we don't need to anger no elvish ghosts!"

Several other guards spoke out against the idea as the lieutenant stood there with a scowl on his face. Finally he turned to Galamir. "Ye don't appear to be in mournin'."

"Do you pack your mourning clothes when you go on holiday?"

The surly lieutenant curled his lip. "'Ave you a pass?" he huffed.

"Aye, your associates were kind enough to grant us passage," he replied, handing the man the piece of paper.

The lieutenant ripped the paper out of Galamir's hand and studied it carefully. For several tense moments we waited and wondered at the delay. Surely I could use the Gifts to help us out of this situation.

Then I remembered once, long before, sitting in a dark, cavernous room, staring at a huge wall where moving pictures told a story of a similar plight in a far distant world. Two cloaked men sat in a contraption magically hovering above the ground, along with two shiny beings made entirely of metal. I realized the same powers were mine to command.

"These elves are of no consequence," I muttered.

"These elves are of no consequence," the lieutenant said.

"You may leave now," I continued, under my breath.

"Begone with ye!"

The other guards parted as we continued across the bridge, and I could feel the constricted place in my throat begin to loosen.

When we were well out of earshot, Galamir glanced at me sidelong. "Whatever swayed him?" he asked when we were well out of earshot.

"Jedi mind tricks!" I answered with a sly smile.

"*Jedi* mind tricks? What, pray tell…?"

"I'm quite certain I cannot explain it to you, even if I were to try."

Above us stood the castle, its windows like eyes gazed upon us as we passed beneath. From inside came the peculiar sounds of hammering and sawing.

The road curved a bit as it ascended toward the castle entrance. We found ourselves in a green, parklike area, long unkempt, looking straight past an iron drawbridge where I could see through a huge front portal standing slightly ajar. Inside the first courtyard of the massive structure I caught a glimpse of about a dozen carts. What sent a chill down my spine was they were all fitted with cages in the cart beds— as if to transport prisoners. There were men and Gargalocs hurrying about the courtyard, and all I longed for was to be well past Stone Harbour, far out of danger's way.

The Silvendell now lay to our right. Another large stone bridge spanned the river, connecting with the road that led up into the mountains to the village of Grandinwolde. Our road, however, remained on this side of the river. Even though we were beyond the end of the city proper, we were still not out of harm's way. Several other dwellings and places of business lay beyond the castle.

As soon as we were well out of sight of Stone Harbour, my chest relaxed for the first time in many minutes. By some miracle we had managed to get through the most dangerous part of the journey with our secret intact.

"You were brilliant!" I exclaimed.

Galamir smiled widely. "And you played the part of my distraught sister quite well. Never have I seen you look so glum."

"Ahem!"

Galamir and I glanced into the cart where the dwarves remained hidden in the coffins. "We are not yet out of harm's way, my friends, and you should remain hidden a while longer, although my spirit is lighter than it has been for a long while," Galamir said. "I trust you have all weathered our ordeal unscathed."

"Aye!" came two slightly annoyed and muffled voices. We waited for a third, but no sound was forthcoming. Quickly Galamir reached across the top of the cart and lifted the lid to the second coffin. Inside lay Froilin, fast asleep.

"'Tis a good thing he doesn't snore—and it wasn't his coffin the lieutenant tried to open!" Galamir slammed the lid shut. We heard a loud bump, followed by a groan. "Serves him right!" the elf exclaimed, as he urged his horse back into the lead.

Galamir caught me trying to stifle a smile, and we both burst out in laughter, releasing the pent-up tension of the previous few hours. But we sobered quickly. We would not be completely safe until we reached the borders of Loth Gerodin.

Loggers were busy in the country we now traveled through. In fact, much of the once-lush landscape was stripped bare, leaving nothing but the stubble of ugly tree stumps littering the hillsides. For several miles we traveled in the open, cringing at the sickening sound of trees cracking and falling to the ground in the distance. Galamir's eyes were mournful as he witnessed the destruction of trees he had probably seen in his youth hundreds of years before.

"If they really want to find us, all they need do is destroy our forest little by little, either by axe or by fire," he said sorrowfully. "We elves cannot remain hidden forever."

As we traveled, we could just make out the curve of Arnuin's Wall, several miles away—the wall built ages ago to keep the Ashkaroth ruffians out of Bensor. Many, many miles to the west was the Guildenmoor Gate, the only portal through the wall, the Gate where I had first appeared in Bensor nearly three years before. It was the first I had seen of the wall since.

In a little while we passed a group of loggers hauling a large cartload of cut timber, accompanied by a lone man in gray who seemed to be overseeing the operation. Thankfully, the loggers and their master seemed much too preoccupied with their work to be concerned with us and our cargo. Otherwise we met no one else along the road.

I could sense Galamir's anticipation as the road crested a hill. Far, far in the distance shimmered the white peaks of the northern Andains. Between us and the peaks stretched a magnificent sea of green. The sight of it took my breath away, and the anxieties of the past days vanished, a vapor in the wind.

CHAPTER 6

"I am enchanted. Even in my dreams I had never imagined a place so beautiful. I do believe my soul has strayed into heaven."

"I present to you Loth Gerodin," Galamir said with a smile.

"It is amazing," I whispered as I breathed in the scent of pine wafting up from the valley below.

After cautiously glancing around the area, Galamir gave a low whistle and the dwarves emerged from their hiding places.

"If I had to spend another minute in that coffin, I do believe I would go mad," said Froilin.

"Aye, I'll have a crick in me neck for the next month to be sure," Goodren added as he rubbed the back of his neck.

"Yes, but those coffins may have saved your hide," Galamir said. "We'd not have made it much past Baeren Ford had it not been for them. We were fortunate the guards at Stone Harbour thought twice about examining our story too closely."

"We heard 'em talkin', we did," Hutto said. "I thought for sure they'd find us."

"Fortune has indeed smiled upon us," Galamir said, "but we are not clear of danger yet, not until we enter the forest. I would therefore suggest you keep your heads low for the remainder of the afternoon."

At the bottom of the hill the road branched off in two directions. The northern fork headed off along the western edge of the forest, through the Greenwaithe and toward Cemnath Androl, the other major elvish colony in the region that lay on the northernmost border of Loth Gerodin Forest along the Sea of Serenia. Yet Isgilith and a host of other, lesser, elvish colonies lay hidden somewhere in that seemingly endless twisting, disorienting sea of green. Galamir turned onto the road that branched off to the east, along the edge of the mountains, soon to meet up and run parallel again with the Silvendell.

Blinking in the bright afternoon sunlight, the dwarves stared at their surroundings, smiling at the sight of the Andains spreading out far to the east and then curving sharply for many, many miles to the north, beyond the forest and beyond the sight of most. Contentedly they lounged back in their coffins, basking in the sun's rays on the back of their heads.

By late afternoon, we reached the edge of the forest. For a while we traveled along the Silvendell once more, passing small, human-occupied hamlets along the way. At this point the river was quite narrow and the water ran swifter, making it impossible to navigate a boat of any size through its waters. It was there the river gave way to a sharp uprising in the earth, at times cutting through narrow gorges lined heavily with trees on either side that allowed little sunlight through to the water's surface at that time of day.

After a while Galamir decided to stop for the night. He had taken once more to humming as he gathered wood for the fire, and that evening under a dark canopy of trees, he played his flute without reservation or fear of being detected. Three horses and riders passed by on the road, yet too intent they were on their business to stop and investigate the source of the music. Galamir commented they were elves, anyway, and not to be feared. Moreover, there were many unseen friends in the forest that would come to the aid of an elf if need be, enchanted creatures who kept themselves hidden, close as we still were to the world of humans.

The next day we continued east along the northern bank of the Silvendell, the edge of elvish territory, on a road rarely frequented by mortals who remained wary of venturing too close to the dark forest rumored to be full of mysterious creatures. The two coffins we abandoned behind a mound of hawthorn shrubs, for it was not unusual for dwarves to be seen traveling along that road. Our mood was considerably brighter. We talked and laughed freely, and Galamir frequently broke out in song with his clear, evocative voice. I even caught Goodren with a hint of a smile upon his lips.

No longer fearing detection, the dwarves sat out in the open, even taking Crumpkin's reins from Galamir. The little horse had proven his worth over and over, and we were all quick to give him a pat and an extra apple from time to time.

Nevertheless, the mood that evening over the campfire grew subdued, for in the back of our minds the dwarves and I knew we would have to part come the morning.

The new day dawned fresh and clean as the dew shimmered like diamonds on the forest canopy above. I awoke on a bed of moss to a chorus of birds flitting about from tree to tree and the sight of ancient trees swaying protectively overhead in the gentle breeze.

Knowing I would meet Galamir's parents later in the day, I took a bit more time that morning making myself look presentable. Stealing behind a thick tree trunk, I changed into the same blue dress I wore when I first arrived in Bensor almost three years before. It was a simple garment for traveling, yet elegant. I also carefully brushed the long locks of my hair and dabbed my neck with a bit of lavender water, thankful my supposed elvish nature kept me from perspiring, or from reeking of any other questionable odor. With any luck, I hoped to appear as though I had not been without a proper bath for several days. On the inside, my heart beat excitedly at the thought of at last reaching Isgilith.

After we consumed the last of the honey wafers, we left camp and continued to head east along the bank of the Silvendell. After a while we crossed over another good-sized river that tumbled down from the north and spilled into the Silvendell below, creating a number of swift eddies at the point where the two waters converged.

"This is the River Triona that flows through my city,"

Galamir commented. "With any luck we shall reach the headwaters by sundown."

It was not long after passing over the Triona that the waters of the Silvendell began to thrash about angrily, fed by numerous tributaries that plunged down from the mountains. Not far ahead a road branched off across a narrow bridge spanning a noisy gorge, and Galamir explained it came down from the mountains and the northern entrance of Grandinwolde. We continued on past the bridge for a little while longer until Galamir brought his horse to a halt.

"This is where we must part," he announced as he dismounted.

I examined our surroundings curiously. There was nothing to distinguish it from the miles behind, other than a gnarled old tree trunk ahead that had no doubt stood there for ages. Unless Galamir had the idea of taking off through the forest without benefit of a road, I thought it a strange place to stop.

The three dwarves eased down onto the ground with the help of a stationary ladder Kiril had fashioned onto the back of the cart. They stood, kicking at the ground and gazing up into the treetops as Galamir saw the wagon was secure in every way. I also dismounted, and a sudden wave of sadness made me realize how much I would miss the dwarves and their antics.

"If you continue east along this road, you should make it into the northern Andains within the next three days," Galamir said quietly. "Draigon's minions still avoid this road and have little to do with the smaller dwarf colonies in the northern Andains. You should be safe there until, Omni willing, our plans succeed and we are all free once more."

"Aye, we've kin there, and 'tis high time we paid 'em a visit," said Hutto with a sniff. "Though Mr. Galamir, Miss Arwyn, we'll forever be indebted to ye for all ye've done."

Froilin then stepped forward. "Miss Arwyn, if it weren't for you, I'd still be rottin' away in Dungard."

I smiled sadly and bent down to embrace my two friends. A tear ran down my cheek as they turned away. Goodren stood in the distance staring into the forest with his arms crossed defiantly, and I could have sworn I heard the sound of sniffling. The dwarf suddenly turned and rushed to embrace me, almost tackling me. The tears streaming down his face into his beard made mine flow all the more.

"My dear friends, I shall miss you all so very much," I said. "The woods of Baeren Ford will seem so forlorn without you there. It pains me to see you leave, yet you must find your life elsewhere."

"Aye, but we shall take ye with us in our hearts," said Hutto, as Goodren and Froilin echoed his sentiment.

"Dear Hutto, Goodren, and Froilin, you may be small in stature but you are giants at heart, and I am honored to call you my friends," Galamir said. "If ever you should need help while you are in this forest, all you need do is call my name three times, and you shall receive it." He smiled. "But please do your best to stay out of trouble from now on."

"Will e'er we see ye again?" said Froilin.

I sighed. "Perhaps our paths will cross again, someday. Only Omni knows for sure, but we can always hope."

With that, the three dwarves climbed back aboard their cart, and I walked over to stroke Crumpkin's muzzle. "And, my dear little Crumpkin, though *you* are small among horses, you are mighty in heart. Thank you for taking such good care of my friends. Now, see them safely home."

Gently Hutto rapped upon Crumpkin's back with the reins. The obedient beast stepped out once more, pulling the cart along behind him and down the road through the trees. Galamir and I stood by solemnly as we watched our three friends disappear in the distance, glancing back longingly every now and again until they were no longer in sight.

For several moments we stared into the trees, and I truly wondered if I would ever see them again.

"It is indeed a miracle we saw them this far. Omni was

surely smiling on us, and let us hope He will continue to guide them," said Galamir solemnly. He then turned toward the old tree stump and, glancing at me with a grin upon his face, spoke words in elvish, invoking the Gifts: "*Caldaril amnuel ochnovan!*"

All at once, the old stump twisted peculiarly, transforming into an elaborate archway of tangled trees through which a narrow road led. I smiled in wonder as we took off on the path that twisted and turned through thick and low-growing trees in a generally northerly direction. The dense foliage allowed little sunlight to penetrate down onto the forest floor below and made it difficult to be completely certain of our direction.

After a while Galamir turned off on one of the seemingly inconsequential paths that split off the main one. We did this several times, each time branching off on what seemed a small deerpath only to discover what appeared a footpath at first glance magically turned into a substantial main road. It was quite disorienting, and I could understand why it would be foolish for anyone to enter Loth Gerodin without an elven guide.

How quickly we traveled once unencumbered by the third horse and the cart, and the miles melted away behind us. After traveling deeper into the forest, I could hear the sound of falling water up ahead. Galamir and I soon came to a sizeable old bridge of stone that spanned the River Triona. Before we traversed the bridge, Galamir slowed his pace and turned to face me.

"Do not be alarmed by the guardians of our wood," he said. "Though ferocious they may appear, you will be in no danger."

I strained my neck to see what Galamir could possibly be referring to. On the other side of the bridge, the path curved around toward the river and came to a dead end at a sheer rock face where the water came tumbling from above. I could see nothing else out of the ordinary but a huge table and two chairs carved from stone that sat to one side of the pathway. Such furniture was much too large for either elf or human.

As soon as we crossed over the bridge, a low voice boomed from above the cliff. "Who's a-darin' t' enter this wood!"

I looked up in time to see two huge creatures bound from the top of the rock face and come flying through the air. The earth shook mightily as they landed on the ground, and even Avencloe, usually so gentle and steady, startled at the sight of them. The two creatures stood before us with giant clubs in their over-sized hands that could easily wipe out a full-grown horse. Over-sized, from their thick hulking bodies to their enormous eyes and grotesquely large noses, one of them sported a mane of shaggy hair upon his head while the other had nothing but stubble, revealing a rather hideous, misshapen skull. Such creatures made Gargalocs appear as gentle as kittens, and I could not help but shrink back in my saddle at the sight of them.

"*Metheuil harberoth!*" Galamir shouted.

The creature with the shaggy head of hair, ambled forward and took a long look at Galamir, the hairs on its chest almost brushing against Calyxa's nose. "Ah, the Master Galamir, indeed it be. Home again!" he said in a low, guttural voice.

"Greetings Guluk, Zigrat. I'm afraid you may have given my friend Arwyn here a start. She is not yet accustomed to trolls and their ways."

"Nay!" the creature bellowed dramatically, slapping his forehead with the force of a felled tree.

"'Tis true, Guluk," Galamir explained indulgently. "There are none left near her home in Guilden."

The creature eyed me curiously, and I wondered if he was considering how to cook and eat me. "Nay, we-um trolls come from dem southlands ancients ago."

"It is indeed a, er, pleasure to meet you—" My voice

cracked. I was not well versed in how to speak to a creature that could easily break me in two with one hand if he took a notion to do so.

"Guluk, where'n is the manners of you?" the other troll chastised. "A slow day 'tis a-been and we're sittin' to tea when the Master Galamir and the lady come up on us all a-quiet. Perchance them to join us, honored we'd be."

I looked up onto the table and for the first time saw a very large copper teapot and two large wooden cups.

"Although we appreciate your hospitality, we must be on our way, or we will not arrive in Isgilith before nightfall," Galamir said.

"Suit'n themselves," the bald one called Zigrat said, "but must'n them come for a visit soon. We's a-have so little news from the wood's outsides."

"That I will," Galamir promised. "Now if you will assist me with your magic."

"For the kind Master, of course, but yes," Guluk replied politely.

I heard a low, rumbling noise and realized it came from the troll, speaking a language as ancient as the earth. There was a long, muted creaking sound that came from inside the rock face before us. The sound grew and became almost deafening until all at once the grinding stopped.

"A-free thems is to pass," the troll announced.

"And grateful to you we are," said Galamir, as he began to lead the way toward the rock face. I followed closely behind, bowing my head with respect as I passed the two gentle giants. They in turn bowed, such ironic creatures with their formidable outward facade.

"Good day to them both and travels a-happy," the trolls said as they waved goodbye.

Galamir led the way to the waterfall. What appeared to be a solid rock surface had a narrow fissure that created the illusion of solidity. Quickly Galamir's horse slipped through the fissure and into a cave beyond. No sooner had Avencloe rounded the turn into the cave than its northern entrance became visible a few dozen yards away. My mind, however, was still reeling from our bizarre encounter. To Galamir it seemed conversing with well-mannered creatures that looked like the side of a small mountain was a common occurrence, and I wondered what other amazing beings I would meet on my holiday.

Though it seemed only a few yards away from the place we had entered the cave, the whole forest appeared all the more alive as we emerged on the other side, and the trees themselves grew denser and hovered protectively over the road, which became much wider. Able to ride abreast once more, Galamir turned to observe my reaction as I entered the inner circle of Loth Gerodin.

"They certainly are a polite, er, species," I commented, nodding back in the direction from which we had just come.

"The trolls? Yes, they are." Galamir laughed. "I'm afraid I should have warned you, yet we in Loth Gerodin tend to take their presence for granted."

"It is their job to guard the forest?"

"They are indeed the guardians of our realm and have been for ages."

"I must say, they would certainly discourage my entrance if I were not meant to be here."

Galamir laughed once more. "I can assure you, no one who is not a friend of the elves gets past their watch. But what do you think of this forest?" He gestured to indicate our new surroundings.

I allowed the wonder to show in my eyes as I took in the beauty surrounding us, and we rode on, speaking lightheartedly as the miles passed. Every once in a while, Galamir and I came upon some elaborate carving in the side of a tree depicting an animal, an elvish face, a doorway, or some other whimsical thing. There were countless footpaths merging with the main road, and each headed off along an enticing trail past gazebos, bubbling streams, and stone structures, placed seemingly out in the middle of nowhere. There even appeared to be a rhyme and reason to the numerous flowers that lined streambeds, pathways, and crevices, as if some very fastidious gardener maintained the whole forest.

And then there were the creatures—all manner of beings, unlike any I'd ever seen before. Creatures that flew through the air, hid among the trees, and scuffled along the forest floor. Some with fur, some with feathers, some on two legs, and others on four. I caught a glimpse of them one moment only for them to mysteriously disappear from view a moment later, making me wonder if I'd really seen them at all. But always I had the feeling of countless curious eyes upon us as we rode along.

After a while, we stopped at a stone table close to the road, beside a cool waterfall that gurgled down from somewhere above. To my surprise, a full picnic basket sat there, complete with bread, fruit, cheeses, and a bottle of wine. I looked inquisitively at Galamir, who smiled.

"The gnomes left it here," he said. "Word has spread throughout the forest of your arrival. This is their way of welcoming you."

"Gnomes, you say?"

"Yes, the little people, tillers of the earth. They are the ones responsible for tending Bensor's Garden, but you'll likely not catch them at work for, you see, they are quite skittish of the big folk."

"What fascinating creatures I have learned of today," I said. "There's no telling what other surprises must lie in store for me in this forest."

"Of that there can be no doubt," Galamir said with a wink.

Together, my friend and I sat down at the stone table beside the stream and ate our lunch. My mood lifted the deeper we traveled into the forest, despite the sting of earlier saying goodbye to my friends being still fresh on my mind. Yet the merriment in Galamir's eyes, the beauty of our surroundings, and the anticipation of at last reaching our destination was enough to make my heart light.

It was midafternoon when two elves traveling south passed us on the path of the River Triona. They greeted Galamir warmly and welcomed him back to Loth Gerodin and were as equally cordial toward me. After that we encountered more elves the closer we came to Isgilith. Where they were off to in the middle of the dense forest was anyone's guess. And they were all of them beautiful, with sparkling eyes, porcelain skin, and hair that shimmered in the splashes of sunlight filtering through the treetops.

It was not until late afternoon, when we rode out upon the top of a ridge and through an ornately carved stone archway, that we looked down on a scene that made me gasp.

"Behold Isgilith!" Galamir announced with a smile.

Speechless, I looked down upon a basin, a horseshoe-shaped indentation in the forest, slightly tilted to the south. On the far side spanned a huge ridge from which flowed three rivers that cascaded down cliffs and converged in the basin below, creating a huge semicircular lake which in turn spilled over yet another drop. Beneath the second plunge sat a perfectly circular island around which the water rushed and then rejoined, forming the River Triona. But it was the island itself that most caught my eye, not only for its circular shape, but for the massive trees growing in perfect formation like columns around its rim.

With all the water coursing about from every direction, it was hard to imagine how anyone could build a city in such a place. Yet as I studied it from above, I could see buildings of gray stone peeking through treetops, walls surrounding hidden gardens, and gently flowing waterways that had been diverted away from the main rivers. Isgilith seemed like a place out of a dream.

"Why do you cry?" Galamir asked, breaking into my reverie with his thoughtful glance.

Was I crying? I hadn't noticed. It was a moment before I could speak. "I cry because my eyes have caught a glimpse of heaven, and now all the things that once held my gaze will appear as gray as ash on a sunless day."

Galamir grinned. "Then let us proceed, for what you see is but a glimpse of hidden treasures."

CHAPTER 7

"I meet Galamir's kin, and they are a delight, yet never could I have expected anything less."

The road we traveled dipped back into the trees and along the circumference of the city, gradually sloping down, and then back up again until we crossed the first of the three rivers on the top tier of the city. To our right, the water disappeared over the ridge, and I could hear it roar as it plunged down the cliff below. To our left, much of the water had been diverted away from the main part of the river and coursed through a labyrinth of buildings, over small waterfalls, and along quiet channels beside peaceful gardens. Were it not for my desire to reach Galamir's home, I ached to get lost exploring the many inviting pathways.

We were almost halfway around the upper ridge when we passed through yet another gate into the busiest and central-most area of Isgilith. Before us coursed the middle of the three rivers through a small lake before it parted and disappeared under the wide road for a bit, only to split and circumnavigate a grand manor before plunging down the cliff behind it. Surrounding the lake was a beautiful stone quay and smaller flowering trees that framed its surface as if the water were a mirror. On the end opposite the grand manor sat a very long and ornate building with patios and hanging baskets of plants and bubbling fountains that cascaded down into the waters below. The glassy surface was covered with graceful swans, ducks, and other waterfowl as well as several swan-shaped boats drifting about leisurely.

Galamir turned down a pebble-covered roadway leading beside the water. Homes made of the same gray stone and adorned with turrets, balconies, and other features lined the lane. Each were surrounded by high walls and private gardens filled with fountains, gazebos, stone pathways, and other such delights. Each house looked like a smallish castle. I felt as though I had stumbled into a fairy tale.

In a matter of moments, Galamir guided us through an opening in the wall beside the road and into the courtyard of a lovely manor. A single turret stood at the point where the two wings of the house converged, and just below a vine-covered balcony was a wooden front door adorned with carvings of various woodland flowers. An elvish youth sat on the front steps and sprang to his feet as the two of us approached.

"Master Galamir, you've returned!" he exclaimed.

"Aye, Androvus, and good it is to be home!"

"Your mother's been expecting you, sir, and the lady as well," the boy said shyly as he nodded in my direction.

"Good! Now if you will tend to our horses, we will..."

The front door of the manor opened and out stepped the most beautiful woman I had seen since my arrival in Bensor almost three years before. She so closely resembled Galamir in the face and her golden hair—long and with soft curls—I guessed she must be his sister, although I had not heard him mention having a sister before. The woman glided effortlessly as she walked down the front steps toward us, her eyes shimmering an unearthly blue that told of her joy at our arrival.

"Mother, at last we've returned," Galamir said, as he embraced the woman and gave her a kiss on the cheek.

"We have been expecting you." Her voice was a breeze blowing through a wind chime. "The birds told us of your safe arrival within the borders of our forest."

Then an elvish man came through the front door into the courtyard. He was also fair of hair, and his eyes were full of gentle merriment, just as his son's. "Galamir, how good it is you have returned safely," he said as he clasped his son's hand.

"Omni was indeed watching over our journey. But come,

I would like you to meet my dear friend." Galamir turned toward me. "Arwyn, this is my mother, Elastair, and my father, Gladigan."

Her rich blue eyes glistening with warmth, Elastair moved gracefully toward me and took my hands in hers. "It is an honor to have you visit our home," she said, and she kissed me on both cheeks.

"You are very kind to have me as your guest." I smiled, already knowing I liked Galamir's family very much. But there had never been any doubts I would.

"Arwyn, your arrival has been anticipated ever since Galamir returned from the south and told us of you," Gladigan added.

"Thank you, my lord," I said, nodding my head respectfully. Indeed I felt honored, though I imagined Elastair and Gladigan were gracious with all their guests.

"Come now," Elastair said. "A special dinner has been prepared in expectation of your arrival. But first let me show you to your room where you may freshen yourself."

With that, the mistress of the manor turned and led everyone through the front door and into a circular foyer lined with stately wood paneling. Above us a balcony spanned the length of the foyer, connecting one side of the house with the other. Elastair led the way up the grand staircase and down a paneled hallway to a room at the end. Inside I looked keenly upon the lavish bed sitting in the middle of the room across from an ornate fireplace and a balcony that looked out over the wall in front and to the lake beyond.

I was most delighted, however, not only to find a basin of hot water had already been drawn for me but also the elves had managed to find a way of incorporating indoor plumbing into their architecture, albeit quite primitive compared to vague memories I recalled from my past existence. How comfortable it all looked after sleeping on the ground and little more than a cot during our stay at the Alliance. I would certainly be well rested once it was time to return home.

"What a lovely bedchamber," I commented with a pleased smile. "I will be most comfortable, indeed."

"I hoped you would like it," Elastair said.

Galamir placed my knapsack on the bed. "You will let us know if you need anything."

With that, I was left alone for a few minutes to unpack and to splash some hot water onto my face. I then returned down the staircase and found everyone gathered in a great room behind the entryway. As I entered, I saw the immense fireplace in the center of the room and the furniture made of fine wood and comfortable upholstery. Everywhere ornate rugs covered the marble floors, and intricate figures were carved in the woodwork surrounding the doorways and in the ceiling rafters. Paintings adorned the room as well as a variety of musical instruments, some of which I had not seen before in Guilden. There were two sets of double doors leading out in different directions to a beautiful little garden behind the house.

Elastair led us through an arched doorway off to the left and into the dining room, where there was yet another fireplace. The long table in the middle of the room was covered with fine china and goblets, candelabra, and eating utensils made of silver. Such finery I was not accustomed to seeing in Baeren Ford. Elastair introduced the young elvish housekeeper, Gwyneleth, who was laying out the evening meal on the table, and then Elastair gestured we be seated.

Dinner was a feast, with plates piled high with roasted duck, fresh spinach, roasted potatoes, nuts and berries, and a bottle of the finest pear wine made right in Isgilith. Based on the richness of the surroundings, I rather expected conversation during the meal to be stiff and stuffy, yet I found Elastair and Gladigan to be a delight, much like their son. At the same time, they retained an air of grace and formality. Elastair in particular was quite the gracious hostess, and I looked with admiration upon the queenly way she sat at the head of the table in her long, flowing gown, directing everyone in sight with little more than a lift of her finger.

Following dinner I retired early to my bedroom, quite ready to peel off my traveling clothes and indulge in a hot bath and warm bed. I walked out onto my balcony and peered over the stone wall surrounding the house to the lake. Thousands of tiny fireflies danced hypnotically to the haunting sound of an elven chorus singing somewhere in the distance, and I thought myself to have already stumbled into an enchanting dream.

CHAPTER 8

"I had hoped coming to the elven city would help to illuminate my true nature."

I could hear Dr. Susan's voice from far away chime in. "And has it?"

I shrugged. "Nay. I am now all the more conflicted within."

I awoke the next morning to daylight pouring into my room through the open doors leading out to the balcony. Outside a chorus of birds flitted about fervently from tree to tree. Drowsily I buried my head into the fluffy down pillows, smiling at the luxuriousness of my surroundings and the sound of the birds' warbling. I could have slept a while longer, but the smell of fresh bacon floating up from downstairs enticed my weary body out of bed. After seeing Elastair's long, flowing gown the evening before, I happily slipped into one of the elegant gowns Loralon had made for me, glad to finally have the chance to wear it.

I went downstairs to find breakfast served in the garden, right beside a bubbling fountain underneath a wooden arbor crawling with honeysuckle. A little later, Galamir took me on a stroll to help me get my bearings around the city. Everywhere we went, the waters flowing through the land had long been tamed and channeled into narrow canals and waterways easily navigated by the numerous swan-shaped boats. Not surprisingly, there were plentiful courtyards and archways adorned with cool green arbors and large urns filled with brightly colored flowers. The scent of roses permeated the air, as did the sound of bubbling fountains.

Galamir then took me to the stockyards to see where the community pigs, goats, and chickens were kept, to the sporting fields, and the archery range. Yet of all the places Galamir showed me, the island beneath the horseshoe-shaped waterfall was the most enchanting.

We walked across one of the bridges spanning the rushing water of the River Triona and onto the circular island in the middle. In the very center of the island stood a gushing fountain, and around its circumference giant elderhorn trees grew in formation, reaching higher into the heavens than even the tallest building on the upper tier of the city. Their sheltering boughs dwarfed us, and in that place I felt a strange peace, like the peace I felt when I visited Arnuin's Hold.

"We are now standing in the very center of Loth Gerodin Forest," Galamir explained, "in the greatest Circle of Omni in all of Bensor, perhaps in all the world." Galamir lifted his eyes to the heights above, as if even he were in awe. "It was in this place Elwei and Arnuin were wed, the most sacred place in all of Bensor."

I glanced around at the Circle. It was quiet except for the thunderous waterfall at one end. We were two of only a handful of elves there. "But why is it so quiet?" I asked. "Why are there not more people here?"

Galamir laughed indulgently. "Dear Arwyn, this place will be filled with all manner of creatures come the Faerenfel, as it is every year."

To me it was no laughing matter. Here the elves of Isgilith could freely gather to sing and dance to Omni in the midst of Loth Gerodin—while those to the south would not dare enter a circle without risking imprisonment—and yet we were practically alone? "I should hope the people of Loth Gerodin do not take for granted the privilege which has long been denied to others."

"Arwyn, I daresay you will not find any people more attuned to the otherworldly realm than the elves. It's just that, well, we attend to such matters privately and do not make a fuss over it."

"Oh, I see." Still, I thought there were certain things over which one *should* make a fuss, but I said nothing further on the matter.

"Come, the high elf, Valdir, wishes your company for the noon meal," Galamir said, offering me his arm. "He has been quite anxious to meet you."

"And what exactly have you told him about me?" I asked curiously.

"Besides the fact that you are an elf living among mortals, he seems quite interested in your association with Eliendor."

I was intrigued. "And I am quite interested in *his* association with Eliendor as well."

"I must tell you of Valdir's wife, lest you broach that topic unnecessarily." Galamir's brow narrowed into a frown. "She was out walking late one night when she slipped into the easternmost of the upper falls, the most treacherous of the three, and was swept over the cliff. Her body was finally recovered several miles downstream."

"How tragic!"

"Indeed." Galamir grew silent for a moment, seeming hesitant to continue. "There were rumors…"

"Yes…go on."

"That the drowning was not entirely an accident."

I gasped. "Murdered?"

"No…suicide," he said. "Before the incident, she was often tearful and had an overall air of sadness about her. Poor Valdir felt helpless concerning her condition and grieved so following her death."

"But why?" I asked, dumbfounded as to why anyone would do something so desperate.

"No one knows." Galamir sighed. "Neither did anyone acknowledge the possibility, mainly for the sake of their sons who were still quite young at the time."

I thought of Callas. What a terrible thing to have lost his mother at such a tender age. I could only imagine it must have been the same for his brother. And under such questionable circumstances!

The noon hour approached as Galamir and I made the

long climb back to the upper ridge and the busy central upper lake where elves were going about their business at a leisurely though steadfast pace. Their actions were slow and deliberate and always with an air of grace.

We climbed the stone staircase up to the grand front terrace of Valdir Velconium's manor, the one I had seen sitting between the two branches of the middle river the day before. As I drew closer, it appeared even more splendid.

A young elf greeted us at the front door, and he led us inside a large foyer lined with windows reaching to the high ceilings above. Two curving staircases on either side led to rooms above, and a pair of golden candelabra hung over a beautiful marble floor. Off to one side of the foyer were windows looking into a grand ballroom where there had no doubt been countless parties and celebrations through the years. On the other side of the foyer stood a large dining hall with windows looking down on the gardens to the west.

The young elf led us down a center hall, which stretched from the front of the manor all the way to the back. A set of large double doors opened onto the veranda behind the house, yet Galamir and I were guided into another room overlooking the garden in back. As we entered, I was startled at the large collection of books lining the walls of the library—the largest I had ever seen.

"My master will be with you in a moment," our guide announced before disappearing into the foyer again.

"His collection of books is quite impressive," I said in a whisper for fear of disturbing the tranquility of the room.

"Yes, that it is," Galamir agreed. "I've not seen its like, even in the homes of Eliendor and Benedrake combined."

I walked slowly around the library for a minute, admiring the workmanship on the huge oak bookcases that extended all the way to the high ceiling. In the middle of the room sat a large mahogany desk, facing windows overlooking the veranda. The imposing desk spoke of its owner's importance to the elvish community. Above the desk was the portrait of a striking elven woman with fine, light brown, almost blonde, locks that draped across her shoulders, whom I surmised must have been Valdir's poor wife as I saw a shadow of Callas in her face. For a long moment I stared at it and felt saddened that life had been snatched from the woman's beautiful bright eyes so soon. But there was something more—she looked oddly familiar, as though I had seen her somewhere before. I dismissed the thought, knowing such was impossible.

Before we were even aware of Valdir's approach, Galamir and I turned to see the shadow of his tall frame in the doorway of the library. The leader of the elven colony appeared to glide across the floor as he entered the room, and the long flowing robe he wore over his tunic of brown made him look quite regal. The finely chiseled features on his face were decidedly masculine, and his dark eyes exuded power and wisdom. His hair was dark with a surprisingly silvery gray tinge, but it was not a gray that reminded me of someone who was old and feeble—although he was certainly quite ancient—but of someone wise and venerable. Yet as I gazed at him, I realized the color had drained from his face, and he stared at me as though I were a ghost.

A bewildering silence fell like a stone inside the room, making me feel quite awkward. "Does my presence not please you, my lord?" I said at last.

"Forgive me," he said with no further explanation. "Arwyn of Baeren Ford, you are most welcome in my home."

Yet in his eyes I saw no welcome. I glanced at Galamir, yet he appeared just as bewildered as I by the elven lord's less-than-warm reception.

"It is indeed an honor to be here," I offered. "Your home is quite lovely."

"I trust our friend, Galamir, is giving you a proper overview of our city, fine young elf that he is," he replied, seeming to ignore my comment.

"Indeed, he spent the morning showing me its highlights, though I suspect we only scratched the surface of its wonders," I said. "Isgilith is even more beautiful than I imagined."

"Come now, I know you must be hungry," Valdir said with seeming effort. "Lunch is served on the veranda."

Valdir led us through the large double doors in the back of the manor and out to a table on a covered porch. As we followed I eyed Galamir, who returned my look with a shrug of bafflement. Several steps led down to a lawn where green grass grew and flowering shrubs surrounded a fountain. On either side of the lawn, the two branches of the middle river plummeted out of sight. Beyond the garden wall, the earth opened up as if ages ago it had simply collapsed, thus forming the basin that stretched out below. From the garden was a stunning view of the vast Circle of Omni and the three converging rivers below.

Valdir motioned for us to be seated at the table prepared for us, yet that same inexplicable silence prevailed until Galamir cleared his throat uncomfortably. "Tell me, my lord, I have yet to see Vandaril," he inquired. "Is he out and about somewhere in particular?"

"He...er...he is currently leading an expedition to the western borders of the Greenwaithe—a surveillance operation if I may be blunt," Valdir answered, all the while avoiding my gaze. "There are rumors of increased Gargaloc activity on the other side, and I sent him to find out what he can of their doings."

Just then one of Valdir's servants brought out three plates of food and placed them before each of us. I looked hungrily at the small feast and took a sip of pear juice from the crystal glass before me.

Galamir shook his head, ignoring the elven lord's bewildering reticence. "That does not bode well."

"Indeed it does not, but whatever the case, we elves must be ready to defend our forest if need be."

"And yet there are many mortals who look to the elves for guidance at such a time, and perhaps intervention as well," I interjected, carefully watching Valdir's reaction. "'Twill be difficult if your attentions are pointed elsewhere."

Still he refused to look me in the eye.

"Yes, but as you saw at the Alliance headquarters, mortals are now taking a more active role in their own defense," Galamir said.

"I only pray it will be enough," I added, dabbing my lips with a linen napkin. "My lord, it was a pleasure to meet your son Callas during our visit."

"I trust he treated you with the utmost in hospitality." What an ironic thing for Valdir to say, as still he would not look me in the eye!

"Why, yes he did. He was quite the gracious host." I gave a quick glance in Galamir's direction, but now he averted his gaze from my own. I would be most relieved when this awkward luncheon came to an end.

"Er, Callas indicated..." Galamir began.

Suddenly there was a loud *clank* as Valdir dropped his fork onto his plate. He brought his napkin to his mouth. "Forgive me, but I must excuse myself," came his muffled words. Valdir rose and walked briskly back through the door into his manor, leaving Galamir and me staring at each other in bewilderment.

My gaze fell to my full plate, and I wondered what I had done to bring about such a strong reaction in the elven lord. In what seemed like hours, a servant appeared to tell us his master had taken ill and would not be returning, but I guessed otherwise. Elves simply did not take ill.

"Was there anything about my words or manner that could have offended him?" I asked Galamir, as we walked back to his home.

"Nay, and of that I am certain," Galamir replied, shaking his head pensively. "Such is not like Valdir. I do not know what could have troubled him so."

"I only wish he could have saved it for after our visit," I said with a gulp. If I elicited such an undesirable response from the leader of the elves, what prospects could I hope to find in the community at large? I was completely flabbergasted, and I wondered that night as I slipped into my bed if there would ever be an explanation for Valdir's odd behavior.

As it turned out, I had only to wait until the following day for an explanation, or at least *part* of an explanation, that came from Valdir himself. Galamir and I had just finished practicing at the archery range and were heading for home when we found Valdir on the lane, looking as though he was waiting for us. When I saw him, I wanted to turn and run the other way, but he walked toward me with such determination I could not ignore him. And this time, there was a smile upon his face.

"Dear Arwyn, Galamir, my friend, how good it is to see you," he began.

Was it really? Such incongruous behavior was hardly convincing and certainly quite baffling.

"Please, I must beg your forgiveness for my less-than-gracious welcome yesterday," the elven lord said with eyes brimming with remorse. He directed his next words to me alone. "You see, Arwyn," he said with emotion, "you very closely resemble someone I knew long ago."

I wondered at his words, for I bore no resemblance to his wife, if the woman in the portrait was any indication. Whoever she was, the memory of her had certainly elicited something quite powerful within Valdir.

"Do you mind me asking who, my lord?" I inquired cautiously.

"An old friend," he said very mysteriously, and it was obvious he would be no more forthcoming than that. "May I join you?"

"Of course, my lord," Galamir replied.

We walked with Valdir between the two of us. "Now, Arwyn, I understand you are friends with Eliendor."

"Eliendor is my friend and mentor," I replied.

"Your mentor, you say?"

"Yes, he has taught me much, everything from Bensorian lore to the healing arts and the elvish language…that is, the nuances of the Bensorian brand of elvish," I added quickly.

"Eliendor must see something quite special in you to have spent so much time with your training. He would not take such an interest in just anyone."

"As I told you, there is something rather special about Arwyn," Galamir said with a wink.

I could tell by his demeanor he was much relieved.

"That there is, Galamir, that there is," Valdir said with a gleam in his eyes.

"And what is the nature of *your* association with Eliendor?" I asked.

"I have known Eliendor for many a year," he replied pensively, "but how far back our association goes is difficult to say, for there have been long periods when I have heard nothing from him and knew not his whereabouts, times when he was no doubt wandering about somewhere far away."

"He *is* full of mystery," I commented. Then again, Valdir himself seemed full of mystery. The change that had come over the elven lord since our first meeting the day before was startling. I much preferred this more pleasant version.

"I believe you were telling me how you saw Callas at the Alliance?"

"Aye, my lord," Galamir said casually. "He even made mention of returning home for the Faerenfel."

Valdir sighed, and I thought there was a hint of sadness in his expression. "That would do me well. It has been long since I have seen my son," he said quietly. Curiously, in Valdir's face I could see no glimmer of his son, and I suspected Callas took more after his mother, both in appearance and temperament. I thought back to what

Galamir had told me about the supposed rivalry between Callas and his brother, and I wondered if those differences had anything to do with his father's sadness.

The conversation turned to less emotionally charged topics before we finally arrived back at Galamir's home. It was there Valdir turned and took my hands unexpectedly in his. "Arwyn, it is my custom to host a gala on the night before the Faerenfel," he explained. "This year I would like very much for it to be held in your honor."

"How kind you are," I said, quite flattered. "I would be delighted."

"Very well, then consider yourself officially invited."

As I stood with my hands still in Valdir's, it seemed for one brief moment as he stared into my eyes he was not staring at me but gazing instead at the mystery woman he held in his memory. It was slightly unnerving, until our gaze broke and he let go my hands.

During the coming days, I settled into the pace of Isgilith, becoming more and more accustomed to the elvish lifestyle—and more and more accustomed to running into Valdir when I was out and about. His manner had become dramatically more attentive than at our first meeting.

Later in the week rain fell for two straight days upon the forest, the kind of rain that fell slowly and soaked into the ground, giving rise to vibrant splashes of color that dotted the forest floor, crept up the sides of the buildings, and adorned the many urns and flowerpots around the city.

Though restricted to indoor activity during those days, I was nevertheless entertained, playing board games with Galamir and listening to his and his mother's musical talents on their numerous instruments. One afternoon Valdir dropped in and, over a pot of tea, asked me all manner of questions about everything from medicinal plants to Bensorian history to the Alliance. Through it all, I had the distinct feeling there was something more to his questioning, like he was sizing me up. He seemed to be over whatever feeling I had elicited in him during our first meeting, yet I found his sudden, intense, subtly flirtatious interest stimulating but slightly overwhelming.

When a third day dawned with no end in sight to the wet weather, Elastair invited several elven maidens over for an afternoon of lacemaking. Lace, as I quickly discovered, was one of the elven city's most sought-after exports, and it was not difficult to understand why after seeing the intricate patterns embellishing Elastair's tables and windows.

The three elven maidens were all tall and graceful, and their faces were framed with long, fine hair adorned with thin braids and delicate ornaments. Galena and Analeth, considered young women by elvish standards, still maintained an air of girlishness and were prone to blushing shyly and giggling. Kyora, however, with her flaming red hair and cold blue eyes, walked into the parlor looking as though she smelled something putrid the moment she laid eyes on me. Her looks were quite striking, but too severe were her intense eyes and her high cheekbones to be considered beautiful. Whether in manner or appearance, Kyora sparked a memory in me of someone I had known once long before, and I did not relish the idea of spending an entire afternoon with her.

As the rain fell steadily on the parlor windows, the five of us cut and threaded and stitched while engaging in polite conversation befitting ladies of distinction. I had watched Loralon embroider intricate patterns into clothing many times, but only a few times had I ever witnessed her doing lacework. The whole process was quite tedious and I felt rather awkward for having to rely so much on Elastair's direction for a craft that seemed to come so easily to the others. Elastair made light of my deficiency when it came to a needle and thread, yet the others looked at me as though an elven maiden who did not produce beautiful lace was somehow less of an elf.

As I attempted to engage in polite small talk with the others, I wished ardently to toss my work into the lake outside and go riding off into the woods. To make it worse, the very nature of our work reminded me keenly of my dearest friend back home, and I suddenly wished Loralon were there.

Although she had engaged freely in conversation with the others for quite some time, Kyora had barely spoken three words to me since her arrival, and so I was rather surprised when she finally directed a comment to me. "Elastair tells us you live among mortals," she said in a rather condescending tone.

"What you have heard is true," I replied.

Kyora's upper lip curled slightly. "But why would you choose to live with humans rather than with your own kind?"

The other two maidens tittered uncomfortably while Elastair, in her elegant and dignified way, gave Kyora a look of displeasure.

"I rather like living among humans," I responded, feeling my heartbeat quicken. "They are hardworking, passionate people, and quite full of life."

"But aren't they a bit, well, malodorous?"

Really?

"Kyora!" Elastair chastised. "I would ask you be more polite to our guest."

"Forgive me, Elastair, but I meant no offense, which I'm sure Arwyn understands. It has been long since I have visited a mortal village, but I remember them as less, well, refined than our cities."

"Elastair," I said, my eyes remaining fixed upon the redheaded vixen, "I can forgive Kyora her ignorance of such matters. After all, the separation of elves and mortals these past years has no doubt created many such misperceptions. Perhaps, Kyora, your memory does not serve you well."

An awkward silence fell upon the group as Kyora coldly met my gaze. Had she possessed the Gifts, she would have seen images floating around in my mind of how I would have gladly knocked her to the floor.

"Elastair, would you have any more tea?" said Analeth, eyes wide with discomfort. How spineless she and Galena suddenly appeared as they sat by so meekly. It was obvious who was the dominant female of the group.

"Certainly," Elastair replied, as she arose from her place on the settee, shooting Kyora a look that dared her to say anything more.

The remainder of the afternoon passed by painfully slowly as Kyora had little more to say to me and tried her best to monopolize the conversation with talk of the goings-on in Isgilith and people I did not know. I thought it quite silly for Kyora to be treating someone she barely knew in such a manner and was glad when the three elven maidens left at the end of the afternoon.

"Did you see her human ears? She is certainly not one of us." I heard Kyora laugh as the front door was about to close. I could take her undeserved disdain for me, but *that* jab stung. Self-consciously I raised a hand to my left ear, embarrassed my secret had been noticed.

"I do apologize for Kyora's less than friendly behavior," Elastair lamented as she closed the front door. "She's a bit, well, uppity. I should have thought better than to invite her this afternoon."

What was it about me that elicited such a rude welcome in some of the residents of the elven city? Still, I shrugged. "You are not to blame for the behavior of your guests."

"However, next time I shall be more careful of the guest list," she said amicably.

I returned her smile and suddenly had a new appreciation for my hostess. Elastair was certainly not meek, yet she emanated grace and dignity, and I was sure at that moment I had found a true friend.

That evening, I retired early to my room and sat on a chair next to the double doors leading out to the balcony, listening to the rain fall gently outside. In my hand was a book I had borrowed from the library several days before, yet my mind drifted off to the events of the past week. Feeling some degree of disillusionment, I longed for my home in Guilden. With the exception of my afternoon with Kyora and my baffling first meeting with Valdir, my time with the elves so far had been most enjoyable, yet I found myself missing the earthiness of life in a mortal village. In some ways the elven way of life was certainly more challenging to my intellect, yet with the absence of illness or disease, I wondered how I would possibly bide my time in such a place. But most unsettling was the thought that I would perhaps never be truly fulfilled in either Baeren Ford or Loth Gerodin.

Furthermore, it was disappointing to come to a place known for being enchanting and have yet to see anyone use the Gifts. In fact, the elves of Isgilith went about their business as mundanely as if they didn't live in a magical forest. Had living in peace and isolation made them complacent? Perhaps living in constant danger and threat of exposure forced one to do the extraordinary. Or was it that only an extraordinary person would bother to risk leaving the safety and security of the forest for the good of all?

My mind drifted to Callas, and I remembered what he said about the elven city being "stuffy." I also remembered our little escapade back at the Alliance headquarters, a hint of a rebellious streak I secretly found exciting, and I could feel a smile spread upon my face. Callas was not afraid to live a little dangerously—like me.

I could understand why Callas did not exactly feel comfortable in Loth Gerodin, and it probably had to do with more than his rivalry with his brother. In many ways, it seemed he and I had quite a lot in more in common than met the eye. He was daring, charming, and slightly rebellious—not to mention physically attractive.

And I knew when he showed up for the Faerenfel, things would become much more interesting.

CHAPTER 9

"It was a perfectly sublime moment, as if I were dreaming the most wondrous dream." I furrowed my brow with irritation. "Shattered in a moment by the presence of an intruder—a mortal at that!"

Sometime that night the rain stopped falling and the skies cleared. I awoke to glorious rays of sunlight shining brightly through the fresh green treetops. I walked out onto my balcony to greet the new day, breathing deeply of the cool, clean air. After spending the previous three days indoors, the whole world beckoned for me to return to the forest and the places that renewed my spirit.

Not long after a hearty breakfast, I threw my bow and quiver on my back and had Avencloe saddled for a ride. Ever since the day of my arrival, I longed for the moment when I could break away and explore the surrounding forest by myself. By midmorning, I passed through the arched entrance to Isgilith and down the road Galamir and I traveled a week before. My heart was light as the beauty of Loth Gerodin enticed me farther from the city gates, and I turned off the main road onto a pathway that led past a gazebo into the forest beyond. Farther along, the pathway followed a bubbling stream through a grove of hemlock and over a forest floor covered with ferns, purple trillium, and wild ginger. Large granite boulders littered the landscape, reflecting the sunlight that shone through the trees above.

After a short distance, we passed over a small bridge of stone to a place where another path split away. The smaller path led up past a hedge of wild azaleas, and I could hear the sound of gurgling water beyond, or…something akin to giggling, and I knew any number of elusive forest creatures were watching us. Curious, I turned off the main path and followed the trail up to a beautiful little pool surrounded by flowering azaleas, rhododendrons, and dogwoods. A small waterfall at the opposite end fed the pool beneath. It was one of the loveliest places I had ever seen.

Quietly I slid down to the ground and tied Avencloe's lead to a nearby tree and then went to sit on the mossy carpet beside the water. Feeling quite happy and contented, I chose to continue ignoring my conflicted feelings of the day before. It was too glorious a day to worry with my troubles.

Being in such an enchanted place brought my Gifts to mind, those supernatural powers of the All, Omni, that he endowed to me in lesser form. To a small, limited degree, the forces of nature were mine to command. It was something I rarely would do back in Baeren Ford, but there in Loth Gerodin, where magical happenings seemed to be part of the landscape, I was more inclined to experiment.

The ground around me was littered with pink and white petals that floated to the ground from the dogwoods overhead. *"Erin dornathel myalim!"* I commanded, and all at once, the petals danced into the air, swirling dreamily as if in the midst of a small whirlwind. Being able to use my Gifts without restraint or fear of what others might think was freeing. I laughed out loud and lay back on the forest floor, basking in the dappled sunshine as the petals fell gently all about me. I allowed the hypnotic rhythm of the falling water to lull me to sleep. How much time had passed when I finally awoke I did not know, but the sun was much higher in the sky.

I stretched contentedly among the white and pink petals and, having no particular urge to leave such a magical place, I lingered awhile, humming to myself in a way I never did when I was in the presence of others. Soon, the hum turned to words, and the words into a song extracted from somewhere deep in my memory.

The rhythm and melody sounded exotic to my ears, unlike any song I had heard either in Baeren Ford or Isgilith. Like so many of my memories that bubbled up at the most unexpected moments, along with the tune came the faint image of a plush armchair where a man sat, book in hands as a silky voice magically emanated from a black box on the floor nearby, the singer nowhere in sight.

A rustle in the bushes broke into my thoughts, and I looked up to see two dark eyes staring at me from across the pool. To my astonishment, a small white horse no more than a third the size of Avencloe stood there, looking as though it was intensely curious about this being who came so boldly into its territory. A single, luminescent, pearl-white horn protruded from its forehead.

I gasped. *Could this be a fabled unicorn?* For a moment it appeared to shrink back a bit, as if unsure of my intentions. I knew very little of unicorns, never expecting to actually meet one, but it seemed to me it liked my singing. So I resumed my song as if nothing were out of the ordinary, all the while keeping a close eye on the creature I had not been certain even existed until that moment.

Timidly the unicorn moved from its spot and daintily traversed the stream on stepping stones, managing to keep its tiny hooves dry in the process.

My heart was pounding as the little horse came within inches of my face and stared into my eyes, as if judging my soul. My voice wavered a bit, and the unicorn backed away for a moment until I began to sing confidently again. To my great surprise, the creature dropped down beside me and placed its head in my lap as if it intended to sleep.

Completely amazed by this turn of events, I reached out gingerly so as not to frighten the animal and began to stroke its neck tenderly. The unicorn closed its eyes and curled its hooves up to its belly as it sighed quietly.

I did not know where the words came from, but I continued to sing from some hidden place in my mind. It was like finding a favorite old blanket in the dark and recognizing its feel and its scent but having no recollection of what it looked like.

Not wanting to move lest I startle the creature, I delicately continued to stroke its neck, inching higher and higher until my fingers found the base of its single horn. I moved my hand along its silky smoothness, thinking all the while how much like an auger seashell it looked and felt.

The unicorn breathed deeply as if it had fallen asleep. I continued to stroke its neck and haunches and though I did not know it at the time, the sound of my voice had caught upon the breeze and drifted farther than I had intended.

My voice trailed off as the unicorn abruptly bolted to attention, its body quivering with vigilance. It sniffed the air, and in a flash it disappeared through the trees. What had frightened it so? My own body stiffened, and I reached for my bow and arrow, which lay by my side on the ground.

I looked over my shoulder to see a mortal man with a large broadsword at his side, staring at me through the trees. His dark shoulder-length hair was tossled about his face, and he looked as though he had not shaved for several days. He wore a plain tunic and leggings of brown, and his complexion looked somewhat darkened by the sun. He altogether appeared a rogue.

I shot to my feet and aimed an arrow at him. For a moment longer he stared at me with no apparent concern I meant to smite him if he dared move an inch in my direction.

"Fair lady, already you have won my heart with your sweet singing. Must you also smite it with your arrow?" he said at last, in fluent elvish. His accent was like none I had ever heard before.

I furrowed my brow and began to lower the bow. The man took a step forward and again I raised it, pulling the string taut.

"Please…no harm I mean you," he said. "Your singing I heard, and I simply came to investigate the source of so enchanting a sound."

Slowly I relented and lowered my bow to the ground, still eyeing him with suspicion.

The man took several more cautious steps forward, his

gaze fixated on me. "You are not some fair vision induced by the weariness of travel, no? Would that you would speak, that I may know you do indeed exist," he pleaded.

"What manner of man are you that the elves have granted you entrance to their forest?"

"One certainly honored by their favor," he replied. "I can assure you I am here with their blessing."

For a moment I stared into his deep brown eyes and sensed he was telling me the truth. Furthermore, I could not imagine how any foe could get past the watchers of the wood uninvited. Hesitantly he took another two steps in my direction.

"Allow me to introduce myself," he said. "I am Allynon of Endara."

"And I am Arwyn."

"Arwyn," he repeated thoughtfully. "Many times have I traveled to Isgilith, but never have I made your acquaintance. You are not from here, no?"

"I have only come here of late. My home is in Guilden."

"Guilden? In you I thought I detected a bit of mortal," he commented.

My expression remained steady even though irritation rose within. Not only had this man interrupted a sublime moment, he was now bringing to light questions about my own nature I would not have addressed on such a glorious day.

"If you do not mind, I shall join you for a time?" he asked, and shifted his weight uneasily. "Far I have traveled and would like to sit for a while before I continue into Isgilith."

"Remove your sword."

"As you wish." He unbuckled the sheath from around his waist and placed it next to a large tree trunk.

"And lest you get any ideas, may I warn you I have taken down men your size before…"

"I do not doubt it."

"And I have friends in the forest who would come to my

aid if need be."

"I can assure you I am a gentleman, if nothing else."

"It's just...uh...you remind me of a rogue I once knew."

"I almost feel sorry for the poor man, for if you would treat a gentleman with such, er, verve, what must you have done to him, eh?"

"Do you wish to join me or don't you?" I asked impatiently, gesturing to the ground before me. He sat down on the mossy bank beside the water, cautiously situating himself several feet away. I thought he bore the scent of the forest after a spring rain.

"Tell me Mr...Allynon sir, what brings you so far from your homeland?"

A dark cloud passed over his face. "Alas, it grieves me that ill news has necessitated my trip to Loth Gerodin," he said. "Even now King Ignathius of Endara lies on his deathbed. It is my mission to return there with the high elf Valdir, for he is like a brother to . . . the king, and the king wishes to see him once more before he departs this life."

I looked into the man's eyes and detected tears welling there, which chipped away at the suspicion of my initial reaction to him and his intrusion.

"I certainly commend you for your loyalty to your king," I said sympathetically.

Allynon looked up with a curious expression on his face. "Few rulers there are more noble than he."

"You must have journeyed far to come here."

"The journey from Endara to Bensor is indeed far, though by ship it can be accomplished in only a few months."

"You came by sea?"

"Yes, and by fortune the winds were with us. We arrived in Maldimire a full three weeks early. I only pray we can return to Endara in time," he said quietly as his voice trailed off.

"And you traveled to Isgilith by yourself?" I said after a moment.

"Nay, I am joined by two crewmen…two who chose to continue into Isgilith without me."

"You say you have journeyed here to Loth Gerodin before?"

"On several occasions, indeed, I have. I, in fact, dwelt here for a time among the elves."

"That explains your command of the elvish language."

"Elvish is but one language I have mastered, for I have spent most of my life at sea, going here and there in the name of King Ignathius and Endara."

"You must have lived an exciting life indeed," I commented.

"Exciting, yes, though there have been times when I was fortunate to escape with my life intact. The nature of my duty to the king has led me into battle against forces of evil that would threaten the freedoms of more civilized countries. More than my share of death on the battlefield I have seen." He sighed. "Even when the cause is worthy and even in those who are deemed the enemy, never have I become accustomed to seeing pain and suffering."

I looked into the man's brown eyes and was surprised to see such sensitivity in someone who appeared such a rogue. "And where exactly have your travels taken you?" I asked curiously.

"Ah, so many wondrous places, lands almost too wondrous to describe," he said, and his face brightened. "Would you believe there are countries far to the south where the color of the natives' skin is not fair like yours and mine, but dark as mahogany?"

"Why, yes, I can believe such a thing."

"Very ceremonial people they are, and odd are their customs. And the animals that roam the land, well, it is difficult to imagine such peculiar beasts, some as large as cottages."

"Do tell me more," I said.

For a while longer Allynon talked, describing the lands to

the south where the large animals roamed. He spoke of golden cities on hilltops, castles, and lands with trees so tall they broke through the clouds above. He described the watery Kingdom of Ta, a group of two hundred islands far to the south where the land jutted out of the sea in tall peaks connected by bridges that spanned the deep channels far below. Mermaids and mermen had created their own cities under the surface of the water in the many caves that sat beneath the places where mortals dwelt, and they could be spotted from boats that sailed along in the clear waters between the mountains.

But his voice—so deep and rich it was and so distinctive, I could have listened to him all day. It was almost hypnotic.

"Although there are many marvelous places in the world, my heart always brings me back to Bensor and Endara. Quite dear they both are to me," Allynon said.

"My, what adventures you have had," I commented.

"Yes." He sighed. "Though of late I have wished for permanence. The days of youthful adventuring have become wearisome to me."

"And I'm sure your wife is not so fond of your long absences."

"But I have no wife."

"Yes, well, I'm sure a man like you has no time for the burden of a family."

"Burden? Nay! But alas, I have yet to find a woman who stirs my soul so deeply."

"Then perhaps my lord is too particular."

"Ah, but Arwyn, one must not compromise when it comes to matters of the heart, eh? Such would only lead to regret. Nay, if it takes another fifty years to find such a woman, one who makes my heart leap at the very sound of her name, then it will be time well spent."

I sat quietly, surprised at his words. So eloquent and passionate they were, especially from someone who looked rather unnervingly like Hamloc, the taverner in Guilden—a man who had no doubt slapped the rumps of many a barmaid in his time.

"Allynon," I said pensively, turning the name over in my mouth.

"Yes?"

"Oh, no, it's just that...well, I was thinking how unfortunate to have a name that sounds like a self-help group for those who indulge too much in strong drink."

Allynon puffed out his chest and looked at me with a crinkled brow. "It was for my great-grandfather I was named," he said with a slightly indignant sound to his voice.

"And a fine name it is," I added hurriedly, turning my head so he would not see me rolling my eyes.

"A very odd woman you are!"

"There are some who seem to think so."

For a moment, the two of us sat together in silence until I noticed the shadows grew long upon the forest floor. "Do forgive me, my lord, but the hour grows late, and my hosts will likely send out a search party if I linger here much longer."

"I would be glad to accompany you on your return," Allynon said. "And...to meet you here again, tomorrow, if I may, yes?"

I thought for a moment. To my knowledge nothing was scheduled for the next day, and I did find myself rather enjoying the intruder's tales of his numerous travels. "Very well," I said, "though won't you be returning soon to Endara?"

"If Valdir is willing and able to go, he will require time to make arrangements for his absence. Yet the nature of my mission necessitates haste, so it is my hope to depart on the day after the Faerenfel."

I shrugged. "And that is just four days hence."

"Yes, refreshed we shall be by then and ready for the second half of our journey." Allynon stood and offered me a hand as I arose from my spot on the ground. "A most fortuitous meeting this has been."

"You have Nat King Cole to thank for that," I quipped.

The man cocked his head to the side. "And happy I would be to do so, but what country is the domain of this, er, King Cole? I do not recall meeting him on my travels."

"He's king of a very small country called Motown."

Together we walked to the place where he had tied his tan-colored horse to the tree beside Avencloe. As he untied Avencloe's rein, I noticed his brown eyes scanning the treetops.

"What is it you seek?"

Allynon smiled awkwardly. "You will think me mad."

"Try me."

Allynon took a deep breath. "As we neared Isgilith, a curious black bird alighted on the head of my horse. Though several times I attempted to shoo it away, it always returned, staring at me and screeching as though trying to tell me something of great importance."

"Oh?"

"When we came to the path leading to this place, it flew to the gazebo and stopped, cawing at me in a rather unruly fashion until I relented and followed," he explained, glancing at me uncertainly. "My companions, they thought I had lost all sensibility and so continued into Isgilith without me."

"This bird...was it a raven?"

"Why, yes, I believe so."

Talthos! Eliendor *had* sent him to keep an eye on me!

"The raven, gradually it led me down the path until I began to question my own sanity." Allynon cocked his head to me with a look of ingratiation. "But that is when I heard your sweet singing."

Of course, one could not be so sure. After all, there were many black birds in the world and most looked very similar. Still...

I glanced at my surroundings. "Do you see this bird?"

"No. As mysteriously as it appeared, it seems to have disappeared." Allynon stopped talking momentarily and looked at me with a sheepish grin.

"And you think *I* am odd!"

Gallantly Allynon held Avencloe's reins as I mounted, and as I did so I caught a glimpse of a large, bluish-green jewel hanging from his neck under his tunic. The thought crossed my mind that perhaps his adventures had led to a bit of piracy on his part before I reminded myself the elves of Isgilith, Valdir Velconium in particular, would likely not associate with a pirate.

I led the way back to the main road where we traveled side-by-side, chatting casually until we at last passed through the archway nearest the middle river. There Allynon nodded to me before he reined about toward Valdir's manor. "Until tomorrow," he said.

"Until tomorrow."

I was afraid Galamir and his family must certainly be concerned about me, so I turned and hurried Avencloe in the direction of the house.

When I walked into the parlor, Galamir looked up and gave me a smile.

"Ah, Arwyn, it seems the treasures of Loth Gerodin have kept you enchanted for the better part of the day," he said. "We were afraid you'd become lost in the forest."

"Nay, I'm afraid I fell asleep for a while beside a stream and lost track of time. And then, well, I had quite a marvelous encounter with a unicorn."

"A unicorn?" Galamir raised his eyebrows. "Why, that is astonishing indeed! Quite skittish they are, and unwilling to be seen by just *anyone*."

"Arwyn, you have returned just in time for dinner," Gladigan said, as he walked through the door to the parlor with Elastair by his side.

"I do hope I have not been cause for concern," I replied.

"Nay," said Elastair. "We have been informed by our son

that it is your habit to spend hours alone in the forest."

"Indeed it is," I said. "In fact, I believe I'll be doing a bit more exploring there tomorrow."

"I would join you, but I must meet with Valdir tomorrow morning," Galamir said.

"Thank you, dear Galamir, but you musn't feel the need to entertain me constantly," I said confidently.

Galamir laughed. "Suit yourself, though I shall send out a search party tomorrow should you be too late in returning."

"You needn't worry. My sense of direction is quite keen," I replied, feeling quite brazen for the secret tryst I had planned. And the fact that tomorrow's companion seemed so world-wise and mysterious made my new adventure all the more daring.

CHAPTER 10

"It is at times surprising how one cannot necessarily judge another based on first impressions. I am certainly glad I did not." I sighed. "And . . . 'tis always good to make a new friend, short-lived though that friendship may be."

I thought little of my encounter with the mysterious stranger that evening and when I did, my mind imagined all the glorious places he had described to me so vividly. How wonderful it must be to travel to such exotic places and to meet so many interesting people. And to have narrowly escaped death on more than one occasion must have been...exhilarating.

The next morning, I stole quietly into the forest soon after breakfast to find Allynon's steed tied to a tree limb just below the pool where we had met the day before. Yet he was nowhere to be seen.

Quietly I climbed up the pathway to the pool, where I spied him sitting on the ground beside the water with a tablet of paper in his lap. He was drawing something with a piece of lead, all the while staring at the dogwood tree under which I had been sitting the day before. His hair was pulled back from his face, fastened with a clasp at the back of his neck, and his face was clean-shaven. For a brief moment, it seemed to me I had seen him, or someone who favored him, at some time in the past. Then it came to me—he, or someone very much like him, had appeared in my vision when I received the Gifts from Eliendor!

So absorbed was Allynon in what he was doing he had not even noticed my presence. "May I see what you are drawing?"

He jumped at the sound of my voice, immediately closed the tablet he held in his hand, and rose to his feet. "Er, greetings, Arwyn," he said rather awkwardly. "How long have you been standing there?"

"Those who are innocent need not startle."

"Perhaps, then, I am guilty," he replied with a smug grin.

"Of what are you guilty?"

His eyes narrowed. "Are you always so exasperating?"

"I simply wondered what you were doing," I responded innocently. "May I?" I held out my hand for the tablet.

With a look of slight embarrassment, Allynon handed the tablet to me, and I turned over the front flap to see a sketch of an elderly woman sitting beside a flower cart. Though old and wrinkled she was, Allynon had captured in her eyes a hint of the beauty she must have been in younger years. I turned the page and found myself looking at a young shepherd gingerly holding a lamb in his arms. I turned the page yet once more and caught my breath as I saw my own likeness, etched in lead. Allynon had captured with precision the moment I had been sitting underneath the dogwood tree with the unicorn asleep on my lap.

"The way you have captured my resemblance is remarkable," I commented, unable to control the surprise in my voice. "How could you have done so after the short time we spent together?"

"Your face, it is not one that is easily forgotten," Allynon said, with an embarrassed grin.

I turned my attention back to the drawing. "You have quite a gift."

Allynon shrugged. "A distraction, it is, that I have long fancied. It helps me to remember those I have met on my journeys," he explained. "There are many more sketches back on board my ship."

"If they are all as good as these, then you must have quite a fine collection indeed."

Could the man be blushing? I thought a hint of red crept onto his face. And what was it about him that had brought out my cheekiness? Yet I was astonished at his talent, particularly with the emotion that must reside in him to have captured his subjects so sensitively. Besides, today he did not appear so much a rogue as he had.

"You clean up well," I commented awkwardly. I turned away to hide the redness that crept into my cheeks, wishing I could take back the words.

"For my appearance yesterday, I do apologize." Allynon smiled. "I gave you a startle, no?"

"Then we are even. Though I do apologize for thinking you a rogue and wishing to skewer you," I replied, with as much charm as I could muster.

"I did wonder there for a moment if I would escape the encounter alive, but it seems Omni has allowed me at least one more day," he said, as he took the tablet from my hands and bound it with a leather thong. "Come"—he gestured upstream—"there is a place I would like to show you. It is a little less than an hour from here on foot, but such a nice day it is I thought you might not mind the walk."

"Indeed it is a beautiful day," I agreed, "and I would love a walk in the woods."

"Very well," Allynon said. "Could you wait here for just one moment?" He disappeared down the path to the place where the horses stood, presumably to put the tablet back into his knapsack. It was not long before he reappeared and began to lead the way along the pathway past the pool and waterfall and up a flight of natural stone stairs into the trees beyond. Together we walked slowly, enjoying the gurgle of the nearby stream and the speckled pattern of morning sunlight that penetrated the thick leaves above and dotted the forest floor.

"Tell me, Arwyn, how it is you came to live in Guilden?" Allynon said at last.

"Well, that is an interesting story in itself."

"I would imagine so, and you have my rapt attention."

What did I have to lose? It was high time I unloaded some of my mysterious past onto *someone*. Why not to a stranger, whom I would never see again after a few days?

I took a deep breath and then told him how I had appeared

in Bensor nearly three years before with no recollection of where I had come from or how I had arrived. I told him of my fright and my sense of aloneness and then how the chance meeting with Frondamein led to my present living arrangements.

"Fortunate, that was, considering the state of Bensor these days. It is not good for a woman to be on her own here as once it was, even one so daunting as you," Allynon said with a grin.

I returned the smile. "And how true I have found that to be," I admitted. "I am convinced Frondamein was sent by Omni to help me, and I must say the arrangement has worked well. And though I am certain Loralon had her doubts about another woman coming to live under her roof, she was very gracious, and soon we became the best of friends.

"It was not easy adjusting to life in the village, for the place from whence I came was, well…different. Not to mention the fact that I had such little recollection of my life before, not even where I lived, my friends…not even my family. That was perhaps more distressing than anything."

"To have no memory of one's own kin, now that would indeed be distressing," Allynon agreed.

I sighed. "I managed to survive those first few months without going mad, but to do so I had to preoccupy myself with other pursuits. I befriended a man named Eliendor, who has been a mentor to me ever since."

"Eliendor…" Allynon said thoughtfully. "Only on occasion have I heard Valdir speak of such a man in Baeren Ford, and usually with an air of mystery, as though he wishes to keep him veiled in secrecy. I can only wonder if his friend and yours are one and the same."

"Indeed that is so." I nodded as I pondered Allynon's words curiously for a moment. "An odd little man he is, but wise in many things. He has taught me so much, and I am indebted to him. Without him and his guidance I would be lost, for it is he who gave me a purpose for which to live."

"And that purpose?"

"He inspired me to become a healer and taught me everything I know about medicinal plants and the art of caring for those who are ill."

"A healer you say? An honorable profession that is, one requiring very special gifts."

"Yes, I do possess certain *Gifts*," I said. My tone was playful. "I would like to think I do some good in the world."

"I have no doubt you do. Despite your overactive sense of vigilance, I sense in you a gentle spirit and wisdom that would make you a gifted healer, yes?" Allynon said sincerely.

"Yes, but I am afraid I'm not always so gentle-spirited," I said with a smile.

Allynon laughed suddenly. "If yesterday is any indication, then I would imagine you are not one to be trifled with."

"No, my lord." I laughed as the blood again rushed to my cheeks.

The terrain suddenly became steeper, and Allynon led the way across a narrow wooden bridge that spanned a small ravine. I looked up the ravine to see a grove of cool, shady rhododendron lining either side of a rocky stream that plunged in successive cascades to places below.

"Would you believe that once, long ago, I visited your village," Allynon said.

"Oh?"

"It was a summer in my youth, just before I became a man. For a time I had been dwelling with the elves when captivated I became by the story of Elwei and Arnuin. Fascinated I was with the tales of Elwei's beauty and so touched and saddened by her tragedy, I knew I must see the famed ruins of Arnuin's Hold where the two had lived and loved for so long. And so with Valdir's son, my dear friend Vandaril, I traveled there. How it moved me to see those silent walls, I was nearly brought to tears."

"I remember having that same feeling the first time I walked between those walls. I always feel a strange peace come over me when I am there." I spoke quietly.

The two of us walked side-by-side without speaking for several moments as the trail twisted and turned underneath the shade of the treetops.

"Now that I know how you came to Baeren Ford, tell me Arwyn, how is it that you came to Isgilith?" Allynon asked curiously.

I glanced thoughtfully at the path ahead before answering. "Last autumn, I was called to heal a sick woman who lived several miles east of Baeren Ford when I happened upon an elf named Galamir while out hunting for food..."

"Galamir, the son of Gladigan and Elastair?"

"Why yes, do you know him?"

"Yes, quite well I know him."

"A fine person he is," I said. "We became fast friends, and he invited me to visit his home in Loth Gerodin once the snows of winter had passed."

"And so now I know how it is you came here and why I have not met you before," Allynon said. Then he pointed to a dark structure that penetrated the ceiling of the forest up ahead. "Ah, we approach our destination."

He led me up the narrow pathway for several minutes until we reached an ancient tower that sat on a ridge in the middle of the trees. "Arin Miraneth this is, built many years ago by the elves. It is one of five watchtowers throughout Loth Gerodin," he explained.

I examined its gray walls from below. They pierced the green canopy above.

"Come," Allynon said, as he led the way around the building to a doorway in the opposite wall. Together we stepped inside the tower where there was nothing but a pile of dried and crumpled leaves that had blown in during seasons past and a winding staircase that spiraled high above the entrance hall. Allynon ascended the stairs, and I followed. Openings in the side of the tower offered enough sunlight and breeze to make the climb bearable until at last we emerged on the flat landing at the top.

I blinked several times in the bright sunlight, amazed to find myself in the midst of a vast ocean of green waves, undulating in the cool breeze. Allynon smiled as he watched me walk to the edge of the parapet and peer out into the distance, seeing nothing but the green treetops and the blue of the sky. I took a deep breath and closed my eyes as the gentle breeze kissed my cheeks. "What a wonderful place this is," I said at last.

"Always I have loved coming here," Allynon said. "It reminds me of the sea."

I let out a sigh as I gazed out over the lonely wilderness of treetops and sky before me. Allynon walked over and leaned his back against the side of the tower. "You smile, and yet there is great sadness in your eyes," he said thoughtfully.

I lowered my eyes to the ground for a moment. "You are very astute," I said. "Indeed I am filled with sorrow, a sorrow that has accompanied me these past three years, a sorrow deeper than simply missing the life I left behind." Looking out over the treetops, I sighed again. "Ever since I arrived in Baeren Ford almost three years ago I have felt my differences from the villagers. I see the way they stare at me and whisper behind my back. Good people they are, but always they have been wary of me, wondering why an elf would possibly choose to live in their midst. Over the years, I have learned to adapt to their way of life, yet there are times when I have longed to find a place where I belong.

"I thought I would feel differently when I came to Loth Gerodin, that I would find the answers I have sought and a place where I truly belong, but I find I do not," I continued. "Instead, I have found being here only makes me feel more mortal, as though I belong more in a human village than in an elven city. I fear I shall never feel at home in either…"

My voice trailed off as a single tear trickled down my cheek. Then I remembered the man standing beside me and felt embarrassed for all I had revealed to him. Never before had I been so open with anyone, not even Loralon. Quickly I looked up and saw him staring at me with a most tender expression on his face.

"I'm sorry," I apologized. "I shouldn't burden a stranger with my troubles."

"Sometimes it is easier to talk to a stranger, no?" Allynon said, and touched me gently on the arm.

I smiled at him and quickly wiped the moisture from my cheek. "I suppose you are right."

After several more moments, we descended the staircase and returned to the forest floor below.

"Tell me more of your homeland," I said as we began the return trek along the pathway.

"Ah, Endara," Allynon began, "the beautiful land of mountains and sea. I can almost smell the salt air of Mir Donaleth, our capital city. How magnificent it is, with its sparkling white buildings and terraced landscape that reaches all the way from the top of Mount Pentamir far down to the Bay of Belmarus below. The palace of King Ignathius sits on top of the mount, commanding a splendid view of the inlet that cuts through the jagged mountains to the north. The white buildings and sun-drenched courtyards of the palace are a sight to behold."

"I take it you have often frequented the palace?"

"Why, er, yes, I have had occasion to go there from time to time." Allynon smiled. For a while longer, he described, in intricate detail, the city of Mir Donaleth and the green rolling hills that sloped down from its mountains for many, many miles until they at last disappeared into the Eleuvial Sea far to the south.

"It sounds as though you have a great fondness for your homeland and that you miss it very much," I commented.

Allynon sighed. "Yes, deeply I love it. Wherever I go,

always it remains a part of me."

"Tell me, who shall lead Endara when King Ignathius has passed away?" I asked, and by the shadow that passed over Allynon's face when I mentioned the king's name, I almost wished I had not broached the subject.

"His son, Ignalius, will ascend the throne," Allynon said, as he choked back the emotion in his throat.

"And does Ignalius favor his father?"

"Indeed he does. A fine ruler he will be, for he will reign with a just and fair hand, as the king has."

"Endara is indeed blessed to have had such a line of honorable rulers. Elderhelm's line has been strong through the ages."

"You know your history, yes?" Allynon said. "Bensor should be so lucky to have such a strong leader, but he who sits on the throne at Maldimire even now leaves much to be desired. It has been several years since last I visited this land, and grieved I am to see all that has deteriorated during his reign."

"But Draigon is not Bensor's true ruler. When our ruler comes, he will be all those things your King Ignathius is."

"I only hope it will happen in time," Allynon said, as he shook his head. "Many times I have sailed past Emraldein Castle, and a dark cloud constantly hovers overhead. I have even heard the evil cries from within, and I know the beast that roams its grounds is afoot and real—not something out of myth and legend. How anyone would be fool enough to dare challenge such a creature for the Sword is more than I can understand. And yet I wish with all my heart it would happen, for I love this land as I do my own Endara and do not wish to see it succumb to those who are wicked."

"We all wish for that day."

The reminder of the growing threat to the south and the unfulfilled prophecy was enough to dampen the mood for a brief moment, until I decided to breach yet another sensitive topic: "Tell me, how did you find Valdir yesterday?" One could never tell with the elven lord. Which Valdir had Allynon encountered—the warm, friendly Valdir or the aloof one?

"Surprised at my sudden appearance," Allynon replied. "Late into the night we talked about all manner of subjects."

"And did he agree to return with you after the Faerenfel?"

Allynon hesistated. "Er, yes…though conflicted he seemed."

"Conflicted?"

"The king's imminent departure from this life grieves him, and he wants very much to see him once more. Yet he appears reluctant to leave."

I shrugged. "With the situation as it is here in Bensor, who can blame him? He feels responsible for his colony." Yet deep down I wondered if there were more to his reticence than concern for Isgilith.

"I did not anticipate the state of affairs in Bensor to have disintegrated so since last I was here," Allynon said solemnly. "Perhaps he needs more time to make arrangements for his absence, or perhaps…"

"You wonder if he should go at all," I said, finishing his thought.

"Yes."

"And you will feel responsible, whether you return to Endara with or without him."

"Yes," Allynon admitted with a sigh. "I did not anticipate the matter to be so complicated."

I smiled gently and placed a hand on his arm. "Do not blame yourself for simply fulfilling the request of a dying man. It is Valdir's choice to make."

Allynon stopped in his tracks and regarded me with a twisted smiled. "Very perceptive you are for someone so odd!"

"You have no idea," I replied with a grin, grateful the solemn mood had lifted.

For a while longer we walked through the woods until we

returned to the emerald pool. To my surprise, Allynon had brought a basket full of bread, cheeses, fruit, and a bottle of pear juice, which he spread on a blanket by the edge of the water. For the remainder of the afternoon we sat there talking about all manner of subjects, and I found myself telling tales of my own adventures with Draigon and even Hamloc.

Allynon burst into laughter at the description of the cocky taverner wallowing on the ground outside Frondamein's cottage. "That and more he deserved, I would say." He chuckled. "No gentleman he was."

"Indeed not!" I said, laughing along with my companion, glad to have found someone with whom I felt so at ease.

"Such would explain your less-than-friendly welcome yesterday," Allynon said with a wink. "Though you have since proven yourself most civil."

I had to laugh out loud. "Please! I only banter with those in whose company I am comfortable."

Allynon cut his twinkling eyes over to me. "Am I to presume you feel comfortable in my company?"

I glanced at him from beneath my eyelashes. "Perhaps," I said.

"Then perhaps I should press my luck and seek your company again tomorrow, yes?"

"I would be delighted, though we'd best not meet in the forest again lest the tongues in the village start to wag. People may wonder why we both seem to disappear for hours at a time."

"Very well." Allynon laughed. "Hmm," he said, as a thoughtful expression rested on his face. "I believe I know what we shall do."

"So mysterious, I wonder what you have in store."

"If it pleases you, meet me on the quay in front of Valdir's home two hours after sunrise," Allynon said with a smile.

The shadows had long since deepened when Allynon and I packed up our picnic and prepared to leave.

"Thank you, my lord," I said, beaming. "I have indeed

had a lovely day."

"As have I," Allynon replied, seeming pleased at my response. He then untied Avencloe's reins from around the tree and stopped to stroke the beast's neck. Avencloe responded by placing his muzzle on Allynon's right shoulder, a gesture I had not seen the horse display with anyone else but me. "What a magnificent horse you have," Allynon said. "Never have I seen one of such beauty."

With deep, dark eyes, Avencloe stared at me over Allynon's shoulder, and the look the horse gave me made me waver a moment. I had always imagined Avencloe to be an excellent judge of character, and it was as if he had looked deep into Allynon's soul. "He is a special horse indeed," I said quietly.

Allynon carefully helped me to my horse's back and then walked over to his own. Out of the corner of my eye I watched as he mounted and, as if blinders had been lifted from my eyes, I was suddenly quite aware of how handsome he was with his dark hair, finely chiseled masculine face, deep brown eyes and tall, lean, yet muscular physique. I quickly turned my head away in hopes he would not catch me staring, and I clicked my tongue at Avencloe, urging him onward.

The two horses trotted slowly into Isgilith, where Allynon accompanied me to the gate in front of Galamir's house. There he nodded his head and bid me farewell until the next morning. I watched as he turned to leave and then rode into the courtyard where I dismounted and left Avencloe with the stableboy Androvus.

The house was quiet inside, yet I could hear from the kitchen the sound of dinner being prepared. I climbed the stairs to my room and walked out onto the balcony overlooking the lake. I smiled as I thought back over my day and the man with whom I had spent it. So mysterious he was and certainly more than a common mercenary. It was obvious he was quite educated and cultured, and I guessed he must be some favored ambassador of Endara to have been sent to so many places in the name of his country. I looked forward to the next morning much more than I wanted to admit.

After I freshened up, I walked quickly down the stairs, feeling rather light on my feet. I saw the smile on my face as I walked past a mirror in the entryway. Galamir and Gladigan looked up as I entered the parlor.

"Ah, Arwyn, we thought we heard you come in," Galamir said cheerfully. "I trust you had a pleasant day out in the forest."

"It was a lovely day." I beamed in response. "And yours?"

"Very nice, thank you. Valdir and I discussed the business of the Alliance for quite some time."

"I'm sure my son would have much rather been out walking in the forest with you than talking with Valdir, but such is the nature of his business," Gladigan said.

"I do apologize for my lack of attention, but the Alliance does demand me at times," Galamir explained. "Valdir asked about you, Arwyn. He was curious as to your whereabouts and if you are enjoying our fair city...Arwyn?"

Seeing Galamir and Gladigan staring at me as though they expected me to say something roused me from my thoughts. "Hmm? Oh...yes, I am enjoying it immensely."

Suddenly Elastair appeared through the door to the dining room. "Dinner is ready to be served," she announced, before Galamir, Gladigan, and I filed past her to the table. "My, Arwyn, the woods must hold a particular fascination for you. We were beginning to wonder if you would make it back for dinner."

"Oh, I could never ignore the rumblings of my stomach," I quipped. "Please forgive me for staying out so long, but I do enjoy the outdoors so."

"An elf's home is in the forest," said Gladigan. "It is where we renew our spirits, and there is nothing odd about communing with nature for a time."

The door to the kitchen opened, and Gwyneleth entered the dining room with two steaming plates of food in her hands. Those seated around the table served their plates and began to enjoy the sumptuous meal.

"I've a bit of news from the house of Valdir," Galamir announced as he put down his fork. Elastair and Gladigan glanced at him anxiously. "It seems Prince Allynon has returned to Isgilith."

Clank!

Everyone looked at me after I clumsily dropped my fork on my plate. I coughed into my napkin. Quickly I took a gulp of water as the family looked on with concern. "Not to worry," I managed to sputter. "A bit of food went down the wrong way." I took another swig of water. "Did you say *Prince* Allynon?"

"Yes, the son of King Ignathius of Endara," replied Galamir. "I know of no more honorable man than he."

"What brings him back to Isgilith?" Elastair asked, as she glanced dubiously in my direction.

"It seems that even now the king lies on his deathbed. He has been sent to take Valdir back to his homeland to see his father one last time before he passes away."

"A pity," Gladigan commented. "His father is a noble king indeed."

"When did he arrive?" asked Elastair.

"They say he arrived yesterday, though I've not seen him. He disappeared early this morning, and where he's been keeping himself is anyone's guess."

Elastair glanced over at me, and I quickly averted my eyes. "And will he be leaving soon?" she asked.

"They will depart on the day following the Faerenfel. I don't believe anyone would want to miss that," Galamir said, as he took a bite of food. "In fact, Valdir's annual banquet this year will not only be held in honor of you, Arwyn, but the prince as well. It shall be the perfect send-off as Valdir prepares to leave us for perhaps as long as a year."

"Valdir must be quite fond of the king to leave Isgilith, especially at such a time as this," I said.

"Valdir has been like an uncle to Ignathius, and is in fact his queen's great-uncle," Galamir explained.

"I see the intermarriage between the elves of Loth Gerodin and the descendents of Elderhelm has remained strong throughout the generations," I remarked, my mind working feverishly to make sense of the connections. Allynon, a prince? How could I have not seen it? It was true he had been surprisingly cultured, well-spoken, and chivalrous—at least compared to my initial *mis*impression— but I had detected no pompousness about him that would have alerted me he was the son of a king. Quite the contrary.

"Yes, it has," Galamir said. "Prince Allynon is a blood relative of Valdir. Although, as you will see, there is little physical similarity as the prince tends to favor his father's side of the family."

"And quite handsome he is, as well," Elastair said with a subtle smile. "Many an elven maiden has pined for him."

"And there have been some he has fancied through the years…" Galamir said.

"Though none have captured his heart," his mother added quickly. "Of that I am quite certain."

"Perhaps you will meet him at tomorrow's hunt, that is, if you would like to go," Galamir suggested.

"A hunt, you said?" I responded, rousing myself from my thoughts.

"Yes, the annual Faerenfel hunt. We ride far into the woods to hunt venison for the Faerenfel feast. It is usually an overnight excursion as we also make camp in the forest, yet we shall return in time for Valdir's banquet the next evening," Galamir explained. "Would you care to join us, Arwyn? Many from the village participate every year."

I glanced at Elastair, who seemed to be waiting curiously for my response. "If you don't mind, I believe I shall remain in Isgilith tomorrow," I said.

"And miss the thrill of the hunt?" Galamir exclaimed.

"I'm sure I will find a way to amuse myself."

"Very well, if it pleases you," the fair elf relented. "Though I feel I am neglecting you."

"Galamir, you needn't worry about me." I laughed. "Please rest assured I am having a wonderful time."

I avoided Elastair's knowing gaze, for surely she suspected my secret. I needed no curious questions, no probing into places I didn't want to go.

And the knowledge that Allynon was a prince made no difference to me. Why should it? The fact that someone happened to be born to someone who happened to be a ruler because he in turn was born into a certain family said nothing about his character. This new information did nothing to change my opinion of him. To me, Allynon was still just a man.

And I was just a woman.

CHAPTER 11

"What a nice surprise to have found such a pleasant friend in Allynon. I so enjoy his warmth and gentle laugh, and I find myself smiling often when we are together."

I hesitated for a moment, long enough for that ubiquitous female voice to make a comment. "And yet..."

I let out a long sigh. "And yet, 'tis a shame it all must end two days hence."

———————————

By the time I walked through the front door the next morning, Galamir and the rest of the hunting party had long since left for the forest. It promised to be another beautiful spring day, and my heart was light as I walked past the stone barrier beside the lake to see Allynon standing down by the water's edge smiling up at me. Beside him in the water floated one of the swan-shaped boats that graced the surface of the lake. An elven youth stood nearby with a long pole in his hands.

"Good morning!" Allynon greeted cheerfully with dark eyes that shined brightly as I walked down to meet him.

"A good morning it is indeed!" I said. "And I can think of nothing more pleasant than a boat ride."

"It pleases you, eh?"

"Why, yes!"

Allynon stepped down into the boat and held out his hand to steady me as I followed and settled into our seat. The elven lad untied the lines to the quay and pushed off.

"What a beautiful day it is!" I closed my eyes and took a deep breath of the cool morning air. Lazily I dipped my hand into the clear water of the lake, making a meandering pattern in the current as the boat drifted by. Allynon watched me with an amused expression, as if he were watching a child discovering the world for the first time.

"To see you so happy warms my heart," he said.

I turned to him and smiled brightly. "There is much to be happy about—the warm sunshine, blooming flowers, and an outing upon the water. Don't you agree, Your Highness?"

Allynon smiled. "You have discovered my secret, yes?"

"Galamir keeps us abreast of all the village happenings, and when he came to dinner last night with news that Prince Allynon had returned to town, I must say I felt a bit taken aback."

"Arwyn, the measure of a man is in the strength of his character, not by virtue of some title he is born into. Therefore, I did not think it important." He shrugged. "The real question is, did that knowledge change your opinion of me, for good or for ill?"

I thought about it for a moment. "Nay, but I would have felt all the more embarrassed had I shot you when first we met," I said with a smile, to which Allynon burst out in laughter.

Suddenly my tone turned serious, and I placed my hand lightly on his arm. "Though now I know why there is such sadness in your eyes. Allynon, I am truly sorry about your father."

Allynon lowered his gaze somberly. "A good king he is, a good father and a good man. Many will grieve his death."

"Tell me more of him," I urged.

"His life deserves more praise than I could possibly give him in a day, but I shall do my best to give you a bit of him in what time we have."

The swan-shaped boat navigated the canals of Isgilith past beautiful gardens and waterfalls, statues and urns overflowing with flowers, and under stone footbridges and cool arbors. With every bend in the waterway, Allynon described to me the life of his father beginning with his honored birth many years before to his ascension to the throne. He told me of his many acts of good will and the love he showed his beautiful half-elven queen, Myathene; his daughter, Melantha; and his three sons Ignalius, Galbritar, and himself.

I heard of his early days of heroism, his own battles against the rising of evil empires in far distant lands, and how Ignathius ardently had numerous Circles of Omni erected throughout the land. Allynon's mother, half-elven niece of Valdir, fell in love with the dashing prince on one of his early journeys to Bensor and returned to Endara with an elven entourage so they could be wed. He recalled how Queen Myathene, a woman of great compassion herself, would take her young sons to the palace gates bearing trays full of excess food to give to the beggars who congregated there. It was little wonder they were so loved throughout the land.

As Allynon talked with such passion and pride for his kin, I watched. It conjured memories in me of another man, a man with slightly graying hair standing up before a large room where many had congregated, each listening intently as he spoke words of hope from a big book with black binding that lay before him. A man I had loved. My eyes misted over momentarily until my mind returned to the man who now sat beside me. In his eyes I saw the same kindness and humility, despite the privileged circumstances from which he had come.

I was hardly aware of the passage of time, so intent I was on listening to my new friend, until the boat, which had been drifting around the canals, finally came to dock beside a quiet walkway on the northern end of the city. Allynon stepped out of the boat and led me along the edge of the canal until we came around the bend to the place where a waterfall splashed into the waterway below. A single table and two chairs sat under a nearby willow tree. Beside the table stood an elven man with a covered platter in his hands, and I could see a bottle of wine waiting for us on the table. Allynon smiled broadly when he saw the delight on my face.

"Oh, Allynon, you've thought of everything to make this day perfect," I said.

We lingered over lunch, our conversation drifting

between any number of subjects as the boats drifted by on the canal. The more we talked, the more this man of irony amazed me. A fine sportsman he must be and a fierce warrior on the battlefield, yet so kind and gentle he was, and behind his eyes I could see the refined intelligence of one suited for exercises more philosophical than physical. The image of a brooding warrior he had struck in my mind only two days before melted away as Allynon shared his thoughts and feelings with me so openly.

As we walked back to the center of the city that afternoon, along a pathway lined with multicolored azaleas, we came upon a group of elven children playing on a grassy lawn. With a simple glance, we jumped into the midst of the game, laughing with wild abandon until we ran out of breath. Brimming with smiles, we continued on our walk passing through gardens surrounded by high walls of stone.

"I understand Valdir is to have his annual Faerenfel banquet in our honor tomorrow night," Allynon commented, still trying to catch his breath.

"That is my understanding as well."

"Always it is a treat to banquet at his home. A feast, he will certainly have." Allynon glanced sideways at me. "You will honor me with a dance later at the ball, yes?"

I stopped in my tracks and lowered my eyes to the ground. "My lord, I would be the one honored, but I am afraid I don't know how to dance in such a manner. I only know the jigs and folk dances of Guildenwood, nothing more graceful than that. I would not wish to embarrass you so."

"Nonsense!" Allynon protested. "More difficult it is to dance a folk dance than a simple waltz. Come, and I will show you," he said, as he took me by the hand and led me onto an open, grassy area surrounded by flowering cherry trees. "First, I will place my right hand on your waist and you will place your left hand on my shoulder, such as this."

I was certain my cheeks began to heat the moment Allynon put his hand on my waist and pulled me close to him. "And I will hold your other hand like this," he said as he took hold of my right hand. "Now when I step forward with my right foot, you will step backward with your left on the first count of three. On the next count of three, it is you who will step forward with your right foot, and I will step back."

"It sounds simple, but the test will be in the doing."

"You need only follow my lead," Allynon coached. "Ready...aaaand one, two, three..."

My left foot failed to step back at the right time, and Allynon plowed right into me.

"My apologies," he said, brow furrowed with concern.

I laughed nervously. "I'm afraid this may require some practice."

"Not to worry"—he smiled—"we've all afternoon. Now let's try again. Ready...one, two, three, one, two, three..."

"Oops!" I stopped cold as I felt Allynon's foot beneath my own. "I beg your pardon, my lord!"

For a moment, a look of excruciating pain passed over Allynon's face, soon followed by a large grin. "Better my foot than yours. I only hope it will be well enough to dance by tomorrow evening."

"How you do tease me." I laughed.

"Come, let us try again," Allynon said, as he again took me in his arms.

There were more embarrassing moments as the two of us muddled through my dance lesson, but they were always followed with peals of mirthful laughter until at last we were sashaying across the grassy ballroom gracefully. As the world spun by, I looked at my partner and smiled, thinking what fun it would be to tell Loralon how a prince taught me to waltz. She would never believe it!

"You learn quickly," Allynon commented.

"I have a good teacher," I said, repaying the compliment.

Humming a tune as best he could, Allynon taught me several other sweeping moves before it was time to head home. Slowly we walked back to Galamir's house. That evening Allynon walked me to the front door, where he lingered a moment before bidding me farewell.

"Thank you, Allynon, for another lovely day. I did enjoy myself so."

Allynon looked up at me as I stood on the first step that led to the front door. He appeared as though he had something of gravity to say, but instead he looked quietly up into my eyes. "That pleases me," he said softly. "May I accompany you to target practice at the range tomorrow morning? You wish to be ready for the archery competition at the Faerenfel, yes?"

"Yes, my lord. I would like the company."

"Very well," Allynon said with a gentle smile. "Until tomorrow."

"Until tomorrow." I turned and walked up the steps to the front door, giving Allynon one last smile before slipping inside. I rushed to the window in the dining room where I watched from the darkness inside as he lingered a while longer, staring curiously at the house before turning to walk through the gate to the road outside.

"Did you have a nice day?" came a voice from behind.

I spun around to see Elastair standing there. "Yes, it was a very nice day indeed," I replied.

"And were you off 'by yourself' again?"

I shook my head timidly.

A knowing smile crept across Elastair's face. "Come, the banquet is tomorrow evening, and you must look absolutely radiant."

Elastair led me up the stairs to her closet where she began to rummage through the numerous gowns hanging there. She handed several to me, and my heart beat wildly as I tried them all on. Each garment fit me like a glove, but it was a slightly off-the-shoulder gown with a tight bodice and full flowing skirt of shimmering burgundy material that caught my eye. "You look stunning," Elastair observed as I studied myself in the full-length mirror.

"Yes, this should do nicely." I smiled as I turned to the side and flared the material of the skirt. "Dear Elastair, thank you. What a good friend you are."

When I woke the next morning, I bounded out of bed. The thought of another day spent by Allynon's side, as well as the anticipation of the upcoming banquet that evening, quickened my steps.

Allynon called on me promptly after breakfast, and with bow and arrows slung across my back, the two of us made our way to the practice range, where we spent the better part of the morning. From a short distance away, Allynon watched intently as I consistently hit my target.

"Now that I see how skilled you are with a bow and arrow, I realize how fortunate I am to have escaped with my life the other day," he said jovially. "Arwyn, there is nothing you do not do well, no?"

"Pray, tell me what you mean, my lord."

"You sing…you are the best marksman, that is, marks*woman* I have ever seen. You heal sick people…you dance."

I looked sideways at my companion to see the huge grin on his face and then had to laugh myself. "You are too kind," I said as my gaze lowered shyly to the ground.

"And you possess many other talents I have yet to discover, yes?"

"A lady must maintain some sense of mystery."

"And that perhaps, you do best of all."

At noon, Allynon led me into a local tearoom situated on the second floor of a charming old building beside a canal. To my surprise, an elderly mortal woman greeted us as we walked into the quaintly adorned room.

Upon seeing Allynon's face, the woman's eyes grew wide, and her wrinkled hands flew up into the air. "Bless my soul! If it isn't the Prince of Endara, returned after all these years!" she exclaimed, as she went to embrace him.

"Velora, how good it is to see you!" Allynon said, towering over her as he gave the woman a hearty squeeze. "I hoped you would be here today."

"You mean you hoped I wasn't in the grave already," she retorted as she gave Allynon a jab in the ribs. "Which I could be had you waited another few years to return."

"Velora, two hundred at least you will live to be!"

I could hardly believe my eyes. A mortal woman in Isgilith? I had no idea such a person existed in the elvish colony.

"Arwyn, I would like you to meet my friend, Velora," he said.

"But you're..." I stammered.

"Mortal, that is correct dear," the old woman said with a smile. "There are a few of us living here in Isgilith. Married an elf I did. I was thirty-one, and he was five hundred and one."

"Where is your husband now?" I asked curiously.

"Killed in Maldimire, ten years past," Velora answered. "Went south on business when he was robbed at knifepoint. The rogues, they killed 'im over a mere ten quiddel."

"I am so sorry," I said with sympathy.

"As for me, I remained in Isgilith, for this is the place I call home now, and the place where our sons live."

I regarded her with compassion. How difficult it must be to live in a place where a mortal was so obviously different from everyone else. It made my own eccentricity seem trivial.

"And you," Velora said, "I had heard we were to be visited by an elven maiden from the south."

I nodded. "You heard correctly."

"How lovely she is, do you not think, Your Highness?" the old woman said, turning to Allynon, who stood there smiling. "And you, dear Allynon, I heard rumors of your return. Though I should say I am grieved at the reason."

"Aye, it grieves me as well. Would that I could have returned for a much happier reason," he lamented.

"And your dear mother, how is she holding up?"

"Strong she is…but mournful, nonetheless. She loves him so."

Velora shook her head. "Tsk, 'tis what happens when mortal and elves wed. The elf remains in eternal youth while watching a beloved wither away into old age. 'Tis I who should have gone first." She sighed. "But you, Allynon, strong elvish blood runs through your veins. You should live to a ripe old age at that."

Allynon laughed heartily. "That I shall hope for," he said. "However, if I am not given nourishment, I will not live much longer. My mouth has been watering all morning in anticipation of your cooking."

"Then come, I shall take you and your friend to the best table in the house," the old woman said as she navigated across the room to the other side and out onto a small balcony overlooking the canal below. "I hope this will suit you well."

"It is perfect," I smiled as I looked through the leaves of a tree and onto a passing boat.

Our meat-filled pastries and vegetables long-since consumed, Allynon sipped on a cup of tea quietly, watching me with a look of amusement as I was so obviously captivated by the comings and goings of the people down below. "I feel I am a spy," I confided with a grin. "This is a grand place to be if you want to hear the town gossip."

I looked to see Allynon staring at me serenely with the hint of a quiet smile on his lips. Feeling my heartbeat quicken, I returned my attention to the scene below in an attempt to suppress the prospects threatening to bubble up to the surface of my imagination. I was so enjoying my brief friendship with the prince, and I wasn't going to ruin it with any thoughts that ventured past the Faerenfel. Our encounter would always remain a sweet memory in my mind.

"Leaving so soon?" Velora commented as we stood to leave.

"I am afraid so," Allynon said. "We must go and prepare for Valdir's Faerenfel banquet this eve."

"Ah, yes," the tearoom owner said. "And what a wonderful evening you shall have, Arwyn. Valdir's banquets are always a treat."

"I have been looking forward to it for days now," I replied.

"But please, do come back and visit before you return home. I do so crave hearing news from the south."

"I would love to," I said, as Allynon led me to the door of the tearoom. With a kiss on the cheek, Allynon bade the old woman farewell, and the two of us walked down the front stairs to the street below.

As we walked to Galamir's home, it seemed to me Allynon's mood had changed since the morning. He had turned pensive and reserved, and I found myself shy and at a loss for words, wondering if the prince's thoughts were thousands of miles away at his father's bedside. For a few moments we walked together in silence. Allynon began to whistle a tune to himself, and the thought crossed my mind that perhaps he had grown weary of my company. After all, we had been together for the better part of the past three days.

As we neared the home of Galamir, he at last spoke. "The time for me to take my leave of you is upon us," he said.

"Indeed it is," I replied uneasily.

"Arwyn, to dance with you will be the wish of every man at the ball tonight, but I do hope you will at least allow me to be the first."

Where had I heard those words before? Sometime, somewhere long ago, and they were tainted by a great sense of disappointment. My heart sank a little at the thought. "Yes, my lord," I said, feeling inexplicably apprehensive.

We passed into the courtyard of Galamir's home and

walked up to the front doorsteps. I turned to face Allynon at the bottom. "Thank you again for a lovely morning."

"Nay, it is I who should thank you," he said, looking intensely at me with his warm, brown eyes.

I avoided his gaze and turned to make my way up the steps. "I must go now to make ready for the evening's festivities."

Suddenly, Allynon took my hand in his and raised it to his lips, kissing it gently. "Until tonight," he said in almost a whisper.

I nodded. "Until tonight."

CHAPTER 12

"What was to be an enjoyable party has turned into a test of sorts. And if Valdir's response is any indication, then I do believe I passed," I said to Dr. Susan. "And yet..."

"Yes, go on," she urged.

"To a lesser degree, the conflict I see in his eyes when he stares at me has returned, much to my utter bewilderment."

"Oh?"

"Though it is of little concern to me at the moment." I could feel the blood rush to my cheeks when I thought of the eyes of another, deep brown ones, staring at me from across the table.

I walked through the front door of the house to find Galamir sitting in the parlor strumming a stringed instrument. "Salutations, Arwyn," he greeted in his usual cheerful manner.

"Greetings, Galamir," I replied. "I see you've returned from the hunt."

"And a successful one it was. We shall dine well tomorrow at the Faerenfel," he said. "I trust you found enough to amuse you here."

"I've been exploring."

"Exploring?"

I nodded. "Yes, and making new friends."

"New friends, you say?"

I could feel the color seeping into my cheeks, so I changed the subject. "Galamir, would you do me the favor of dancing with me—right now?"

He cocked his head to the side. "Certainly."

"Good. I'm not accustomed to dancing and could use the practice." In truth, being able to dance with Allynon was no guarantee I would be able to dance with anyone else. If my newfound ability transferred to another partner, then I would be less likely to embarrass myself that evening.

"Ah, and no doubt you will be kept busy this eve on the ballroom floor, so you must be ready."

Galamir lay his instrument down, and the two of us walked into the entryway, where we went through the same motions Allynon and I had the day before. Though it felt awkward at first, the movement was basically the same, and it was not long before we were sashaying across the floor. The debonair elf smiled at me, and with him I found myself laughing out loud, though I did not feel in his arms the way I did when I was in Allynon's

Satisfied my dancing skills would indeed transfer to other partners, I was ready for a rest. "Galamir, all this dancing has made me quite weary. I must go and freshen up a bit, or I'll not be worth anything this evening."

Galamir's merry eyes smiled as I ascended the staircase. "Go and catch your breath for a while. You'll need it later."

Up in my room, I fell upon the bed and spent the better part of the afternoon staring at the tree that stood outside my window, watching how its leaves danced about in the breeze as conflicting thoughts danced about in my mind. "What has become of me?" I chided myself. It was not like me to act this way.

An abrupt knock sounded on the door. "Come in," I called.

The door opened and Elastair, with young Gwyneleth at her side, walked in carrying the dress I was to wear that evening, along with several irons retrieved from the hot coals of the fire for the purpose of curling hair. For the remainder of the afternoon the three of us chatted lightly as I sat before a mirror while the other two helped with my grooming.

Reaching into the pocket of her gown, Elastair brought forth two bejeweled combs and used them to pull my hair away from my face and over my ears. Although it was flattering, I quietly reached up and removed them, letting the loose tendrils fall onto my shoulder. "He'll...they'll see my…"

"It becomes you," Elastair interjected. "All anyone will see is how stunning you are."

I relented, nodding my head as a smile slowly crept onto my face. Elastair placed her hands on my shoulders and leaned over, whispering into my ear, "Be you elf or mortal, you are destined for greatness, Arwyn of Baeren Ford. Do not be afraid of who you are."

All dressed in our finery, I walked with Galamir and his parents to the lane beyond their front gate, where we joined many other elves making their way to the home of Valdir in great anticipation of the events ahead. I spotted Kyora, Analeth, and Galena walking past. Much to my relief, the three elven maidens appeared much more intent on where they were heading than to see me standing there, but I was nevertheless disappointed Kyora had received an invitation to the gala.

To make matters worse, I caught enough of their conversation to know competition for the prince's attention would be thick.

"I hear Prince Allynon is in town," Kyora said with excitement.

"Though I wonder where he's been keeping himself," Galena commented.

Analeth sighed. "I thought he would have been on the hunt."

"I don't care where he's been, as long as he dances with me. How handsome he is." Galena giggled girlishly.

Kyora turned up her nose and glanced dubiously at both her friends. "But darlings, he won't be dancing with you if he's saving all his dances for me," she said in jest, though it seemed to me Kyora probably hoped such would be the case.

"She speaks out of both sides of her mouth," I whispered to Elastair. "She looks down on mortals, until it comes to a prince. No doubt she has her sights set on becoming a princess."

Elastair shrugged her shoulders. "You needn't concern yourself with Kyora. Prince Allynon is sure to see through her wiles."

I, however, was unconvinced. The whole situation seemed all too familiar, though for what reason I was unsure. For me, the heart of a man remained unfettered until he proved otherwise, and I knew to guard my own heart as well. How I wanted in that moment to use the Gifts to make Kyora tongue-tied or to give her two left feet, but I could imagine Eliendor's disapproving gaze. And I truly did not wish to incur the wrath of Omni for using His Gifts for something so, well, petty. Nay, if Allynon's head could be turned by a woman as wily as Kyora, then he was not the man I thought he was.

As we reached the steps leading to the front terrace of Valdir's manor, I felt a knot in my stomach. We joined the banquet guests standing in line to enter the grand foyer until at last I found myself on the top step inside looking down on the gathering below. There stood Valdir greeting guests and beside him was Allynon, looking quite dashing cloaked in royal blue. An eager Kyora curtseyed before the prince as he gave her a slight bow. I strained my ears, but all I could hear was "Pleasure to see you again, Kyora."

Suddenly I was aware a hush was rippling over the crowd standing in the foyer and many turned their eyes to where I stood. No doubt word of my arrival had spread through Isgilith, and as I had remained so elusive the past few days, I was certain there were those who wondered if the famed elven maiden of Baeren Ford really existed. Slightly unnerved by all the attention, I hoped I wouldn't embarrass myself by tripping down the steps.

Then my eyes locked with those of Allynon. He stared at me the same way he had when first he saw me sitting in the forest. I forgot about everyone else in the room.

"Greetings, Arwyn, what a joy it is to see you," Valdir

said, as he walked halfway up the stairs to greet me, drawing my gaze from Allynon. On the high elf's face was a broad smile, and he seemed slightly out of breath. "Welcome again to my home."

My, how vastly different *this* greeting was than the first time I visited him there! The high elf took me by the hand and led me down to the bottom of the steps to the place where Allynon stood. It was a moment before he allowed his gaze to stray from me. "Er, Arwyn, I wish to introduce you to one who is like a son to me, Prince Allynon of Endara."

"Actually, Arwyn has been party to my insufferable company these past days," Allynon replied with a wink.

"I would hardly call your company 'insufferable,' my lord," I said with a smile.

Out of the corner of my eye I saw a slightly stunned expression pass over Valdir's face. "So this is where you have been keeping yourselves," he muttered softly.

Allynon took my hand in his and brought it to his lips. "Absolutely dazzling, you are," he said.

"You flatter me, my lord."

"My lips can only profess the truth of what my eyes see."

I could feel the blood rise to my cheeks, and my eyes lowered to the floor with a discreet smile. Galamir, who stood next to me, watched the entire interchange with a puzzled look on his face, though his mother looked on with a coy smile.

"Galamir, how good it is to see you," Allynon exclaimed, as he clasped the hand of his old friend.

"And it is indeed good to see you as well," the elf replied cordially, "though I am quite grieved by the nature of your visit."

"Thank you, my friend," Allynon said with sincere gratitude in his eyes.

Two mortal men walked into our circle. "Arwyn, I would like you to meet Inago and Endegar, two of the finest and most loyal crewmen on my ship. It was they who accompanied me on my journey here."

I caught my breath as the man called Inago walked up. He was a tall, robust man who looked as though he could strangle an ox with his bare hands. But it was not his size so much that caused me to gasp but the color of his skin, which was the color of night. On his left ear dangled a golden earring and his head was clean-shaven. He wore loose pieces of exotic, shimmering cloth that draped his hulking body, exposing the huge muscles of his arms. I felt rather diminutive standing next to him.

Upon seeing my reaction, Inago let out a deep, hearty laugh. "De lady has not seen one like me before, no?"

"Actually, I have," I replied, "in Maldimire only last autumn. The city is a melting pot of humanity."

"A *melting pot*, eh? A fitting description, that is," Allynon said thoughtfully. "My friend Inago hails from the kingdom of Shakracar, far to the south. Many years ago he saved me from what would have been an unfortunate accident involving four hooligans I met alone along a city street late one night. Quite young and foolish I was back then and believed I could take on the lot of them. Inago here stepped in and saved my hide, for which I am eternally grateful. For his reward I offered him a chance to sail with me and see the world…"

"Been with His Highness ever since—fifteen years now to be exact. And I can tell you, my lady, there be no finer man than he."

I could not help but smile when I looked into the twinkling eyes of the gentle giant and heard his deep, booming voice. But there was something more in those eyes—a searching soul that seemed to stare into mine with the same curiosity, as if he were sizing me up. I realized he possessed the Gifts, too. I turned away quickly, not ready to reveal my soul to one I had only just met.

"One of my most trusted crewmembers…and friends Inago is," Allynon said. "An uncanny way he has of reading the hearts of others, which comes in useful in diplomatic situations. Indeed I would trust him with my life."

Ah, notion confirmed!

"Are you saving all your praise for this old oaf?" Endegar protested. The fit young man, shorter than his two counterparts, sported a thin mustache and goatee, and his sly eyes gleamed in a most devilish manner as he bent over to my hand.

Allynon smiled at his crewmember's brazenness.

"The truth is," Endegar continued, "Inago here is only kept around for his charming disposition. Why else do you think we brought him all the way from Maldimire through hordes of Gargalocs? He can talk his way out of any unfortunate circumstance."

"I do believe it is of yourself you speak." Allynon grinned. "As a lad, Endegar came on board. Putting him to work, we thought, would be much more productive than letting him loaf about the docks making nothing but mischief. An honest man we have made of him."

I laughed. "It is indeed a pleasure to meet you both. But tell me, who is watching the ship in your stead?"

"I can assure you, my lady, it has been left in good hands," Endegar commented. "Though we can only hope our comrades have not found too much trouble in Maldimire."

Valdir remained quiet until that moment, yet I was keenly aware he studied every glance, every spoken word, every gesture between the prince and me. With some degree of effort, he grabbed two goblets of wine from a passing servant and handed one each to Allynon and me. "May I have your attention," Valdir announced. In a moment the room came to a hush. "It is my distinct pleasure to welcome you all to my home, but in particular I am happy to welcome Prince Allynon back into our midst and our new friend, Arwyn, who has traveled from Guilden to dwell with us for a time. I hope you will each have an opportunity to greet them both later in the evening."

Almost everyone in the room looked on approvingly, that is, except for Kyora. I briefly glanced at the elven maiden and caught the icy glint in her eyes as she stared at me.

"It is also at this time I announce my imminent departure for Endara. Even now Allynon's father, King Ignathius, lies on his deathbed, and it is my desire to see my dear friend for one last time before his spirit departs this world. Though I will be away from you for many months, I leave my son Vandaril to guide you through these dark days." A dull murmur shot through the crowd as the implications of the high elf's announcement began to sink in. "We must therefore make merry this eve, for it will be the last I am with you for a long while. Come now and let us dine together," he said, gesturing toward the main banquet hall.

Slowly the crowd filed into the adjacent room where we situated ourselves around the enormous table in the middle already covered with platters piled with succulent meats, vegetables, and an array of breads and cheeses. Off to the side of the room sat a table loaded with tempting pastries filled with cream and lathered with chocolate, cakes of every variety as well as an assortment of fruits and nuts. I could not remember ever seeing so much food in my life.

Valdir took his place at the head of the table, gesturing for me to be seated at his right hand and Allynon directly across from me at his left. Galamir took a seat beside me with Elastair and Gladigan just to his right, and Allynon's two crewmen took the places next to their master.

"I trust you have been enjoying your stay here," Valdir said as he passed me a platter of mushrooms boiled in saffron and broth, though the statement seemed almost forced.

I glanced quickly over at Allynon, who smiled at me subtly. "I am indeed having a lovely time," I replied. "The prince has been seeing to that."

"Ah, so dat be where His Highness has been a-hidin' himself these past few days!" exclaimed Inago.

Valdir made no comment, but with fork and knife in hand,

he hesitated a moment and exchanged glances with the two of us as if he were struggling with some internal debate regarding my friendship with the prince.

On my other side, Galamir raised an eyebrow. I, however, refused to meet his questioning gaze, though I laughed inwardly, relishing the idea he was no doubt stewing over my having kept a secret from him.

My attention soon turned to my conversation with Valdir. The expression on his face had turned strangely stoic, and the conversation always seemed to come back to the Alliance and Bensorian politics. Why he was so enraptured by my opinion was beyond me, yet he seemed to hang on my every word. Either he was a gracious host trying to make me feel welcome or he really did care what I thought. Or the subject of politics was much safer to discuss than what was *really* on his mind.

Eventually Galamir was drawn into the conversation, though he kept a close eye on Allynon the entire time. However, it was all I could do to keep my mind from drifting whenever my eyes met with that of the prince's.

Our meal had almost come to a conclusion when a servant whispered something in Valdir's ear. The elven lord's face brightened, and he turned in time to see a lone elven man enter the banquet hall. "Vandaril, my son, how glad I am to see you," he said, standing to embrace the latecomer. It was then I saw the resemblance. The younger elf's facial features were stoic and masculine, closely resembling his father, and like Valdir, his dark hair hung straight down his back. The contrast between the two of them and Callas was quite striking.

"I was afraid I would miss the Faerenfel altogether this year," the regal elf said with a deep voice. Vandaril's eyes widened as the guest seated beside his father stood to greet him. "Allynon, bless my soul! Is it really you?" he exclaimed, as Allynon stood to give his friend an embrace.

"So good it is to see you, my friend. It has been a long

while!" Allynon exclaimed.

"At least four years since you were last here, if I recall correctly. What brings you back to Loth Gerodin?"

A shadow crossed Allynon's face. "Would that I could have come under happier circumstances, but my father is quite ill," explained Allynon. "His physicians give him little less than a year, and already several months have passed since then. I have come in haste in order to return your father to Endara, for it is my father's wish to see him one last time."

"I am loathe to hear such news. All of Endara and, indeed, many others will certainly feel the loss of so great a king." The younger elf's eyes met mine, and he walked around to the other side of the table, smiling broadly. "Ah, the elven maiden of Guilden. It is indeed an honor to at last make your acquaintance," Vandaril said, bowing low and kissing my hand.

"The pleasure is mine, my lord. Galamir has told me much about you."

At that moment, Galamir stood to warmly clasp the hand of his friend.

"Ah, Galamir," Vandaril said, "we are indeed grateful to you for bringing such an honored guest into our presence."

"How are you, my friend?" Galamir smiled.

"None the worse, despite the gravity of our mission these past two weeks."

"What news have you from the Greenwaithe?"

A hush fell over the entire banquet hall as we awaited Vandaril's reply.

"Yes, son, perhaps you can share your findings with us all," Valdir suggested.

The crowd murmured in agreement, and both Galamir and Allynon settled back into their chairs to hear the news.

"Alas, the news I bring does not bode well," Vandaril began. "In recent weeks, a number of Ashkar and Gargaloc forces have mustered just across the border, yet our spies have been unable to penetrate far to determine the nature of their business."

"Do you think they mean to invade?" sounded a slightly alarmed voice from someone in the crowd.

"No, they do not have the numbers. At least, not at the moment."

"Could it be a decoy? A ploy to keep our eyes from the south?" Galamir interjected.

"A decoy?" Vandaril replied thoughtfully. "Such could be a possibility, though from what are they drawing our gaze?"

"I've no idea. After all, it is no secret Ashkars and Gargalocs are now entering Bensor at will through the Gate farther south," Galamir said as his brow furrowed with concern.

I thought immediately of Frondamein, who had long said his presence there at the Gate meant little, only a ruse for maintaining the appearance that our country was being well guarded.

"Perhaps such would be an important question for our spies at the Alliance to investigate." Galamir concluded his observation.

"What of the Alliance?" said a voice from the crowd. "Does it remain secret?"

"Draigon still knows nothing of its presence," Vandaril answered. "Am I right, Galamir?"

Galamir nodded. "By all accounts, our mission remains clandestine."

Vandaril continued to address the question concerning the Alliance between the elves of Loth Gerodin and the men to the south as I leaned over and whispered to Galamir. "Do you think it wise to discuss Alliance business here?"

"No need to worry," Galamir whispered back. "We are among friends. Everyone in this room has been training to fight for the Alliance when that day comes. Moreover, you will find our kind most resistant to corruption."

But that did not mean elves could not be corrupted. I

remembered Eliendor telling me when an elf did fall to darkness, it rendered him altogether evil.

"I only hope this new threat along the Greenwaithe will not necessitate that the Alliance turn its gaze away from the upcoming battle in Guilden," Galamir added, breaking into my thoughts.

"Would such jeopardize the rebellion to the south?" I asked.

"Nay, it will still go forward, with or without the elves of Loth Gerodin, though we had hoped for the aid."

"We have stockpiled armaments in safe places throughout the forest," Vandaril continued, "including here in Isgilith, and with cooperation from our brothers and sisters from Cemnath Androl and other such colonies, I believe we would have the masses to thwart an invasion from beyond the Greenwaithe." The look upon Vandaril's face was solemn. "Perhaps Galamir can comment on news from farther south."

Galamir stood once more to address the gathering. "Even now, preparations are being made for the rebellion against Draigon, and yet news that our attentions must necessarily turn to our northern borders is grievous indeed, for it will take our gaze from Maldimire and those other pockets of evil to the south that need to be scourged first."

Again a murmur rippled through the crowd. "Why should we give aid to men from the south, many of whom no longer have any use for the elves, when we have woes at the borders of our own lands?" cried an angry voice from farther down the table.

I could not see who had spoken, but the words elicited a strong reaction from several, making me stir uneasily in my chair. No doubt my friends and neighbors from Baeren Ford, good people who simply wished to live their lives and who held no elf in contempt, were included in their estimation. Did they all look upon me with the same mistrust as the one who had spoken?

Valdir rapped on his wine goblet to restore order in the room and to my surprise he turned to me. "Arwyn," he said, "hailing from Guilden, you must have a unique perspective on Bensor's current state of affairs."

Suddenly every pair of eyes in the room was upon me, and I had the strange feeling Valdir was putting me to the test. Now was my chance to begin the work of the Alliance that I had been asked to do. Very well. I would take the bait.

"Indeed, now is the time for all Bensorians to unite against our common enemy. For far too long Draigon has been allowed to weave a web of mistrust, a mistrust that has in turn bred fear, a fear that is morphing into hatred—all to drive a wedge between us. For Draigon knows the longer the peoples of Bensor remain divided the weaker we will be.

"How do mortals now esteem us?" came another voice, the speaker I could not see.

"There are indeed pockets of contempt toward the elves, though they seem to be limited to Draigon's strongholds, namely Maldimire," I explained. "However, I can assure you most in the south still lament the lengthy separation with this fair race and even now long for help from the north."

A young elf with straight, golden hair stood and looked directly to Galamir and me. "With all due respect to you, my lady, and to Galamir, but it seems our interests are better served along our own borders. We cannot afford to lose our own in the troubles to the south."

I stood to my feet in order to see the speaker more clearly and to address the entire group that had assembled. "Are we not all Bensorians?" I argued. "Any threat that compromises the well-being of one group should be considered a threat to all. We must come together for the sake of all, elves, men, *and* dwarves, as well as the myriad intelligent creatures who call this forest their home."

"Yes, but *dwarves,* my lady?" One of the elven men who had appeared most displeased stood. "They have retreated to their mountains, caring only for the riches of their mines and little else. Of what use are they to us? And for that matter," he went on, not giving me time to respond, "why have we allowed a complete stranger into our fold at such a time as this?" He turned to me and with his sharp eyes stared at me with suspicion. "It is rumored you have only lived in Baeren Ford for three years. I, for one, am curious to know from whence you came before then?"

A murmur arose from the crowd and all at once I felt my stomach tighten. From the corner of my eye I could see a smirk on Kyora's face.

"Have you heard nothing?"

I looked across the table at Allynon who had spoken, his voice raised slightly on a note of frustration. "The very mistrust Arwyn has so keenly pointed out, you demonstrate."

"But, my lord, one cannot be too careful at such a time."

"Would you then question me?" Allynon continued, standing to his feet. "What claim have I on your trust? A foreigner I am in this land, yet you have always embraced me. You will extend that same grace to others, yes? Or is it as Arwyn has said, that Draigon has succeeded in driving a wedge of mistrust among you?"

"But, sire, you are long known to us, and Bensorian blood runs thick through your veins."

"Yes, and that is why to travel through Bensor and see the eyes of the people grieves me, for they are crying out for relief from the tightening vice that threatens the land. Or you have become so comfortable within the confines of your forest you have given little thought to the suffering of those to the south, no?"

"And as for the dwarves, I would hardly call being held prisoner and forced to do the work of slaves in one's own mines 'retreating,'" I said, feeling bold. "You would do well to understand their circumstances before you pass judgment, otherwise the elves may very well find if the south falls, then it will be only a matter of time before they penetrate your borders and enslave you as well."

"Nay! No one could reach us here! Isgilith has long remained secret to all but our friends, and so it shall remain," the elven man argued.

"Arwyn is right!" Galamir said. "With fire and ax, they would one day reach us. Are we willing to fight now for our home…nay, for the whole of Bensor, to ensure we will all be free?"

Several enthusiastic "hear, hears" and "ayes" erupted from the crowd. There was nodding of heads and a general feeling that the fires of justice had been stoked.

I looked over at Allynon, whose jaw was clenched with determination, and I was certain in that moment I caught a glimpse of his father's greatness.

With a look of anguish, Valdir put a hand on Allynon's shoulder. "It grieves me to make this decision, but the situation here in Bensor is much graver than I had anticipated. As much as I wish to see Ignathius again, I'm afraid I must remain here to lead our colony, and therefore shan't be accompanying you on your return to Endara."

"Nonsense, father," Vandaril said as he walked to his father's side. "You must return with Allynon and fulfill the wishes of a dying friend, a friend who has been a faithful ally to us for many long years. Have you not been preparing me all these years to lead in your stead? Are there not other strong leaders here in Isgilith—and in other parts of the forest—who will see that Loth Gerodin does not fall? In the end, we here will be victorious."

"Yes, my son, you are indeed ready to take my place." Valdir sighed and placed a hand on Vandaril's shoulder. He then looked at me sadly, and I again had the strange feeling he was not seeing me but the mystery woman he had spoken of before. "Yes, and there is truly nothing left here for me but memories. I suppose my absence will make little difference to the outcome of our conflict. Omni's will shall triumph regardless of anything one elf can do when there are others who are able to lead."

"Then you will go?"

There was a long pause before he spoke. "Yes, Omni help us, I will," the elven leader relented.

Vandaril walked around the table to me. "Dear Arwyn, if it is within my power, the elves of Loth Gerodin will not forget the suffering of our friends in other parts of Bensor who have long endured the brunt of Draigon's brutality, and we will continue to give aid to the Alliance in whatever way we can. After all, my father and I have a rather personal stake in its success," he added with a grin. "Indeed, if for no other reason we wish for my brother, Callas, to be successful."

Callas? For the moment, my memory jarred when he came to mind. I had fully expected him to show up for the Faerenfel. Yet…it did not matter so much to me anymore.

"Come," Valdir said, addressing his guests, "my time with you wanes and the road ahead appears dark, but for that which we have left, let us make merry." He then walked over and offered me his arm. "Arwyn, I would be most honored if you would accompany me to the ballroom."

I took Valdir's arm and walked to the door where I glanced behind me at Allynon. He was talking to Kyora, and my knees suddenly felt numb.

CHAPTER 13

"I am reticent to acknowledge the stirrings I feel deep within, and yet with every passing hour I feel them more keenly."

I am quite certain in that moment Dr. Susan saw an expression on my face that was something akin to a mixture of grief and surrender. It was several moments before I was able to speak again.

"His presence washes over me like a flood, and in that flood I would gladly drown."

The guests of Valdir poured into the grand ballroom where a group of elven musicians sat playing their instruments softly. I waited expectantly by Valdir's side and was relieved to see Allynon enter the room chatting with Elastair and Gladigan, *not* Kyora.

"Allynon," Valdir gestured toward the door. "Do join me here," he said, leaving my side to meet the prince in the middle of the room. "May I have your attention please?"

A sudden hush swept the crowd and the orchestra stopped playing for a moment.

"Allynon, we would be honored for you to begin the festivities. With whom do you now choose to dance?"

Kyora and her friends had volleyed to the edge of the crowd and were smiling hopefully in Allynon's direction. But Allynon was not looking at them. He was looking at me. He walked toward me with his hand extended. My heart skipped a beat as I placed my hand in his. Together we walked onto the ballroom floor where Allynon placed his hand on my waist and, giving me a nod of encouragement, stepped forward. My own foot followed suit, and all at once we found ourselves twirling about the floor like a spinning top. Feeling the eyes of the entire room upon us, as well as the cold stares of Kyora and her friends, I beamed with triumph that my feet were moving as I wished.

"For someone who learned just yesterday, you dance amazingly well," Allynon said when we were out of earshot from the crowd.

"I did have an excellent teacher."

Allynon gave me a wink. "'Twill be our little secret."

"Yes, my lord." I laughed.

It was not long before Valdir gestured for the other guests to join us, and soon the ballroom floor was filled with other couples twirling in the soft light of the candelabra. When the first dance ended, Allynon walked me to the edge of the crowd close to Vandaril, who had managed to change into more suitable clothing than those he had arrived in minutes before. No sooner had I caught my breath when the elf walked up and offered me his hand.

"Allynon, you're not going to keep this enchanting woman all to yourself this evening, are you?" he said.

Allynon bowed in deference to his friend and placed my hand in his. As I walked out onto the ballroom floor by Vandaril's side, I already could see Kyora inching her way casually in Allynon's direction, a vulture waiting for a leopardess to abandon her kill.

"Galamir has told us much about you," Vandaril replied. "How could you have lived in Guilden all these years without making your presence known to us, I wonder?"

"Why did it take an elf so long to travel there to find me?" I replied. "Perhaps then I would have made myself known much sooner."

Vandaril laughed. "Had we but known of your presence, I'm certain we would have taken you into our fold long before now."

But I wasn't certain I wanted to be taken into their fold.

As the crowd went by in a blur, I managed to glance over in Allynon's direction. Indeed he was talking with Kyora, yet every few moments his gaze strayed out onto the ballroom floor, and so far he had made no move to go there himself. Suddenly I realized Vandaril had asked me a question.

"Pardon me, my lord, but I could not hear you over the music."

"I asked if you had a pleasant visit to the Alliance," the gallant elf replied as we spun around rapidly.

"Oh, yes, I did indeed. Your brother was quite the host."

"Ah, my brother Callas." He smiled. "Quite the charming one he is."

"He told me he would attempt to return home for the Faerenfel."

"Now that would be surprising indeed if he appeared. He is much more, er, worldly, shall we say, and thinks the ways of the forest too provincial. He much prefers the passions of men to the refinement of the elven way of life."

I nodded understanding, remembering how eager Callas seemed to shake the shackles of Loth Gerodin. At last the number ended, and I found myself on the opposite side of the room from where I had started. I was carrying on a conversation with Vandaril when another of the guests, an elf by the name of Heronium whom Galamir had introduced me to several days before, asked me to join him for a dance. Willingly I obliged, becoming more and more comfortable with the performance of my feet in this new endeavor.

Luckily the dance ended on the right side of the room, but Allynon was nowhere to be seen. I thanked my partner politely for the dance before quickly scanning the ballroom floor for any sign of him. I was at once relieved to see Kyora standing close by talking to another male guest while glancing around as if looking for someone. Her eyes landed upon me, and I could see a faint glint of triumph in her eyes.

How silly! She was not my rival. Why had I become hers? This entire situation seemed much too familiar, and a faint uneasiness stirred inside me.

"'Twould be a shame for the host not to dance with his special guest." I turned to see Valdir, and he offered me his arm.

As we danced together, so lightly he stepped, I guessed he had years of practice. In awe I watched his ancient eyes, so out of place they seemed in one who still looked so young. It was hard to imagine living to be thousands of years old.

"And how are you finding the people of Isgilith?" he asked.

"Oh, they are most gracious and have been very kind to me."

"And one in particular, from what I understand." Valdir smiled, but the smile seemed forced, and behind his eyes I could detect conflict.

"Yes, my lord," I replied, attempting to stifle the satisfaction that it was *my* company the prince had desired.

"I wondered where the two of you had been keeping yourselves, though I already had my suspicions," he said. In his voice I detected a note of surrender.

Had he hoped I would have spent my time with him? Or had he hoped to play matchmaker for Vandaril? I had to think quickly of something safe to say. "The prince is a good friend, and I am grateful for the attention he has shown me since he came to town." Quickly I averted my eyes so Valdir could not see the emotion there.

In the distance I caught sight of Allynon talking with the leader of the orchestra, but no sooner did I walk off the ballroom floor with Valdir than Galamir appeared at my side to offer his hand. There was a mischievous gleam in his eye as he walked me out into the midst of the other couples.

"Why do you stare at me so?" I asked, knowing.

"I needn't have worried about you being alone after all, it seems. 'Exploring the forest by myself' indeed!" he said with a twinkle in his eye.

"Can you ever forgive me for not being entirely truthful concerning the company I've been keeping," I said with a demure smile.

"I can, though I do feel responsible for your well-being

while you are here. I do hope the prince has been seeing to that."

"Indeed he has," I replied.

After several more spins around the ballroom floor, the song ended and Galamir walked me to the edge of the crowd. Together we stood for a moment until a young elven maiden smiled at him from across the room.

"Arwyn, if you will excuse me, I am being summoned," he said.

"By all means, you musn't keep her waiting." I laughed, as the flirtatious elf hurried to offer the maiden his hand.

Allynon had disappeared again, and frustration came as quite a surprise. Friendship was all I could dare hope for from him. After all, he would be gone from my life in a matter of days. Yet the feelings he had sparked in me were difficult to ignore. In fact, no one before had ever made me feel the way I did when we were together.

I watched as a host of handsome couples dressed in finery and long, delicate gowns in an array of colors moved in synchronization across the ballroom floor to the steady rhythm of the music. Such a beautiful scene made me smile with delight.

"You are thirsty, yes, with all the dancing you have done?" I turned to see Allynon, and I beamed as he handed me a glass of wine.

"Yes, my lord," I replied, accepting it gratefully. I took several sips of the sweet liquid, peering at Allynon from above the rim of my goblet.

"With all the attention you are receiving, I was afraid I would not catch up with you again this evening. Every man here would wish to dance with you...that is, if I would let them."

Suddenly the rhythm of the music changed to a slower pace, and Allynon took the goblet from my hand and placed it on a table nearby. "Come," he whispered as he led me onto the ballroom floor for the second time that evening.

Slowly we began to sway to the melody, and I was suddenly aware of how close Allynon held me. We danced together in silence, moving rhythmically to the sound of the music. I could feel Allynon's gaze upon me, and for a while I attempted to avoid looking at him directly.

It was no use to resist. Soon he drew me in, and my own gaze was consumed with Allynon's penetrating eyes, gazing intensely into mine. For several moments the world beyond the ballroom floor ceased to exist, becoming nothing more than a blur in the background. Lost in his deep brown eyes, I realized suddenly how deep my breathing had become and how flushed my face felt, and I came to a slow halt.

"I'm sorry…I seem to have lost my breath," I said.

"Perhaps we should step outside for some fresh air, no?" Allynon suggested.

I nodded slowly as he placed his hand on the small of my back and guided me through a glass door leading out to the front veranda. For a moment an awkward silence fell between us.

We came to a stone bench outside the manor on the veranda overlooking the lake, and Allynon gestured I be seated. He sat down next to me. Hundreds of fireflies danced in the shadows nearby, and the distant sound of music penetrated the cool evening air.

"I don't remember ever seeing so many stars before," I commented, though my breath was heavy with emotion.

"Starlight becomes you," he said gently. My gaze lowered to the ground, unable to face him lest my eyes betray me. He took a deep breath. "Arwyn, I…"

Suddenly there came the sound of two people talking noisily nearby, completely shattering the moment. We looked in the direction of the disturbance and saw Inago and Endegar walking toward us in the darkness. "Ah, Your Highness, there you be! We been lookin' all over for you," Inago exclaimed.

Allynon gave me an apologetic look and stood up. "What

could be so urgent?" he said in a tone that was none-too-pleased.

"Your Highness, do forgive us," said Endegar, glancing around the prince's shoulder, "but we did not see the lady. We only ask a moment for you to settle an issue Inago and I are debating."

"We been debatin' de day we be a-leavin'," Inago interrupted. "'Tis de day after de Faerenfel, no, as I be tellin' Endegar here?"

Allynon gave an uncomfortable glance in my direction and nodded. "Yes, the day after tomorrow we will leave," he replied impatiently.

"Is that not what I told you, Inago?" Endegar exclaimed with a look of triumph on his face. "That the prince has spent enough time here as it is and would be anxious to return home."

"But I was a-tellin' him, what with…" Inago began.

I am quite certain the blood had all but drained from my face. Listening to the debate, I felt a knot form in the pit of my stomach, as if someone had punched me, and I felt ill.

"Gentlemen, *another* time we shall have this discussion."

Crestfallen, I quietly slipped away from the gathering and hurried toward the door into the ballroom.

"Arwyn, wait!" Allynon called behind me.

I fled into the gathering inside and made my way through the crowd. In my hurry I happened to brush past Elastair.

"Arwyn," she said anxiously, grabbing my hand, "are you feeling ill?"

I turned to her and pleaded. "I must leave immediately or I will be."

"What has troubled you?"

"I cannot tell you now. I only know I must leave."

"Very well," Elastair said as she put her arm around my shoulder and led me into the entrance hall.

Valdir stood inside the doorway talking to one of his guests when he saw us approaching. Immediately he excused himself and stepped forward with a look of concern upon his face. "Arwyn, are you not feeling well?"

"No, my lord," I answered, glancing around nervously. "I'm simply not accustomed to so much dancing. I do hope you'll forgive me, but I must retire for the night, though I wish to thank you for a lovely evening."

"It was my pleasure. I hope you will feel well enough to attend the Faerenfel tomorrow."

"I do as well, but for now I must bid you a good evening," I said desperately as I saw Allynon making his way through the crowd, eyes scanning left to right.

"Arwyn, what on earth troubles you so?" Elastair asked once we were both outside and well beyond earshot of the manor.

By then the tears were streaming down my cheeks. "I don't know!" I sobbed. But I did know, and I could not suppress my feelings a moment longer. "I...I couldn't bear for him to see me cry."

"The prince?"

I nodded.

"Did he upset you?"

"Yes."

The look on Elastair's face was one of confusion. "I cannot imagine the prince ever being unkind."

"No, it was nothing like that."

Elastair stopped in her tracks and took me by the arm. "Arwyn, you're in love with him."

I looked tearfully at Elastair in the light from a streetlamp. "What a fool I am to fall for a man I can never have!"

"What makes you say that?"

My mind was a jumble of conflicting thoughts and feelings, so difficult to put into words. "Though it seems he fancies me," I began hesitantly, "there are no doubt many women he has fancied, and many he has said goodbye to." I threw my hands in the air and continued walking down the lane. "I have deceived myself into thinking I may be something more than a distraction during his stay here. His father is on his deathbed, for heaven's sake! He has more important things on his mind than courting."

"Arwyn, the prince is not the type of man to dally with a woman's heart, especially under such circumstances," Elastair said with a serious note in her voice. "Besides, it was obvious to everyone in the room how he looked at you."

I wiped my cheek and looked squarely at my friend. "And how was that?"

"Dear, he could hardly keep his eyes off you! But it was much more than that. Arwyn, he looked at you the way a man looks upon the woman he loves. And when you last danced with him—it was to a traditional elvish song of love—one typically reserved for those who are wed or betrothed. For him to have danced with you then was quite a bold declaration!"

I felt stunned. He had taught me that dance in the garden only the day before! Why would he do something so bold if he only meant to leave me in two days? One more day seemed hardly enough for true love to take root, not enough for a commitment I would fully trust. How could I entrust my heart to someone I had only met days before, someone who would then disappear once more?

I shrugged my shoulders and walked through the front gate of Elastair's manor. "What does it matter? In two days he will be leaving—I heard him say so himself. Knowing someone for five days is too short a time on which to base any promises, and Endara is such a long way from Bensor. I should not expect much."

"Perhaps you should leave it to the prince to make that decision," Elastair said, as she opened the front door of her home.

Yet even as my reckless heart longed for his embrace, every bit of my cautious, sober reason begged for temperance. On some level of consciousness, I seemed to vaguely recall an incident from my previous existence when

I had exposed my heart ever so slightly only to have it trampled upon, and that experience did not even compare to what I felt with Allynon. Nay, I would not be so foolhardy again.

Yet, what hope had I to again find a man, either in Isgilith or Baeren Ford, so strong, intelligent, and kind-hearted, not to mention so dashing?

"I will not make a pitiful spectacle of myself, like those other females who are fawning over him. He has been so kind to me, I truly do not wish him to feel any guilt for having created a thirst in me that he cannot quench. Nay, he must not see the strength of my affection."

"And you would miss the Faerenfel?"

I considered the possibility for a moment then shook my head. "No, after all, to attend the Faerenfel is the reason I came to Isgilith, and I would not wish to disappoint dear Galamir. And yet, I will do what I must to protect my heart."

"I understand, but I advise you to give the prince a chance to make his own heart known."

Elastair sighed. "Come." She walked toward the dining room. "Let me make you some tea to help you sleep. You must be rested, for you don't know what tomorrow may bring, and your way of looking at things may be much different by then."

CHAPTER 14

"Like the stag that will be served at the feast this eve, I feel I have been pierced through the heart. And if that is not enough, I must now pretend to make merry and somehow keep my heartache from being a spectacle for all to see, especially him."

For a long while I lay awake, replaying the evening over and over in my mind. My restless night was filled with images of Allynon, and as the morning sun rose I wondered how I would possibly face him without revealing my heart for all to see. How much easier it would be for him to slip out of town quietly, making the past few days nothing more than a pleasant dream. Yet the thought of never seeing him again made my heart ache all the more.

Almost every elf from Isgilith flocked to the playing fields on the edge of the city that morning to begin the day's festivities, and I hoped somehow to become lost in the crowd. Much to my relief, the earliest event of the Faerenfel was one in which I found myself shielded in the midst of a group of female elves, all weaving garlands of flowers and greenery to adorn their hair and the manes of the horses that were to participate in the competitions. Underneath the trees we worked, and an undercurrent of excited chattering rippled through the gathering.

Elastair sat close to me as I worked glumly on a wreath of white foxglove for my hair. Much to my dismay, Kyora and her entourage came trotting up and placed themselves strategically between us and the main path.

"Did you not have a wonderful time at the ball last night?" Galena giggled as she glanced over in my direction.

"Indeed I did," replied Kyora. "The prince was so charming. He seemed to love the way I dance."

"And he's watching you right now!" Analeth exclaimed

as she looked toward the path.

Elastair leaned over and whispered, "Don't let them fool you, dear. Galamir informed me the prince appeared shaken after you left and retired early to his room. Moreover, it is you he seeks out now, and not those three silly girls sitting over there."

Pretending to be in search of a bright ribbon to add to my wreath, I looked out of the corner of my eye and could see Allynon sitting a short distance away on the back of his horse, with Valdir and Vandaril slowing their horses to a stop behind. I turned away and went back to my weaving.

"Silly girls they are indeed!" I said, trying to control the emotion in my voice. "I would not have expected such from an elven woman."

"But women they are not," Elastair replied. "Though they may appear as you and I, they are still quite young in elven terms and have much to learn yet about the world. I doubt any of them have traveled far beyond the borders of Loth Gerodin."

"I must say everyone else has been most kind to me, the way I would expect a lady to behave." I glanced in the general direction of the path and could see the brown mare Allynon had been riding was gone. Only Valdir remained. My gaze locked with his briefly, and I saw a spark of questioning there that I did not dwell upon long enough to try to understand. I turned back to Elastair. "How is my wreath?"

"Lovely. It will look beautiful with your green dress," Elastair said as she took the wreath and placed it in my hair. "As I said, you look lovely."

Throughout the day there were all manner of competitions and demonstrations of skill from jousting and juggling to wrestling and foot races. From the back of the crowd, I watched as Allynon took part in a mock sword battle, admiring the way he moved as nimbly as his elven opponent, taking command of his weapon with ease. So masculine he was I could feel my heart rate quicken, and the sight of him stirred in me those longings I so desperately wished to suppress.

By late morning, the crowd made its way over to the archery range where I had already committed to compete, though I was in no frame of mind for competition. As I walked up to the line when my turn came, I happened to glance out into the crowd of onlookers to the place where Allynon was talking with Galamir. The two of them were looking in my direction. What on earth could Galamir be telling him? Had Elastair told her son my secret—that I had been absolutely miserable since last night? Nay, I knew better than to suspect Galamir would betray me. If anything, I knew he would protect me.

The pressure was almost unbearable. The elvish crowd was no doubt curious to see the newcomer's skill with a bow, and all stood in rapt attention as I nocked my arrow. Trying to force the image of Allynon's brown eyes from my mind, I lifted my bow and took aim at the target. A hush fell upon the crowd until the only sound was a thwap! and the whir of the arrow as it hurled through the air. With a sharp thud it hit its target, though at least an inch from the bull's-eye.

Unnerved, I nocked another arrow and took a deep breath. *Concentrate, Arwyn*! I closed one eye to line up my target with the sight. In a flash, I released another arrow, and this time it landed even farther from the center.

A little more than disconcerted, I knew I had one more chance to prove myself on the archery range. I could just imagine the smirk on Kyora's face somewhere in the midst of the bystanders until suddenly a thought occurred to me. The Gifts! Of course! I had been relying too strongly on my own strength at a time when it felt weakest. But until that moment, I had not been disciplined enough to clear my mind of all distractions.

Banishing my troubles for the moment, all my will was

bent on the very center of the target. Calmly I lifted my bow one last time and steadied my breathing. With a quick release of the string, the arrow flew through the air and hit the target dead center. A collective gasp echoed through the crowd followed immediately by loud applause. I bowed my head and returned to my spot beside Elastair.

"That was quite a performance," Galamir said as he walked up. "You may yet win this competition."

"My aim was off," I lamented.

"But not by much. Your opponents will still be hard-pressed to surpass you."

"Even you, Galamir?"

"Yes, even me," he said, smiling encouragingly. He looked at me as if he knew a secret, yet he was no more forthcoming than that.

The contest went on for quite some time until Kyora stepped confidently up to the stand.

"You did not tell me she would be part of the contest," I whispered to Elastair.

"I did not wish to alarm you, for she is one of the best archers in Isgilith," my friend explained.

We watched as one, two, three, Kyora shot three arrows into a spot no larger than my thumbnail in the very center of the target, much to my dismay.

Galamir was the last to compete, though it was clear Kyora would in all likelihood receive the top prize. When her name was called, the elven maiden approached the winner's podium with a smile of self-satisfaction. Galamir fared a little less well, earning himself the second place award. Considering the circumstances, I was glad for my third place rank, but I knew in my heart I could have performed much better. And as if to add insult to injury, my adversary stood there with a gloating smile as she stared directly at me.

As the crowd at the archery range dispersed, I slipped through the throng and back into the woods to the place where Avencloe was tied to a tree. The horse relay was little less than an hour away, and I wished to prepare him for the event. With brush in hand, I stroked his mane, whispering into his ear words of affection and praise.

"You must fly like a falcon this afternoon," I coaxed. "Grant me the joy of the wind in my hair that it may strip away my sorrows."

After a while I mounted Avencloe and made my way over to a vast clearing in the forest. Spectators lined the edge of the long playing field, waving banners and shouting cheers as the four teams made ready for the race. Avencloe stamped his hooves impatiently, as if he longed to feel the rush of the wind through his mane.

The relay teams had been divided randomly among the contestants, and I recognized one of my teammates as a guest from the banquet the evening before. Amidst cheers of encouragement, I rode over to the place where we made ready for the race to begin.

Waiting patiently for the other teams to line up at the starting gate, I looked over to see Kyora was again among the competition. As the redheaded elven maiden joined her team, she happened to catch me staring in her direction. With a cold glare, Kyora snapped the reins harshly against her horse's neck, causing the animal to quicken its pace. Allynon was nowhere to be seen, although I suspected he must be watching from somewhere in the crowd.

During a quick meeting with my teammates, it was decided I would go last, being the lightest of us all. We all lined up before the starting gate to await the lowered flag. Feeling extreme confidence in Avencloe's abilities, I stroked his neck and whispered the words of encouragement I always whispered to him before beginning a hard run.

There was tension in the air until the starting flag dropped and the first riders took off across the vast field. They became but moving dots on the far end before turning around and heading back. Already Kyora's team was out in front by a length, and that gap soon widened the closer they came to the starting point.

Amidst a din of cheers from the crowd, the second group of horses and riders took off. My team already lagged behind. My heart thumped in anticipation of the ride as I wondered if even Avencloe could make up such a vast gap. These were elven horses he raced against, and though some were slower than others, by whatever magic the elves possessed, their horses were overall faster than the average.

By the time the second group of horses returned to the starting gate, the gap had widened even more with my team still in dead last. Only two more groups of riders to go and the fate of the race would be determined. The third group took off consecutively as their teammates crossed over the starting line, with Kyora's team in a firm lead.

I poised myself at the starting line, my body tense for the ride ahead. I glanced over to see Kyora also waited at the ready with intense eyes willing her teammate onward. With a look of triumph, Kyora turned and glanced at me right before her horse shot away across the field. The two other teams were next to come in, and the last of the riders took off from their starting positions.

Kyora was almost midfield when at last it came Avencloe's turn to begin his leg of the race. The gap between him and the other horses was wide, and yet he seemed almost happy for the challenge. My heartbeat quickened with excitement, and for a few moments I felt alone and free again, as if galloping across the windswept fields of Guilden with not a care in the world. How good it felt to have my hair blowing wildly in the breeze behind me and to see the world passing by in a blur.

By the time I reached the turnaround point, we had almost caught up to Kyora's horse, and it was not long before we passed it completely, leaving all of the other contestants in the dust. Gasps of disbelief came from the onlookers as I sped down the final stretch far ahead of everyone else. A huge cheer erupted when Avencloe crossed the finish line. My teammates rushed to me in an onslaught of gratitude for bringing them a victory against such steep odds. I smiled at them obligingly, but deep in my heart it was an empty victory. Allynon was nowhere to be seen.

Following the celebration, I headed back to Galamir's home to freshen up for the evening. The festivities were not yet complete, and perhaps the most magical part of the Faerenfel was yet to come. Yet it was with a heavy heart I wished for the day to be over.

Galamir, Elastair, and Gladigan had apparently remained at the playing field throughout the afternoon, and I debated whether or not to attend the evening festivities at all. Then I thought of Galamir and how he had so wanted me to come to Isgilith especially for the Faerenfel, and I decided I could not let him down. Besides, I knew I might never again have the opportunity to see the mysterious spectacle promised for the evening.

A host of elves walked in the direction of the giant Circle of Omni on the lowest tier of the city and to the Faerenfel feast that would be held there. I, however, walked alone, feeling a twinge of regret for the way I had carried on that day. Who had behaved like a silly schoolgirl? It was not very womanly to run away from one's fears, avoiding Allynon as I had. In truth, I did indeed fear opening my heart to love— and the possibility of having it trampled.

Perhaps Elastair was right, perhaps I should leave the door of my heart open until I learned the prince's intentions. With a sigh of remorse over a wasted day, I wondered if I would even have that opportunity.

"Hello, Arwyn!" A male voice called to me from behind.

My heart sprang to life and I turned with a smile. I looked behind me and was both startled and disappointed to see Callas walking up beside me with a spring in his step.

"Hello, my lord," I said politely, trying to hide my

frustration behind a half-hearted smile. "This is indeed a surprise."

"I told you I would be coming to the Faerenfel, did I not?" Callas replied cheerfully. "And I am not one to go back on a promise."

"Yes, my lord."

"I trust you are having a nice visit in our fair city?"

"Indeed I am."

"Good, good. And you have met my father?"

"Yes, he has been very..."—*hmmm, confusing, mysterious, conflicted*—" gracious to me," I replied. "And your brother as well."

"Ah, the favored child," Callas commented with no further explanation.

"When did you arrive in Isgilith?"

"A while ago, actually. Glad to have made it in time for the evening's festivities."

"You almost missed the Faerenfel altogether."

"Ah, yes. Would that I had arrived in time for the elderhorn scale for, though I am normally disinclined to boast, I must admit I do excel in the sport," he said, leaning toward me with a captivating smile. His light brown hair, tinged with splashes of auburn, seemed to catch fire in the light of the late afternoon sun. "Yet even more fortunate I am to have chanced upon you here."

I smiled weakly in response as my eyes darted to the ground.

"Shall I accompany you to the feasting place?"

"Yes, my lord, it would be an honor," I said.

Following the throng of other feast-goers, Callas and I walked down the cedar-lined way to the Circle of Omni, and it seemed to me we walked into a lofty building. The light from the setting sun cast rays through the tree trunks, giving the appearance of shining through windows as they hit the grassy earth beneath. Looking above to the soaring roof created overhead by the coming together of the treetops, the spirit of the place moved me even if my companion did not in the same way he had the first time we met.

I could not deny Callas's presence stirred me. It wasn't that I didn't like Callas. In fact, it was easy to be seduced by his alluring smile, his boldness, and the way he looked at me with those mischievous pale gray eyes...but he wasn't Allynon. Besides, his presence elicited feelings of confusion that were a bit more than I wished to deal with that evening.

From somewhere nearby came music, and already a horde of elves danced merrily in the midst of the trees. The dance was one I had learned in Baeren Ford, and I guessed many of the old folk dances were the same across Bensor.

"Would you care to join me?" Callas said, offering me his hand.

"Of course," I replied as we joined the others out in the clearing.

It was certainly a livelier jig than those the night before, and it took my breath away to be spinning around so fast. My feet were at least more familiar with what was expected of them than they were with the slow waltzes. Callas smiled at me in his captivating, flirtatious manner with every turn we took, and it soon became clear how truly different he was from his more stately brother and father.

We danced together for yet two more numbers, and Callas showed no sign of slowing down until a point came in the second for the female dance partner to shift one partner to the left. Gladly I shifted to someone else, and I was happier still the dance called for yet another such change. With any luck, at the end of the dance I would become lost in the crowd.

The time to switch partners came once again, and just as I sashayed to the left, I looked up to see Allynon stepping into the dance from outside. The next elf down appeared stunned that I had been stolen away so abruptly and was about to protest when the oncoming dancers forced him to move out of the way to avoid a collision.

Allynon grabbed me by the hands and spun me around. "I have missed you today," he said boldly, as I turned to face him again.

"Forgive me, my lord, but the day has held many distractions," I replied.

"Come with me," he said as he took me by the hand and led me from the midst of the dancing. When we were some distance away, he stopped and turned to me. "Arwyn, there is a matter I must discuss with you."

"Yes, my lord."

"I wish to ask your forgiveness if I have offended you."

"Offended me?" I repeated, feeling quite stunned. "Why, you have not offended me in the least."

The lines on Allynon's face visibly relaxed. "Then..."

"Hello, Allynon," came a voice from nearby. Together we looked up to see Callas standing there. A smile was upon his face, showing no hint of irritation for having his dance partner stolen out from under his nose.

"Callas, how good it is to see you again." Allynon's tone was formal, hinting nothing of the warmth that had characterized his greeting of Vandaril the evening before.

"And what a surprise it is to see you," Callas said. "What is it that brings you back to Isgilith?"

"I come for your father. It is my father's dying wish to see him before he leaves this world."

"You father is ill? Indeed, I am grieved to hear it," Callas replied. "Has my father agreed to return with you?"

"Indeed he has."

"And who will lead Isgilith in his absence, for surely he will be away for a long while?"

Allynon glanced uncomfortably at me. "I believe he has spoken with Vandaril about leading the colony in his stead."

"Ah, Vandaril, of course." Suddenly Callas grew pensive as he stared into the distance. "My, this is an interesting turn of events indeed," he said quietly, and I wondered by his tone of voice the exact meaning behind his words. Callas broke from his pensive gaze and turned back to Allynon. "I see you have met Arwyn."

Allynon glanced at me. "Yes, I have."

"And will you be joining us for the feast?"

Allynon looked at me as if searching for an invitation. I smiled at him encouragingly, the first genuine smile that had been on my face all day.

"Yes, I will join you."

The three of us walked past the treeline to a long table where Valdir and Vandaril were already seated and speaking jovially with a young servant who had placed two plates of roasted venison before them. It was the first I had seen of Valdir since early that morning. They looked up as we approached, and their eyes widened to see Callas.

"Callas, my son, this is indeed a wonderful surprise!" Valdir exclaimed as he stood to his feet and went to embrace his son warmly. "What made you decide to come to the Faerenfel this year?"

Callas glanced subtly in my direction and smiled. "I had a feeling it would hold a particular interest," he said.

"No matter the reason, I am just glad you are here!" Valdir said. He was obviously pleased, though behind Valdir's eyes there was a hint of apprehension.

"Callas!" Vandaril said, as he walked up behind his father.

"Hello, brother," he responded without making a move in Vandaril's direction. The unspoken tension in the air was most uncomfortable, and I wished to escape the exchange altogether. "I understand our father is to be away for a while and is leaving you in charge of the colony," Callas commented rather nonchalantly.

"With you away at the Alliance, it seemed only fitting," said Vandaril.

"Yes, my son," Valdir added, "your calling is to the south. That is where you are most needed now."

"Yes, Father, I'm sure you are right as always!"

Suddenly Galamir walked up. "Hello, Callas!" he greeted. "I was beginning to wonder if you had been held up on your journey, so late you are arriving at the Faerenfel. You almost missed it altogether."

"I was distracted along the way with Alliance business," Callas replied.

"Perhaps you can apprise me of recent happenings over dinner," Galamir suggested.

Taking that as an invitation to be seated, we all took our places at the table where Valdir and Vandaril were dining, and I found myself in the awkward position of sitting between Allynon and Callas. Luckily, Galamir sat next to Callas on the other side and, whether out of strategy or necessity, he kept him distracted for a while with talk of the Alliance. Not that having Allynon's attentions all to myself was any more comfortable, and the two of us found ourselves having to endure awkward silences throughout the evening as we struggled to find trivial topics to discuss that would not breach any emotional boundaries.

The fact that Allynon would be leaving the following morning still weighed heavily on my heart. I could not bear to ponder that at the moment. Callas, who was no doubt puzzled and perhaps slightly irritated by Galamir's sudden sociability, was eventually able to remove himself from that conversation now and then to carry on polite chitchat with me.

To my relief, the spectacle of the Faerenfel itself was enough to be a distraction for most of the evening. Young elven servants had seen that the host of long tables along the perimeter of the Circle were laden with platters of venison, nuts, berries, and candied yams. The pear wine flowed freely, and there was a feeling of general merriment in the air.

Long after the last rays of the early evening sun had disappeared into the west, darkness descended upon Loth Gerodin, and something magical happened. Under the soft glow of the lanterns hanging from the boughs above, the clearing filled with the most amazing creatures I had ever seen. Half-human, half-animal fauns and centaurs leapt into the middle of the clearing, followed by a parade of gnomes, sprites, and wood nymphs. Unicorns of all sizes with their single horns protruding proudly from their foreheads walked shyly into the middle of the gathering.

Suddenly I heard the whir of tiny wings like those of a hummingbird's next to my ear. I looked in time to see a fairy dance through the air, alighting on my shoulder, and then onto the table before me, where it stayed only a moment before flying off once more. The whole clearing was soon aglow with the lights of several hundred of the little creatures floating hypnotically over those who danced on the ground. I could not help but smile in wonder at the sight before me.

Allynon leaned over and whispered in my ear, "Do you know the origin of the Faerenfel?"

"Please tell me," I replied, even though I had heard the story several times before from both Eliendor and Galamir.

"Legend has it the Faerenfel began ages ago with the marriage of Elwei and Arnuin, who were wed one starry spring night here in this very clearing. This clearing is said to be at the very center of Loth Gerodin," he explained. "As they did on the night Elwei and Arnuin were wed, the creatures of the forest have come together every year thereafter to celebrate their union once more."

"How absolutely wonderful," I said with a tender smile. A smile spread to Allynon's face as well, and I knew even if these were to be our last moments together, I was at least glad I was experiencing the Faerenfel with him.

We then turned our attention back to the middle of the clearing where the host of mythical creatures twisted and turned methodically in a primitive dance to stirring music curiously emanating from deep inside the waterfall partially encircling the far end of the island. It was a sound unlike anything I had ever heard before—a mixture of high female voices singing haunting words in an ancient language to a deep, droning sound that pulsated through the entire gathering. For a long while time stood still as the creatures danced in synchronization, back and forth and in circles— dances they had known from the beginning of time, for these beings were older even than the elves.

Then, one by one, the creatures dancing in the center of the clearing stopped abruptly as though sensing the presence of a hunter in the woods. I soon realized their reaction was something more akin to hearing one's name being called in a crowded room. Slowly they all turned in the direction of the table where we sat, as a stunned murmur stirred amongst the onlookers. Paying no heed to the host of elves surrounding them, the forest creatures collectively bowed low to the ground. Trembling unicorns fell forward to their knees; fauns and centaurs lowered their heads in reverence; the forest gnomes removed their hats and stood still as stone; and even the fairies' fluttering diminished.

I leaned over and whispered to Callas, "Your father certainly commands the respect of all forest creatures."

Callas turned to me, appearing quite baffled. "But never before have they demonstrated it in such a way," he said.

I looked to Valdir, who sat to the left of Allynon, and to my great surprise I found him staring straight at me with eyes that spoke of awe.

With a crescendo the music picked up again and intensified. In a manner that seemed almost giddy, the creatures of the forest danced in the clearing, jumping and turning with such intensity a buzz of bewildered whispers arose amongst the onlookers.

Following a rather dramatic climax, the music quieted to a steady rhythm as one by one the creatures in the middle of the clearing disappeared, signaling the end of the annual coming together of all those who dwelt in the forest. In a few moments they returned to their elusive existence, seeming more illusion than reality. I smiled with delight, still in awe of the spectacle I had witnessed.

"Might I accompany you on your walk home this evening?"

The voice of Callas brought me back to reality and the gravity of the moment. I glanced sidelong at Allynon, trying not to be obvious, though my heart pleaded for a sign from him. With a slight nod of the head, it was evident he had heard Callas's request and was handing me over.

What? You're practically giving me up to another man! Will you not fight for me? I wanted to scream at him.

So there was my answer. Perhaps I truly *had* been only a mere distraction.

I turned back to Callas. "Yes, my lord," I said numbly, feeling the anguish rise in my throat.

Gathering what pride I could muster, I flung my head back and turned to Allynon, determined to hide the hurt and anger in my eyes. "I presume..."

"Arwyn, I need..."

We had both spoken at the same moment.

"Please," he gestured.

"I presume this is goodbye," I said. "You'll be leaving in the morning."

Allynon looked at me with his deep brown eyes and smiled gently. "I am afraid you are mistaken."

What? Had I heard correctly? I was fairly certain my heart stopped beating momentarily as I waited breathlessly for an explanation.

"I have decided to remain in Isgilith a while longer."

I was stunned. Barely had I the time to soak in this announcement when I felt Allynon's fingers curl around mine.

"After all...how could I possibly leave the woman who has so completely captured my heart?"

Slowly I lifted my head, hardly believing what I had heard. As I looked deep into his eyes I found a reflection of myself engulfed in his warmth and tenderness. My heart quickened as did my breathing, and I felt a tear of joy trickle down my cheek. I turned my head slightly, and out of the corner of my eye I could see Callas was absorbed once more in conversation with Galamir. He had heard nothing of what Allynon had whispered. I imagined it had been Galamir's intention all along to lure the prince's rival away.

The last of the fairy lights disappeared from the clearing, signaling the end of the Faerenfel. With subdued reverence, the audience made their way from the area. The midnight hour had come, and it was time to return home. As we arose from the table, I saw Galamir pull Callas off to the side. Callas glanced over his shoulder, appearing slightly perturbed, as he no doubt had other things on his mind than even more talk of the Alliance.

I turned to Allynon, who grabbed my hand and whispered fervently in my ear. "Meet me in the forest tomorrow, two hours after sunrise."

"I will," I promised, nodding breathlessly.

For a moment longer our fingertips touched, then I willed myself to walk away. Even as I moved beyond his reach, I looked back at Allynon to see him gazing at me, motionless, as I slipped into the night.

All else forgotten, I walked silently through the crowd of ghostly elves returning home for the night, having completely forgotten about Callas until he caught up to me.

"I do apologize for my, er, distraction this evening," he said. "Your friend Galamir does not know when to let matters of business rest."

I nodded and smiled weakly. "He is quite single-minded," I replied.

For the remainder of our return to Galamir's home, Callas made light talk to which I replied with yeses and noes, indeed nots, and nods of the head. I was glad to finally reach the front door of Galamir's home, where I could excuse myself from Callas's presence and retreat to the guest quarters to ponder this turn of events.

After a polite good night to Callas, I slipped into the darkened house and up the stairs to my room. My hosts had lagged behind at the celebration, but it was not long before I heard the front door open downstairs and the family entered. Soon the house was silent but for the occasional calls of a nocturnal bird outside the window. With great anticipation I lay awake far into the night, my thoughts centered on the man I was to meet early the next morning.

CHAPTER 15

"If I am dreaming, then may I never wake."

The sunrise did not come soon enough. At first light I jumped out of bed and nervously changed into a gown of green. The minutes ticked by painfully slowly as I paced the floor of my room, resisting the urge to go dashing off into the forest too early. But as the sun made its ascent through the eastern sky, abandoning all my arguments against my irrational heart, I had Avencloe saddled.

Without even a bite to eat, I mounted my waiting stallion and took off at a slow gallop past Valdir's house where I thought I spied Callas out on the front steps talking to a couple of early risers who were passing by on horseback. Hurriedly I passed by, hoping he hadn't spotted me. I could not let anything delay me seeing Allynon.

With heart beating wildly, I was too distracted to take much notice of the hoofbeats that followed me. I turned off the main road and onto the path beside the gazebo when a thought suddenly occurred to me.

What if last night had been but a dream, an illusion brought on by the hypnotic effect of the Faerenfel? What if Allynon were not there to meet me? That he had in actuality left early this morning for Endara? Pushing such notions out of my mind, I pressed on into the forest, only vaguely aware of the beating of a horse's hooves still some distance in the direction from which I had come.

Up ahead through the trees I could just make out a brown mare. All anxiety melted away instantly when I saw Allynon. As I drew near, without a word he took Avencloe's reins to steady the horse. I flung my leg over Avencloe's back and, placing my hands on Allynon's broad shoulders, slid to the ground and into his arms. Allynon's hold around my waist remained firm as he pulled me even closer.

Gingerly he lifted his hand to my cheek. I closed my eyes for a moment, luxuriating in the feel of his touch upon my skin.

Breathing heavily, I opened my eyes to see him now so close. "How I have longed to touch your face," he said, "and to kiss your sweet lips." With that, Allynon pressed his lips to mine in a tender, lingering kiss.

I could have stood there forever, succumbing to his embrace. This was an ecstasy I never wanted to end. And yet, after another blissful moment Allynon pulled away and opened his eyes.

"Arwyn," he began, gazing at me with passion, "so in love with you I am."

"And I with you," I whispered.

With a smile of utter elation on his face, Allynon once more pressed his lips to mine. Gladly I accepted his embrace, abandoning all reason and any preconceived notion of how falling in love should progress at a more sober, respectable rate. I only knew I longed to hear those words from him again and again.

"Come with me," Allynon said at last. He led me by the hand up the path to the pool where we had met only several days before.

As we sat upon the mossy carpet, Allynon gazed at me while he caressed my cheek with his fingertips. How warm his hand felt against my skin. With that he leaned over and kissed me once more, very slowly and deliberately.

"I could not bear to leave you," he said at last, still caressing my cheek and the tresses of my hair with his hand.

"And I could not bear for you to go," I admitted, as tears of joy flowed from my eyes.

"When we were atop Arin Miraneth," said Allynon, "how I had wanted to take you in my arms and remove the pain of your loneliness. It was then I knew I loved you, and the thought of leaving you became unbearable."

"As it did for me," I replied. "So much that I had to shelter my heart against the pain of our parting."

"Though leave you I did not. I am still here with you," he said as he pulled me closer, wrapping me in his arms.

"But your father," I said, all the while dreading what must certainly be an urgent need to depart.

"My dear Arwyn, always thinking of others." Allynon gently guided my chin so my gaze would meet his own. "But no, on our journey over the sea, the winds were with us, making our arrival in Bensor three weeks earlier than expected. The gain affords me the time to linger here in Isgilith, that is, until our path is made clear to us, yes? And then we shall see, though I know what my heart desires," he said tenderly. "Until then, let us not be burdened with the thought of parting."

Being enveloped in Allynon's warm embrace was all that mattered at that moment, and all the uncertainty of the previous day melted away like snow on a glorious spring day, leaving nothing but beauty in its wake.

"But, pray tell, why did you let me go with Callas last night?"

Allynon chuckled. "I cannot say the thought of striking Callas and then dragging you away over his unconscious body did not cross my mind, but to act in such an unchivalrous manner is not the way I wish to win your heart." He then grew serious. "Arwyn, your happiness is my desire, whether with me or another. That choice only you can make, although...I have great confidence in your ability to determine which of us would love you best. Besides," he went on with a gleam in his eye, "the sight of Callas pouting is not pretty, and I did not wish to end your first Faerenfel so unpleasantly."

"Or perhaps you should have, and made my choice all the easier." I laughed and leaned in for a kiss, to which he willingly obliged.

The next two weeks were the happiest I could ever remember. Every waking moment Allynon spent by my side until it became common for us to be found talking quietly in the cool of a garden, walking hand-in-hand along a forest pathway or under the moonlight beside the lake.

Every moment I spent with Allynon, the more fettered my heart became. His kindness, his dry sense of humor that often brought laughter to my lips, his honor and humility, and his gentle, even-tempered manner—all from someone I would have expected to be rather pompous—never ceased to amaze me. How could a man be all those things? I had to pinch myself to be sure he wasn't a figment of my imagination. And yet...there was something about him I couldn't quite place my finger on—a deep sadness perhaps, as if he carried a great burden in his heart. I assumed it had to do with his father's imminent death. Still, the hard lines etching his face only three weeks before were replaced with smiles of joy.

But not everyone in Isgilith shared our joy. Everywhere we went we saw the elves of Loth Gerodin preparing for battle. Elven men bore swords and engaged in mock swordplay, and the archery range was filled from morning to night with both men and women practicing their skill with the bow. It seemed the elves had taken to heart the debate at Valdir's home the night before the Faerenfel and had decided not to leave the fate of their forest to chance. It was a sobering reminder of all that was happening beyond the borders of the forest.

Kyora's sudden absence in that part of the city was also quite noticeable, to me at least, although there was at least one occasion when the elven maiden chanced upon Allynon and me walking hand-in-hand while she was out gathering berries in the forest with her friends. The encounter had lasted but a moment, yet it so flustered Kyora, she turned and left the scene and her friends without uttering a word. As far as I was concerned, she had only herself to blame for her silly behavior.

And then there was the issue of Callas, who slipped away abruptly on the day following the Faerenfel with little more than a word to his father concerning his hasty departure. With a sting of guilt, I knew the reason he had left. But what could I do? After all, I had made my choice.

Two weeks had passed since the Faerenfel, and still Allynon made no mention of his plans for departure. Then one evening at sunset, he and I strode together under the massive elderhorns of the giant Circle of Omni. Allynon had seemed greatly preoccupied the entire day, and it made my heart sink to consider the possibility that his time in Isgilith grew short. Yet I knew the task he had been sent to do weighed heavily on his mind, and I could not expect him to linger much longer in the forest. Beyond that…well, I had thought little of it, as if I were living under the illusion that life beyond Loth Gerodin had come to a standstill and would remain that way indefinitely. It was much easier to deny the reality of passing time than to face an inevitable goodbye.

Still, I gathered my courage and took a deep breath, preparing for the words I dreaded. "You seem lost in your thoughts—you have been all day," I said, placing my hand on his arm. "What troubles you?"

Allynon stopped and turned to look at me in the golden sunlight that shone between the massive trunks of the elderhorns. There was a pensive smile upon his face as he took my hands in his. We were all alone except for the birds that had come to roost in the branches above. As Allynon cleared his throat, I braced myself for the worst.

"My dear Arwyn," he began, "there *is* something I wish to discuss with you, though admittedly difficult it is for me."

I held my breath and looked at him anxiously.

"Arwyn, these past few days have been the happiest of my life," he began. "To complete a task, I came to Isgilith, yet little did I know I would find a treasure unlike any other in the world." He lifted his hand to stroke my face. "And now that I have found you, I cannot let you go." There was a pause as he choked back the emotion in his voice. "Marry me, Arwyn!"

Had I heard him correctly? I stood there for a moment in stunned silence. "Marry you?" I exclaimed. This was all so sudden. The last thing I had expected from my holiday in Loth Gerodin was a marriage proposal!

I gasped and turned away as the reality of our situation came crashing into my awareness, making me feel as though I were waking from a pleasant dream. "Marry you—why, you are a prince! I am but a simple peasant from Baeren Ford. I rank not with nobility."

"Fair lady, but no," Allynon whispered as he walked up behind and stroked my arms, pressing his lips against my ear. "What makes you noble is not your rank but that which is in your heart. Such purity, such compassion and tenderness I see in yours. Your strength and courage far surpass even the greatest, and in your eyes I find a peace that calms my soul like nothing else. Marry me, and I will make you queen of my heart."

I turned slowly to face him, but in my eyes were tears of apprehension. "How you honor me! But, Allynon, there are still many things you do not know about me, things that make me, well, different from most."

"And to discover those secrets is something I greatly anticipate," he said with an impish grin.

"You don't understand!" I protested. "Come with me," I said as I took him by the hand and led him to the edge of the fountain standing in the middle of the circle around which grew bushes covered with perfect yellow roses. I stopped before one of the bushes and closed my eyes. "*Memnon arya othelos!*"

In the waning sunlight, we could see a tinge of red appear at the base of the flowers. In a matter of seconds the red had spread throughout the tender petals, leaving no hint of the yellow that was there before.

Allynon's brow furrowed into a frown, and he sat down slowly on the edge of the fountain. "So you possess the Gifts," he said quietly.

Yes, that was me, oddity that I was.

It was several moments before Allynon spoke, and in the meantime it seemed by the anguished look upon his face a battle was going on inside him. So there it was—my dream was ending.

"What I already suspected of you, it is confirmed," he said at last. "The moment I laid eyes on you, I knew you were special. Unicorns only approach the purest of souls." He looked up to me with eyes full of anguish. "The truth is . . . the truth is, *I* am not worthy of *you*."

"What do you mean?" I asked, astonished.

Allynon took a deep breath as if gathering his will. "Many years ago, it was," he began. "I was barely a man and thought I knew what it meant to be a man. I had traveled to the country of Anghara to meet with the king on official business of Endara. The king took kindly to me, as did one of his daughters, and invited me on a hunting party to his lodge in the mountains, several days journey from the capital.

"Along the way we camped close to a river, and as the others broke camp the next morning, his daughter and I rode on ahead across the bridge," Allynon explained, glancing uncomfortably at me. "Suddenly the skies opened and there came a downpour like none I had ever seen before. A flash flood raged down from the mountains and washed away the bridge, trapping us on the other side away from the party, who would have to travel an extra three days to the nearest bridge that led to the lodge. The daughter and I, we arrived there in but a few hours.

"All alone in that large manor, we found ourselves. She fancied me as I did her…though I did not love her. However, she was young and willing, and I was young and curious and, well…"

I could feel the blood drain from my face as I considered

the thought of him in the arms of another woman.

"After three days the rest of the hunting party arrived, but I could see the suspicion in her father's eyes, and it was more than I could bear. Unable to handle the guilt I had brought upon myself, quite abruptly I packed my things to leave." Allynon's voice trailed off and it was a moment before he could speak again. "Though never will I forget the look upon her face, nor how she told me she loved me and pleaded tearfully for me to stay. Yet being the coward I was, I left."

I stood there, at a complete loss for words.

"But that is not the worst of it," Allynon said, his voice choked with emotion. "To wipe the image of her tearful face from my mind, I returned home to Endara and busied myself with all manner of worthy distractions. Then, months later, a diplomat from Anghara arrived at my father's court. And there, before everyone, he revealed how I had impregnated the king's daughter and left her. To hide her shame, she married a man she did not love, only to lose the child before it was born."

"Oh, Allynon," I whispered.

"A wound it is that never heals," he said, shaking his head in sorrow. "In one reckless act I brought dishonor to myself, to my family, and to the poor young woman who bore the consequences of my indiscretion." A faraway look clouded Allynon's eyes as he stared into the distance. "Mercy and forgiveness my father showed me, even though disgrace I had brought upon our family. Yet how could I forgive myself? In everything I have done, from the works of service to my kingdom, to my fighting battles against the forces of evil, to my diplomacy in foreign lands, I have sought redemption. Would that I could find it, but alas, I believe I shall wear an invisible badge of guilt on my chest until the day I die."

For several moments, neither of us spoke. What could I possibly say to take away his pain? No words came to mind that seemed adequate.

"To keep myself from incurring more pain and anguish, I even vowed to forsake all other such relations with women until I found the one to whom I wished to give myself—*all* of myself, my heart, my life. And now that I have found you, I would rather risk losing you than for you to not know the truth about me. But, as you see, I am not the man of honor you deserve."

Deep inside me a wound that had not quite healed began to ooze once more, and hasty words said in anger echoed in my ears, revealing my own guilt. I walked up to him and whispered in his ear. "I would expect nothing less than for a man of honor to feel guilt over such a thing." He looked at me, surprise written on his face. "Would that I could take away your pain."

Allynon took one look in my eyes and pulled me close. "Could it be—you still love me?" he murmured.

"If you would still love me, plagued though I am with my own afflictions, then why would I not offer that same grace to you? Allynon, love is less a feeling than an act of will."

"Though I would wager you have done nothing so heinous."

The memory was quite vague, but I knew there was once a boy of light brown hair whom death had stolen from me too soon. It was enough for me to still feel its sting. "To betray one whom I loved with hateful words spoken in a fleeting moment—that is the guilt I bear, now with no opportunity for atonement. Would you now discard me that I have shattered your illusion I am in any way special as you say?"

"Sorry I am for the guilt you feel you must bear. But you tell me nothing about yourself I have not already guessed, for you are stubborn and high-spirited, yes?"

Taken aback, I gave Allynon a sidelong glance and could see a faint mischievous grin on his face—as well as a look of relief. "And weird," I added. "Really, really weird. You have no idea."

"But it is this—how you say—*weirdfulness*, I find so charming, as well the way your beautiful green eyes alight when you talk of the people you love. To find another woman like you would be a difficult task, impossible even! So why should a man who has been searching his entire life for a priceless treasure then discard it when he finds it is perhaps a bit tarnished? He does not discard it. No, not ever!" he said, taking me in his arms and pressing his forehead to mine.

"And when I look at you, I see a man who could easily have excused his past indiscretion as a privilege of his position. Instead, you have become a better, wiser man."

"I am truly humbled, for I do not deserve your favor. But if you will have me..." His mouth found its way back to my lips, where I met him with full surrender. "Never have I wanted anything more than I want you," Allynon murmured as, trembling, he pressed me even closer.

Suddenly, out of nowhere, I felt myself being snatched from Allynon's arms. In horror I could see my own body as if I were an onlooker standing several feet away. It had gone limp, and Allynon was frantically calling to me, struggling to lift me to my feet. All at once, I found myself in the midst of a deep memory, drowning once more in a sea of bright yellow light. A deep, pulsating sound came from its center, as did a fervent whisper meant for my ears alone. I believed I would go mad if it continued.

Suddenly, all went dark and silent. I opened my eyes once more to see Allynon standing before me, his face pale with alarm. "Arwyn, are you well?" he said anxiously. "I was holding you in my arms, and it was as though you...died for a moment."

Quite shaken, I pushed myself away from him and shook my head. "I cannot marry you," I said, as tears streamed down my face.

A look of anguish clouded his face.

"No, it is not what you may think," I said with despair. "I

cannot leave Bensor. For whatever reason I was brought here to this land, this is where my destiny lies. I am…forbidden to leave and therefore cannot return with you to Endara."

"I do not understand," Allynon said slowly.

"For nearly three years I have attempted to understand, yet the answers are not forthcoming."

"Then perhaps it is time to move on."

"Please, my heart wishes more than anything to return with you, but it is my duty to remain. I *must*. I made a commitment to the Alliance—I gave them my word!"

"Arwyn, you would be much safer in Endara. If you remain here, I fear for you greatly that some harm may befall you in my absence. And then, what would I do if I returned and found…why, I can hardly bear to think of it."

"Any argument you have against my remaining in Bensor would be far more rational than my arguments to stay. Yet I feel if I were to leave, my very legs would sprout roots and plant themselves into the ground," I said tearfully.

"Arwyn, there is a place for a sense of duty, but do you not think Galamir and the Alliance will fare well without you?"

What was I to say? He was right, after all. What difference could one person make?

But it was *forbidden.*

I shook my head. "I'm sorry. I think Omni *wants* me to stay, or…someone else…not of this world."

Allynon sighed and looked deeply into my eyes, and I dreaded what he would say next. For a long moment I waited in silence for him to speak. "Very well, if stay here you must, then I will return for you."

"You would leave your homeland for me?" I said, shocked.

Allynon took me by the hands. "My home, it is with you, wherever you may be, and," he said resolutely, "Bensor *is* as much my home as Endara, yes?"

"But your family, your duty to your country…"

"All the family I require is *you*. And as for Endara, Ignalius and Galbritar are quite capable of running things in my absence. As it is, I will only be in the way."

"It is too much for you to sacrifice…"

"Shhhh," Allynon said as he wrapped his arms around me. "To live life without you would be the far greater sacrifice. It is of no consequence whether we live in Endara or Bensor. Though…" he said, as a cloud darkened his face. "I must warn you my return to Endara with Valdir, though temporary, will take many months. A year, perhaps, we will be parted, and that grieves me terribly."

"How difficult it will be for me to see you go, not knowing if I will ever see you again. If only…" I said with resentment, suddenly regretting my overriding sense of duty and honor. How frustrating to not even be sure of my purpose in Bensor, a country that seemed to be coming apart at the seams! Yet how could I abandon my friends at such a time?

"Unbearable it will be to remain away from you so long, and I shall worry about you so."

I smiled reassuringly. "You know I can take care of myself."

"Omni help the Gargaloc who crosses you." Allynon laughed. Then he grew quiet. "You will marry me then, yes?"

I looked into his eyes full of tenderness and love, and I had but one answer. "I will."

For a moment we embraced under the light of the moon as it rose through the trees until Allynon reached under his tunic and retrieved a chain of gold from around his neck. On the end of the chain there rode a rather sizeable stone of aquamarine surrounded in pure gold. I had only caught glimpses of it before, but seeing it dangling there in all its glory made me gasp. "An heirloom this is, given to me by my father at the time when I became a man," he said. "I want you now to have it. Know whenever you look at it I will return for you and that death alone would forbid our reunion." As Allynon stared at me, his eyes burned intensely as if to emphasize his words. "But hear me now, Arwyn, as long as there remains breath in my body, I will use that breath to return to you." With that, he placed the aquamarine jewel around my neck.

"Such a gift is priceless," I said, having to catch my own breath. "But, Allynon, I am afraid I have nothing but myself to…" Just then, the light of the moon struck upon my hand as it lay on his shoulder. I looked curiously to see it reflecting off the ring I had worn there ever since the day I had first come to Bensor. It was my only link to that previous existence…but none of that seemed to matter any longer.

Slowly I slipped the ring off my finger and placed it in Allynon's hand. "This is all I have to give you," I said. "It is all I brought with me from the place I lived once long ago, but of that I have little memory."

Allynon uncurled his fingers from around the purple stone and stared at it tenderly. "Too precious this is for you to give away," he said as he attempted to place it back in my hand.

For a slight moment I wavered. After all, the ring was the only physical link I had with that other life I had left behind. But I had not only left it behind, I was letting it go. Nay, my life was now in Bensor. With him. "No, please, I wish for you to have it now. It will mean more to me if it stays with you."

Allynon smiled and looked at me lovingly. "Very well. I shall then put it on a chain around my neck and whenever I look at it I will see your beauty, until the day when I can gaze upon your face once more," Allynon said as he slipped the ring into his pocket and then placed his hands around my waist. Passionately he kissed me until I felt as though I might melt into his body. "Have you now found the home you have been searching for?" he whispered.

I nodded. "I know I have, and it is right here in your

arms."

CHAPTER 16

"Alas, the morning has come and my dream has ended. I wake to the reality of our imminent departure and of a most treacherous way lying ahead."

During our last days in Isgilith, Allynon and I went about the task of preparing to leave, bittersweet though it was, and we cherished our last moments together in that magical place. Our glad news brought smiles to the faces of Galamir, Elastair, and Gladigan, though Galamir seemed most happy I would be remaining behind in Bensor.

On the evening before our departure, Vandaril hosted a farewell banquet in honor of his father, inviting many of the most prominent families in Isgilith, including Allynon's aged mortal friend, Velora. However, I was happy to see Kyora and her entourage noticeably missing from the guest list.

The banquet itself was held on the rear veranda of Valdir's manor overlooking the gorge below. Dozens of candles set upon tiered candelabra were placed about the patio, creating a warm, intimate feel to the gathering. As the guests congregated around the dinner table, the mood felt somewhat subdued as if the question of what would come to pass between then and the next time we would all be together plagued the back of everyone's mind.

Over the course of the evening, several in the crowd gave eloquent speeches in honor of Valdir until the time came for him to pass the leadership of Isgilith over to his son. "It is with a full heart I bid you all farewell, yet I go to Endara with confidence, knowing my son, Vandaril, will lead you well in my stead. In fact"—his voice wavered—"regardless of when, or even if I ever return, I mean at this moment to permanently make Vandaril my successor."

A rush of surprised gasps echoed through the gathering,

and I could tell by the look on Vandaril's face the announcement had taken him by surprise as well. "But, Father..." he started to protest.

"I have made my decision!" Valdir's response was resolute, even if his downcast eyes betrayed a struggle within. "Nay! For many ages I have led this colony, but the time has come for one...for one far more worthy than I to lead it, and I have every confidence you, my son, will be a better leader than I." I could tell by the stunned gazes others sensed what I had—Valdir was not simply being modest—there was some internal conflict going on inside that made him truly question his own worthiness. It was enough to make the crowd stir uncomfortably.

"Father, how you honor me," Vandaril replied. "I can only hope to lead Isgilith with the same loyalty, the same passion and bravery as you have." A chorus of solemn "hear! hears!" arose from around the table, along with the sound of clinking glasses as father and son embraced warmly.

"Lord Valdir," Galamir said, rising to his feet and raising a glass, "you will always have my allegiance, but my allegiance to you has always extended to your son, Vandaril. I give it to him now unreservedly, as I know you are as determined as I to see a unified Bensor and our enemy deposed."

"May the blessing of Loth Gerodin go with you, Galamir, my friend, as you leave tomorrow to fight this battle on the front to the south, even as we fight it on our own borders." The crowd nodded and murmured in agreement until Vandaril clinked his glass for their attention. "My dear friends, though it is a solemn occasion we honor, I would be remiss if I did not acknowledge a bit of happiness in our midst."

A slight murmur of anticipation mounted. With that, Vandaril turned to Allynon and me. "My friends, I am proud to announce that Allynon, Prince of Endara, son of Loth Gerodin, has become promised in marriage to Arwyn of

Baeren Ford."

A collective gasp rippled through the crowd, followed by delighted smiles and nods of approval. I glanced at Elastair, who smiled at me smugly. I then turned to Allynon and had to catch my breath, for the sight of him smiling at me so lovingly with his dashing, sensitive dark eyes made my heart skip a beat.

"Congratulations, friend," Vandaril said as he clasped Allynon's hand. "You are indeed a fortunate man. Fortunate, that is, you discovered Arwyn first. Were it not for my detainment on the Greenwaithe, I may have had a few days advantage on winning her heart, though she may now think herself all the more lucky," Vandaril jested as he gave me a wink.

"Lucky for me too," I replied, "that you saved me the exasperation of having to choose between two such fine gentlemen."

"No doubt there is many a man who will grieve the loss of your heart," Vandaril added.

Valdir had remained quiet throughout the proceedings, his fixed gaze revealing nothing of what was happening behind his eyes. He cleared his throat uncomfortably. "Indeed, I rejoice in the fact that Allynon has at last found his treasure," he interjected politely, giving a nod in our direction.

With no further comment from the elven lord, Vandaril addressed the gathering once more. "Now, ladies and gentlemen, let us raise our glasses to Prince Allynon and Arwyn," he proposed. "May the months of your separation be as a moment, the day of your wedding come swiftly, and all the years following be filled with joy."

More "hear, hears" echoed across the veranda as the sound of clinking glasses permeated the air. There was no doubt that Vandaril's toast had raised questions, but it was not until the food was served there was any mention of them. As we dined I tried to answer their politely phrased questions concerning my reasons for remaining behind in Bensor as best I could.

But how could I explain why I was letting the man I loved leave Bensor, risking the possibility I might never see him again? To aid in the cause for Bensor was certainly admirable, yet I wondered if deep down they thought I was a fool for not leaving certain peril behind to enjoy the life of a princess. But a princess I was not, and how could I enjoy such a life with the knowledge I had abandoned my friends at the time of their greatest need?

The overall mood of the evening was one of subdued merriment. Inago and Endegar, who gave Allynon much ribbing for keeping such a secret from them, amused the gathering with tales of their adventures in foreign lands and were quick to boast of their master's numerous feats of bravery.

"And then there was the time when His Highness led the siege at the Ford of Bruhainen, reclaiming the city for the peaceable Bromelans after it had been invaded by their barbaric neighbors to the west," Endegar said, pointing a fork at Inago.

"Aye, de sight of His Highness comin' at dem with death in his eyes kin make any scalawag quake in his boots," Inago remarked, followed by a booming laugh.

"Mighty is His Highness in battle," Galamir said. "I'll not dare cross him after hearing years ago how he single-handedly defeated the black sorcerer of Calispell, thereby lifting his curse on the poor mountain people there. Such took more than mere strength of arms, but sheer cunning as well."

"And they be forever indebted to his bravery," Inago added.

Allynon lowered his gaze and smiled modestly as his two crewmen talked a while longer about their master's many courageous acts. I could but listen in wonder to their tales, for Allynon, unpretentious as he was, had not mentioned them before except in terms of his involvement in the collective efforts of many.

Never before had I heard of the pivotal role he had played on many such occasions, and although hearing such wonderful stories made me respect Allynon all the more, it also raised doubt in my mind. How could such a man, who had had such glory bestowed upon him and who had accomplished such great things in his life ever be content living a simple, pastoral existence somewhere in Bensor? Could I really give such a man a life that would bring him the kind of fulfillment he had become accustomed to? Why, oh why could I not simply board his ship several days hence and be done with all uncertainty?

As the evening wore on so did the goodbyes, until at last Vandaril alone remained talking quietly to Allynon at the banquet table that was all but emptied. Valdir returned from the foyer where he had bidden the last of the guests farewell, and I waited for him to appear through the door. I had seen him only a few times since the Faerenfel, and always with Allynon by my side, but I needed to speak with him alone.

"May I have a word with you, my lord?"

"By all means," Valdir replied courteously. "Come, let us stroll down by the water," he said as he led me down the back steps of the veranda and onto the dew-covered lawn. Together we walked to the edge of the overlook and gazed down upon the plummeting water as it thundered into the darkness below.

"What is it you seek, Arwyn?"

"My lord, you are indeed full of wisdom, and in many ways you remind me of my dear friend, Eliendor. That is why I now seek your counsel," I began, allowing my eyes to wander to the place where Allynon and Vandaril were still talking. Taking a deep breath, I began. "Although my happiness is great, I am also troubled."

"You doubt your decision to remain in Bensor, and you

wonder if it is all for naught."

How perceptive the elven lord was, like Eliendor, and I found it both comforting and unnerving all at once. "Why would I let Allynon sail away and risk never seeing him again? For me to remain in Bensor is to face almost certain peril. Moreover, of what benefit could my presence possibly be?" I asked, sincerely hoping he would talk some sense into me and tell me it would be understandable should I abandon my heroic inklings and overblown sense of duty.

For a moment Valdir looked as though he were thinking of a proper way to respond. "Arwyn," he finally said as he looked intently into my eyes, "do not underestimate what one person can accomplish. You may yet have a role to play in the Alliance that you cannot foresee. If you feel you have been brought to Bensor for a purpose, then you must do what you must to discover it."

He was right, of course, and he only confirmed what I already knew in my heart. There was really no sense fighting it. "Then please, while you are away, watch over Allynon. Bring him back safely to me...that is, if you truly believe life with me here in Bensor would bring him fulfillment."

Valdir pursed his lips and looked at the ground as if conflicted by the thoughts going round in his mind, like there was some obstacle that kept him from being completely happy for us. Yet in someone so well versed in the Gifts, I found it very difficult to read what was *really* going on in his heart.

After a moment he looked up at me tenderly. "Arwyn, you need a strong man, a man with a passion to match your own, a man who loves not only you, but one who is willing to sacrifice all else to live in a country wrought with peril and difficulties as you are so determined to do."

My heart sank. "And you do not think Allynon is truly willing to make such a sacrifice?"

"I know he thinks he is..." Valdir hesitated, again trying to find the right words. "He is an Endaran prince, beloved by his family, his people. To leave that life behind for a life of uncertainty here in Bensor will be difficult, no matter his love for you. It would sadden me to see you heartbroken should he choose not to return."

I could feel tears welling in my eyes. Valdir sighed deeply upon seeing my distress. "And yet…if there is a man worthy of you, then it is he," he conceded. Valdir closed his eyes momentarily as if summoning the strength to continue. "Arwyn," he began with some difficulty, "you have my word that if it is within my power, he will return safely to you."

I gave the elven lord an uneasy smile, not certain what to make of all his mixed messages. He was indeed a perplexing man, no matter how wise and kind he was esteemed to be.

"Ah, but I must admit I *had* rather hoped when you first arrived in Isgilith that you would fancy…er, that you would fancy…my son, Vandaril. It is an odd turn of events yet one for which I give my fullest blessing."

"Thank you, my lord," I said quietly. Funny how he had made no mention of *Callas* being worthy of me. Was it any wonder Callas harbored such a grudge against his brother?

"Now I shall take my leave of you," Valdir said politely. "If leave in the morning we must, then I suggest we all get our rest."

As the elven lord walked back toward the manor, I turned to stare out at the inky blackness below that marked the place where the huge Circle of Omni stood in the middle of the valley. I could just make out the silhouette of the trees surrounding the island as they loomed black against the dazzling celestial display above. I could hear an elven chorus in the distance, yet as enchanting as it all was, the conversation with Valdir had unnerved me. Did he really question whether or not Allynon would return to Bensor to marry me? Should I?

Allynon walked up from behind and wrapped his arms around my waist. "I saw you talking with Valdir."

"Yes, he so reminds me of my friend, Eliendor: slightly

mysterious, as if he knows a secret he is not quite willing to share," I said, hoping he wouldn't notice the quivering in my voice.

"Mmm, yes," Allynon said pensively. "The same thought I recently had myself."

I turned to face him. "What do you mean?"

"A long talk he had with me the other evening," Allynon said with furrowed brow. "It seems he has been concerned ever since it became obvious we had feelings for one another."

"Oh?"

"He told me your *compulsion* to remain in Bensor, it is something I should not interfere with, and…"

"Yes," I said anxiously.

"I do not yet know what it will mean to marry you."

"Does he think I am so difficult?" I laughed.

Allynon chuckled a moment. "A complicated woman you most certainly are, but such would never stop me from loving you…or from sacrificing all to be with you."

"Valdir *is* like Eliendor, always speaking in riddles," I said with a defiant huff

"Shh," Allynon whispered, pulling me close and kissing my forehead. "This is not the end. Someday, together we will return to this place…I am quite sure of it." For a little longer he held me there, staring out over the lake as the fireflies danced in the darkness, and all the while it relieved me that the darkness hid the uncertainty in my eyes.

In the weeks since I had come to Isgilith, time ceased to exist for me. Now I wondered what had happened in the south since I had left home, making the urgency of return weigh heavily on my heart. I thought of Isgilith, and my friends there and knew if the realm to the south fell to darkness, then no elvish army, not even the magical creatures of Loth Gerodin would be able to keep the city and its location concealed any longer under a veil of green. And by the same token, if Loth Gerodin fell first, then what hope did we in the south have?

Even Galamir, normally so serene, seemed eager to be on his way. We all knew the coming days would bring many trials, and I hoped our respite in Loth Gerodin had given us the strength to face them.

Early the next morning before the first light of dawn peered over the mountains to the east, a ghostly fog covered Isgilith as our small company congregated in the courtyard of Galamir's home. Avencloe stood alongside Calyxa, both of them saddled and laden with provisions for the long journey. Allynon had come for us, yet he thoughtfully remained in the background tending to his own horse as Galamir and I said our goodbyes to Elastair and Gladigan. The mood was solemn, for none could foretell when, or even if, we would ever meet again.

"Mother, father, I do not know the day of my return to Isgilith," Galamir said. "After I see Arwyn safely home, I must return to the Alliance. The time to act is almost upon us, and my assistance there is needed."

"My son, we do not begrudge you the path you have chosen, for you serve a noble cause," Gladigan said as he embraced his son one last time. "We can only pray for Omni's grace to see you through these days."

With tears in his eyes, Galamir turned then to Elastair, who embraced her son with a tenderness only a mother can give. "Though a mother's heart will always long for her child's safe return, I do not fear for you," Elastair said. "You have a light in you that will see others through these dark days. Use it well until we meet again, when times are happier."

Galamir looked into his mother's eyes and smiled reassuringly one last time before turning to leave.

Fighting my own tears, I approached Elastair and Gladigan. "Dearest Elastair and Gladigan, how do I begin to thank you for all you have done for me, and how do I now possibly tell you goodbye?"

"Fair lady, you have honored our home with your presence, and you will always be most welcome in it," Gladigan said. "You may thank us by returning to visit again someday."

"My husband speaks the truth. It is you who have honored us," Elastair said. The elven matriarch stepped up to regard me squarely in the eyes and with a solemn note to her voice she whispered with great conviction, "You are destined for greatness, that I can tell."

I was taken aback as the words rang in my ears. Somehow, somewhere deep in the recesses of my mind a memory tickled, as if I had heard them once before.

"*You* are a woman of greatness, and I am honored to call you my dear friend," I said as we embraced.

In my mind I saw another young woman of fair hair, someone who had also been very dear to me. "Will I ever see you again, dear Reggie?" I muttered absently. "That is...dear *friend*." The tears flowed down my cheeks.

"Do not be dismayed, Arwyn, for someday our paths will cross again," Elastair assured. "Perhaps the next time we meet it will be at your home."

In spite of the somberness of the occasion, it seemed rather humorous to wonder where such company would find a place to sleep in Frondamein's tiny cottage. The thought brought a smile to my face. "It will be a happy day indeed when elves...our kind may travel freely throughout the land. May Omni be with you until we meet again."

I forced myself to break away. I turned toward Avencloe and found Allynon standing there, quietly offering an arm to envelop me, to help take away the sting of parting. It was only a matter of time before he would take his leave of me, though I could hardly stand to think of that farewell.

Together Allynon, Galamir, and I rode out under the stone archway separating the courtyard of the house from the road. For a brief moment we stopped and turned to salute Gladigan and Elastair one last time. Without a word, we urged the horses on down the lane toward Valdir's manor where the elven lord waited alongside Inago and Endegar, all three on horseback. I could barely make out through the fog the dark shape of Vandaril standing near his father's mare, Willomane.

"The time has come for us to part," I heard Valdir say. "Take courage, my son. Lead our people well in my stead."

"I only pray you will reach Endara's shores in time and that Omni will see you safely back to your own," said Vandaril.

"Aye, may Omni be with us all." Valdir said as he clicked his tongue, urging Willomane onward.

With a nod of farewell to Vandaril, the six of us disappeared into the fog, phantoms taking flight. Surely the return trip, with the absence of the dwarves, would be marked by less peril, or so I hoped. Yet it was with a heavy heart I turned to look upon the giant elderhorns surrounding the Circle of Omni one last time. They were quiet, and I wondered if Omni Himself would remain quiet or, for that matter, if He had even heard the cries of this land.

The elderhorns emerged from the fog like a ship's mast in the trough of a wave only to slowly disappear into the grayness of the morning as we rode into the trees, beyond the border of the elven city.

For a long while we rode in somber silence until the morning sun began to break through the mist covering the land to reveal a bright blue sky above. With the shadows the solemn mood permeating our departure also began to lift, and it was not long before Inago, who rode up ahead, began to sing. The other members of the party exchanged smiles as our leader bellowed lively old folk songs with his deep, resonating voice, and we all chatted freely as we rode south.

Later that afternoon the cave, which led under the waterfall, loomed up ahead. I recognized it immediately and leaned toward Galamir. "Will we be encountering your, er, 'friends' today?"

"It is difficult to say whether or not they will be about," the elf replied, with a smile. "They are much less concerned with those leaving the forest than with those who enter. But for us, well, we'll wait and see if they put in an appearance."

With a click of his tongue, Galamir took the lead as the traveling companions entered the cave, following behind him one-by-one. In a few moments we reappeared on the other side, blinking in the bright sunshine. We looked around, but the trolls were nowhere to be seen. I could not help but feel a little disappointed, wanting to see them one more time.

"Ah, I see they have left us a treat," Valdir said as he climbed down from his mare. He walked over to the giant stone table where a basket lay on the ground underneath. Inside was an assortment of nuts and berries, along with bread and jam and a jug of cider. Beside the basket was a huge, troll-sized teacup filled with water for the horses.

For a while we lingered under the cool shade of the trolls' table, enjoying the small meal and the break from our journey, none of us eager to leave the heart of the forest. Yet as the afternoon wore on, so did the need to press onward. As we mounted our horses, Valdir and Galamir turned to salute their unseen friends, and from somewhere deep within the rock, I thought I could hear a low rumble.

The conversation waned as weariness began to set in, yet it enthralled me that on the return journey, what had appeared upon our arrival in Loth Gerodin as narrow, haphazard deer paths had magically turned into one single road that after many miles led directly to the main road through the forest.

"We'll travel a while longer before stopping for the night," Galamir announced. Having traveled that way so many times before, Galamir almost knew the way blindfolded and certainly knew the best and safest places to camp along the road, so no one questioned his judgment.

In a short while, we passed the bridge leading over the Silvendell and traveled another mile or two beyond. As it turned out, we camped for the night in the exact location Galamir, the dwarves, and I had camped the night before our arrival in Isgilith. It was not far from the road, yet no one truly feared what eyes would see us as long as we were within the borders of Loth Gerodin.

The group went about the task of gathering firewood and settling in for the night. In little more than an hour, the sun slid behind the trees to the west and out of sight. A merry fire crackled on the ground, above which three quail and one rabbit were skewered and roasting. The mood was light, though I felt a little awkward being the only woman in the midst of five male traveling companions. Would that there had been another female to accompany us, but such was not practical under the circumstances. Not that my escorts acted in any way other than in a respectable manner, and I knew I could trust them to protect my honor, but it felt different than it had when it was only Galamir, the dwarves, and me. Perhaps it was because I was not as familiar with Inago and Endegar as the dwarves, and it seemed they were still in the process of sizing me up. I could tell they were quite loyal to Allynon, and it was understandable they would scrutinize anyone their master determined to marry.

That night I slept in a makeshift tent beneath a low-hanging tree branch, with Allynon and Galamir sleeping protectively nearby.

The following morning, Inago resurrected the fire and everyone lingered over mugs of hot tea, perhaps as a way of putting off the inevitable departure from Loth Gerodin.

"These honey cakes, they are quite good," Allynon commented, as he munched on his breakfast, "and quite filling as well."

"We've enough to supplement our diet until we arrive in Maldimire," Valdir commented. "After that..."

Suddenly the group froze as we heard the unmistakable

sound of hooves galloping furiously in our direction from the road to the west. We were only a short distance from the road, yet several large trees concealed our presence. Galamir sprang to his feet and made his way in that direction, careful to remain hidden behind the forest underbrush. The sound of galloping was now quite close, and we all waited anxiously to know whether the rider was friend or foe. In a moment, a broad smile crept onto Galamir's face. "Hail, Astragon!" he called as he stepped into plain view.

The rider pulled back on the reins when he heard his name and turned to see Galamir. "Galamir! It is indeed fortunate I have found you," he said. "Where is Lord Valdir?"

"Come, follow me," Galamir urged.

Those of us who had remained around the fire stood as the elf named Astragon rode into our midst, and I recognized him as one of the attendees of the Faerenfel banquet several weeks before. Nimbly he dismounted his horse and walked up to the elven lord. "Salutations, Master Valdir, I come bearing urgent news from Stone Harbour." I could feel my stomach tighten at the mention of the city.

"Speak quickly," Valdir urged.

"The road through the city has been closed to travel. None may now pass there," Astragon said.

"What kind of new devilry is this?" Valdir demanded.

"Draigon is apparently thwarting any travel, and thus any communication, between Loth Gerodin and the south," said Astragon. "If you attempt to pass, then you will be arrested."

"And what chance would we have if we attempted to circumvent the city?" the elven lord asked.

"Little to none, my lord," Astragon replied. "The region lying between the southwestern corner of Loth Gerodin and Stone Harbour is now a wasteland of felled trees. One could not travel cross-country unnoticed, especially with all the servants of Draigon about."

A stunned silence descended upon the group. Who would have thought it would come to this? Draigon had somehow managed to isolate the elves of Loth Gerodin from the rest of Bensor. Had this been his game all along—to deal one final blow to a people he loathed by completely shutting them off from any involvement in Bensorian affairs? And what did it have to do with the presence of Ashkar troops along the Greenwaithe? Did he mean to attack the elves of Loth Gerodin?

I could tell by the grave expressions on the faces of my companions these same questions raced through their minds.

"Is there no other way?" I said, suddenly anguished that perhaps our prolonged sojourn in Isgilith had cost Allynon and Valdir the ability to leave the forest.

"There *is* another way," Galamir said, though the look on his face was one of great hesitation.

"What way is that?" I asked.

"The Dinwiddle Stair," Valdir answered skeptically. "In the mountains there is a narrow gorge through which flows the River Dinwiddle. Along its western banks is an even narrower path leading from the river's headwaters at Grandinwolde for twenty miles, until it eventually plunges down onto the Elwindor plain below at Floren. The way is most treacherous, for the path is narrow and follows a course over slippery stone, especially so this time of year with the spring melt coursing from the mountains above. A faulty step could send one plummeting into the rapids with little hope of rescue."

"That road I have traveled before, though not in the spring," Allynon said. "The more perilous way it is, yet not impossible."

"And what of Grandinwolde?" Valdir said. "The castle is a bastion of Draigon, crawling with Gargalocs, yet to reach the Dinwiddle Stair we must go right past its front door."

"It sounds as though taking that path could backfire on us."

All five of my companions turned to look at me quizzically, and I realized none of them had any clue what I was talking about. Such an advanced weapon that backfired had not come to that world—and I prayed it never would.

"The road between here and the village is seldom traveled these days, and with any luck we would be able to reach it by nightfall," Galamir suggested. "By cover of night we would have a greater chance of slipping through unnoticed. There is a safe house at the southern end of the lake where we could rest for the night."

For a moment the group remained silent as we pondered this ill-fated turn of events.

"I say we take our chances and take the Stair, yet I will go along with the wishes of the group," Galamir said. "All in favor, say aye."

A chorus of reluctant ayes arose, not one of us daring to consider what could befall us should our choice prove a poor one.

"Your decision grieves me, for I do not wish any of you to come to harm," said Astragon, "though I know it can be no other way."

"Hasten now back to Isgilith," Valdir said solemnly, "and alert my son of this news. It seems Draigon has made yet another move in a game of his making. We know not its rules or its objective, yet the time for the elves of Loth Gerodin to act is nigh. It grieves me I cannot stand with you all, yet death will not wait for the end of this conflict."

With an anguished look upon his face, Allynon spoke, "My lord, you *must* remain here in Loth Gerodin. Now is not the time for any leader of Isgilith to depart on a long journey."

"Nay, Allynon," Valdir sighed. "My time as leader of Isgilith is over, and I was right to pass it on to Vandaril. The battle for Bensor is now his to fight, and it is time for him to take his rightful place as leader of our colony." The elven lord's gaze turned to me, yet from the faraway look in his eyes, it seemed he wasn't really seeing me. "What is more, once long, long ago I made a promise to another that I would

keep the bonds between the people of Bensor and those of
Endara strong. That, perhaps, as Vandaril himself reminded
me, is one of the most important contributions I can make to
the welfare of this country."

"As you wish, my lord," Allynon said quietly, bowing his
head.

"Come now," Valdir said as he glanced at our long faces,
"such dismal outlooks will not make our journey any easier.
Let us now take to the road, grateful this meeting has perhaps
saved us from any number of troubles."

CHAPTER 17

"So miserable I am, I would almost knock on the front door of the Ashkar-infested castle for a chance at a warm, dry bed."

With little chatter, we went about the task of preparing to leave. It was not long before we saddled our horses and headed back in the direction from whence we had come the evening before. Astragon rode with us as far as the bridge over the Silvendell, where he took a somber leave and headed along the forest road toward the east.

As we neared the river, the din from the raging water became almost deafening. Up ahead a bridge made of large, sturdy lodgepoles spanned the gorge below. As our company crossed over, I marveled at the noisy deluge as it tumbled over falls and down into pools and swirling eddies. Huge boulders flanked the edges of the water, as did large conifers with delicate needles shimmering in the light of the morning sun. Despite my earlier gravity, I was secretly delighted to take the path through the Andains.

Throughout the morning we followed a road that wound up gradually into the mountains through pine forests and groves of lacy-leafed aspen until at last we ascended a bluff where we stopped and looked back. I could not help but gasp as I looked down upon the whole of Loth Gerodin at my feet, for all I could see was a seemingly endless sea of green, bordered far to the east by the northern branch of the Andains and to the west by a brown wasteland.

With a jolt of awareness, I realized I was staring into the land of Ashkaroth with its stark mountains rising up far in the distance above a featureless plain. As if a region could take on the personality of its ruler, the green of Bensor ended abruptly, contrasting with the lifeless brown landscape on the other side.

A chill went down my spine as I gazed into that land, knowing it bred the fiercest of men and most gruesome of half-breeds. In the distant mountains beyond the plain was the lair of the one who had infected that foul realm, and I hoped necessity would never bid me venture into such an accursed place.

Our group stopped to rest beside a small stream trickling down from the mountains. We had met no one on the road the entire morning, and it seemed we would not until we reached Grandinwolde. Allynon had been particularly quiet that morning, and he went to stand a short distance away staring pensively across the vast forest below.

I touched him on the arm. "Your eyes tell me you are troubled by guilt," I said gently.

He took a deep breath. "To take Valdir away from his people at such a time, how can I not feel responsible?"

"It is his choice to go."

Allynon sighed. "Perhaps he is right. Perhaps it is time for Vandaril to take over. However, as much as I esteem Vandaril, to imagine anyone leading Isgilith but Valdir is difficult, no?"

"Change *is* difficult to accept, even change that is good."

"I know what you say is true, but two different matters it is to know it and accept it in one's heart."

"Time alone can take care of the latter," I said gently. "Give yourself that much at least before you continue to doubt yourself."

Allynon turned to me and smiled as he gazed into my eyes. "Yes, and there are some things that will only grow stronger with time," he said as he took my chin in his hand, guiding my lips to meet his momentarily. "Perhaps we should rejoin our friends. If I know Galamir, he will not wish to linger here much longer."

Allynon and I returned to the others, and it was not long before we were on our way once more. As we journeyed, the road rose before us through a cleft between two mountains.

"Turn and look once more," Galamir said, "for this is the last view some of us may have of Loth Gerodin for a long, long while."

We halted our progress for a moment to turn and gaze back to the forest, now far below. I looked quickly at Valdir and thought I saw his lips move in silent petition to some unseen force. At last he turned resolutely in his saddle and did not look back.

I stared nostalgically out over the sea of green, remembering with pleasure the joy I had found under its leafy boughs, and I wondered what would become of the elves' home. Suddenly saddened, I turned away and proceeded up the road and into the cleft that was the gate into the Andains.

All afternoon we rode, passing through alpine forests teeming with deer, elk, foxes, and rabbits, as well as several small hamlets and a few isolated cabins. Yet we seemed to be the only travelers. How laborious this path into Loth Gerodin would have been, had we come this way pulling the dwarves' cart along behind us, even going downhill toward the forest. As it was, we made good time on our steady climb into the mountains

Late in the day dark clouds gathered above, and after a while the rumbling sky opened and a torrent poured down upon the earth. Showing no sign of letting up, it continued on for the remainder of the day, slowing our progress. Miserably I sat in my saddle, trying as best I could to ward off the rain with the hood of my cloak. My efforts were of little avail. It was not long until the moisture soaked through and clung to my skin.

In silence we pressed onward, wishing for a hasty arrival at Grandinwolde, which still lay several miles away. It was not until darkness fell that we saw the first signs of the village in the illuminated windows of its northernmost buildings.

"The downpour may actually be to our advantage,"

Galamir remarked. "With any luck, there will be few people out on such a night. Leastwise the darkness will cloak our arrival."

As we rode into the village, I looked longingly into the windows and caught glimpses of cozy fires and people sitting around their tables eating hot meals. It made me wish all the more that the day's journey would soon come to an end.

Farther along, we came to a rather sizeable mountain lake flanked by a jumble of crooked, half-timbered buildings lining narrow, cobbled streets. A lone lantern lighter stood on the quay beside the water, trying his best to protect his light source from being doused. He hardly looked up as we passed, obviously more interested in finishing his task and returning to his hearth than on the comings and goings of any visitors. We passed only one other villager leading a packhorse along behind him, but he paid us little heed.

Up on the hill to our left loomed the castle. So tall and dark it was, even against the black sky. Small windows dotted its turrets, firelight flickering within, and I shivered to think it housed dozens, perhaps even hundreds of Draigon's servants. Yet it appeared none were out and about that night. What revelry or secret planning must be going on inside?

On the southeastern side of the lake, the waters spilled into the headwaters of the River Dinwiddle. Our horses clip-clopped across the wooden bridge spanning the waterway, and once again we found ourselves on a street lined with a myriad colorful signs hanging above the entrances to quaint shops.

For all the noise our horses' hooves made on the narrow cobblestone streets, we would have fared as well announcing our presence with horns and trumpets. I was quite relieved when we turned from the main road onto a series of back streets until we came to the back of an out-of-the-way house and a blacksmith shop, near the place where the Dinwiddle disappeared into the gorge beyond.

Quickly Galamir dismounted and went to rap on the back door. In a moment the door opened slightly, revealing a middle-aged man on the other side. The man peered out suspiciously until he saw Galamir.

"Ah, Master Galamir! Thank goodness, 'tis a friend," the blacksmith said as his face brightened. Cautiously he peered into the darkness and saw us, sitting anxiously on our horses. "I see ye've brought friends," he whispered. "Come, come, the lot of ye. Get yerselves in out o' the damp."

"Gasperon, we are in need of your services, your *discreet* services, if you will."

"Indeed, indeed," the blacksmith said as he lifted a lantern to illuminate the pathway. "I'll tend to yer hairses in a moment. Come get yerselves in out o' the weather."

"What brings ye to the village on such a night and after so long an absence?"

"There is no time to explain at present," said Galamir.

Gladly we dismounted and entered the inviting house. The blacksmith's eyes grew wide at our motley group, and what a sight we must have been—three mortal men, one of whom looked as though he could make at least two of the others, another elven man of obvious high standing, and then there was me—the lone woman. And all of us drenched to the bone.

Suddenly footsteps sounded on a flight of stairs at the back of the parlor. A woman wearing a long sleeping gown and robe, with her hair tied up in braids under a nightcap, appeared from the floor above, carrying a broom in a most threatening manner.

"Not to worry, me dear," Gasperon reassured. "We've guests for th' evenin', friends of Master Galamir, the elf."

"Galamir? Well, why didn't ye say so?" the woman said as she lowered her weapon.

"Please forgive me wife," the blacksmith said. "She's been a bit skittish o' late, what with all the comin's and goin's o' those who reside up the hill. Come, Rohana, and let us make introductions all 'round."

The blacksmith's wife crept down the stairs until she stood before her guests. Soon all introductions were made, Valdir and Allynon's titles purposefully omitted. The less known about our identities, the better, in case anyone were to later come around inquiring about us. Rohana looked at me and shook her head.

"Tsk! Ye poor dear, soaked to the bone," she said, as she took me by the arm. "I'll draw ye up a nice 'ot bath. There's also a bit o' stew left on the fire, though it'll not fill the lot o' ye. 'Twould take much more than that small morsel," she said, looking with wonder at the size of Inago. "Still, we've some freshly baked bread and dried meat in the pantry. And there's the huckleberry pie I was savin' for tomorrow. Ye'll not starve."

"Indeed we will not," said Valdir, "and we are most appreciative of your hospitality."

Gasperon gathered a cloak around him and disappeared into the damp darkness of his back lawn as Rohana gathered blankets for us. We sat before a blazing fire, glad for its warmth, the feel of the soft blankets, and the taste of substantial food. Conversation was sparse, so drained we were from the day's travels.

It was not long before Rohana returned from upstairs. "Miss," she said, "there's a bed prepared for ye in what was our son's room when 'e lived at 'ome. Now that he's got a wife and three little ones, he's no need of it. Ye may use it this eve, though I'm afraid the gentlemen must sleep in the secret place, that is, unless one of 'em be yer 'usband."

I glanced quickly at Allynon and smiled. "Not yet."

Everyone comfortably full, we followed Rohana to the second level of the modest yet nicely apportioned house. At the foot of another staircase that disappeared into the dark attic above there hung a large tapestry. Rohana pulled it aside to reveal a tiny fissure in the wall. With a gentle push, the wall swung open. In a narrow storage area were several cots and sleeping rolls for such occasions.

"'Twill be a tight squeeze, 'specially for five such robust men," Rohana said, again staring at Inago. "But 'tis a safe and dry place to lay yer 'eads. Me husband will sleep in the parlor tonight," Rohana explained, turning her attention to me. "If there be trouble, ye'll be awakened, miss, and ye'll need to hurry into the room by this way. There's a bolt on th' other side o' the door what can be used to keep it shut tight."

I nodded understanding as I watched my companions contort their bodies to fit into the secret area. Allynon lingered behind the others. Giving me a reassuring smile, he touched my cheek gingerly. "Take yourself a nice hot bath and get some rest—you will need it for tomorrow," he said.

Rohana cleared her throat. "Er, miss, yer room's at the end o' the hall. I'll set yer bag inside and fold the bedcovers down."

"Thank you," I replied, handing her my travel bag.

Allynon and I suddenly found ourselves alone in the dark corridor. Urgently he pulled me close and kissed me with fervor. "All day I have been waiting to do this," he murmured in my ear.

All at once, I glanced over his shoulder and saw Valdir standing there, his face glowing in the light of a candle he held in his hand as he stared at us. His expression was something akin to anger, which I found quite unnerving. Abruptly he turned and disappeared behind the tapestry.

"What is it?" Allynon asked, having not sensed Valdir's presence. "You look as though you have seen a ghost."

"No, but I think someone else has." Allynon's look was questioning, but I put a finger to his lips before he could speak. "I think it's time we get some rest."

I turned and found Rohana down the hallway in a bedroom with a cozy fireplace that sat at the foot of a comfortable-looking bed. Steam rose from a tub in the corner of the room, and I couldn't wait to climb in.

"It's modest, but 'twill do," said Rohana, fluffing a pillow.

"It looks like a room fit for a queen after the traveling we have endured today," I commented.

"Ye'd best get yerself out o' yer wet clothes. I've an extra gown ye can borrow if yers be soaked through."

"I would imagine all my clothes are, but I can put them before the fire to dry tonight," I said, as I began to take my clothing out of my traveling pack. I was surprised to discover the leather pack had done an adequate job of keeping out the moisture, much to my relief.

Elastair had given me one of her finest garments, and it especially I treasured and did not wish to be ruined. I sighed as I saw how wrinkled it was, yet that could not be helped. "Actually, they are not as wet as I had feared," I commented, suddenly realizing Rohana lingered in the room as though she wished to ask a question but was afraid of being impolite.

"What's it like, that is, to be the only woman travelin' in a group of all men?" she finally stammered.

I thought for a moment before answering. "It was a bit awkward at first, but they have all been quite respectful of me."

"And the one with the dark hair, the handsome one—he's yer love?"

"Yes," I smiled. "We are promised to be wed."

"Ah, a lucky one ye are. E'en an ol' woman such as meself can recognize a good catch when I see one," Rohana said with a grin. "But listen at 'ow I babble on, and ye tired and soaked to the bone! I'd best leave ye be."

"Thank you, though, for everything."

"'Tis no bother. Now get yerself a good rest," Rohana said, as she walked to the door. "And don't be shy if ye need anythin'."

With that, the hostess disappeared through the door, at last leaving me alone in what seemed a luxurious room compared to sleeping out on the ground. There was something to be said for sleeping under the stars, but on such a wet night I was happy to have a solid roof over my head and a hot bath and warm bed to enjoy. Sleepily I peeled off my traveling gown and laid it out before the warm fire. I made certain my bow and quiver were close at hand, should we receive unexpected visitors in the night.

The hot water of the bath felt so luxurious, it was almost enough to distract me from the thought of Valdir's unsettling gaze, and yet I could not erase the image from my mind. What had angered him so?

When I finally dragged myself into bed, it did not take long for sleep to take hold, and I fell into a deep slumber to the sound of the rain pounding against the windowpane.

By morning, the rain had stopped, but a thick fog hovered above the surface of the lake. My well-rested traveling companions and I congregated in the dining room before daybreak, where we enjoyed a hot breakfast of eggs, sausage, and huckleberry muffins. Rohana worked busily at the hearth as Gasperon entered through the back door.

"Worked long into the night, I did, seein' to the hairses' shoes," he announced. "There were a couple what needed some work, but all in all they looked quite good. They've been fed, and I'll see to their saddles in a bit."

"How can we ever thank you for your hospitality?" said Valdir cordially, all indication of his apparent irritation from the night before vanished.

"'Tis a good and just cause we fight for, each in 'is own way," Gasperon said. "I remember the Bensor of old, the Bensor where there was no need for secrecy as we were all free to come and go as we pleased. That is the Bensor I wish to see again, though if 'twill ever be so, only Omni knows." He turned to Galamir with gratitude. "You, Master Galamir, 'ave always been a champion for the cause, and though I've ne'er known the exact nature o' yer business, I know 'tis important, and therefore wairthy to protect."

"I only hope no harm will come to you because of it," Galamir said.

"Pish! Them what live there on the hill don't scare me one bit, they don't," Gasperon said indignantly.

In a few moments, we pushed ourselves away from the table and made ready for our departure. I stood in the front parlor looking out the bay window but could barely see the row of buildings along the lakeshore, such a thick fog had settled into the valley. Allynon came up from behind and put his hands on my shoulders.

"Would that the fog were not so thick," I lamented.

"But the fog, it shall conceal our departure."

"Yes, though I would have liked to get a glimpse of the castle in daylight."

"It is very beautiful, the castle, or at least it was many years ago," he replied. "And, if you like, I shall build you one just like it."

"'Twill only happen if the Alliance is successful," I commented gloomily. "And if it is not, then I am afraid there is little point in dreaming of such glories."

I turned to look at Allynon and found a frown upon his face. "And what then? If the Alliance fails and I am fortunate enough to return and find you still alive, would you then return to Endara with me?"

Slowly I nodded. "If all else fails and there is nothing left here," I said quietly.

Yet there was more that troubled me—the doubts I had felt it in my heart those past few days. "Even if it succeeds, what is there for us here? I would go back to healing people, but *you*...a man needs a purpose in order to feel he is a man. Marriage to me would not be enough to give you that kind of satisfaction."

"You underestimate the satisfaction that comes from being a good husband and father...and yet you speak the truth." So now it was out in the open. Allynon had acknowledged my innermost fears, that marriage to me alone would not be enough to satisfy him. "However," he continued with a thoughtful gleam in his eyes, "I have a very strong sense that life with you will always be filled with much purpose."

I swallowed hard and lowered my gaze to the floor. He certainly had more hope than I did at the moment.

"Make ready to depart. It is to our advantage to make use of this fog while it lasts." Allynon gave my hand a quick squeeze and a smile of encouragement before he turned back to the window.

But his countenance abruptly changed. "Quickly, Arwyn, go and hide yourself!"

From inside the dark parlor, I glanced out the front window and could see four shadowy men dressed in gray approaching rapidly from a cleft between the buildings. "Galamir, Valdir, to the hiding place!"

In a flurry of activity, I grabbed my traveling pack, bow, and quiver and hurried to the top of the staircase with Valdir and Galamir and into the hidden entrance as the others in the household scrambled to assume an air of normalcy. As the secret door bolted shut, we heard a loud knock on the front door, and I could hear Gasperon walk slowly to the door and turn the squeaky handle.

"And a good mornin' to ye, gentlemen. What brings ye out so early? I don't see ye've any hairses what need shoein'."

From my perch in the secret compartment, I could easily hear everything.

"We've not come for yer services," one of the men said rather rudely. "Word has it several visitors were spotted going in the direction of your 'ome last night."

"Aye, you and yer people don't miss a thin', now do ye?"

"We'd like a word with 'em," came another voice, equally gruff.

"Suit yerselves," Gasperon said, as I heard multiple footsteps enter the parlor below, "but I don't think this one 'ere is up to an inquisition."

Through the rafters, I could hear Allynon moan.

"Indulged 'imself a bit too much last night at the tavern, if ye know what I mean," the blacksmith explained.

"I do wish you men would do somethin' about this one, lyin' about me parlor as if 'e owns the place," Rohana complained. "I don't run an inn 'ere. 'Twas out o' the goodness o' me 'eart I let 'em stay last night, seein' as they were in no shape to be runnin' about in the rain tryin' to find a place to lay their 'eads."

"Good morning, gentlemen." Endegar's voice rumbled from the doorway to the dining room. "Has our appearance in your fine town created a disturbance?"

"State your business here at once!"

"Our business?" Endegar replied as three of the men shuffled into the dining room.

But where was the fourth?

On the high dining room wall was a shelf Rohana had filled with vases and other knickknacks, and behind one of those vases was a hole no bigger than a mouse. I discovered in my crouched position I could easily peer down, at least partially, onto the room below. I could barely see the tops of two of the men's heads as they stood staring at the dark figure of Inago, who sat at the far end of the table. Calmly he looked at the intruders and popped an entire muffin into his cavernous mouth.

"Truth be told," Endegar continued with a sly look as he moved closer to the lieutenant, "we are but three sailors from Shakracar on shore leave while our master does business in Maldimire. You *have* heard of Shakracar, have you not?" Endegar asked, his cunning eyes maintaining a steady gaze.

I could only guess the other two were shaking their heads in response.

"You've not heard of our fair country? 'Tis no surprise actually. Lies far, far to the south, it does. Yet, and I did not wish to mention this in front of our hostess," Endegar confided, as he glanced toward the entrance to the dining room. "Rumors of the beautiful women of Bensor have reached its shores. The women of the mountains are said to be especially buxom with soft, milky-white skin. I'm sure you gentlemen can appreciate the nature of our quest and why we were so anxious to make the journey all the way from Maldimire."

For a moment, I heard some muttering from below, and it seemed the two soldiers were nodding a grudging agreement.

"What traveler would stay at the home of a blacksmith and not at the local inn?" the lieutenant asked impatiently.

"Our horses required some attention after our long trip, and so we thought it best to bring them here," Endegar replied. "However, our friend in the other room, who consumed a bit too much ale, was in no condition to go a step further. Were it not for our kind hosts who took pity on our state, he would have awakened in a puddle of water."

"But where are the others? We were told there were several more in your party." The lieutenant's eyes narrowed with suspicion.

"Eh, such is the nature of a dark, rainy night," Endegar shrugged. "Such a deluge can surely play tricks on the eyes. Nay, there were naught but three of us that came up from Maldimire, though my friend here is certainly big enough for two men."

Suddenly I heard the fourth soldier enter the house without bothering to knock. "I checked the stable," he announced. "Seven horses I counted."

Gasperon, who I could only guess had been standing somewhere nearby, huffed in exasperation. "Do ye think it odd that a blacksmith would 'ave a few extra hairses about 'is stable? Three belong to me guests, two are mine, and the others were sent to me for new shoes. Now if there be anythin' suspicious in that, then…"

The leader walked across the room close to Inago's seat

and stared coldly at the two unlikely traveling companions and then at the soiled plates lying on the table. "That's a lot o' food for two men to consume," he grunted.

Slowly, Inago rose to his feet and crossed his arms over his chest. The sight of the giant, brooding man who easily towered over the others caused the other three to shift their weight uneasily.

"Er, he's rather sensitive about his hearty appetite," Endegar quipped. "Eats enough for all three of us, he does."

The one soldier whose reddening face I could see, looked in frustration at his comrades for having not yet found an excuse to arrest our hosts. "Nevertheless, we'll still have a look around."

From inside the secret room Valdir, Galamir, and I sat tensely in the darkness, listening as the three soldiers poked around the upstairs quarters just inches from where we were hidden. Rohana hummed a tune as she went about changing the bed I had slept on the night before. The muffled sound of Endegar and the blacksmith talking about the flood the night before wafted through the rafters.

Soon we heard footsteps going up the stairs into the attic and then the sound of shuffling feet above our heads. I caught my breath as I noticed a rather sizeable crack in the ceiling and a dark figure hovering above it.

For a tense moment, the soldier stopped to listen, but he seemed not to notice the fissure at his feet. "Nothin' up 'ere but some old trunks full o' blankets," one said, and he and the two others joined the lieutenant back down in the parlor.

I breathed a little easier as I glanced at Galamir and Valdir. In the darkness I could just make out their silhouettes, both sitting cross-legged in the cramped space. "We found nothin' out o' the ordinary upstairs," one of the men in gray announced.

"Tell me," said the lieutenant, "'ow is it ye came to Grandinwolde?"

"By way of Stone Harbour," I could hear Endegar reply.

"And 'ow is it ye got past the sentries on the road?"

There was a moment of silence, and the sound of coins rattled on the tabletop. "Never underestimate the power of gold," Endegar said, and I could only guess they transferred into the hand of the lieutenant.

"Aye, sorry to 'ave troubled ye," he said.

Through the hole, the lieutenant emerged into my view once more as he walked to the front door.

He stopped and turned menacingly on Gasperon. "We may 'ave found nothin', but I don't care for the rumors I hear concernin' yer friendship with elves. The cunning and devious creatures are not to be trusted and need to stay in their forest where they belong, not associatin' with the likes of us mortals."

"I'm not exactly sure who's been tellin' ye that pack o' lies, but I'd like to have a word with 'im meself," said Gasperon indignantly. "Cavortin' with elves, indeed!"

"Nevertheless, we'll keep our eyes on ye." With that, the four men in gray strode to the front door, past Allynon, whom I could hear snoring loudly. In a huff they slammed the door shut as they left.

"They're gone," Gasperon said after a moment.

"But only for now, perhaps," Allynon said, sounding suddenly recovered from his debauchery. "Though a stellar performance you gave, my friend, it may not be enough to keep them at bay."

"Ah, but you gave quite a performance yourself," Endegar said.

From right below the place where I hid, I could hear Inago laugh so loud it echoed throughout the house. "Never have I heard such snorin' from His Highness. If he did snore so loud, never would we sleep a wink."

The sound of such mirthful laughter coming from downstairs was enough to entice Valdir, Galamir, and me from our hiding place. I for one was glad to be out of such close quarters with Valdir, who had yet to meet my gaze following the troubling look he gave me the night before.

"Although I wish we had the luxury of reviewing your fine performances, we must now make haste before they get another inkling to investigate your story," he said as we descended the staircase.

"Yes, my lord," Allynon said. "Come, much there will be to tell when our travels are over this evening, but first we must face the Dinwiddle Stair."

"The Dinwiddle Stair?" Gasperon said, as a look of concern appeared on his face. "Are ye sure ye should attempt it, what with the rain we 'ad last night?"

"There is no other way," Galamir asserted.

"I'm afraid he's right, Master Gasperon," Valdir said.

"Then ye'll need certain provisions to be sure, aside from the food me wife 'as prepared for yer journey," said the blacksmith. "Come now to the stable. The fog'll protect ye from pryin' eyes, but ye still must make 'aste afore it lifts."

Gasperon disappeared out the back door to check the stable and seeing no one, motioned for the group to follow. When we entered the stable, he shut the door tightly behind us and whispered, "Ye'll need to walk the hairses o'er runnin' water, and ye'll need a couple or so ropes as well, somethin' strong in case one o' ye loses 'is footin' and ends up o'er the brink. The hairses would not fare as well, but their weight would 'ave th' advantage on slippery rock."

"But where are our saddles?" I asked, noting that Avencloe, Calyxa and Willomane's were nowhere to be seen.

"Hidden, and a good thing, too, as it turned out. 'Ad the enemy seen the elvish workmanship on those saddles, 'twould 'ave meant doom for certain," he explained, digging through a pile of straw until he retrieved the three saddles.

Hastily we brushed them off and saddled the horses as our host rummaged through a crate for two coils of rope, which he handed to Galamir. Suddenly the stable door opened. For a brief moment, we held our breath until Rohana appeared carrying two sacks full of food. She handed them to Galamir and then walked over to me.

"Miss, sorry ye couldna see the castle proper, what with all the fog and secrecy. Thought I'd give ye a reminder of Grandinwolde, nonetheless, to take with ye," she said, handing me a handkerchief embroidered with a likeness of the castle. "Used to be the pride o' Grandinwolde and still would be, were it not for them what lives there now. 'Owever, 'tis still a sight to behold, and I hope ye shall, someday."

"I hope for that day as well," I replied with emotion. "Thank you for your hospitality and for the beautiful gift. Whenever I see it I will remember how you opened your home to us."

"'Tis the least I could do," Rohana said. "Now ye'd best be on yer way, but do take care on the Stair."

Gasperon opened the stable door slightly and gave a quick glance at the surroundings. "Ye'd best be gone—the fog's a-liftin' fast. May Omni be with ye," he said as he swung the door open wide.

The six of us headed out into the lifting fog. Gasperon and Rohana's house sat close to the headwaters of the Dinwiddle. Cliffs rose abruptly on either side of the river, making ambush from anywhere but the front of the house unlikely. Our biggest concern was how the lifting fog could expose us to prying eyes from the castle's towers. The unexpected delay we had encountered could prove detrimental.

We only had a short distance to go before we would be out of sight of the castle, but if the fog cleared, that distance might as well have been a hundred miles. And yet to hasten down a treacherous path could very well prove tragic with one false step.

Out of the corner of my eye, I could see a white tower looming above the remaining fog, and I hoped those who stood sentinel there would by some miracle have their gaze be drawn elsewhere once our cloak vanished altogether.

CHAPTER 18

"Such a place of beauty it is, and yet it is difficult not to think that around every bend lies potential death."

With the Dinwiddle on our left, we entered a narrow canyon with a floor not yet kissed by the morning sun. The road on which we traveled had been carved from the granite cliffs and was flat and smooth, but it was also wet and slick after the night's soaking. Slowly we traversed the slippery path, barely wide enough for the horses in some places, knowing one false move on the slick surface could send us and our horses tumbling into the raging, muddy waters with little hope of rescue. To make matters worse, rivulets from the mountains above cascaded down the walls of the canyon across the narrow trail, making passage all the more treacherous. My heart pounded as we rode at a walk. I was not so nervous about my own mount, knowing how surefooted Avencloe was, but my brow creased with concern for my companions.

A little further and we would move beyond sight of the castle's highest tower. I glanced behind and had to catch my breath when I saw it. In the full light of the sun, its white spirals pierced the lifting gloom against the backdrop of Mount Kinareth, with no hint of the residents inside. I could not help but smile to admire such a beautiful structure so like a swan rising from the mists of the lake on a crisp morning, and yet I wished to be out from beneath its gaze as quickly as possible.

As we rode along, no one spoke. The gravity of our precarious situation weighed heavily, making the thought of undue chatter nerve-racking at best, and with the threat that our voices would echo throughout the canyon, we dared not spook the already nervous horses into a bolt.

The roar of the rapids only a few feet to our left was

deafening. To our right was a sheer cliff face, certainly unscaleable for all except Callas, and even that I doubted. An expanse of only fifty feet or so separated the two walls of the gorge. Our only escape, if we were being pursued, was forward. Nervously, I looked behind me once more, in time to see the castle spires disappear from sight as we rounded a bend in the river. My heart rate began to slow.

Galamir, who kept his ears and eyes concentrated on the path ahead, rode in the lead yet was careful to turn his head every few minutes to check on the company that followed. Inago rode behind him, followed by Valdir, then me, Allynon, and finally Endegar in the rear.

For a long while we rode in this manner until at last the rays of the sun made their way high enough into the sky to look down upon the granite staircase. The sunshine, along with gusts of wind that blew up from the vale below, helped to quickly evaporate the remaining moisture on the trail. Yet there remained the small rivulets that tumbled down the cliffs from above, creating small hazards along the way. Most were little more than trickles and easily traversed, yet there were a couple that required each of us to dismount and walk the horses through.

Several hours passed, and the sun was high overhead when the sight of a natural bridge—carved by countless years of onslaught by wind and water and spanning the width of the canyon—loomed ahead.

"Ah, the Dinwiddle Gate at last. We are little less than halfway through," Galamir announced. "Perhaps we should stop for a rest and a bit of food."

"What if we are being followed? Should we not continue on as quickly as possible to make our way into the open?" asked Endegar.

"They likely would not send anyone after us, for they would be at as great a disadvantage on the Stair as we," Valdir replied. "Nay, they would likely hope we encounter some obstacle that would force us to turn back, and so lie in wait for our return."

"No turning back, eh?" Allynon said. "Then I say we rest."

We all concurred, weary from the physical and emotional strain of the morning.

The place where we stopped to rest was an alcove in the cliff, which formed a platform of sorts wider than the path on which we had been traveling. It allowed the members of our company, as well as the horses, a short respite from the raging waters. The mood was one of subdued relief for having made it so far without incident. Endegar lay on the ground a few feet away with his hat covering his face as the others sat about the platform on small boulders eating the meal Rohana had provided.

"I rather like the Stair," I commented, admiring the beauty of the rock formations above and the way trees grew out of the most unexpected cracks and crevices along the way, ornamenting the canyon with bright splashes of springtime color. There was a fresh scent in the air, and the sun provided a bit of warmth to the damp gorge. "It would be a pleasant hike were it not for the conditions."

"The Stair, it *is* beautiful," Allynon agreed. "When first I traveled this way, I remember thinking as much, though it did not hold the peril it does today…or perhaps in those days I was younger, more daring, and more foolish," he added with a smile.

"I do not like dis place at all. 'Tis suffocatin'," said Inago, his dark eyes darting upward. "Glad I will be to rest my head on de bare earth tonight, just to be out from between de cliffs."

"To see the Elwindor Plain will be a relief, yes?" Allynon commented.

"No," Valdir said. "On the plain we will be thrust out into the open with no place to conceal ourselves come nightfall."

"Is there no place in Floren to stay for the night?" I asked, remembering with pleasure the feeling of a warm bed from the night before.

"Nay," the elven lord answered, his eyes fixed upon the slice of bread he held in his hand. "Once we exit the Stair, we must make haste while there is still light. Floren is the official outpost of Draigon's army in Elwindor, being one of the largest villages in the region, and Galamir has informed me there are no safe houses for miles."

"Then should we be traveling through that village at all?" Endegar said.

Galamir stood alone at the edge of the river, staring down the road to the south. "It does not have the reputation of Stone Harbour or Grandinwolde, for that matter," he said. "They have little need to watch the southern entrance of the Dinwiddle Stair, especially at this time of year. We could easily slip into the village and slip out the other end, perhaps with time to travel a good distance more before dark, although that is doubtful if we encounter more obstacles on the Stair." Galamir returned his gaze to the road ahead.

"Galamir, what is it you see?"

The elf frowned. "My lord," he replied to Valdir, "there appears to be some sort of obstruction in the road beyond the Gate."

"Can you tell what it is?" Valdir said, rising to his feet.

"It looks like a rockslide, which would not be surprising after the rains of last night."

"Only one shovel we have in our provisions," Allynon said.

"Then come, our time of rest is over," Galamir said. "We've work to do if we plan on making it to the Elwindor Plain by sundown."

Renewed and somewhat invigorated by the short respite, we mounted our horses to begin the second half of our journey through the pass. It was not long before we rode underneath the Gate, craning our necks to marvel at the massive arch at least one hundred feet above the canyon floor. On either side of the river its sheer granite walls rose, meeting in a pinnacle at the top where vines and lichen clung to its moist underbelly. In comparison to the giant structure, the six of us were miniscule.

After passing beneath the Gate, the roadblock ahead came more fully into view. A pile of mud and rock sat heaped upon the narrow path, no doubt a result of the night's deluge, making easy passage all but impossible. Our company dismounted and set about the task of removing the obstacle from the path. With only one shovel, wielded by Inago, and everyone else working together to clear the larger rocks from the heap, the task took the better part of an hour.

"We've lost time," Galamir said wearily, as he mounted his horse. "We would be lucky indeed to make it to the bottom of the Stair and to put a good distance between us and Floren by evening, yet we must still try to get as far beyond the village as possible."

The afternoon's pace seemed much faster than it had that morning. With the waters still raging to our left and small streams cascading down from the mountains above, our situation remained perilous, yet I could not help but be enchanted by our surroundings. The road, which began at the headwaters of the Dinwiddle, had gradually sloped downhill throughout the day on its twenty or so mile trek to the place where it spilled out onto the Elwindor Plain. We had long since passed out of the coniferous forest to the north and were riding through country with cliffs on either side that were steep, though not as sheer as the ones we had passed through earlier. The gentler slope and the lower elevation allowed for a profusion of deciduous trees to grow along the way, all framing the river quite masterfully, and I thought what a spectacle it would be to see in the autumn.

The sun had long since sunk out of view when for a moment the road ahead appeared as though it opened out into clear blue sky. Inago let out a hoot when he saw the opening, knowing the end of the grueling journey was in sight. Glad the most tense and tedious part of the journey was almost behind us, we began to rejoice in the day's good fortune. With little less than a mile to go, we rode eagerly for the southern entrance, glad that, with the exception of the mudslide, most of the impediments we encountered that afternoon we passed with little effort.

For a few minutes the light-filled cleft disappeared as the course of the river turned slightly to the east. Yet as we emerged from around a sharp bend in the cliff face, we were met with a sight that turned our blood cold.

From the overhang plummeted a sizeable stream about eight feet in width that surged noisily onto the road before finding its way into the Dinwiddle, leaving a space of less than a foot between it and the short drop-off into the rapids of the river. Though likely only a few feet deep, the Dinwiddle roiled furiously at that point, offering no footholds should any of us find ourselves swept into it by the gush from above.

"Ah, now the reason we have met no one coming from this direction is clear," Valdir said calmly.

By then all in our traveling party had dismounted before the falls that blocked the way, apprehensive about how best to proceed—if it were even possible.

"Surely there must be some way around it," said Endegar.

"Nay, even if we were to scale these slopes, what of the horses?" Galamir replied.

"Yet returning to Grandinwolde would slow our journey, not to mention we could ride right into a trap," I said. "Regardless, it would be folly to attempt to go through Stone Harbour."

"And the stream, we cannot wait until summer for it to dry," Allynon lamented.

We stood silently for a moment, our fear and frustration growing with every second of daylight that ticked away.

"But make it through…it be possible."

We looked up to see Inago standing at the edge of the falling water, studying it carefully.

"Inago, this is more than the mere trickles we have encountered thus far," said Galamir. "One false step and we would end up over the brink. The distance is too far even to leap."

"The current, it is swift, but Inago is right. If it did not empty into such a torrent, we would think little of crossing such a stream by foot," Allynon said. "The horses could make it, yes? The weight they have, but we would need to lead them across."

"For that matter, Inago has the weight as well," said Endegar with an impish smile. "He could go first and help the rest of us across."

"Ah, but do not be surprised if I have not de strength to see you safely across, Master Endegar," Inago jested.

For a moment we all fell silent, pondering our options until Valdir spoke at last. "Omni help us." He sighed. "But it may be our only chance." Reluctantly the rest of us nodded our heads in agreement.

"Then settled it be," said Inago, "and I shall be de first to cross."

"Take with you the most sure-footed and least spooked horse. It will show the others the crossing can be accomplished," Galamir suggested.

"That would be Avencloe," I offered.

"Aye, but Avencloe will only follow you across," Valdir replied. "Perhaps Willomane should go first. She is a calm and steady mare, and Avencloe seems to have taken a liking to her." I glanced quickly at Valdir's horse and realized I had seen the two horses often standing side-by-side touching muzzles and Avencloe had always seemed eager to follow the beautiful, honey-colored mare. "With any luck, Avencloe and the others will follow suit."

After a little more plotting, we geared ourselves up for the task ahead.

"Remove your boots, and walk across in your stockings. That is, if you're wearing them," Galamir said with a wry smile.

"Master elf, I may seem a brute of a man, but I can assure you no barbarian am I," Inago said good-naturedly, as he sat down on the ground and began tugging at his boots. He rolled up his trouser legs and with a heavy sigh rose to his feet and took a long look at the watery path before him.

Galamir uncoiled a strand of rope Gasperon had given him that morning and handed one end to Inago, who coiled it tightly around his forearm. The exotic man then stepped forward into the rushing stream and let out a shriek as the ice-cold water splashed against his side. Gritting his teeth, he moved forward step-by-step, holding firmly to the rope anchored by Allynon, Galamir, and Endegar. In a few more steps, Inago reached the dry stone on the other side.

Allynon pulled the rope back and tied one end to Willomane's lead. He then threw the other end across to Inago, who coaxed the horse forward. In a few strides, the mare easily trod through the rushing water pouring down upon her right side.

The company heaved a collective sigh of relief after proving the stream could indeed be traversed. Yet the greater part of the group had yet to make the crossing, and we knew the time to celebrate was yet to come.

As those remaining behind removed their boots, I stepped up to Avencloe, who placed his muzzle gingerly on my shoulder. I looked him in the eye and narrowed all my thoughts to him in the way he understood best, telling him the stream must be crossed and he had to help lead the way for the others. Avencloe neighed gently as if he would readily obey.

Galamir was next to attempt the crossing. Inago threw the rope across to him, and he at once looped it under his shoulders and around his back. The gentle giant then planted his feet firmly on the path and nodded. Effortlessly Galamir placed one foot in front of the other as if he were merely walking down a city street until he reached the far side safely.

I then began to take off my shoes, and Allynon kneeled down before me. "My darling, I do not wish to see you as wet and miserable as you were last night, but it cannot be helped. Nor do I wish to see you swept away in the torrent, so I shall assist you across."

"You would do well to tend to your own crossing and not worry yourself with me," I protested.

"For you I will provide assistance, even if I must throw you over my shoulder and carry you."

I looked into his eyes and could see he was determined.

"Allow me the opportunity to display a bit of chivalry," he said with a smile.

"Very well," I said slowly, rising to my feet, "but I am not averse to going it alone."

"That I know. Much too independent you are, but if we are to be wed, then you must become accustomed to me taking care of you every now and then."

I sighed. He was right, of course.

With that, Allynon caught the rope Inago threw over to him and tied it around his chest. Endegar retrieved the other rope that remained in Galamir's pack and tied the end around me. Allynon then clasped my hand in his and took a deep breath. "You need not worry—much I have to live for. That will be enough to see us both across," he said with a smile. Allynon then stared resolutely at the path before him and cringed as he took a first step into the cold, swift water.

I followed closely behind, keeping a firm grip on his hand, yet the shock of the cold water as it coursed onto my hip made me gasp. The momentary diversion was enough to make me lose my balance, and my feet shot out from under me. I could hear the others shouting with alarm as Allynon struggled to steady me without losing balance himself. Calmly he held on as I flailed about in an effort to regain my footing.

At last I steadied myself with the help of his rocklike arm, soaking wet but standing upright. I had not considered my weight, being lighter than the rest, would make such a difference in my ability to withstand the deluge.

With a determined look, Allynon continued on, waiting with every step until he was certain I had my footing.

"Bravo!" came a chorus of relieved voices as we reached the other side. Lovingly I beamed at him with a greater appreciation for his strong masculine physique.

"Send over the horses now, beginning with Avencloe," Galamir shouted across the torrent.

At the sound of his name Avencloe pricked his ears and, seeing me on down the path past the falling water, casually walked through the stream before Valdir and Endegar had a chance to tie a rope to his lead. I held my breath as the great beast approached and gently stroked his muzzle in welcome as he came to my side. "That's my Avencloe," I whispered. "Now go to Willomane and call your friends to you."

"If they were all so easy," Allynon said, "but I am afraid the others will not cross over so effortlessly."

The next two horses to cross were those of Galamir and Inago, both of which made the journey with little more than gentle coaxing and a steady hand on the lead rope. The two remaining required a little more persuasion.

"Whoa, girl...steady." Valdir raised a hand to Endegar's mare with fingers outstretched toward the horse's eyes. He then began to use the Gifts, speaking in the elvish tongue as he kept his gaze fixed on the eyes of the beast.

"What he be doin', Your Highness?" Inago whispered.

"Elves, they have a mystical way with all creatures, a way of bending them to their will," he answered. "Many times I have seen it before."

Slowly, hesitantly, the horse that had been rearing her head and pawing nervously at the ground took a few timid steps through the water, when suddenly her rear hoof slipped out from under her. The mare quickly regained her balance and hurried to the other side so quickly that those of us standing there had to jump aside to keep from getting trampled.

"Our task is not yet finished," Galamir said as he looked across the stream to the tan-colored horse that was Allynon's mount. It reared and glanced about wildly, despite the efforts of Valdir and Endegar to calm it.

"I be fearin' 'twill take more dan elven magic to get de beast across," said Inago.

"Aye," said Galamir, "his eyes will need to be shielded."

"Then someone must walk him across," Allynon said.

"I will," came a voice from the other side.

"Lord Valdir, the crossing would be too dangerous," Galamir protested.

"Someone must see him across."

"It should be me," Allynon offered. "It is my mount, after all."

"Nonsense," Valdir said. "You are already safely across. Moreover, as you have already pointed out, we elves have a way with animals you mortals lack."

"Very well, my lord, but you will have a rope tied about your chest, as did I."

"As you wish," the elven lord said as he caught the rope Allynon threw over to him and slipped it under his arms. "Come now, my fine young stallion, your turn has come whether you desire it or not." Valdir threw a blanket over the horse's eyes and took the lead firmly in his hand, speaking to the beast in the elvish language. As if in a trance, the horse, so frantic only a moment before, calmly stepped into the cold water with little more than a quiet neigh until both stood once more on dry ground.

Allynon walked up to the stallion and rubbed its muzzle. "A loyal friend you have been on this journey, and I am glad you will be seeing me to its finish," he said, the relief evident in his voice.

"All safely across," Inago said. "Glad I will be to leave dis place now."

"Ahem!" came a voice from the other side of the stream. "Forgetting something?"

"Ah, Endegar! How could I be forgettin' you?" Inago laughed.

To see such a man snickering so hard that he shook was enough to make the rest of us exchange smiles.

Endegar, however, was none too pleased. "You would do well to remember me. After all, it is I who saved your hides back in Grandinwolde."

"Come now, stop your complainin' and get yourself over here." With that, Inago threw the rope to his comrade across the stream.

Endegar grabbed hold and stood at the water's edge. "You'd best hold tight to your end. If there be any funny business, I'll have your head, especially if my favorite pair of trousers are ruined."

The young man rolled up his trousers higher before he stepped into the cold water. He took several steps toward us, but he weighed little more than I. His wiry legs gave way, slipping out from under him, sending him sliding down into the river in the blink of an eye. Allynon and Galamir, who stood closest to Inago, rushed to the giant man's side to help him hoist the rope in as Endegar flailed about, struggling to keep his head above the rushing water. It was only several feet deep, but the force of the rapids made it impossible for him to stand. Already he had floated several yards downstream, and the three who held the other end of the rope lurched forward. Endegar sputtered and gasped for breath, as he was dragged up a bank of slippery boulders to the path.

Inago collapsed on his haunches, trembling, as sweat poured from his bare brow. Everyone else scrambled to help Endegar who lay on the ground. I grabbed a blanket from a nearby pack and placed it around his drenched shoulders. It took a moment for him to collect himself before he finally spoke.

"Did I tell you not to mess my trousers?" he called to

Inago.

Inago appeared surprised for a moment before a mighty, bellowing laugh escaped his lips. "You be lucky, escapin' with your life, my friend. So we be even from this mornin's escapade?"

"For the moment at least." Endegar grinned.

We all looked at each other and laughed heartily, half at the jesting of our friends and half with relief that we had narrowly avoided tragedy. Galamir glanced at the cleft leading onto the plains below. The shadows had already inched their way up the far wall of the gorge. "Come," he said anxiously, "change quickly into dry clothing, for we must make haste while there is still light. There will be time enough for celebration later."

The leggings I wore beneath my riding gown were respectable and many of the elven women in Isgilith wore them without an outer skirt. And at the moment, mine were drier than my riding skirt, and though it felt not the least bit feminine to wear them alone, comfort won over, and I removed my soaked outer layer. My wet bodice would have to remain.

The men, likewise, changed quickly into dry trousers as I turned my head, and we all put our boots back on, glad they had managed to stay fairly dry through our ordeal. There was little time to do more. We simply *had* to get well onto the Elwindor Plain by nightfall, for the town of Floren at the southern gateway to the Stair held its own dangers. I remembered all too well Galamir's warning that it was one of Draigon's outposts.

Still, it was with lighter hearts and a renewed strength we mounted our horses, glad the end of the Stair was in sight. As we approached the bottom, we were met with the vast Elwindor Plain. To our left the Dinwiddle plunged down into a succession of four pools before it began its journey through Elwindor, starting at the village of Floren that lay on the vale below. For as far as I could see were gentle rolling hills dotted with orchards, fields of wheat, and vineyards that would soon be brimming with luscious red and golden grapes. Scattered about the landscape rose fortified towns perched atop granite outcroppings. They appeared much less vulnerable to attack, unlike my own Baeren Ford that sat exposed in the open. The thought gave me a shudder.

To the west lay the Silvendell and the beginning of Guilden's forests beyond. From that vantage point, we could see far in the distance to the mountains surrounding Lake Gildaris and the place where the Lower Silvendell emerged from the eastern branch of the great body of water. From there it began its course through Fernwood Forest and on south where it would eventually empty into the sea at the castle that had stood silent for two centuries.

I looked toward the hills far to the south that sheltered the bay at Emraldein and with my sharp elvish eyes thought I could distinguish a dark cloud above that region. How it contrasted with the clear amethyst beginning to settle into the sky above. A chill traveled down my spine as I looked at the dark speck on the southern horizon, and my heart filled with sudden fear, forcing me to tear my gaze away.

"There lies Floren," Galamir said, nodding at the village. "We can only hope for safe passage."

"Is there no way around?" I asked, trying to shake the image of the dark cloud to the south.

"Nay," Galamir replied. "To the east lies the Dinwiddle, and as you can see there is no place to traverse it safely before it travels into the village. To the west, the land sloping down into the vineyards is very steep. Nay, we must take our chances and go through town."

"And what of the enemy?" Allynon asked.

Galamir paused. "We must keep our hoods tight about our heads and make eye contact with no one. If we appear as six men on important business then perhaps we will attract little attention, especially coming and going as swiftly as we are," Galamir said. "Arwyn, keep to the center, and we will do our best to surround you."

"Let us go, then, and be done with it," said Endegar. "I am ready for a warm fire and some meat in my belly."

Suddenly glad to appear more masculine with my leggings on, I nevertheless thought it unfortunate to wear my cloak and hood on such a fine evening, but knew I had best follow Galamir's advice.

Together the six of us started down the long, twisting, sometimes steep road that led from the foot of the mountain down through fields of heather. People out walking along the road looked up with astonishment as our hooded selves emerged from the Stair, a place where no mortal would dare tread at such a time of year. When it appeared we meant no harm, they seemed content to let us pass without incident. It was not long before we entered the northern gates of the village. We rode with urgency and with such an element of surprise we hoped to catch any soldiers who may be about off-guard.

I fought to keep my eyes glued to the road that twisted down the side of the steep hill. What an exasperating place it must have been to live in and traverse every day! More vertical than horizontal, the village had been built on the banks of the Dinwiddle in tiers that sharply sloped downward as the river made its way to the floor of the plain. The meandering river and its offshoots twisted and turned under archways and through huge waterwheels before plummeting down into a central lake.

Other than the many stares we received while traversing the village, we were met with no resistance. However, as we trotted through the central square on the lowest tier of the village, I was dismayed when we came upon a small group of surly looking men who looked up as we passed with a mixture of surprise and spite. They were all of them quite sordid, sporting scraggly, ill-kempt beards, greasy hair, toothless scowls, and the gray of Draigon's soldiers. I felt none too comfortable we had chanced upon them and did not like at all the malicious gleam our sudden appearance sparked in their eyes. Still, they made no move to halt us, and it wasn't long before we passed through the southern gates of the city.

On beyond lay the sprawling golden fields of Elwindor and what we hoped would be a place to rest our heads for the night.

CHAPTER 19

*"My innocence is lost," I said, as a tear of remorse
trickled down my face. "I have human blood on my hands."*

*"It doesn't sound as though the blood you shed was so
'innocent,'" Dr. Susan said softly.*

*"Nay, yet who am I to test the will of Omni in matters of
life and death? Still," I admitted, "any other outcome would
have been unacceptable."*

Once we had cleared the southern gates of Floren, I had
to resist the urge to kick Avencloe into a gallop down the
road. For so long we had been within the confines of Loth
Gerodin's dense forest, and I longed to fly with abandon
across the vast fields before me.

As if he could feel my yearning, Avencloe let out a loud
neigh and bobbed his head up and down as if urging me to
give the signal for a full gallop, but to leave my friends far
behind would have been foolhardy. Still, I was glad when
Galamir urged his own horse to pick up the pace, anxious to
set up camp as far from Floren as possible before nightfall.

We were able to put several miles between us and Floren
before the last light of day flickered in the western sky.
Galamir reluctantly called a halt to our travels. Camping out
on the open plain, so close to Floren, with little hope of
finding substantial cover in the rolling fields, was a situation
we had all wanted to avoid.

Under a blanket of stars bursting forth from the growing
darkness above, our company set up camp several hundred
yards from the road behind an outcropping of gray rocks that
shielded us somewhat from the eyes of anyone who might
pass by. Driftwood from the banks of a nearby stream
provided fuel for the fire, and once a blaze was started I went
right to work preparing a cup of hot tea for Endegar, who
had been shivering ever since his ordeal on the Dinwiddle

Stair. Galamir had the task of skinning and skewering two hares and a pheasant he had shot along the way as the others saw to the horses and the gathering of firewood.

In a little while the mood was much more relaxed. Everyone had changed into dry clothing, and we were able to sit back with full bellies and make light of the day's exploits. I relished the feeling of Allynon's sheltering arm around me as I placed my head on his shoulder. Contentedly I gazed into the dancing flames of the fire and up at a galaxy of stars sprinkled like pearls from far horizon to far horizon. Up above I could see Elwei flickering silently in all her golden glory.

There was a faint rustling nearby. We all looked in time to see a big black bird take off from a bush at the edge of the light and meld into the darkness of the night sky. Our heartbeats returning to normal, we settled back into the coziness of the fire when I heard a faint whisper on the breeze.

"Arwyn, beware!"

My body twitched and I sat upright.

"Arwyn, is there something the matter?" Allynon whispered over the sound of Galamir's voice as he continued singing a mournful tune.

I turned to look at Allynon. How could I dare tell him I had just heard a voice, seemingly from nowhere? Yet even more disturbing was its message.

From somewhere in the darkness came the faint, barely audible sound of a twig cracking. Allynon stiffened as he sat upright, listening and scanning the darkness around the fire. The elves had heard it too, and we all jumped to our feet. Several of the horses began to neigh and paw nervously at the ground. The men were already drawing their weapons when I realized my own bow and quiver of arrows was on Avencloe's saddle, which sat past the edge of the light where the horses were gathered. How foolish! I thought, chastising myself for my lack of vigilance.

"Arwyn," Allynon said calmly, "remain close to me."

My companions stood poised to battle an unseen foe. Valdir and Galamir aimed arrows into the darkness on opposite sides of the fire circle, and the three men had drawn their swords. I had the urge to run into the darkness to retrieve my weapons when from it came a bone-chilling cry that sounded like a howl, answered by a host of other high-pitched cries. We were surrounded, but by *what* was still unclear.

"Do what you must to protect Arwyn! Keep her surrounded!" Valdir yelled, as the dark figures of mortal men and husky Gargalocs emerged from the shadows, running and shrieking into our midst.

The sound of arrows whirring through the air and hitting their mark with a *thud* filled the encampment for an instant, but there were too many invaders for even the elves to kill before they reached the circle. Chaos ensued as I found myself in the midst of clanking swords as metal clashed with metal. Frantically I turned my head, trying to find someone I could aid when suddenly I felt the sickening feeling of unfamiliar arms wrapped around me as Allynon yelled my name. Next, I saw him running toward me, sword drawn and ready to strike the man who held me when out of the darkness another attacker intercepted his path.

My assailant was tall enough to lift me slightly off the ground in the struggle to carry me into the darkness. With all my might, I heaved forward and delivered a crushing blow to his kneecap with my right foot. For a moment, as the man cried out in agony, I found a chance to plant my feet firmly on the ground, lower my body, and bend over, sending my assailant into the dirt.

Resisting the urge to retrieve my bow and arrows, I knew my attacker still had plenty of fight left in him and would follow me into the darkness beyond the firelight—something I had to avoid at all costs. Quickly I turned as he sprang to his feet, and as I caught a good look at his face, disgust more than fear filled me.

He was a tall, lanky man with dark hair tinged with streaks of gray that fell down below his buttocks. On his face he sported a long beard that fell in a braid down to his chest. With wide, leering eyes he regarded me as I stood there waiting for him with clenched fists. Lustily he licked his lips and ran to grab me once more. At the last second, I pivoted, dodging my assailant before I delivered a fierce blow between his shoulder blades.

The assailant spun around, dazed, having surely not expected such a telling blow from a woman. He had much to learn about women, elven women in particular. Still, he would not let me get the best of him. "Elven wench!" he yelled, right in time for me to grab his ample beard, forcing his face down as I thrust my knee into his nose.

Groaning and barely able to stand straight, the man gazed up into the night sky holding his nose as blood gushed forth. He did not see the final blow coming, for I had pivoted on my right leg and sent, with my left one, a final jolt to his ribs, knocking the wind out of him and sending him sprawling to the ground. Thank goodness I had removed my riding gown and was wearing my leggings or my movement would have been severely hampered.

He would not be as quick to recover, but my best bet for taking him down for good would be with my bow and arrows. All around me my companions were fighting fiercely, some against multiple assailants. Galamir and Valdir had come to my aid as best they could, yet all the men were preoccupied with their own battles, and Allynon had been forced away from my side. I certainly did not want anyone to risk his life to save me. My survival would have to be my own doing.

In that moment, I saw the chance to make my way to the place where the horses stood, desperately trying to escape their bindings. Several had already broken free and were running about wildly in the darkness. I heard Allynon calling my name and wondered if I were already being pursued.

In the darkness I could just make out six short piles of saddles and traveling bags, and I ran to the place where my belongings lay. As I hurriedly reached for my bow and an arrow from my quiver, I turned to see my attacker stagger to his feet. The battle raged on around him, making it impossible to shoot without risking the life of one of my friends.

Enraged, my assailant looked through the commotion surrounding him until he spotted me out in the darkness. "Wench!" he yelled as he licked the blood from his lips, setting out to where I waited in the shadows. Suddenly he stopped in his tracks, my arrow lodged firmly in his chest, and fell face forward to the ground with its tip protruding from his back.

Barely had I the time to consider what to do next when I heard footsteps approaching from behind. Quickly I turned and shot another intruder barely six feet from the place where I crouched before frantically directing my attention back to the campfire.

Two dark figures lay crumpled at the feet of Allynon and Inago, yet they were in the midst of fighting two more. Valdir and Galamir had resorted to swords and were engaged with three of the attackers, one of them a Gargaloc. I attempted to aim my arrow, but I would have risked hitting one of my own. Suddenly I detected movement on the far side of the circle and saw another Gargaloc running in the direction of the battle. For an instant, the way cleared for me to let loose with my arrow. With a sharp *thud* it found its mark, and the Gargaloc tumbled to the ground.

Allynon fought nearby, sword locked together with that of the enemy in a dangerous dance of brute strength and will. Violently the two fell against a giant boulder and I could see Allynon wince in pain, all the while holding his adversary steady against the rock until the brute found the strength to push Allynon away momentarily, clearing the way for me.

In an instant the man's body gave a violent jerk, and he gave up the struggle, slumping to the ground with an arrow in his chest. Allynon looked up in surprise to see me standing several yards away, my eyes narrowed with vengeance. He quickly turned his attention to Endegar, who was fiercely combating an assailant dangerously close to the fire. Allynon ran to his aid, and together they were able to turn the villain's back to the flames and to distract him with their swordplay. Little by little he inched closer to the fire until he caught himself coming perilously close to its edge. By then it was too late. Allynon and Endegar were both upon him, and he was no match for the two of them together.

With a cry of horror, he lost his balance and toppled over into the flames. From the midst of the fire he rose screaming to his feet and ran off into the darkness where he suddenly fell to the ground with an arrow from my quiver protruding mercifully from his back.

The next thing I saw was the look of dread on Valdir's face as he turned from a fresh kill to look at me. "Arwyn!" He yelled, in the time it took Galamir to nock an arrow and send it flying through the air to a ruffian who had emerged from the darkened fields beyond with the intent of fatally striking me with his sword.

Allynon, who had also seen the assailant, ran toward him like a crazed man, causing Galamir to adjust his aim at the last millisecond. The arrow planted itself in the attacker's shoulder, and though it slowed him momentarily, he continued to rush toward me until Allynon positioned himself between us. Allynon delivered the first blow, met with the clanging sound of metal upon metal as his lunge was blocked.

The assailant looked around and saw he was the only one still alive. Still, it was obvious he was not going to go down without a fight. Several times he and Allynon went round and round in a deadly dance of lunges and pivots, when at last the arrow lodged in his shoulder began to show its effect.

Allynon saw his opportunity, dodged a blow, and stabbed the murderous villain in the back. With eyes bulging, the man slouched to the ground as Allynon pulled his bloodied sword from his flesh.

For a moment the six of us stood on the battlefield, bracing ourselves for another attack. We were all standing, none of us bearing significant wounds, at least from what I could tell upon quick glance.

Somewhere in the darkness came the sound of someone running toward the road. In an instant Galamir raised his bow, tracked the footsteps with his uncanny sense of hearing, and let an arrow fly into the inky black night. In the distance there was a muffled cry, and the footsteps came to an abrupt halt.

Breathlessly the company scanned the darkness beyond for any other sound or sign of movement.

"Could there be others?" Allynon said at last. "We cannot let them return to Floren for reinforcements."

"Come with me, Allynon. The rest of you remain here close to the fire," Galamir said, as he took off into the darkness toward the road with Allynon following closely behind.

Still quite shaken, I turned to look at Inago, Endegar, and Valdir, who all stood rigid against the possibility of another attack. I felt the urge to do something useful, anything, to keep myself occupied during this tense time of waiting. For a long while Galamir and Allynon were gone, and I began to worry they had perhaps been ambushed down the road.

To keep my mind off of my fears, I surveyed a wound Endegar had received on his right shoulder. I then asked Inago to fetch water from the nearby stream so I could begin boiling water for the marigold petals I kept in my medicine bag, as they were particularly good at cleaning fresh wounds and keeping infection from setting in. Endegar's wound was not deep, but it was several inches in length and had already begun to clot. Inago and Valdir had fared better, having sustained no visible wounds. Together they began to round up the horses that fled during the attack, and I was relieved to see the white phantom that was Avencloe appear at the edge of the firelight.

Nearly an hour had passed when Galamir and Allynon reemerged from the shadows. "There are no more, it would seem," Allynon announced as he walked into the firelight. "The lot of them, they came in two wagons, but they left no one to tend to the horses. The horses, we led them around a knoll far from the road and set them free."

I stood and went to him. Allynon took me into his arms and held me protectively. "Are you well?" he whispered.

"As well as can be expected," I answered, as I wept quietly onto his shoulder. It took several moments before I could speak again. "Though I sustained no physical wounds, it may take a while for my soul to heal," I said, as I shivered. "Allynon, three have lost their lives at my hand. How can I ever be at peace again, knowing I have human blood on my hands, even from ones so heinous?"

Allynon gently put his hand on my chin and guided my eyes to meet his own. "To kill a man, I can tell you it is never easy," he said solemnly, his body stiffening in pain, "no matter how much it may be justified."

"I believe only a good man would feel that way," I said, as I wiped my eyes. "But what of you? It was a nasty fall you took against that rock."

"It can wait, no? I must help the others with the dead."

"You'll do no such thing, even if I have to throw you over my shoulder and make you show me your injury," I added, with a wry smile in an attempt to lessen the gravity of the moment.

"And you would do it too," Allynon said, returning the smile. "Arwyn, I must admit that when I heard the tale of your, er, *confrontation* with your taverner friend in Baeren Ford, I thought it surely a...shall we say, a slight exaggeration. I see now you are indeed not a woman to be trifled with."

"I'm glad I have convinced you. Now come and let me take a look at your wound."

Obediently Allynon pulled his tunic over his head. I could feel my cheeks flush at the sight of his bare masculine chest and my heartbeat quickened, yet I could not ignore the angry red area on his left rib cage. "Oh, Allynon, you must be in such pain!"

The prince touched his ribs carefully and winced when he came upon a slight irregularity in the bone. "My rib, I must have fractured it."

I studied the wound with concern, my mind already working through the list of medicines to use. "Comfrey! I need a comfrey poultice to help the bone heal faster, yet I have none with me, and do not recall seeing any nearby," I said, half to Allynon and half to myself. "Horsetail would be good to mend your rib, but…arnica! Yes, arnica is good for bruises, and we rode through fields of it on our way here! Wait here and I shall fetch some."

"The others, they need my help. We cannot leave these rotting carcasses strewn about our camp until the morning," Allynon said, slipping his tunic over his head.

"You are in no condition to be dragging around dead bodies." I sighed. "I could use the arnica on Endegar's wound as well. At the very least you can come and protect me on my search."

"As you wish. I would not want you poking about in the shadows alone."

"Do you think more will come?"

"It is hard to say," Allynon replied. "I believe none escaped, but that is not to say others will not follow."

"Who were they?"

"Ashkars," came a voice from the darkness nearby. "With a few renegade Bensorians mixed in the pack, to be sure, as well as a few Gargalocs." Valdir stepped from the shadows, his timeless countenance not reflective of the fatigue the mortals felt so keenly. "They are men from the lowlands of Ashkaroth, once like the men of Bensor but so poisoned they have become by their evil queen that they have chosen the path of wickedness. They are cunning, without mercy, and are worse than the mindless half-breeds they have enslaved to do their bidding."

Valdir only confirmed my impression that Gargalocs were more childlike than anything, though formidable they could be. They were not to be feared as much as those who looked like men but acted as beasts.

"But why? What quarrel had they with us?" I asked. "They did not seem intent to rob us or they would have done so when we were all preoccupied."

"Most likely, they attacked us for sport." The wise elf sighed.

Allynon and I remained silent for a moment; I pondering soberly the depths to which the human heart was capable of descending.

"How many?" Allynon asked.

"Galamir, Inago, and I have counted fifteen so far, yet we know there are at least two who are unaccounted for."

"How may I be of service?"

"Arwyn is right—you are in no condition to aid us with this task. Go with her to gather her medicines."

I was surprised the elven lord was aware of our conversation, yet with the keen hearing of the elves it was also not out of the question to expect such a thing. All in all, it was a little disconcerting to think we had been overheard. I went and gathered an empty pouch to hold the yellow flowers I sought. Allynon and I then went out into the shadows where we found an abundance of arnica in the starlight. For a long while we worked to gather enough of the flowers to last several days.

When finished with that task, the two of us walked down to the stream for more water to boil. We found the charred remains of one of the attackers only five feet from the water's edge. Quickly we alerted Galamir, who had since discovered two other bodies in the darkness himself.

Shaken from the gruesome discovery, I returned to the fireside and set some of the arnica petals to boiling. I soaked a clean cloth from my pack in the concoction and pressed it to Allynon's ribs, keeping it in place with one of the long pieces of colorful cloth Inago sometimes used to wrap around his head.

It was a little past midnight when I went to check on the progress of Valdir and the others who had tended to clearing the place of corpses. After a brief debate concerning what to do with the bodies, we decided it best to bury them rather than to burn them and perhaps give away our location to anyone who may come looking when our attackers didn't return to the village.

In pity I looked at Inago who stood below in a shallow pit he had dug with the one shovel we had with us. Though he had received help digging from both Galamir and Valdir, the large man had suffered the brunt of the heaviest labor that day, and he appeared weary. Gratefully he accepted a drink of water from a flask as beads of sweat poured from his brow.

It would have been prudent for us to move our camp, but after a short discussion, we determined the effort would be too great for the few remaining hours left of darkness. Someone would have to remain on watch for the rest of the night.

For at least two more hours the men took turns digging the pit. From the campsite nearby I could hear them laboring far into the night to dig a pit large enough for eighteen bodies. I had long since made a preparation to help ease Endegar's and Allynon's pain and to help them rest. Endegar at last settled onto his sleeping roll and appeared to be asleep, yet Allynon refused the concoction for the moment.

"Get some sleep," he said. "A long night it has already been, and you need some rest."

"It is you who needs the rest," I answered soberly.

"I will be fine. Furthermore, I must feel useful. Another pair of eyes and ears to detect any movement in the darkness may prove critical."

"But…"

"Later tonight I shall drink some of your tea before I lie down, but for now I wait and watch."

I could see it was no use to try to convince him otherwise, and I was too weary to try. I spread my sleeping roll close to the place where Allynon sat and lay down upon it, bow and quiver close at hand. I fell asleep fast, yet my sleep was fitful, and I awoke several times throughout the next few hours. Each time I opened my eyes I could see Allynon sitting there, his dark eyes piercing the shadows for any threat.

At some point I was aware that the activity at the mass grave had ceased and all five of my companions now rested around the fire. An uneasy rest descended around the campfire, and though eyelids drooped, it was evident that all ears remained alert to any sound coming from the darkness beyond.

CHAPTER 20

"I have had enough of adventuring for now and am ready to see the valley beneath Arnuin's Hold once more."

"It seems you have had more adventure than you bargained for," came the ever-present voice.

"Yes, I can only hope to return to a more quiet existence, yet with the upcoming rebellion and the cavernous void I shall feel when Allynon departs, perhaps I should not hope too much."

When I awoke the next morning, I found Allynon sleeping soundly beside me. Quietly I arose and went to the fire to begin boiling water for morning tea. Only Valdir and Endegar were awake, and I greeted them with a nod before walking in the direction of the stream. It seemed Valdir watched me somewhat anxiously as I headed off into the swelling dawn, though I was careful to keep my bow and quiver close, having been reminded of their necessity the night before. Then, it suddenly occurred to me how protective he had been during the attack. Valdir had been so vocal in his concern with my safety. Was it due to mere chivalry? Or was there even more to it?

I had reason to doubt any fondness he harbored for me, still so aloof he was at times. I remembered the way he looked at me with such anger two nights before, causing me to wonder if he secretly despised me. Or if the reminder of his poor wife's untimely demise kept him distant from women in general, fearing further pain and loss. Yet there were other times when he could be quite warm, protective even. There was clearly something about me that elicited in him very powerful emotions, perplexing enough to make me avoid him as much as possible.

As the sun rose in the eastern sky, its golden fingers stretching across the plain, Allynon awoke to find me busily cleaning and applying an herbal tincture to Endegar's wound. Still reeling from the night's events, the company was slower to stir, yet when Galamir awoke soon afterwards, it was clear he was anxious to be underway.

"Taking into account the events of last night, we must consider our next course of action carefully," he said while sipping a cup of tea. "If we make haste, we could cross the Silvendell by nightfall, but then we must decide where to rest our heads this evening."

"What are our options?" Allynon asked, as I reapplied his compress. In the morning light his bruise appeared much darker, and he easily relented and drank my pain-killing tea.

"We could risk exposure again and camp in the woods along the East Road…or, and I know 'twould most likely be too far out of the way, and we would have to make very good time indeed, but we could always find safe haven at the Alliance."

The group was silent for a moment as we pondered Galamir's suggestion. No one wanted to risk another episode like the night before, yet we did not relish the idea of having to travel so far out of our way, which could create dangers of its own. Furthermore, I thought of Callas and how awkward it could be if he were there, for I knew in my heart the handsome elf fancied me and was quite certain his discovery of my feelings for Allynon explained his hasty departure from Isgilith so soon after the Faerenfel. And in truth, his bold and charming ways I knew could be too much of a distraction—a distraction I dared not entertain. Still, the thought of a hot bath and a warm bed to sleep in made the option almost attractive.

"One other option there is," Allynon offered. "On our way to Isgilith, two or three miles south of the ferry we stopped at an inn on the west bank of the Silvendell. The innkeeper, he seemed a good man, and I was surprised at how, once he discovered we were foreigners, he kept complaining about the 'ruffians and disagreeable sorts' that had taken over his country. Sympathetic to the enemy he certainly is not, and I believe he would provide safe refuge."

We were all silent for a moment. I envisioned the prospect of a hot meal, hot bath, and a warm bed in a real place of rest, not in a cave, comfortable though it was, shrouded with the weight of a secret mission.

Galamir spoke at last. "All in favor of spending the night at this inn, say 'aye.'"

The suggestion was met with unanimous approval from all but Inago, who remained snoring on his sleeping roll. Endegar glanced at the sleeping giant with a raised eyebrow.

"'Tis a pity, and with him sleeping like a babe at that," he said with an impish gleam in his eyes, "but someone must wake him." Endegar nonchalantly walked over and poured a cup of cold water from the stream onto Inago's forehead. He bolted upright, sputtering and spewing curses at his mischievous companion.

Still rather dazed from his sound sleep, he arose slowly and staggered off in the direction of the stream, returning in a few moments for the last of the morning's provision of honey cakes and some of my tea.

As the others prepared to leave, I applied salve and bandages to Inago's hands, blistered from hours of shoveling the night before. "Your hands will be as good as new in a few days," I commented, tucking the end of his cloth bandage into place.

Without warning, he grabbed my hands and held them firmly in his, causing me to gasp. I looked up into his big, soulful eyes and found them staring intensely into mine. I remembered what Allynon said about his ability to "read" people, and I had the distinct feeling he was reading me. I wasn't sure I wanted him to peer inside my soul, to see the person beneath, but I could not look away.

After a moment, his eyes grew wide, excited even, followed by an unexpected contortion into confusion.

"Inago, I can tell are a wise man, a seer," I said, nervous.

"May I ask . . . what did you see?"

"Dear lady," he answered breathlessly, "for years I been a-lookin' for a soul so pure, but I seen nothin' but darkness in de hearts of men. Den I look into your eyes, and I see a light so bright it outshines de stars even. But . . . but it be hidden behind a curtain."

All activity at the camp had come to a halt, everyone having turned his attention to Inago and me.

"Remember!" Inago said insistently. "You must remember!"

"Remember what?" I was at a loss.

"You must remember de light, from where it comes. Only den will de curtain come down and de light will shine so bright."

No one moved, no doubt trying to figure out what to make of me. Even Valdir looked nervous.

Allynon was the first to speak. "I told you she was special, no?"

It was not long before we were underway, taking off in a southerly direction on the road that led from Floren. For the greater part of the day we traveled through rolling, rainbow-hued countryside covered with a plethora of wildflowers waving in the gentle breeze, eventually giving way to sprawling farmsteads and fields of golden wheat, orchards brimming with the beginnings of ripening fruit and olives, and vineyards where the famous wines of Elwindor originated. Inviting stone farmhouses dotted the landscape, some quite large and others more modest, yet they all exuded the typical Bensorian love of nature, charm, and orderliness.

Already the rising sun sent its warming rays to the earth, and it was not long until we shed our heavy cloaks. I had been away from Baeren Ford for almost seven weeks, a month by the Bensorian calendar, and I was suddenly aware of how most of the spring had passed. Summer was only five weeks away—summer, and my third anniversary in Bensor.

Rarely now did I think of the life I had left behind three years before. It might as well have been a million years ago, so distant it felt.

For the greater part of the day, we rode farther and farther to the south and west until the southern slopes of the Andains began to shrink behind us. Allynon spoke little throughout the journey, and I could tell he was in a great deal of pain. Endegar's wound continued to throb, yet he said the pain-killing tea I gave him earlier had helped to ease the hurt to a dull ache.

By midafternoon, Galamir spotted the East Road, over two miles ahead. A cloud of dust rose from that direction, and he motioned for the group to halt as he stopped to watch and listen. Until then, we had met no one but the locals going about their daily business. But the sight of several riders galloping toward us was cause for concern.

"What do you see?" Endegar asked.

"Riders, six to eight at least. According to Alliance spies, Draigon's adherents seem to have concentrated in Guilden and in the mountains, though he still has strong pockets of supporters in Elwindor. Who knows if those riders be friend or foe, but I am not willing to chance another meeting with the enemy," Galamir said. "If we take off cross-country, perhaps we can avoid them. Such would nonetheless be to our advantage if we are able to save some time as well. The landowners in this region do not take kindly to strangers cutting through their property at such a time as this, yet it cannot be helped." With that, Galamir rapped his horse's reins and turned away from the road. The rest of us followed suit and it was not long until we had left the road behind us, keeping out of the open by following a long hedge to a stand of trees.

Once we were certain the riders had passed without veering off course to search for us, we continued onward, galloping over heather-covered hills until at last we came upon the East Road. With no one in sight but a lone farmer leading a mule with a heavy load on its back, we eased our horses down onto the road. Several miles to the west lay Fernwood Forest, and within an hour we reached its green borders.

For one last time, I looked to the north and saw the southern slopes of the Andains rising into the blue sky above. From that vantage point they did not appear as massive, yet it was only yesterday I had ridden beneath them, filled with awe at how their peaks seemed to soar up to the very throne of Omni.

Without a word we slipped beneath the green canopy of Fernwood, and in an instant were transported to a cool world of lofty branches set high above the road. Fernwood felt so light and airy, much different from Loth Gerodin, where the trees grew in greater proliferation. Each forest claimed its own type of beauty, and I marveled at how many different personalities the land of Bensor harbored.

The six of us followed the East Road through the trees, and the heavy mood from the night before lifted. Galamir was certainly more relaxed as we entered the cover of the forest, though he mentioned the local lore supposed it to be haunted. After a short while we came to a bridge spanning the Lower Silvendell. On the eastern side of the river a road branched off to the south, marked by a high stone archway. Partial elven runes, chipped away in recent years by vandals, were barely distinguishable at the top of the arch.

"Long ago it said 'Fenrother, Southern Kingdom of the Elvish People'," explained Galamir, who rode beside me. "The city lies almost fifty miles to the south, about halfway between here and Carona, where the road eventually ends."

"Fernwood must be quite a large forest," I commented.

"Long and narrow it is, though broader in the south. From there it follows the Lower Silvendell north where it eventually tapers to an end close to Stone Harbour. We have but a short distance, twelve miles at most, until we pass beyond its western entrance."

"Tell me of Fenrother," I said.

Galamir was more than willing to describe the beautiful elvish city that lay nestled among the trees below the great falls of Calyxa—for which his horse was named—where the Lower Silvendell plunged over a hundred and fifty feet down a sheer drop on its trek to Carona. It was considered the northern gateway to Carona and in its days of glory, the summers there were long and filled with the sounds of music, bubbling fountains, and the constant roar of the falls. Unlike Isgilith, the city was not hidden from the outside world, and both mortals and dwarves often frequented it. It was abandoned, when it was clear Draigon would make life difficult for any elf refusing to relocate to Loth Gerodin. Skirmishes broke out, but in the end it seemed more sensible to make Loth Gerodin home rather than risk any more elvish lives.

I noticed as Galamir spoke, he failed to mention anything about Callas. Yet I remembered the story he told me before about how Callas had tried to reestablish the colony at Fenrother only to meet with failure, which I believed must have contributed to a stifled bitterness I had sensed in Valdir's youngest son. It was something I knew was best left unsaid. There seemed to be enough tension between Callas and his father than to open old wounds that had yet to heal, and I also guessed much of Callas's bitterness had to do with his rivalry with Vandaril, whether real or imagined, for their father's approval. It was obvious to me that Valdir had complete faith in Vandaril's abilities, yet he was generally quiet when it came to his intense auburn-haired son.

I pondered these things for a long while until the forest abruptly ended and we found ourselves looking out over a meadow less than a mile in breadth to a clump of trees in the distance. The afternoon sun was suspended just above the western horizon, and there was only a little while left of sunlight.

The anxious crease on Galamir's brow returned as we

approached the eastern banks of the great river, for the only way to cross was by ferry. According to my elvish friend, the nearest bridges spanning the river were in Stone Harbour, which was certainly out of the question, and more than eighty miles to the south closer to Maldimire. Either option would put us at least two days behind schedule and would harbor dangers of its own. We simply *had* to cross the river by ferry.

The deep flowing waters of the Silvendell soon came into view, as did a large wooden raft secured to the dock by a large chain. Sitting propped against one of the pilings was an old man who appeared to be asleep. As the sound of horse hooves clopped against the wooden planks of the dock, he opened his eyes and sat upright.

"Er, didn't see ye comin'."

"How could you with closed eyes, old man?" Galamir said with a congenial smile.

The ferry operator ignored Galamir's comment and stood up, eyeing us curiously. "I suppose ye'd be needin' me services."

"Aye."

"Some o' ye be elves, that I kin see e'en with these old eyes."

"That is our business."

The old man glanced nervously toward the opposite bank. "Look, I've nothin' against yer kind, but I've been threatened within an inch o' me life if I let ye cross the river."

"Perhaps we can persuade you otherwise," Galamir said, as he pulled a gold coin from his tunic.

"And I'm to alert them 'igher ups should I see any elves in th' area."

"Very well," Galamir said, shaking his head. "For your trouble and your silence. Either you take us across now or we tie you to that tree over there and confiscate your craft. 'Tis your choice." As if to emphasize his elvish friend's words, Inago began to finger one of Gasperon's ropes in his hand.

The old man greedily grabbed the gold coins from Galamir. "They'll all be at the tavern by now regardless."

"Which tavern?"

"Just north o' here near the lake is a tavern they 'specially like. Spend the whole evenin' there, they do." At least it was in the opposite direction of the way we were heading. "The taverner there, he hates 'em. A rowdy bunch they are when they're filled with brew."

"That bodes well for us. We will be well on our way to Wittering by the time they return," Galamir lied. "Come now, and let us be on our way."

"Aye, but I kin only take three hairses at a time. Jittery they kin be on the water, and I'll not 'ave too many on board to get nervous all at once."

It was decided that Inago, Endegar, and Valdir should go on the first crossing, followed by Galamir, Allynon, and myself. The two mortals, along with the elven lord and their three horses, boarded a raft with a large chain threaded in the center of the vessel through two holes and a winch and up to an iron pillar on the dock. The old but burly ferry operator closed the gate and began to crank a winch that slowly raised the chain up from the bottom of the river, beginning a motion that propelled the vessel forward. The going appeared painfully slow to those of us who lingered behind, as we watched the last rays of sunlight disappear behind the trees across the river.

Once our friends were safely across, the old man took his time returning to the eastern bank but eventually pulled up to the dock. Allynon, Galamir, and I led our horses onto the ferry, and with a loud shudder as the gate shut behind us, we were on our way.

The ferry driver immediately turned the crank, and I watched with fascination as the chain lying submerged on the riverbed was pulled to the surface and through the jarring, gnashing teeth of the winch only to slowly descend into the watery depths of our wake. Around us the river swirled and eddied in the gentle current and, were it not for the chain that held us, we would have been set adrift downstream. We sloshed through the water at a tediously slow pace, until the ferry came to rest against the dock on the western side of the river.

Galamir turned once more to the ferry operator. "You have been most helpful," he said as we disembarked. "And if you are questioned, you can tell them *we* threatened you within an inch of your life if you did not allow us passage."

"Aye, though I'm glad it didna come to that," he replied as he watched us mount our horses. "I wish ye luck on your journey, where'er ye be headed."

Eager to be on our way in the waning daylight, we turned and travelled down the road, trying to put as much distance between us and the ford as possible. The road that turned south toward Maldimire was a short distance past the river and the inn only a few miles down the road. As darkness fell, we were glad to see the inviting, lamp-lit stone inn sitting off the road down a tree-lined lane. Allynon dismounted, walked to the front door and rapped on it firmly. In a few moments the door opened, and a short little man peered out cautiously.

"Master Faxendor, it is I, Allynon of Endara. With my associates and three friends, I have returned in search of lodging for the night."

The innkeeper peered around the tall man to the five travelers who stood on his front lawn. Seeing the rather unlikely combination of persons there, his eyes grew wide, and he called inside. "Myrdal, 'tis the three gentlemen from Endara, and ye'll not believe who they've brought with 'em!"

An older woman with curly blond hair piled upon her head appeared at the front door. "Elves!" she cried. "Why, we've not seen yer kind in these parts for ages."

"We come in search of lodging," Allynon repeated, suddenly appearing quite weary.

"Aye, aye, that ye'll find 'ere," said Faxendor. "We've enough beds for the lot o' ye, seein' as 'ow business 'as been slow o' late. In fact, ye'll be our lone guests this eve."

"All the better," Allynon replied. "We have traveled far and have encountered hardships along the way and would be grateful for a safe place to rest our heads."

"Ye've come to the right place, and we'll keep yer presence discreet," the innkeeper added, glancing at Valdir, Galamir, and me. "Now come, come. I'll tend to the hairses. Myrdal will see ye're fed proper and each given 'ot baths. By the looks o' ye, ye could all use one . . . er, beggin' yer pardon, miss." The little man blushed suddenly as he looked at me. "I was referrin' to the gentlemen."

Suddenly the sound of footsteps came from around the corner of the inn and a young man, probably no more than eighteen, appeared pushing along a wheelbarrow filled with firewood. He was slightly taller than Faxendor, yet there was no mistaking he was the innkeeper's son. "Ah, Riddoc. Come lad, and 'elp yer da see to these hairses."

Obediently the young man took Avencloe's lead, smiling and blushing sheepishly when he took it from me awkwardly. It was enough to make my companions exchange knowing smiles.

"Thank you, kind sir," I said in an effort to make poor Riddoc feel less self-conscious about his moment of adolescent infatuation.

Together the group of weary riders filed through the front door and into a cozy and spacious parlor. Myrdal then led us up a flight of stairs to our rooms. "There's already enough water 'eated for one bath," she said, as she opened the door to a room at the top of the staircase. "Per'aps the lady would care to bathe first?"

"Thank you, but there are others amongst us who have fared worse than I. Perhaps they should be first," I said.

"That should be Allynon," Galamir suggested.

Allynon began to protest but saw it was useless as the rest

of us all agreed with Galamir. "Very well," he said quietly.

I said nothing, though my concern for his pain and weariness had been growing throughout the day. Allynon, however, had traveled that long distance on horseback without once complaining of the pain he suffered. Such stoicism, coupled with his selflessness and willingness to pull his own weight seemed so ironic in one who had been born to privilege. When I considered his numerous other qualities, was it any wonder I had fallen in love with him?

After we had all settled into our sleeping chambers, Allynon bathed in a large cast iron tub sitting in the corner of his room while the rest of us met in the dining room downstairs to discuss plans for the next day's travel.

"With any luck, if we arise before the sun and set out early, we will arrive at Fendred's house by dark," Galamir said.

"Why, it took us the better part of two days to make the same trip before," I said as I dressed Endegar's wound with clean bandages.

"Aye, but we will not have the burden of a wagon laden with two coffins filled with dwarves. That should speed our progress considerably, though it will still be a long day," Galamir explained. "Moreover, Fendred offered to keep us on our return journey."

"Yes, though he will surely be surprised to see our company has grown to six," I said. "Still, I know he and Helice will be glad to take us all in."

"Who is this Fendred?" Endegar asked curiously.

Valdir had already heard the story of how Galamir and I had met, yet he sat quietly and listened as I recounted the story for the benefit of Endegar and Inago. After a while, Myrdal appeared at the door to the kitchen bearing platters full of steaming food, which she placed on the table before her guests. She disappeared for a moment before returning with a covered tray, which she handed to me.

"Miss, would ye be kind enough to take this to the

gentleman upstairs? 'E seemed in no mood to return downstairs for dinner."

"Certainly," I replied, happy for the excuse to be alone with Allynon. "And would you mind bringing a pot of boiling water and an empty mug upstairs when you have the chance?"

"Aye, that I'll do, miss," Myrdal replied.

I took the tray from Myrdal and walked into the main hall and up the stairs. Allynon beckoned me to enter when I rapped on the door, and I found him sitting on the edge of his bed, staring at the fire in the fireplace. The clothes he wore were clean and his hair was damp. Altogether he appeared somewhat refreshed but weary, and he smiled when I entered.

"Ah, food," he said. "I would almost rather spend this time at rest, yet if you will stay and dine with me then I could be persuaded to put off sleep a while longer."

"You need to eat," I said as I placed the tray on the bedside table.

Allynon lifted the lid to reveal two plates piled high with meat, potatoes, cooked carrots, and a basket full of rolls. "There is far too much food here for me to eat alone. It would be a shame for it to go to waste."

I smiled coyly. "Very well. Although I enjoy the company of the others, I still much prefer yours."

Suddenly there was a knock on the door. At our beckoning, Myrdal entered carrying a tray that held a mug and a pot of steaming water. The innkeeper's wife promptly dismissed herself.

I poured the hot water into the mug along with a small mesh bag filled with horsetail, which I had been delighted to find during a brief rest that afternoon in Fernwood. Allynon compliantly drank the tea as the two of us sat on a rug before a now-roaring fire and consumed our meal, talking quietly together about the day's journey—it was the most Allynon had spoken all day. When we were finished, I rose and went to the pot of hot water where I had a compress of arnica soaking.

As I prepared the compress, I was intensely aware that Allynon's breathing became heavier as he stood there watching my every move. In the firelight, our eyes met, and I was aware of the familiar yearning rising in me every time I peered into his deep brown eyes. His gaze fell to the place where the neckline of my dress dipped, slightly revealing the cleft beneath. I could almost see the battle raging behind his eyes—after all, I felt it too. And although I knew the reason he turned away, I could not help but feel grief that my thirst for him would not soon be quenched.

Realizing all thought of the compress had been momentarily forgotten with the heaviness of my own breath, I felt blood rush to my cheeks. I turned back to my task just as I heard the sound of footsteps passing by in the hall outside. By the heavy sound, I imagined it was Inago on his way to the room he and Endegar shared. It would not be long before Galamir retired to the bed on the far side of the room.

Methodically, I squeezed the excess water from the compress, though I let out a faint gasp when Allynon removed his tunic. His unfettered dark hair fell loosely about his muscular shoulders, and I felt my heart rate quicken. I knew I shouldn't even be there, flirting with temptation. Still, I could hardly ignore the angry bruise on his side. I swallowed hard and walked over to quietly apply the compress to his bruised rib.

Allynon lifted his arms as I wrapped his chest with a long piece of cloth to keep the compress in place, a process requiring me to be next to his bare skin. It was almost too much for me to bear, and for a long moment we stared at each other with eyes full of desire, until I heard the sound of another set of footsteps coming up the stairs, passing into the hallway beyond.

"You'd best get in bed," I said quietly.

Allynon nodded and climbed beneath the covers. I sat

down on the edge of his bed and stroked his brow as he smiled drowsily and closed his eyes.

"You must love me very much to go to such trouble on my behalf," he murmured.

I said nothing but leaned over and gently kissed his lips. Then rising from the bed, I went to place the empty dishes on the tray. Before I turned to leave, I could see he had opened his eyes once more and was watching me. Smiling, I quietly left the room, careful to close the door gingerly behind me. I met Galamir on the stairs and bade him good night before taking the tray downstairs to our hostess. Wearily I climbed the stairs once more and retreated to my own room, glad to find a hot tub waiting for me there.

I awoke to find Allynon sleeping peacefully beside me. We lay in a large bed sitting in the middle of an opulent room fit for a king. At the foot of the bed, a balcony opened up to the sky, and from somewhere below I thought I heard a sound like the muffled roar of crashing waves. I stretched contentedly in the light of the moon, dangling close enough to reach out and grab, and a warm breeze wafted in and tickled my brow.

With an intense longing to feel Allynon's touch, I rolled over to wake him—only to find the spot beside me empty!

Panicked, I sat up in bed and glanced around the unfamiliar room until my eyes rested on a dark spot—a pool of blood on the floor beside the bed. A scream rose from my belly, becoming lodged in my throat where it dissipated into no more than a whisper as a blood-chilling wail came from closeby. The next thing I knew, I was running through a dark, cavernous room, tripping over objects in my way while being pursued by something in the darkness, something so close I could feel its hot breath upon my neck and the sound of furious, unearthly snarling in my ear. I was cornered like a mouse.

I awoke in a tangle of bedsheets, panting. Trying desperately to get my bearings, the comforting sounds of hooting owls and croaking bullfrogs outside my window grounded me back to reality. My heart still pounded as I fought against the urge to flee.

The inn was deathly quiet. I placed my head on my pillow once more and lay there for quite some time—an hour at least—trying to shake the images haunting my sleep. Were they simply the product of a weary brain firing neurons willy-nilly? Or did they mean something more? And the thought that sent the sharpest chill down my spine—would Allynon come to a bloody end before we could be reunited . . . or would I?

Trying to banish such worrisome thoughts from my mind and return to sleep, I was on the brink of unconsciousness when all at once I had the distinct feeling I was not alone. I opened my eyes and glanced toward the door where, even in the darkness I could just make out the levered doorknob turn slowly, quietly. Breathlessly I watched the door inch open, revealing a dark figure on the other side.

"Allynon!" I whispered.

Before I knew it, my feet hit the floor and I ran to fling the door wide open—only to find the hallway curiously empty and silent. Carefully I padded down the hallway and pressed my ear to Allynon and Galamir's bedroom door, but I detected no movement on the other side—only the sound of methodic breathing. Could the darkness of the corridor simply have confused someone seeking the privy in a state of half-sleep? Or—and the thought jolted me—had someone intentionally attempted to enter my room while I slept?

Shivering uneasily, I returned quickly to my room, careful to turn the key in the lock behind me, but the combination of my disturbing dream and uninvited visitor left me cold and trembling for some time after. It was a long while before I could sleep.

The next morning at breakfast, I found myself watching Riddoc reproachfully over the rim of my teacup as he entered the dining room with a heaping pile of firewood and proceeded to place each piece in a neat row upon the hearth. Looking up, he saw me sitting there and gave me a wide grin—certainly not a behavior I would expect from a peeping tom who had been caught red-handed.

"Mornin' to ye, miss," he greeted cheerfully. "Sleep well?"

"I've slept better," I replied. "And you?"

"Mum's always said a good day's work's the best remedy for a sleepless night. Guess 'tis why I always sleep like a babe from dusk 'til dawn."

"Really? No midnight wanderings for, say, a bite to eat? Or to go to the privy?" *Or to spy on unsuspecting women travelers?*

"Hmph! Da would skin me alive were I to wake the customers!"

"Indeed," I managed to emit, disappointed my theory of adolescent infatuation run amok had not produced a culprit.

No time had I to further ponder the mystery of my midnight intruder when Galamir herded the rest of my traveling companions into the room, traveling bags in hand, determined to get on the road as soon as possible in order to make it to Fendred and Helice's home by dark.

As for my "visitor", I decided it best to dismiss the entire incident as a case of a weary mind blurring the distinction between dreams and reality.

Throughout the day, we rode hard along the East Road across the Guilden countryside. Both Allynon and Endegar appeared to be in better spirits, even quite jovial, talking more freely, and I was glad my medicines were having the desired effect.

As we travelled, the landscape became more and more familiar, and I came to realize how much I had missed that land so fragmented by stone fences, broad patches of woods, tranquil ponds, and meadows where cows and sheep grazed peacefully.

By midday we arrived in Wittering, where we passed through with little more than a few brief glances, so accustomed had the residents become to travelers coming in and out of town. The fact there were elves among our party seemed worthy of no more than a passing stare, and then not by the wrong sort—that is, not until midafternoon when a small band of men in gray passed us, going in the opposite direction. By a stroke of good fortune, we outnumbered them, and I could see in their wide eyes as they stared at Inago's burly physique and the huge broadsword by his side they thought better of causing any trouble for us. Thankfully, the only others we met along the road that afternoon were farmers and shepherd boys going about their daily business.

Only an hour of sunlight remained when we arrived at the home of Fendred, Helice, and Rumalia, and what a welcome sight it was. Fendred, out chopping firewood on the front lawn, looked up with surprise and a hint of apprehension as the six of us approached on horseback. But when he laid eyes on Galamir and me, a broad smile spread across his face.

"Master Galamir, Miss Arwyn, a glad sight it is indeed to see ye've retairned!"

"Greetings, Fendred!" Galamir called. "We have indeed—and brought friends with us."

"That I kin see," Fendred said as he walked over to Avencloe to help me dismount. "And I'll say, if they be friends o' yours, Master Galamir and Miss Arwyn, then they are welcome 'ere, humble though me home may be."

The front door of the house opened, and Rumalia ran outside to embrace me joyfully. Helice also appeared, beckoning us inside. "So glad ye made it at last. We've been expectin' ye these past few days," she said. "Although we've not much on the fire, we'll share what we have."

"Not to worry," said Galamir, holding up the carcasses of

two pheasants and three quail. "We've already seen to our dinner."

The six riders dismounted and introductions were made all around. Inago offered to help Fendred with the horses while the others went inside, and it was obvious when they returned to the house Fendred was in awe of the large, dark-skinned man. Even Helice and Rumalia had difficulty keeping their eyes off of the exotic foreigner.

Long after the evening meal had been consumed, we sat around the table with our hosts, sharing tales of our adventures. They listened politely to news that Endara's king had taken ill, and I smiled to myself as I imagined how they would feel if they knew the king's son was sitting right in their parlor. Some secrets were best left unsaid—but then there were those secrets I gladly shared. News that I was to wed the handsome stranger was met with smiles of delight, yet the family had difficulty understanding why I would not return to Endara with him. Indeed, it was a decision that defied rational explanation. What words could adequately express this gnawing conviction that would not let me go?

My fellow travelers and I were not the only ones with stories to share. My companions listened attentively as Rumalia recounted our ordeal in Dungard. Although Allynon had heard it all before, I was confident he had quietly assumed my tale was a bit embellished. After all, few who went into Dungard ever lived to see the light of day. Even his companions listened, wide-eyed, as if they weren't quite certain what to make of the woman their master intended to marry.

Of tidings from Baeren Ford, Fendred and Helice had none to tell except that there had been no rain in the region since the day I had left and that there were rumors of some strange construction going on several miles south of Baeren Ford, but nothing more. It was only on occasion Fendred traveled into the village, and then it was to purchase supplies and not to carouse with the locals. Yet surely he would have heard if something too momentous had happened, and in that I found comfort. My thoughts drifted to Loralon, and I suddenly felt anxious to arrive home, hoping she had fared well in my absence.

That night I shared Rumalia's bed while my five male companions slept on the parlor floor. I had almost drifted to sleep when I heard Rumalia whisper. "Ye love him, don't ye?"

"Hmm?"

"Your intended, ye know, the handsome one with the long, dark hair."

"Yes, very much," I answered sleepily. Rumalia sighed in the darkness, and I realized she wanted to talk more. "What is it?" I asked patiently.

Rumalia hesitated a moment. "Arwyn, do ye think I'll e'er be wed?"

"Yes, I would imagine so. You're a sweet, attractive young woman. Someone will fall in love with you someday, when the time is right."

"Do ye really think so?"

"Yes, I do," I answered, suddenly recalling vague memories of adolescent self-doubt. "I once had those same fears myself."

"You?" Rumalia said in disbelief.

"Yes, even I."

Silence descended upon the room for a few moments . . . long enough for my mind to drift off somewhere between wakefulness and sleep. The last I remembered of our conversation, Rumalia started to ask me a question. "Arwyn, what do you think about . . . Arwyn?"

Her words faded into the background of my mind, and I knew no more until the morning.

CHAPTER 21

"You sound conflicted," Dr. Susan commented.

"Indeed," I admitted. "I am reminded one part of my heart belongs to Bensor and my family here. The other, to Allynon. The closer we come to Maldimire, the more I feel it tearing apart."

"That is a very difficult load to bear."

"And what if I cannot bear it? What if, in the end, it shall be the death of me?"

"I think you are much stronger than that," Dr. Susan replied sympathetically. "Now, as you were saying..."

After such a late night, everyone was slow to rise. Even after consuming the huge breakfast Helice and Rumalia had prepared, we lingered for a while around the table sipping hot tea. It was about midmorning when I became anxious to leave, ready to return home and know Loralon and Eliendor had fared well in my absence.

As we all stood on the front lawn preparing our horses to depart, Rumalia gave me one last embrace. "Do tell, er, Kiril I sent greetings," the young woman said, almost shyly. "And Loralon as well," she added quickly.

I wondered at my friend's sudden shyness until a knowing thought came to mind. "I will be most happy to tell them both that you send greetings," I said, with a smile.

The last of our "farewells" said, we mounted our horses and rode to the main road. I turned one last time to wave at the family, and a sudden wave of sadness washed over me at the three of them standing there on the front lawn, along with a vague sense of impending doom. It troubled me greatly, though I spoke of it to no one.

At such times, having the Gifts proved frustrating...and slightly disturbing, especially when I had no particular reason for my sudden epiphanies. Had I truly experienced a premonition, or was my feeling simply the product of imagination? And if I were to warn them, what was I to warn them of?

After such a late start, we pressed onward throughout the morning and early afternoon, stopping only for one brief respite until we came to the deer path that veered through the substantially smaller bog, having had little rainwater to feed it over the previous month. After passing the cottage of Kiril's uncle, Leoric, and crossing the two bridges that spanned the river south of town, I had to resist the urge to go galloping off in the direction of the cottage at the edge of the woods. There would be time enough to see Loralon later.

My traveling companions and I came to the Baeren Ford Road, glancing cautiously to the north and south, though there were no visible signs of the enemy in either direction. We slipped across and into the woods to the west, heading along the trail that led to Eliendor's cottage. When we arrived, it relieved me to find the lore master outside, pruning dead, fruitless branches off a cherry tree and throwing them onto a small fire in the corner of his yard while Talthos, the raven, performed his own bit of weeding nearby.

Eliendor looked up as we approached, seeming not the least bit surprised by our sudden appearance, though his eyes twinkled with delight when his gaze landed on Valdir and the three unlikely mortal men who accompanied us.

"Bless my soul!" he exclaimed, rising to his feet. "If this is not a welcome meeting!"

The elven lord dismounted and walked over to Eliendor, where he clasped the old man's hand in the fashion of elves and gave him a warm pat on the back. "How long has it been, my friend?"

"Much too long!" Eliendor replied.

"And I see you are still looking rather old, at that!"

What an odd thing to say! But even odder was Eliendor's response, for he practically burst into a giddy kind of laughter I had never seen from the normally stoic man. I didn't know what had gotten into him. Even Galamir looked stunned.

"Ah, yes, well the clock has yet to rewind," Eliendor said, glancing in my direction, at which time his expression turned to one of relief. "Arwyn, it pleases me that you have safely made the journey to Loth Gerodin and back again."

"Yes, though it seems a curious black bird kept appearing, and I wondered if you had sent Talthos to keep me in line," I said accusingly as I dismounted.

"You would be surprised how far the eyes of Talthos can see," Eliendor replied, with no further explanation. "I knew you were in good hands with Galamir at your side, though such explains neither the presence of my old friend, Valdir, nor of the other gentlemen who have accompanied you. To what do I owe this pleasure?"

Taking the lead, Allynon walked up to Eliendor and bowed. "Master Eliendor, please allow me to introduce myself," he began. "I am Allynon, son of King Ignathius of Endara, and these are two of my ship's crew, Inago and Endegar."

"Greetings, one and all," Eliendor replied thoughtfully. "Ignathius…yes, I have heard Valdir mention your kin on various occasions. Your father is a man of great honor, from what I understand."

"Yes, but sadly, on his deathbed he now lies. Several weeks past, my ship docked in Maldimire, from whence we traveled to Loth Gerodin on a mission to bring Valdir to Endara so, before the end, my father may see his dear friend once more."

"I am truly sorry. It grieves me to hear such news."

"Yes, all of Endara shall grieve his passing," Allynon said, to which everyone standing around nodded with concurrence.

"But that is not the only news," I said after a moment, walking up to stand beside Allynon. All at once, my stomach began to churn, so much it felt like I was bringing my intended to meet my father for the first time. I truly hoped my news would please him, yet I suddenly found it quite difficult to speak, so choked with emotion I was.

"Master Eliendor, I came to Loth Gerodin on a mission of my father, yet little did I expect to meet Arwyn on my journey." Allynon took my hand in his and stared into my eyes. "She is the most enchanting woman I have ever met, and never will my heart be the same for it." I held my breath for what was to come next. "She has agreed to marry me."

Eliendor stood silent and motionless for several moments, as if he were in shock. Endegar and Inago shifted their weight uneasily in the interim.

"This is…quite an unexpected turn of events," Eliendor said at last, eyes fixated in an almost accusatory manner on Valdir, of all people.

Valdir cleared his throat. "Though you must understand, dear friend, Arwyn feels rather *compelled* to remain in Bensor to help with the cause of the Alliance until such a day as Allynon can return to wed her."

I am not certain Eliendor had taken a breath in those few moments, yet upon hearing Valdir's words, his chest heaved with apparent relief.

"That is most wise," he replied. "If your love is true, then it will stand to the months of separation and the tests that will surely come."

Eliendor then did something quite unexpected, positioning himself right in front of Allynon and putting his hands on either side of Allynon's head, staring intently into his eyes. "Is Arwyn alone your heart's desire?"

Allynon did not flinch. "Arwyn's happiness is my heart's desire."

For another long moment Eliendor stared, searching, and I knew he was peering into Allynon's heart. "You fear for her."

"Yes," Allynon admitted. "For her to remain in Bensor at such a time grieves me."

"And though you doubt her decision to remain, you are prepared to bid her farewell when you leave Baeren Ford tomorrow."

"Tomorrow?" I exclaimed, feeling as though someone had punched me in the stomach. I was barely prepared to bid Allynon "farewell" two days hence when he would board his ship, much less the following morning.

"Surely you did not expect to accompany Allynon to the lair of the enemy, especially after your escapade there last fall?" Eliendor argued.

"I had hoped to do so somehow, though in my heart I know it unwise," I admitted.

"Arwyn, I am not entirely certain your exploits with the dwarves have not aroused suspicion in your direction. Loralon came for a visit soon after you left. It seems two of Draigon's lieutenants had come through, intent on discovering your whereabouts. Gave her quite a scare, they did."

"And?"

"She tried to convince them you had gone for good, back to your 'kin' in the northern forest."

So, I was still being treated like a criminal, but then I suppose that was what I was in their eyes. It was enough to make my knees go weak.

"Then, perhaps Arwyn *should* go to Maldimire and make a spectacle of boarding Allynon's ship and, in fact, set sail, leading them to believe she has indeed gone for good before doubling back to…say, Galymara."

We all looked over at Valdir, who had spoken, but it was Galamir's face that brightened at the possibility. "Where I will be waiting with the horses!"

"Endegar, he shall go with you."

The young man twisted his head to stare at Allynon.

"Managing two extra horses alone would be difficult, even for an elf, yes?" Allynon added. "Having a mortal go along would further keep you from drawing attention as a lone elf traveling through Guilden."

For a moment, we all grew silent, pondering the possibilities of this latest scheme.

"A bit risky, yet it may work, at that!" Valdir exclaimed.

I looked over at Eliendor, who was eyeing the elven lord dubiously. Valdir and he then exchanged a peculiar look as if they were in some sort of conspiracy. "I will make certain she disembarks safely in Galymara," Valdir commented pointedly to Eliendor, as if he had just read the old man's mind.

Eliendor shook his head as he gazed up at me. "You certainly have a way of complicating matters."

"Er, Eliendor, I've never seen your garden look so beautiful," I said in an attempt to change the subject. But the truth was, after traveling through countryside noticeably affected by drought, the fact that Eliendor's garden flourished with an abundance of springtime colors was quite remarkable.

"Ah, spring," he replied with a spark of delight in his ancient eyes. "'Tis my favorite time of year. A time when that which seemed dead comes alive again."

Everyone else concurred, glancing around and commenting on the glorious spectacle of nature before us—everyone but Valdir, who I found gazing quietly in my direction. When our eyes met, he looked away only to find Eliendor's gaze upon him, narrow and perceiving, causing the elven lord to lower his eyes as a momentary look of sorrow and shame crossed his features. "My dear friend, we certainly have much to discuss after so long an absence," Eliendor commented pointedly, and with what I thought was an air of compassion.

Valdir smiled briefly and nodded. Whatever had been plaguing the elven lord, I truly hoped Eliendor could say something to bring him peace.

***

Allynon and I soon took leave of our traveling

companions and headed in the direction of town.

I smiled as we emerged from the woods and gazed upon the familiar scene of the valley that had happily changed little in my absence. Anxiously I led Allynon down the lane to the cottage at the edge of the village and to the stable's entrance. There we dismounted and tied our horses to the hitching post outside, Allynon all the while surveying the cottage with interest.

"Your home, it is charming," he said.

"It is small but comfortable," I replied, glancing around the garden and front lawn. "It seems Frondamein has been home recently. Everything appears quite tidy. It would be surprising for Loralon to have seen to it all on her own with a toddler in tow. Come," I said, taking Allynon's hand as my stomach tightened with excitement, "let us go and find her."

"Uneasy I feel to meet those who are like family to you." Allynon shuddered. "Eliendor, well, it felt as though he was looking into my soul."

"Yes, he has a way of doing that. Though I don't believe you'll have difficulty meeting Frondamein and Loralon's approval," I said as I stepped up to the front door and turned the knob. "Funny, but the door is not usually locked." Softly I rapped upon the wooden door, feeling suddenly uneasy. I looked at the window and noticed the curtains had been drawn. After a moment I heard footsteps on the other side.

"Who is it?" came a muffled voice.

"It is Arwyn. I have returned!"

The door flew open, and Loralon stood there with a broad smile upon her face. "Arwyn, at last!" she cried, as she reached to embrace me. "I'd waited so long, I was afraid ye'd not be retairnin' at all."

"Nonsense! You know I could not stay away forever."

"Ah-wyn!" came a tiny voice from inside the house. I knelt down as a small child with flaming red hair like his mother's ran across the floor and into my waiting arms. I stood up and twirled him around, smothering his face with kisses.

"Amerigo! What a little man you've become," I said excitedly. "How I have missed you—how I have missed you both!"

Loralon became suddenly quiet as she noticed the tall, dark-haired man standing outside her door. He was smiling at her, and based on the quizzical expression on her face, I could tell she was trying to determine what on earth he was doing there.

"Loralon, there is someone I very much want for you to meet," I said, stepping aside. "I would like to introduce you to Allynon of Endara. Allynon, I would like you to meet Loralon of Baeren Ford."

"A pleasure it is to meet you at last," Allynon said as he bent over to kiss Loralon's hand. "Arwyn has told me much about you."

Loralon's face turned crimson. "My, 'tis a long journey what brought ye here from Endara," she stammered.

"Yes, it was long indeed."

"I met Allynon in Loth Gerodin. He was there on official business for King Ignathius," I explained.

"Ah, ye kin pull the wool o'er me eyes some o' the time," Loralon said, glancing quickly at me, "but seein' ye there, I knew ye wairn't elvish, though I would've expected ye to be, what with the company Arwyn's keepin' these days."

"In truth, I am one-quarter elvish, at the very least," Allynon replied. "My grandmother, she was elf-kind, and through my father's line I have several elvish ancestors, though you are quite perceptive to see that mortal blood does run strongest through my veins."

Loralon raised an eyebrow as she looked first at Allynon and then at me. "Now, 'ow is it 'e come all the way to Loth Gerodin on official business o' the king, only to wind up 'ere in Baeren Ford?" she asked curiously.

The smile on Allynon's face grew, yet he looked to me to take the lead. "Come, let us go inside first and all will be explained," I said.

"Where are me manners? Aye, there's no sense in the whole o' Baeren Ford 'earin' yer business," Loralon said. "Do step into the parlor."

Allynon followed as I walked inside the cottage, besieged by the familiar scent of lavender I had so missed over that past month. I lowered Amerigo to the floor to play, but I could tell Loralon's curiosity was about to overflow. Suddenly, seeing the two people I loved most standing together in my home was more than I could bear, and tears of joy began to flow down my cheeks.

"Arwyn, are ye alright, dear?" Loralon began to ask, when suddenly her eyes grew wide as she first noticed the bluish-green jewel hanging around my neck. I had not felt comfortable flaunting the expensive necklace, yet when I wore low-cut necklines, there was no way to keep it subdued, and I had refused to take it from around my neck during our journey for fear of losing the precious gift. "Arwyn, the jewel 'round yer neck—why, ne'er 'ave I seen anythin' like it. It must be wairth a fortune! Where did ye e'er get such a thin'?" Loralon exclaimed.

"It was a gift from me," Allynon said gently as he took my hand.

"Ah, I could tell it, I could, that ye fancy Arwyn," Loralon said as her eyes began to mist. "Could see it in the way ye look at each other."

"Loralon, though on a mission from King Ignathius, what I found in Loth Gerodin was a great and unexpected treasure, more precious even than this stone," Allynon said poignantly. "When I met Arwyn there in the forest, I knew in my heart I would never be the same, and I am indeed fortunate she has come to love me as well and has agreed to be my wife."

Tears flowed from Loralon's eyes as she listened to Allynon's words, followed by a cry of excitement. "Bless me soul, Arwyn's to be married!" she exclaimed as she rushed to embrace me. "Arwyn, 'ow lucky ye are! Why, no man's brought me to tears so since Frondamein asked me to be 'is wife—and what a handsome one 'e is at that!" Loralon winked.

Suddenly the young woman stopped talking and a look of sadness swept over her face. "Tch! I suppose this means ye'll be leavin' us for Endara," she said quietly.

I reached out and took Loralon's hand. "No, I shall not be leaving Bensor," I said soberly. "This is where my duty lies."

Loralon shook her head, almost as if she were willing herself to protest. "Nay, yer duty here is done! Ye must go now with yer love. I'd only have wished Frondamein could've seen ye one last time, but 'e just left o'er a week ago for the Gate. He'll not return for a month."

"No, you don't understand. My duty *to Bensor* is not done. Were I to try and leave its shores, I know I would regret it deeply." I looked to Allynon, but his eyes were downcast and he remained silent.

"But what life 'ave ye here?"

"Loralon, I know you do not completely understand, and in truth, neither do I. But I have made a promise to help bring about healing and reconciliation in this land, and there are those who seem to think I alone am in a unique position to do so, living among mortals as I do." I smiled weakly, trying to be brave, all the while wishing we coud leap forward to the time when the rebellion would be done and all would be made right.

Loralon looked at Allynon with tears in her eyes. "Ne'er 'ave I heard anythin' so sad in all me days," she said at last.

"Let us not dwell on sadness, at least not for now, or I shan't be able to stand it," I said. "On the morrow we leave for Maldimire. There I will board Allynon's ship and make it appear as though I am leaving Bensor for good, for I hear Draigon's minions have been looking for me."

"Aye."

"We will then sail to Galymara, where Galamir will meet

me and see me safely home."

"Galymara? Why, ye kin stay with Frondamein's sister, Maerta, and 'er 'usband, Fergil!"

"I've heard so much about them—I should like to finally meet them," I said. "But, come, I have so much to tell you from my journey, so many wondrous places I have been and things I have seen that I wish to share with you."

Loralon's face brightened. "I kin only imagine what grand stories ye have to tell. Now sit yerselves down and tell me all while I prepare the evenin' meal."

Allynon gently took hold of Loralon's arm and guided her to the settee. "Please sit here with us. Arwyn tells me the food at the Blue Willow is still good, as is their ale, and I would be honored if you both, and Amerigo, of course, would accompany me there this eve."

The look on Loralon's face was pleased. "So ye've been to our fair village afore, 'ave ye?"

"Years ago I visited when I came to see Arnuin's Hold. So taken I was with the story of Elwei and Arnuin, I had to see it for myself."

"That pile o' rocks," Loralon shrugged. "Seems all 'tis good for now is a place for the children to play, although I know Arwyn's taken to it."

"Perhaps she will take me there after dinner, yes?" Allynon said, glancing at me with a smile. "I should like to see it again."

Little Amerigo, who had remained close to his mother's skirt, stared shyly at the stranger. Suddenly he saw the shiny hilt of Allynon's sword and, overcoming his shyness, went to investigate. Allynon picked up the child and placed him on his lap, letting him run his fingers along its artful workmanship. It was not long before the toddler warmed to Allynon and was proudly bringing him all sorts of odds and ends for his perusal. Allynon was quick to humor the child and asked him all manner of questions about the objects, to which he sometimes received amusing one-word answers.

Loralon looked on with approval as she watched the rather stately, masculine man reduced to a pretend horse on which her son climbed, squealing with laughter.

All the while, she listened intently as I described in detail my journey to Isgilith, the marvels of the elven city, and finally how Allynon and I came to meet and fall in love, yet I was not completely forthcoming regarding Allynon's true identity. It was one thing for Loralon to know but quite another for the other villagers.

Nay, I would wait to tell Loralon when the time was right.

CHAPTER 22

"Glad I am Allynon is a man of honor," I said, vaguely aware of the heat creeping upon my face. "By a mere glance into his dark eyes, a touch of his hand upon my skin, a kiss from his lips, and I am tempted to relinquish all thought of virtue."

It was late in the afternoon when Allynon suggested we depart for the Blue Willow. After such a late breakfast, we had not bothered to stop for lunch along the road, and we were both starting to feel emptiness in our bellies. With Amerigo riding upon his shoulders, Allynon escorted Loralon and me up the road to the tavern.

"My, Mr. Allynon, ye've certainly got yerself a way with the wee ones," Loralon commented, as we walked along.

"With two older brothers and an older sister, I have several nieces and nephews to keep me entertained when I am home."

"A large family ye have, do ye?" Loralon said. "They must miss ye somethin' terrible when ye're gone."

"Yes, and I miss them as well," Allynon replied.

I remained silent as we walked along the road. Being reminded of Allynon's great fondness for his family made me wonder once again if it were too much to ask him to leave his homeland to marry me, and the thought left me with an apprehensive feeling in the pit of my stomach.

Many of the villagers had already gathered at the Blue Willow for the evening, yet we were able to slip in and take a seat in one of the small dining areas flanking the more central one. Loralon had informed me there had been several rumors circulating as to my whereabouts those past few weeks, but it was generally assumed I had returned to live with my kind in the northern forest. My sudden reappearance in the tavern was therefore cause for a wave of murmurings to spread throughout the gathering, and rumors continued to emerge in the coming days of my unexpected return with the rather human-looking "elf lord."

As we sat around the table attempting to ignore the stares of the fellow tavern-goers, our conversation was interrupted by the sound of a familiar voice.

"Miss Arwyn, ye've retairned!"

I looked up to see Kiril, with four frothy mugs in his hands. "That I have, and how good it is to see you, my friend!" I replied warmly.

Kiril leaned closer and whispered. "Say, did our scheme with them dwarves turn out as planned?"

"Yes," I answered, also in a whisper. "They have safely returned to the Andains, thanks to your help."

"Ah, this must be Kiril, whom I have heard so much about," Allynon said heartily.

"Don't believe I've 'ad the pleasure," Kiril responded cautiously.

"Kiril, I would like you to meet Allynon of Endara. I met Allynon during my visit with the elves," I explained.

Kiril eyed the newcomer suspiciously. "Beggin' yer pardon, sir, but ye don't look much like an elf."

"So I have already been reminded of once today," Allynon said, as he winked at Loralon.

"Arwyn and Mister Allynon are to be wed!" Loralon blurted out. Silence descended upon the table, and several sitting nearby overheard the comment, sending another wave of murmurings spreading throughout the tavern.

Kiril's face turned a bright shade of red. "Er, if ye'll excuse me, I've got to see to me duties," he stammered, and walked away.

"I do not believe I made much of an impression," Allynon said.

"Not to worry," I replied. "He's quite protective, though I would imagine he'll come around in time."

"That I hope. I would hate to think we could not be wed

until all your many friends approved our union." Allynon laughed.

Kiril returned to the table several times over the course of the evening to deliver food and drink. Allynon responded to him in his warm, congenial manner until at last Kiril pulled up a chair to chat as business began to die down for the evening. With all the excitement and interest surrounding my visit with the elves and sudden return with the mysterious stranger, there had been little discussion on the happenings in town over the course of my journey.

"What has come to pass in Baeren Ford during my absence?" I asked, finally breaching the subject.

Kiril hesitated for a moment as he glanced toward Allynon. "I've not seen it meself, but they say them what's in Draigon's service 'ave built a fort o' sorts to the south, off the main road. Why is anyone's guess."

My mind returned to the previous fall and our return from Maldimire when we came upon a place in the woods that Draigon's minions appeared to be in the process of clearing. "Since ye left, seems they pass through but 'ave no cause to linger, thanks be," Loralon added. "But still, it's like they're up to somethin'."

"Aye, they were in 'ere right after ye left, askin' about the elven woman who lived up the road. Told 'em ye'd gone north for good, I did," Kiril said. "But I suppose ye'll now be goin' off to some far distant land where ye'll 'ave not a care."

I glanced at Allynon, whose brow had furrowed into a frown. "No," I said slowly, "I will remain in Bensor until such a time Allynon can return for me." Even as I spoke the words, I felt my heart sink and wondered if I should indeed simply sail off into the west.

"Ye're not leavin'!" Kiril exclaimed with obvious excitement. He then caught himself and attempted to calm his voice. "What I mean is, well, ye're the best 'ealer this town's e'er seen. All the folks know it, e'en them what blamed ye for all the troubles a while back, and I'd daresay e'en they've missed ye since ye've been gone."

"I will not abandon you," I replied quietly, wishing to change the subject.

For a while longer we sat and talked until Allynon looked at the growing darkness outside and suggested we make for Arnuin's Hold before the hour grew too late. Standing up, he withdrew a small pouch from his tunic that jingled as he reached in for two coins to give Kiril.

I watched as Loralon peeked into the pouch, where she saw more than a few pieces of gold.

Quietly she leaned over and whispered to me as Allynon saw to the charge for the meal. "'Andsome *and* a man o' means! Why Arwyn, you've got yerself quite a man there," she exclaimed.

"But of even greater consequence is that he is a *good* man—as good a man as your Frondamein," I replied.

"Ah, well then, ye've been blessed beyond measure, ye have."

"I will consider myself even more blessed after we are wed."

"Aye, what a pity ye must wait so long. 'Tis 'ard when ye're in love and must be parted—'tis like there's a hollow place in yer soul what grows more with each passin' day."

"Perhaps we can lean on each other at such a time," I said.

"Miss Loralon, Mister Allynon 'ere's asked me to escort ye home," Kiril said.

"Aye, go now to the Hold," Loralon said. "Spend some time alone together afore ye be parted."

Just as I was about to walk through the front door of the tavern, Kiril stopped and pulled me to the side. "Might I have a word with ye?"

"Yes, Kiril," I said as I moved out of the way to let Loralon and Allynon pass through the door. "What is on your mind, or can I already guess the nature of your concern?"

Kiril glanced outside the tavern to make sure we were out of earshot of Allynon. "Miss Arwyn, are ye sure ye know this Allynon fella well? I mean, are ye sure he's *wairthy* o' ye."

I tried to stifle the smile creeping onto my lips. "Yes, I am quite sure of it."

"It's just, well, ye canna be too sure o' strangers these days," he stammered.

"For good reason you should feel that way, yet I can assure you Allynon is a man of honor," I said gently. "You need not fear for me."

Kiril looked into my eyes and seemed to find the reassurance there he needed. "Verra well, then I shall be happy for ye," he said as he turned toward the door.

"Kiril, I just saw a friend of yours," I mentioned casually. "Oh?"

"Rumalia sends greetings."

Kiril turned his head quickly, and I thought I could detect blood rising to his cheeks.

"Is she well?" he asked.

"Yes, she's doing quite well actually."

The two of us walked outside to the road where Allynon and I took our leave of Kiril and Loralon and headed, hand in hand, in the direction of Arnuin's Hold.

"Your friends, they are quite loyal to you, no?" Allynon commented as we walked along.

"And I to them," I added quickly. "They are like family to me, the only family I have known these past three years."

The last light of day was fading into the dark void of night as we passed beneath the ancient walls of the Hold. I led Allynon through the maze of ruins, up the hill to the crumbled building and the Circle of Omni.

"I come here often when I need to renew my spirit," I said, glancing up—beyond the four towering walls surrounding us—into the night sky. "The peace and tranquility I find here stirs my soul as nothing else."

"When first I stepped between these walls many years ago, I remember how it affected me the same," Allynon commented. "It is like it still holds the spirit of those who once roamed its halls. If you listen closely enough, it almost feels as though you could hear its very stones whispering." He stopped and looked at me, though I had grown suddenly quiet. "Come, let us linger here a while. We have had such little time alone these past few days."

I nodded and sank to the grassy carpet, noticing the slight wince on Allynon's face as he sat down beside me.

"With all the excitement of the day I'm afraid I've not thought of your wound, though you've appeared to be on the mend," I said. "Let me see how you're faring."

Obediently, Allynon removed his tunic. Even in the dim light of dusk I could see the bruise did not appear as dark and angry as it had even two days before.

"The pain, it has eased a great deal," Allynon said. "It seems your medicine is working."

I placed my hand gingerly on his ribs. To feel his bare skin beneath my fingers and to smell his masculine scent so close was irresistible, and I found my hand straying across the coarse hair of his chest to the base of his neck, where I felt the rumble of a moan rising to his lips. With eyes burning with desire, he stared at me, and my mouth found his, open and waiting eagerly for mine.

What if we were never reunited? This could be my only chance to know him in *every* way.

Allynon wrapped his arms around me and gently lowered me to the ground. For a moment, he gazed into my welcoming eyes. "Oh, woman, how I want you!" he whispered into my ear, the sensation of his hot breath upon my earlobe sending delicious tremors through my body like a wave.

I let out a moan as Allynon tasted the soft flesh of my neck, slowly traveling down its long sinews, down past the place where the bluish-green jewel lay upon my chest to the mounds below. My body rose to meet his as my fingers plunged into the dark locks of his hair, causing them to become unfettered and to fall loosely about his face.

I held my breath for a moment. Did I really want our first time together to be tinged with the guilt of leading a good man to act against his conscience? Of giving my virtue away to a man who was not yet completely mine?

My internal debate raged on before I realized Allynon had raised up and was sitting, trembling, beside me. I sat up and looked at him questioningly until he finally spoke.

"Arwyn, every ounce of my body *aches* to know that of yours, but I shall do what is honorable and wait until we are properly wed."

I sat there silently, not knowing whether to feel disappointed...or relieved.

"Arwyn," he said slowly, "there is something about you, something I dare not dishonor. And even were it not for that...I feel I must somehow atone for my grievous error of the past. And that is why I cannot."

"Then let us be wed," I said, half-seriously and half in jest.

Allynon took my hand in his and kissed it, though the expression on his face remained solemn. "To leave you is difficult enough. If you were my wife, I could not leave you, and certainly not if there were any possibility you carried our child."

I looked away mournfully. "I pray you will forgive my weakness. 'Twas foolish to light a fire only to extinguish it."

"Nothing there is to forgive. After all, long before now that fire had been lit," Allynon said, with a smile. He remained quiet for a moment, and it seemed to me he hesitated to speak. "There is another way," he said tentatively. "The day after tomorrow, you could always board my ship and sail away with me to Endara where we will be wed in splendor."

"You know I cannot," I said defiantly, rising to my feet.

"Woman, you are stubborn!" Allynon argued vigorously as he followed suit. "Nothing there is for you here—nothing but a crumbling dream falling down about you piece by piece! Try as you may, one person cannot put Bensor back together."

I stood with my back to him for a moment as tears came dangerously close to erupting. "What of you, with all your talk of honor?" I said quietly. "Would you abandon your friends at such a time?"

The sound of silence echoed within the ancient walls until I felt a familiar warmth surrounding me. With his strong arms, Allynon enfolded me, and we stood silently there in the dark.

"It is that I worry for you so," he said at last. "I worry that when I return for you, all I will find is a pile of ash, and you gone…or worse. Who knows what evil Draigon has in store, and my dreams, they are plagued with fear for you."

"And I worry you will not return at all," I admitted, surprising myself with the raw honesty of my words. "That you will be reminded of your love for Endara and choose to remain there with your kin," I said passionately, as tears began to stream down my face. "I could certainly not cast blame if you were to choose that path. I know what I ask of you is too great a price for anyone to pay."

Allynon placed his hands on my shoulders and turned me around. The look on his face was unyielding as he gripped my arms and looked me in the eye. "Hear me now, Arwyn," he said, eyes burning with resolve. "With all my heart, I love you. To the ends of the earth, I would go if that is what it takes to be with you. Even if I must scale the very lair of the unspeakable one to the north, I would do so. So do not think for one moment anything barring death would prevent me from returning for you."

"I'm sorry," I cried. "I am so sorry things are as they are. What I wouldn't give if they were different."

"Yes," Allynon said as he drew me to him. He kissed my

forehead tenderly as tears flowed down his own cheeks. "The die, it has been cast. Somehow, some way we can only trust Omni will bring us together again."

CHAPTER 23

"I take a great risk to travel to the lair of Draigon."
"Is it worth the risk?" asked Dr. Susan.
"To gain more precious days with Allynon—yes. To succeed in deceiving my enemies—yes," I replied, my hands twitching with trepidation. "Yet if our plan fails, then there is nothing that would have made it worth the risk."

Early the next morning, I climbed down the loft ladder with my traveling bag, now much lighter than in recent days, into a quiet parlor where Allynon stood rolling up his sleeping blankets. I was beginning to wonder where Loralon was when I heard the unmistakable sound of Inago's voice booming across the front lawn.

"Dear lady, would it please you to inform de Prince Allynon and de Lady Arwyn of our arrival?"

I looked outside the front window in time to see Loralon at the well, staring with her mouth wide open at the unlikely group of visitors—the young, debonair, fair-haired elf and the ancient elf in the long, flowing robe of shining burgundy who sported long, fine hair dappled with streaks of gray and a face shimmering with unearthly beauty; two humans, one with a bright blue quill sticking out his broad-rimmed hat, who had the look of a cad in his gleaming eyes, and a dark-skinned man with exotic, brightly colored cloth wrapped loosely around muscles that looked strong enough to choke the horse on which he sat. I couldn't help but smile.

"I...beg yer pardon?" I could hear her stammer.

"De Prince Allynon," Inago repeated patiently. "Please inform His Highness dat we be here."

Without a word, Loralon turned and ran to the front door, dropping the pail of water on the way. She rushed into the cottage to find Allynon putting the last of his belongings into his travel bag. Awkwardly, she walked up to him and bowed to the floor.

"Your Highness, welcome to me...er, *my* humble home," she said, her voice shaking as she carefully pronounced each syllable.

"Please, there is no need," Allynon said, as he touched her gently on the shoulder.

"If I'd 'ave known I'd be entertainin' royalty, I'd 'ave 'ad a more proper welcome, me lord, given ye a more suitable place to rest yer 'ead at least."

"As it was, I slept like a baby," Allynon smiled, "and a most gracious hostess you have been."

Loralon turned to me with a look of exasperation. "Ye didna inform me ye'd brought a prince under me roof, and I'd not prepared a lick!" she scolded. Her furrowed brow turned to a smile as she gave me a hearty embrace. "Arwyn's to marry a prince. Why, a princess ye'll be!"

"Yes, not that it will be of much consequence here in Bensor." I shrugged. "I shall be happy enough to be Allynon's wife. However, I think it best to keep this in confidence. I do not think it wise for such news to reach the wrong ears."

"As ye wish," Loralon said reluctantly. "Though I've a mind to prove 'em wrong, them in the village what told me several years ago takin' in a stranger, an elf at that, would only cause problems."

I gave my friend a sidelong glance. Loralon had confirmed my suspicions, but I had to admit they had been partially right about my penchant for trouble or, at least, my proclivity for exploring all opportunities, as I liked to think of it. Loralon's eyes grew wide. "Oh, but I'm forgettin' meself. There's some gentlemen awaits ye both outside."

"That I assumed, seeing as how my secret has been discovered." Allynon grinned.

Allynon and I were saddling our horses for the journey when Loralon walked inside the barn, Amerigo trailing closely behind his mother's skirt. "Give this to Maerta," she said, handing me an envelope sealed with wax.

I nodded. "Yes, it's not as though we can call ahead and let her know we're coming."

Allynon and Loralon stopped what they were doing to stare at me. "Just a bit of my, er, *weirdfulness*," I explained, with an embarrased smile.

"Accordin' to Frondamein, she and Fergil live on a quiet cove east o' the village, below the cliffs. At the end of a row o' fishermens' 'ouses, ye'll find a white one what ye enter through a courtyard."

"That sounds simple enough."

"Aye." Loralon sighed. "Do send 'er greetin's. 'Ow we wished to go for a visit ourselves, but I've little 'ope of it."

"Chin up, Loralon. Perhaps you will, sooner than you think," I replied, trying to be optimistic.

"Aye, we kin always 'ope, we kin."

Loralon followed us out the barn door, Amerigo in her arms, and I introduced her to my new friends, her round eyes bulging as she stared with unrestrained amazement at the unlikely assemblage.

"Waird 'as it, the place where the East Road meets the road to Maldimire's bein' watched," Loralon warned. "Ye'd best avoid it, if ye kin."

"Very well," Valdir said with a nod. "We shall take that under advisement and avoid it at all costs."

"And the fort, as well," I added.

"The fort?" Galamir asked.

"It seems Draigon has built an outpost about twenty miles south of here, though for what reason is anyone's guess."

Galamir was quiet for a moment, working through the possibilities in his head. "'Twould be too far out of the way to take another road."

"For much too long already, I have been away from my ship," Allynon lamented. "Time, it is pressing."

"Then we shall have to go around."

"I believe I could recognize the area before we come upon it," I offered.

"That will have to do, though 'twill be a nuisance to go off through the woods without benefit of a path. But I suppose, 'tis better than our other options." Galamir clicked his tongue at Calyxa. "We'd best be underway."

I started to mount Avencloe but, catching myself, turned to embrace Loralon before leaving.

"I wouldna blame ye if ye sail away to Endara day after tomorrow," she whispered in my ear. I knew she was trying to be brave, but her quivering voice betrayed her true feelings.

Was I really strong enough to let Allynon sail into the west without me? I hadn't truly convinced myself I was.

The thought sent a convulsive sob from the pit of my stomach, up my throat where it became lodged, feeling as though it would choke me. I clung to Loralon, my wet tears falling into her hair. If I wasn't, this would be the last time I would ever see her, Amerigo, and the valley beneath Arnuin's Hold.

I couldn't speak.

Tenderly I kissed Loralon on the cheek and Amerigo on his forehead, wondering if this was truly the end.

Determined to not let my eyes betray my heart's distress, I quickly wiped the tears from my eyes with Rohana's handkerchief. I could not bear to look upon Loralon's tearful eyes a moment longer, or my heart would be torn in two even more than it already was.

I tried to force the lump in my throat back down into my gut as I mounted Avencloe, but it remained, burning, convicting me of my heart's guilty longings and the torment that would follow should I heed them.

Without looking back, we headed into the woods to the south and then took a sharp turn east, across the river, and onto the deerpath. In a while, we came to the East Road, and, seeing no one in either direction, ducked into the woods to the south, heading in a generally southwestern direction through the bush. Our going was slowed, but we eventually emerged on the road to Maldimire more than a mile from the checkpoint.

On we rode to the south for a while, closer to the mysterious encampment we knew lay ahead. I thought for certain I would recognize our surroundings in time for us to skirt off the road before we reached it, yet when we rapidly came upon a wasteland of felled trees where a forest had recently stood, I was so disoriented that we were not able to avoid it. We were exposed, out in the open, yet even before we had the opportunity to discuss our options, Endegar gave a low whistle from behind.

"We've company," he muttered.

I resisted the urge to look back.

"How many?" Galamir said calmly.

"Three."

"How far behind us?"

"Two hundred yards," Endegar replied, "too close to make for the woods and circumnavigate this place without drawing considerable attention to ourselves."

"Then we press onward and hope our numbers discourage them from any mischief," Valdir said, but I could see his body tense as he fingered his hilt.

My heart sank as we rode through the once-lush landscape, now stripped of all vegetation. Men and Gargalocs were going about, hacking to pieces felled trees in a clearing littered with ugly tree stumps. We pressed onward, though no one seemed to pay us any mind. Nearby a dozen or so workhorses pulled carts bearing large logs behind them. Beyond the clearing and set farther back from the road was an area several acres in size that was surrounded by a high fence, behind which came the sound of sawing and hammering.

The sense of secrecy surrounding the place evoked an eerie feeling as several men in gray stood about, guarding its borders. The company stared silently as we hurried to pass it by, and I was suddenly reminded of a similar sight I had witnessed in Stone Harbour. What sort of devilry was going on in secret inside those fortresses?

By some fortune, we passed by without incident, yet several more times that day we passed groups of men clad in gray, each so consumed with their business they barely gave us a second glance. Although this in itself was fortunate, there was something about it that also felt slightly disturbing. What distracted them so?

Yet what most surprised me about our journey was Valdir's sudden willingness to engage me in conversation during our less guarded moments—mostly concerning the weather and other inconsequential matters. According to Galamir, he had spent half the night in deep conversation with Eliendor, and I wondered if anything the lore master said had brought about the sudden change. I could still detect in him a twinge of sadness, but he overall seemed more at peace, at least enough to push aside whatever had been plaguing him those past days.

Before darkness fell, we found the same grassy meadow I had camped in during my previous trip to Maldimire and settled in for the night behind the rocky knoll and away from prying eyes. Soon we sparked a fire, and everyone sat around consuming the provisions offered by both Loralon and Eliendor.

As I helped to clean the campsite after our meal, Allynon bade Galamir to follow him to the edge of the gathering place. The look on his face was serious, and it had seemed to me he had been preoccupied throughout the day, though there was no doubt as to the reason for his melancholy mood. I watched them on the edge of the firelight, and they were just far enough away to make it difficult for me to hear them, though I wondered what they were discussing. I could only guess, by the way they took turns glancing in my direction, that it had to do with me, and I saw Allynon hand Galamir his pouch of coins, which the elf promptly slipped into the pocket of his tunic.

That night I slept with Allynon's arm around my waist, savoring the comfort of his presence for as long as I could. Nearby our friends rested, each taking turns throughout the night watching and listening to the darkness beyond the small fire. My rest, however, was broken from time to time by the disconcerting sound of wagons creaking by in the distance. What anyone could be doing traveling at such an hour was more than I could understand.

The following morning burst forth with a brilliant sunrise through the treetops to the east. It promised to be a warm day.

Allynon donned his stately royal blue garb, the same he had worn at Valdir's banquet the night before the Faerenfel. With Inago in his exotic-looking draped attire that accented his substantial brawn, they both looked like foreign dignitaries—no one to be trifled with.

We rode throughout the morning, stopping only briefly to rest the horses and eat lunch.

By midafternoon, we came to a road that branched off to the west, crossing the River Goldenreed only a few miles north of the city. It was there that we took our leave of Galamir and Endegar, but not before Valdir said a poignant goodbye to his mare, Willomane.

"You have carried me well, dear friend. Go now with Galamir, and find your way home," he said. "There wait for me until I someday return for you."

As Valdir mounted Endegar's rented horse, I reluctantly handed Avencloe's reins over to Galamir. "You must also go with Galamir to Galymara, and there wait for me until tomorrow when we shall be reunited," I explained. "He will care for you well until then."

"I will look after him as if he were my own," Galamir said, reassurance in his eyes.

"I've no doubt you will." I gave Avencloe one last stroke on his muzzle, feeling as though I was sending part of myself away. "May Omni go with all of you."

"And with you, until we meet on the morrow."

We watched as the three horses and two riders disappeared from sight over the bridge before I climbed atop Allynon's horse, hoping with all I had our scheme would work.

After all the shuffling of horses and riders, we set out once more to the south, me with my arms firmly around Allynon's waist. I was not the least accustomed to riding in such a manner, yet it was not long before we crested the hill that looked down upon our final destination. Maldimire looked much the same as it had when I visited the previous fall, at least from that vantage point. The sight of the sparkling city on the hill, beautiful though it was, still sent a chill down my spine as I remembered the ugly secrets beneath.

"It is a miracle we have made it this far," Valdir said pensively as he looked upon the city.

"The *Windsong*," Allynon said, with a smile, "you can see its mast above the buildings down on the bay. It is where I left it."

I stared down toward the place where the Silvendell emptied into the blue Eleuvial Sea and saw the masts of not one, but at least three tall ships. "How can you tell which is yours?"

"Like a mother knows her child, a captain knows his ship," Allynon said. "And what is more, you see the standard of Endara waving from its tallest mast, yes?"

I looked again and even my sharp eyes could barely make out a red and purple flag with the majestic bluish-green eagle crest of King Ignathius flapping in the ocean breezes. It was at that moment when I remembered the wave of sadness that had come upon me when I first looked upon the bay with its tall ships months before. It had been a harbinger of this very day, and I now knew why the sight of it had almost brought me to tears. There were times when it was very difficult to have this uncanny intuition, and yet, I also suspected I had best pay close attention to it.

We made our last ride together down onto the plain below and across to the northern gate of Maldimire. There we were met by guards who stopped all but local merchants. All at once I wished to disappear, yet I knew this entire ruse rested on leading the powers that be to believe I was leaving Bensor for good.

"Halt!" one of the chief guards demanded.

Not wishing to draw any more attention than was necessary, we came to an obedient standstill before the city gate.

"What business have you in Maldimire?" he asked with a sneer.

"I am Allynon, Prince of Endara, son of Ignathius, king of Endara, and captain of the *Windsong*. I have in my party the honorable Inago, emissary of the Kingdom of Shakracar, Master Orfindel of the Serenian Sea clan, and Lady Arwyn of Baeren Ford."

"That tell me who ye be, but what be yer business?" the guard said gruffly.

"Bensor no longer welcomes travelers from foreign lands, no?" Allynon said. "It was not so long ago when I did business in this very city without having to suffer an interrogation just to enter its gates."

"You are welcome here in our fair city, but not the elves," he added, his lip curled as he eyed Valdir and me.

"Gentlemen," Allynon began calmly, "with my bride and her kin, I shall board my ship and begone swiftly from this land. To do so peacefully is my wish, though should anyone hinder me, they shall answer to the king of Endara himself, and to an Endaran fleet awaiting me even now in the Straits of Eragoon. Quite certain, I am, that they would come swiftly and with great force should need arise." Allynon's hand went to the hilt of his substantial sword for added emphasis. "Does your master truly desire a visit from the Endaran navy?"

The guards stirred uncomfortably at the mention of the king and his naval fleet. Who would want to to incite a dispute with such a powerful country?

The captain of the guard turned and whispered to his comrades, who were all looking at Valdir and me in a way that did not make me feel at all comfortable. I then saw one of them slip away, through the gate. Had he gone to alert his master of our presence?

"Begone with ye, then," the captain said at last. "'Tis best ye see to yer business and leave for Endara by nightfall."

Allynon nodded and clicked his tongue at his horse. We all followed him through the gate, though instead of taking the road straight up and across the gorge into the center of the city, we turned on the road leading west along the bay. I was glad to be going away from the heart of the city. Almost suffocating it felt, a vulture looming over us, and I breathed much easier the deeper we rode into the cluster of buildings that hugged the bay of Maldimire. I would rather encounter a whole fleet of pirates and scalawag sailors in the back alleys of Maldimire than the dictator on the hill who was potentially seeking my demise.

"How many long years has it been since last I was here?"

I looked over at Valdir and could see a strange expression on his face that was a mixture of deep sorrow and unease.

"Lord Va...that is, *Master Orfindel*, how long *has* it been?" I asked, curious.

"Since the days soon after Draigon came to power," he replied. "I shall be glad when we are safely aboard the *Windsong*." He then looked back uneasily at the Palace of Lords. "You are not the only one against whom *he* holds a grudge."

I pondered Valdir's words, certain there must be quite a story there. Feeling ill at ease over the guard who had slipped away and what he was up to, I, also, wished to be safely aboard the *Windsong* and out to sea.

In recent years, the borders of Maldimire had stretched farther west across the Goldenreed and into the marshland where a hodgepodge of multicolored buildings had been built on a multitude of tiny islands, connected to each other with a series of bridges and canals. The place had a bad reputation, so frequented it was by pirates and others of ill repute. Still, I thought it would be a pleasant place should someone take a mind to clean it up.

We crossed the bridge over the Goldenreed and meandered through cobblestone streets, eventually emerging on a broad quay next to the bay. The air was thick with the smell of fish, and dozens of small fishing boats lined the quay with their morning catches for sale.

Keeping the water to our left, we followed the curve of the bay to the west. Eventually, the road crooked back into a maze of buildings, but it was not long before we crossed yet another bridge to one of the islands in the marsh, and I marveled that anyone had thought to build a city in such a place. We rounded a corner, where we were met with the sight of the *Windsong*, gently rocking to the steady rhythm of the swells entering the bay. Everywhere, people who had come from all over were going about on foot. Even Inago, notwithstanding his size, could easily blend in with so many from foreign lands.

The road ended at the wide jetty, next to which the *Windsong* was docked. As we approached the sailing vessel, I could see several men about the deck in various states of work and leisure. There was at least one swabbing the deck and another busily fumbling with a bunch of coiled ropes. One man fished from the bow, and another napped behind him, next to the bulwarks. Still others were sitting around playing some sort of dice game, while others were kicking a ball about the deck.

A lone crewman smoked a pipe on the starboard side of

the ship, looking over the bustling dock below. He saw us and blinked his eyes in disbelief. "It's...it's Master Allynon! He's returned!" he said excitedly. "The Master's returned with Inago!" he yelled.

Immediately all activity on board ceased as the crew rushed to stand at attention as Allynon dismounted. The crewman who had first spotted him, an older man with a ruddy complexion, ran down the gangplank to greet him.

"Bless you, Master Allynon! Inago!" he cried. "So long you have been gone, we feared the worst."

"Please forgive the delay, Pindarus. In Loth Gerodin, I encountered a...distraction," Allynon said, glancing at me.

"Your journey, it was successful?" Pindarus asked, glancing first at Valdir and then at me.

"More, even, than expected," Allynon replied, cutting his eyes to me with a smile. "All is well with the ship, I trust, and the crew, they have avoided trouble in Maldimire, yes?"

"Yes, sir. Everything is as you left it."

"Good. We must set sail in haste while we are able," Allynon said, glancing anxiously toward the city. "Now get the crew to work!"

"But, sir, where is Endegar?"

"Endegar, we will meet him tomorrow up the coast, but that I shall explain later," Allynon said with an air of authority. "Inago, return the horses and see that you get a good price for them."

"Aye, Your Highness."

"And the crew, they are all aboard?"

"Some are out carousing in the city."

"Find them and tell them to return to the ship or risk being left," Allynon commanded.

We gathered our belongings from the backs of the faithful horses that had carried Allynon, Inago, and Endegar so well those past weeks and made our way up the gangplank to the ship's deck.

By that time, all of the crew had gathered on deck to

witness their master's return, and judging by the smiles on their faces, they were relieved to see him and Inago. I could see the curiosity in their eyes as they noticed me, for surely they were not expecting Allynon to return with a woman in tow.

"We set sail by evening!" Pindarus yelled up at the crew. "Now get yourselves to work!"

"My lord Valdir," Allynon said, "I shall show you to your quarters, modest though they may be." He then took my hand. "Come, my love, I would like to show you my ship."

Allynon took Valdir to his modest, but comfortable sleeping quarters and then took the time to show me his ship from bow to stern and everything below deck. The belly of the ship held the crew's quarters, the galley, and storerooms filled with casks of food and other provisions, all neatly stockpiled and smelling pleasantly of aged wood and exotic spices.

"Ready we are for a hasty departure, should need arise in hostile ports," Allynon explained.

"And Maldimire?"

"Worse I have encountered, though Maldimire, it can be a dangerous place for foreigners, but far more dangerous it is for those who reside here—or those wishing to escape, eh?"

Allynon escorted me lastly to the armory. "One last thing to you I give," he said, opening a cabinet that held a bright array of weaponry. He retrieved a sheathed dagger attached to a leather strap. Allynon unsheathed the dagger, revealing a sharp blade and hilt that was encrusted with the insignia of Endara. "Take it, and if need arises, use it!"

Apprehensively I took the dagger from his hands. "Let us hope there will never be such a need."

Up on deck, the bulwarks smelled of varnish and reflected the late afternoon sun, and above my head, a web of ropes crisscrossed the *Windsong* from one end to the other. It was obvious the crew had kept things in top-notch condition during Allynon's absence, either from habit or sheer boredom. I could not help but be impressed with how orderly everything was.

"You will use my quarters," Allynon said, pushing open a door in the ship's stern, off the deck. Inside was a cabin with rich, comfortable furnishings, including a bed, table, chairs, settee, and armoire.

"But..."

"Only the best for you," he said, placing his finger to my lips. "And I shall sleep on deck, as often I do when the stars are bright and the seas calm."

"Very well," I relented. "I know I will be most comfortable."

"Come, we are readying to leave, and you must see Maldimire from the water." Allynon guided me back onto the deck.

Everyone went about busily to prepare the vessel for departure, but I could tell by their sidelong glances they were quite curious as to what I was doing there. At last, Pindarus stepped up tentatively to Allynon.

"Sir, the lady, will she be joining us on our voyage?"

Allynon looked at me sadly. "We will see Arwyn safely to Galymara, and from there we will take our leave of her and continue our voyage to the west," he said at last, "though there will come a time when we will return to these shores so the lady and I may be wed."

"Wed, you say?" Pindarus smiled with delight. "His Highness is to be married? Bless my soul, never did I think I would live to see the day!" Several crewmembers milling about close by began to murmur excitedly among themselves at the news.

"Please," Allynon said in a hushed tone, "Too grieved I am at our parting for celebration. It weighs heavily on me, and I wish to spend this last day together with few distractions."

"As you wish," Pindarus said. "The questions, I will keep

them at bay for as long as you like."

I stared numbly up the ship's tallest mast. As long as we had been on the road together, the fact Allynon and I would be parted always seemed an event that would occur in the future. Now that we were on board his ship, the full weight of the impending separation came crashing down upon me. In the bright light of late afternoon, I squinted and lowered my eyes to hide the tears welling there.

The missing crewmen, who had been found at a local tavern, returned to the ship along with Inago. Last-minute provisions for the journey were hastily purchased in the nearby marketplace, and at last the swarthy-looking crew hoisted the ship's sails, which immediately ballooned in the stiff breeze, ahead of schedule—and not a moment too soon.

Down on the docks below a commotion arose. Several soldiers in gray came thundering on horseback onto the quay, guarding a black carriage that rode in their midst. My heart skipped a beat as the carriage came to a halt in front of the *Windsong*. I knew the dark figure sitting inside must be Draigon. Immediately I felt my legs grow weak, as the entourage watched the *Windsong* with malevolence in their eyes as it slipped away from the dock and into the waters of the bay. Valdir, who stood next to us, turned abruptly and left at the sight, the blood drained from his face.

One rider in particular caught my eye, and the sight of him made my blood cold—Halthrax, Draigon's chief lieutenant, the same greasy-haired minion who had been witness to my arrest and incarceration months before. I knew from the look in his dark eyes he recognized me. Indeed, he was looking for me. I had not been forgotten. Nay, they remembered me all too well.

How easy it would have been in that moment to reach for the bow hanging constantly from my back and to fling an arrow at his heart, but I thought better of it. I did not wish to be single-handedly responsible for inciting a war between Bensor and Endara. Besides, I could not bring myself to kill in cold blood, even one so loathsome.

For a moment, I could feel my heart pound inside my chest, until I reminded myself it was for this reason I had come to Maldimire.

Our plan had worked. With Allynon's arms wrapped around me as we stood on deck, watching Maldimire melt away in the distance, there would be no doubt in the minds of my enemies I had left Bensor for the life of an Endaran princess, and oh, how appealing that option suddenly seemed.

And I knew there was still time to change my mind.

CHAPTER 24

"With every mile that brings us closer to Galymara, I am consumed with greater uncertainty."

"You are unsure whether or not you have made the right choice to stay behind," Dr. Susan commented.

"Deep in my heart I know 'tis the right path, yet at the moment I do not desire to do what is right. Only by sheer will do I remain...but I curse this day should I never lay eyes on my love again."

Had our departure been delayed longer, I could only imagine our fate. As it was, I stood my ground on deck, determined not to be swayed by the intimidating gaze of Draigon and his minions. Allynon was at my side, I was aboard his ship, and I was safe—for the moment. And with summer only a few weeks away, it would not be long until the rebellion, when Draigon would be ousted for good.

We watched as the city of Maldimire slipped away. How majestic it looked from the water, soaring as it did to staggering heights on the cliffs above. Even the Palace of Lords appeared deceptively grand and regal—but I knew the ugly truths it hid inside those decaying, whitewashed walls.

After a few moments, we all descended the staircase to the quarterdeck where we found Valdir sitting on a bulwark. He was trembling and his head drooped to his chest.

"Lord Valdir," Allynon said, placing a hand on his arm. "Are you not well?"

"It seems the ghosts of my past have returned to haunt me," he replied with some effort, "and I cannot say I am not deserving of it. Please," he said, glancing at me, "take me far from these shores that I may at last find peace."

Allynon's brow creased. I knew he sensed conflict within Valdir—and knew it had something to do with me—yet he had not breached the topic with me, nor had I pursued it.

However, I knew it must have been difficult for him to receive a half-hearted blessing of our union from one he looked to as a father. The thought gave me no comfort, making me wonder if I could truly trust Valdir to see Allynon safely back into my arms.

"Master Pindarus," Allynon called to his first mate, who stood at the helm, "head for the Straits of Eragoon."

"But what of Galymara? What of Endegar?" he asked.

"If by chance we are being watched, followed even, we must appear to be heading due west, where easy it is to lose any pursuers, yes? From there, we change course for Galymara. But take care to stay far north of Tarsham."

"Yes, the accursed place we should avoid at all costs," Valdir added.

"Yes, Your Highness!" Pindarus replied.

I was about to ask about this place called Tarsham and why it was to be avoided when the ship hit open water and began to roll and pitch in such a way I had to grab onto the bulwark to catch my balance. But something else happened, something that had not happened to me since my very first night in Bensor.

I felt sick. Not just sick—violently ill. So suddenly it came on, all I could do was lean over the side of the ship in time to expel the contents of my stomach. Still, no relief came. The sight of the churning water below only made me feel worse.

"Arwyn, you are not well, no?" Allynon asked with concern, placing his arm around me.

"Not at all." My apparent elvish nature had made me so unacquainted with sickness or physical discomfort for so long that this sensation came as quite a surprise.

"The swells, they are difficult for one who is not accustomed to them," he said. "Perhaps it would be good for you to lie down."

I nodded, desperate to put myself on any steady surface. Allynon held onto me securely as a swell hit the front of the ship, causing it to lurch upward unexpectedly. My head spun, and I wondered how I would survive the next day with my dignity intact.

In Allynon's cabin, I fell onto the bed, but little relief did it provide. He opened the portholes for fresh air, and such did help, yet every time I lifted my head I at once felt ill.

There on Allynon's bed I remained, unable to move, unable to eat, unable to do anything but wish for the entire sickening, dizzying experience to end. Nowhere in my bag was there a remedy for such seasickness.

Remaining flat on my back helped, but still I could not rest. Inago and even Valdir came and went from time to time, delivering water and cool cloths for Allynon to apply to my forehead, but no food could I endure. As I watched Valdir come and go, I recalled only days before when he had given Eliendor a look seeming to say he would do whatever it took to keep me from sailing to Endara for good. Was this sickness merely coincidence? Or had the two somehow conjured this affliction? Nay, I thought, it made no sense for them to inflict such misery upon me, unless Valdir truly meant to sabotage my marriage to Allynon. But such did not explain why Eliendor would go to such lengths to keep me from my life with Allynon just to aid the Alliance?

But would I ever be able to journey to Endara as Allynon's princess? Or would my traitorous stomach keep me on solid Bensorian soil forever?

Allynon remained in the chair next to the bed, the waning light filtering through the portholes revealed the creases of concern on his brow.

"This is not how I wished to spend my last day with you," I muttered.

"It cannot be helped, my love," he replied. "Is there anything I can do to increase your comfort?"

I closed my eyes and shook my head, wishing he had the power to keep his bedchamber from rocking back and forth.

In the following hours, I fell into a fitful sleep until I woke sometime after midnight, thankful beyond measure the rocking had stopped. I stole out of bed and, through the darkness, made my way onto the main deck where I discovered we had anchored in the bay of some island, its outline dark against the backdrop of a star-filled sky, each one reflecting off the glassy water in the cove. I wished to share that moment—one of our last together—with Allynon.

I sighed when I found him crumpled up on the grate above the cargo hatch, fast asleep. He appeared very uncomfortable, and I doubted he ever *really* slept there by choice. I smiled to myself, grateful he cared so much for my honor. What had I done to deserve the love of such a good man?

And then the thought came to me—*perhaps I didn't deserve it.* Quickly I brushed the notion out of my mind.

It was not long until I retreated back into his cabin, where I fell into a deep sleep troubled with images of the dreaded moment the following day when the *Windsong* would sail into the west—without me.

It was midmorning of the next day when I awoke to find Allynon once more sitting in the chair beside the bed, staring at me serenely. "How long have you been watching me?"

"*Studying,* to be more precise—the curve of your chin, the way your dark hair contrasts with your fair, porcelain face, and now, the way your eyes shimmer like jewels when you look at me—so that in my darkest moments without you, their memory will bring me light."

Allynon shifted over to the bedside to wipe a tear from my cheek.

"The drawing I made of you, the ring you gave me—they will remain close to my heart, until the day we are together again," he said, pulling a chain out from under his tunic from which dangled my amethyst ring. "Gazing at them, it is not the same as gazing into your emerald eyes or holding you in my arms, yet precious they are to me."

"And when I feel your jewel around my neck, I will feel your love from afar," I said, fingering the aquamarine stone that fell just below the base of my neck. "It will give me strength…" My voice trembled as Allynon wrapped his arms around me, holding me tightly, silently, for several moments.

The familiar doubt plaguing me in recent days crept back into consciousness, making me wonder if I should simply suffer through the months of seasickness to sail west with Allynon and be done with it. But could I really endure months of being with Valdir in such close quarters?

Though I was loathe to admit it, I wondered if our farewell would be forever. And for what, *really*? Was I fooling myself with some grandiose sense of self-worth, believing I could actually make a difference to that land? Yet the thought of leaving Bensor tormented me. Nay, desire the easier path though I might, I would remain true to my word and stay where I could perhaps be of some use to a troubled land.

The sea was calmer throughout the remainder of our voyage. Though I still felt ill, I choked down a few bites of bread and managed to go on deck when we neared the coast in the late afternoon. After a while, the village of Galymara came into view, appearing to tumble down the side of the cliff into the sea. Much smaller than Maldimire, it was still a substantial fishing village, though according to Galamir, not crawling with the enemy.

As we sailed into port, it relieved me to see on the jetty Galamir and Endegar sitting on Calyxa and Willomane, along with Avencloe, his white hide and golden mane shining in the late afternoon sunlight. The waters at last grew calm and my queasiness disappeared, though I still wondered if Valdir had played any role in my ailment.

The crew hailed Endegar heartily as Pindarus eased the vessel up to the dock. There was a flurry of activity as they lowered the gangplank, and Endegar came aboard amidst raucous greetings and pats on the back.

"Ever since that night in Loth Gerodin when I asked you to be my wife, I have dreaded this moment," Allynon said, putting his arms around me. I could hear the emotion in his voice, even over the noise.

"Would that it did not have to be this way," I said mournfully.

"Do not torment yourself. Look instead to what lies ahead. This is surely not the end for us." Allynon sighed. Pulling me closer he kissed my forehead.

The time had come for me to let him go.

"Come," Allynon said as he took me by the hand and led me to the gangplank where Inago and Endegar stood quietly.

"Master Endegar, it is a relief to see you and Galamir, and I thank you for safely escorting him and my dear Avencloe here," I said. "I've a feeling you are much less a rogue than you are a loyal friend."

"*Someone* must keep these scoundrels out of trouble." Endegar removed his feathered hat and bowed low. "My lady, it has been an honor to travel with you."

"And with you," I replied. Next I turned to Inago, whose smiling eyes twinkled in the fading light. "Master Inago, behind your daunting facade lies the heart of a true prince."

"The lady, she be kind," he replied. "Now, don't you be a-worryin' yourself about His Highness. Even if Endegar and I must row d'entire distance ourselves, we'll see dat His Highness returns safely to you."

I could not help but smile as I embraced the two. How fond of them I had become. "I shall miss you both and the way you always seem to wriggle out of any sticky situation." I laughed through my tears. "I am indebted to you for all you have done."

For the first time, Endegar's face flushed crimson. Even Inago's dark skin appeared tinged by a hint of red.

I hesitated upon seeing Valdir standing there, waiting to speak to me. What would he possibly say? What would I?

To my great surprise, he took my hands in his and stood there for a long moment as if studying them. He then looked me squarely in the eyes for the first time since the evening before we left Isgilith. "May Omni go with you through the trials that lie ahead," he said to me in elvish. "May you find that which you have been searching for, the peace of at last becoming the person you are destined to be. You are strong, my dear Arwyn, stronger than you know. Take heart and look to what the future holds, which may be more than you ever dreamed."

My eyes filled with conflicted tears. For a moment I caught a glimpse of the greatness he could be—of the greatness he was—and it saddened me that for whatever reason he had thwarted his greatness in my eyes over those past weeks. My Gifts had betrayed him, but one so well-versed in the Gifts himself had easily hidden the rest. I wondered if I would ever be privy to the secrets plaguing him.

"Thank you, my lord," I managed to say. "May Omni go with you on your journey."

"We will only be gone a moment," Valdir added.

I realized that to an elf who had lived a thousand years already, a year *was* but the blink of an eye. However, to those who had not had the privilege of having lived so long and who waited under the shadow of doubt, a year could seem a thousand lifetimes.

Gently Allynon placed his hand on my back and walked with me down the gangplank to the cobblestone quay where Galamir waited. "In your care, I now place her," Allynon said to Galamir. "See her safely home."

"That I shall do," the elf replied solemnly. "I give you my word."

Allynon smiled as he clasped Galamir's hand, giving him a pat on the back in a genuine display of friendship.

"May the winds be with you on your voyage to Endara," Galamir said, "and may they return you safely to these shores."

Allynon's eyes brimmed with emotion as he turned to embrace me. After a long moment, he finally spoke. "Never have I told you, but from my father's palace in Endara, far in the eastern sky I can see Elwei ablaze in all her glory," he said, staring tenderly into my eyes. "Elwei, she will lead me back to Bensor, back to you."

I smiled and nodded even as tears flowed down my cheeks. "A celestial GPS of sorts."

Allynon cocked his head to the side. "Weirdfulness?"

"Yes," I said, laughing through my tears. I buried my head on his shoulder once more and for a long moment did not move.

"How can I say goodbye to you when I cannot even let you go?"

"By knowing my heart goes with you," I said, as I wept quietly onto his shoulder.

"Death alone would prevent my return to you, and such will not happen," Allynon said. "As long as there is breath left in me, I will spend it returning to you, for in your arms is my home."

For a long moment I gazed into his eyes one last time, memorizing their color, how they looked so lovingly at me, knowing the memory of them would be all I would have to cling to in the coming days. Not caring who watched from nearby, I succumbed to Allynon's fervent kiss for a long moment until he at last tore himself away.

"I *will* return for you!" he said. With that, he turned to the gangplank and ascended to the deck of the ship.

In that dizzying moment, I wished desperately to follow him on board, to abandon all sense of honor and duty to be with the man I loved forever. Yet also in that moment the gangplank was raised, and the dockhands had already begun to uncoil the huge ropes fettering the *Windsong* to the pilings at the edge of the water.

I stood there weeping and feeling quite alone until

suddenly I felt the comforting arm of Galamir around my shoulders. Together we watched in silence as the large vessel drifted out into the bay and unfurled its massive sails that immediately ballooned in the ocean breeze. Allynon stood on the ship's stern, unmoving as he stared out over the bulwark.

It was not until the *Windsong* hit open water that we mounted our horses, and although I was happy to be reunited with Avencloe, my relief at seeing him was tainted by a sudden emptiness. With Willomane tethered to Calyxa, we rode up the main avenue, where our view of the sea was blocked by a long row of buildings. At last we came out above the village at the top of the cliffs.

Far below, already heading out to sea, the *Windsong* seemed but a child's toy in the midst of the vast ocean. One lone figure we could see on the ship's stern. As the sky to the east turned to a deep shade of amethyst, he raised his arm in salute once more. I waved in response as a tear trickled down my cheek.

For a long while we watched in silence, until the sun hung low over the western horizon. A chain of volcanic islands loomed to the south and west like darks mounds against the amber sky, the same archipelago from which we had set sail early that morning. It was then the *Windsong* pitched toward them in a southwesterly direction.

As the ship was engulfed in the growing darkness upon the water, Galamir turned his horse away from the sun as it kissed the horizon. "Come, let's pay a visit to Frondamein's sister."

CHAPTER 25

"Sadness continues to roll over me like waves in the ocean, and I am helpless to stop it."

"I took the opportunity when Endegar and I arrived in town this afternoon to do a little business for the Alliance," Galamir explained as we made our way east of Galymara down a steep road to a cove beneath the cliffs.

"Oh?" I replied despondently, hardly caring at that moment about the Alliance.

"My sources tell me another of Draigon's mysterious fortresses has been built just to the west of here. Fortunate for us, his minions reportedly retreat there come nightfall."

Another fortress with sawing and hammering going on in secret behind high walls? What on earth were they plotting?

"Still, it will be all the better when we find shelter for the night," he added.

At the bottom of the cliff, a group of houses was nestled behind a stone wall and next to the shore. Just as Loralon told us, at the end of the row we found a doorway that led through the wall into a courtyard sitting in front of a white house at the base of the cliff. I wasn't exactly sure how sister Maerta would feel about hosting two unexpected guests, nor could I be entirely certain she still lived there, so long it had been since Frondamein visited his sister.

Galamir pulled a rope hanging next to the entrance, and we heard a bell ringing on the other side of the wall. In a moment, a young man with curly brown hair and overgrown stubble on his sun-tinted face entered the courtyard from the house and peered at us with wide eyes through the bars on the door.

"Fergil?" Galamir began.

"Aye, what is it ye want?"

"I am Galamir, and this is Arwyn. We were sent here by

Frondamein's wife, Loralon, who has sheltered Arwyn in her home these past years."

At the mention of Frondamein and Loralon, the man's eyes grew wide. "Maerta!" he yelled over his shoulder, gaze still upon us, yet a woman whose eyes closely resembled Frondamein's had already appeared at the door into the house.

"Ye know me brother and Loralon?" she said, rushing to the courtyard entrance. "To come all this way, the news canna be good..."

"You needn't worry," I replied with effort. "They are as well as can be expected, considering the difficult position in which Frondamein has found himself."

"Aye," Maerta replied knowingly.

I reached into my bag and retrieved the letter Loralon had told me to give them. "This is from Loralon," I said, handing the envelope through the bars on the door.

Maerta immediately tore it open and read the note inside. When she was done, her expression was still one of confusion. "Me brother 'as dealin's with elves?"

"Yes," I said, reaching over to pull up the hem of my skirt—and the embroidered sprig of lavender signifying Loralon's work. "I owe Loralon for my fine wardrobe."

Maerta's lips turned upward into a smile. "Come, come, ye're most welcome 'ere, ye are," she said, glancing around before opening the courtyard door.

"We will be gone by morning but would be most indebted to you for safe shelter this eve," Galamir explained. "I am afraid my friend has had a trying day and is in sore need of rest." We led the horses into a courtyard surrounded by the house on two sides and the cliff on the other. The branches of a sprawling tree growing at the courtyard's center shaded the entire area.

"Aye, we'll tell the wee ones to mind their manners," Fergil said.

As soon as he spoke, four young children, two girls and

two boys, ranging from about two to seven, poured out of the house into the courtyard, mouths agape as they stared at us.

"Lads and lasses, what ye're seein' are two elves in the flesh," their father explained.

"Elves!" chimed a chorus of excited voices.

"Aye, we've not seen yer kind since Beldorf's poor elvish wife fled for Loth Gerodin. Didna make it, though, rest her soul," Fergil said, ushering us into the small house. "Worked for the man, I did, until Draigon's men destroyed his fleet o' fishin' boats. After that, well, I kin 'ardly make ends meet, workin' on me own, what with six mouths to feed."

"Er, we have brought you a small token of gratitude from the market, though I'm afraid 'twas all that was left," Galamir said, opening a sack filled with clams and five fish.

"A fine gesture, indeed! Now throw it in the stew, woman, whilst I see to the hairses!" Fergil said, as he gave his wife a kiss on the cheek.

"Ye'd think I know what to do with clams and fish, married to a fisherman!" Maerta retorted with a playful jab to her husband's ribs.

Seeing the obvious affection Fergil and Maerta had for each other only made the throbbing in my heart ache all the more.

"Now come, sit, and tell me news o' Loralon and me brother."

We all crowded around a long table in the main room of their small house, all four children sitting very mannerly as I mustered the effort to answer all their many questions.

"They've a young son, Amerigo, who will turn three this autumn," I explained.

"A wee one!" Maerta said. "Ah, 'tis a pity we canna see 'im."

"Aye, but the winds, they are a-changin'," Fergil said with a glimmer in his eyes that made me wonder if he knew of the rebellion. "But, pray tell, where'd they get such a name as 'Amerigo'?"

"I believe he was named for an explorer," I answered, my mind drifting to that place I had come from, the memory of it now flashing before my eyes with greater regularity.

"'Tis odd, to be sure, but I like the sound of it," Maerta commented.

As kind as Maerta, Fergil and their children were, I was relieved when they finally showed us to our sleeping quarters. Galamir slept on a cot in the adjacent boathouse, but they gave me a sleeping mat on their rooftop terrace. Down below in the courtyard the horses rested under tree boughs that spread up and over the spot where I lay. Beyond the leafy branches I could see Elwei shining, and I wondered if, out at sea, Allynon were gazing upon her, also.

And though the tears I had fought hard to keep at bay all evening yearned to be released, I dared not weep for fear if even one fell, I would be helpless to hold back the torrent that would surely follow.

Three evenings later, I found myself once again overlooking the small valley beneath Arnuin's Hold. The sight of the ancient ruins and the village brought tears to my eyes, though not for reasons of nostalgia. For the first time, the sight of the fortress's crumbling walls brought me no comfort, the neat little cottages under its shadow, no sense of safety and security. A weight had been growing in my heart, a sense of foreboding—and it was only partly to do with Allynon's departure.

Galamir paused beside me, his brow furrowed with helpless apprehension as he glanced at me. After all, I had spoken little since we left the home of Maerta and Fergil. We had traveled along the back roads of Guilden to Baeren Ford, stopping the first night to sleep in an abandoned cottage along the way. Galamir built a fire from old furniture left in a state of disarray and tried to make the accommodations as comfortable as possible. Yet in my despondence, I could but stare into the flames, refusing all offers of food and drink.

On the second night we camped out in the woods, far from the road. I forced myself to be slightly more communicative, and Galamir managed to get me to eat a bite or two, yet sadness pervaded my entire world. I knew he cared about me greatly, yet how could I assure him I would be well when I was suddenly certain of nothing myself, wondering deep down if the cause we served would be for naught in the end, if Draigon had something up his sleeve that would doom us all. *Something* just did not feel right.

Following yet another day of vigilance, it was a relief to at last look upon the familiar village, if for no other reason than it signaled the end of our long journey. Did Galamir know as he sat there watching me stare at the valley that there was more than mere sadness in my eyes? In me was a feeling of dread, particularly as I stared at the Hold, its walls looming ominously against the northern horizon.

With a slight shift of my weight, I urged Avencloe on toward the small cottage at the edge of the village. Loralon practically tackled me in her relief when I walked through the front door, having convinced herself I had gone for good. Smiling numbly I accepted her embrace, though in my heart I felt no joy at our reunion. In fact, it was hard to feel anything at all.

Early the next morning, as the first light of dawn cast an eerie glow upon the mist rising from the lake, Galamir emerged from the woods to the southwest and onto the front lawn. Loralon had already risen and had taken Amerigo with her to milk the cow and gather eggs for breakfast. I kept watch from the window in the parlor until I saw my elvish friend walk across the lawn to the front door.

"Greetings, Arwyn," he said, as he stepped inside at my invitation. "How good it is to see you this morning."

"And good it is to see you," I answered. "Though I find this brief meeting bittersweet."

"Aye, I am afraid my travels will be dark indeed without your light to help guide me."

"Would that I could come with you," I said, dreading the thought of having to remain in Baeren Ford, feeling useless. "Can my bow not be of use to you?"

"Arwyn," Galamir spoke resolutely, "I made Allynon a solemn promise to keep you safe, although he did not ask me to do anything I would not have done otherwise. I would not wish…"

"You know I am not averse to battle," I interrupted. "Was this not the reason I remained behind in Bensor—to help with the Alliance and the rebellion? Besides"—I lowered my gaze to the floor—"being on the road again would keep my mind off my heartache."

"In due time, there will be a way for you to help. For now, you must remain here with Loralon and the child until I come for you."

"Loralon will never leave without Frondamein, and he is not expected until the new moon."

Galamir grew pensive. "That may be too late. The date for the rebellion has surely been set. You must convince Loralon that Frondamein would *want* her and Amerigo to come with you to safety."

"I shall try." It was useless to argue, and I was much too weary to do so.

Although I certainly wished to see to Loralon and Amerigo's safety, this was not exactly what I had in mind when I chose to stay behind to help in the fight against Draigon. I turned my face away as tears welled in my eyes.

"How is our friend, Eliendor?" I asked quickly, as I went about setting the table for the morning meal.

Galamir did not answer immediately. "He appeared rather…er, glum actually," the elf replied. "For as long as I have known him he has always been of a rather serious bent, yet his thoughts were weighed down with great care, more so than I have ever seen in him."

"It is the times in which we live," I replied sadly. "No one knows more about this land than he. It cannot be easy to see that which you love crumbling at your feet."

"Aye, I see it in his eyes, just as I see it in yours," Galamir said, as he moved to my side and touched my sleeve. "It is not the prince's departure alone that prompts your sadness."

"How well you know me," I whispered.

"You have at last allowed yourself to fall in love with a land and a people whom you fear will be lost. You have risked the love of your life to remain true to an even deeper love."

I placed the remaining dishes on the table and abandoned my task as tears flowed down my cheeks.

Galamir smiled gently and took my hands in his. "'Twas not your sense of duty prompting you to remain in Bensor but the guidance of your heart," he said as he looked deeply into my eyes.

"And all I love is fading beyond my grasp." My voice trailed off. "Will you not stay for breakfast?" I asked in an attempt to put off yet another inevitable goodbye.

"Nay, the road beckons," Galamir answered. "For too long I have neglected my duties at the Alliance, and now I must return and prepare for the battle ahead. But first, Allynon wanted you to have this." Galamir reached in the pocket of his tunic and withdrew Allynon's pouch full of gold coins.

"Thank you," I managed to say, truly grateful, knowing how my own stash of coins had been depleted in recent days. "My dear, dear Galamir, how difficult it was for me to see the prince sail away. Now I find the empty place in my heart grows ever greater as I face yet another loss," I said sorrowfully. "You remind me of someone I loved very dearly once long, long ago—someone I lost forever. I fear losing you as well."

In an unusual show of physical affection, Galamir took me in his arms in a warm embrace. "Do not fear, Arwyn," he said with all tenderness. "I am bound to you forever even though we must be parted for a time."

Yes, I had felt it, too—a bond with Galamir unlike any I had felt before. Not romantic, but much deeper than friendship, like we were cut from the same cloth.

"Look for me to come for you, Loralon, and Amerigo in several weeks ere the tempest, and take you all to safety. But do not be dismayed, my dear, brave Arwyn," Galamir added, with a gentle smile. "The path you seek will be revealed to you when the time is ripe."

"I can only hope what you say is true."

"Though we must first walk through a bit of shadow, there is always hope, so fear not. Until I return for you, whatever these days may bring, think upon your time in Isgilith and those who love you, and that will give you strength."

With one last warm embrace, the fair-haired elf turned abruptly and disappeared through the front door of the cottage. I followed him as far as the doorway, where I stood and watched as my friend walked to the place where Calyxa and Willomane waited. Adroitly he mounted and, turning one last time, raised his hand to me in salute. "Farewell, dear Arwyn, until our next meeting."

I walked out to the road, watching in silence as Galamir rode away with Willomane following close behind, before vanishing into the woods like phantoms in the creeping dawn. For a long while I stood staring in the direction of the forest.

With Galamir gone, what was there now to reassure me the events of the past months had not been merely a dream? Slowly, my hand traveled from the hard lump in my throat to the concealed necklace hanging from my neck, and for a moment I felt comforted.

Beyond my memories, however, there was little to give me comfort. The anguish of self-doubt gnawed away slowly at my soul, and I could sense Baeren Ford had changed in my absence. As I stood beside the fence separating the front yard from the road, I stared out over the village. It appeared no different than it had before I left, yet a kind of despair had settled into the quiet valley like a plague. It was nothing I could put my finger on, just a silent hopelessness in the eyes of those who passed by so early that morning. Up on the hill above town my eyes were drawn to the looming sight of Arnuin's Hold. Oppressive it seemed to me now, and as I stared, its gray walls towering above suffocated me with their crushing presence.

And then I thought of the prophecy foretold by the wizard, Amiel, surrounding the Hold:

"From the shadow of Arnuin's Hold,
Where river bends and reeds shine gold,
Elwei's heir shall wake the light
Of Veritana's stone so bright."

The notion that Bensor's true ruler—the only one who could wield the abandoned Veritana sword at Emraldein castle and live—would emerge from the shadow of the ancient ruins brought me no comfort. "Only a fairy tale," I whispered.

"Are ye alright, dear?" Loralon asked tentatively.

I had not heard her walk up from behind, so lost I was in my thoughts. I realized how my breathing had become staggered and my heartbeat had quickened. Tears formed in my eyes as I saw Loralon standing there, the sight of her safe, familiar face a beacon in the darkness.

"Come inside, won't ye now, and 'ave yerself a cup o' tea. Yer 'eart aches, as well it should, but it's nothin' a spot o' tea can't ease a bit."

I nodded gratefully and followed Loralon inside, though I was in no mood for conversation. Together we sat in silence, sipping tea beside the hearth as little Amerigo played at our feet.

Later that morning the two of us toiled together in the

parched garden. No rain had fallen in Baeren Ford since the day I had left for Isgilith, and the early summer's crop did not hold much promise. Everywhere in Guilden the story was the same—streams running low and gardens withering from the uncharacteristic heat and dry weather.

Loralon stopped pulling weeds momentarily to stretch her back, and, turned her gaze northward. "Arwyn, look!" she said, pointing to the northern horizon. "P'raps we'll soon see an end to the drought."

I stood and looked to the north. Black clouds billowed, a slow wave, engulfing the land. Sinister they appeared, not as the soft gray clouds that rolled in from the west, bringing with them showers to water the earth. Nay, these were not clouds bringing replenishing rains, but only despair. All across the village people stopped to stare at the wall of formidable darkness spreading from horizon to horizon, eventually blotting out the light of the sun. A huge bolt of lightning flashed across the sky like a giant whip, followed by an agonized crack of thunder, as if the heavens had cried out in pain.

"Those are no rainclouds," I muttered under my breath. "Come, grab Amerigo and let us take shelter."

Loralon grabbed Amerigo from the place where he played nearby in the dirt. The little boy had already begun to whimper as the sky rumbled overhead. Everywhere in the village people stopped what they were doing to tremble under the encroaching shadow. After a while the streets were deserted and silence descended upon Baeren Ford.

Loralon and I sat nervously with Amerigo in the parlor, wondering what evil would befall us from above. I wanted desperately to visit Eliendor that afternoon and tell him all about my visit with the elves of Loth Gerodin, yet the climate was much too foul to dare leave the safety and security of the cottage.

That night I tossed and turned in my bed, haunted by dreams of a white leopard and a black panther standing atop a high mountain shrouded in a blanket of clouds. The two beasts circled each other with bared teeth, snarling menacingly for what seemed like ages. Suddenly the black panther struck the leopard with its razor-sharp claws, drawing blood that oozed red down its snow-white mane. The leopard cowered for a moment in pain and then with a low growl that turned into a wail, it sprung upon the panther, engaging it in a deadly dance of piercing fangs and claws ripping flesh.

I woke with a start, breathing heavily while staring into the darkness. Outside a bolt of lightning flashed, answered by the boom of thunder, yet still no rain pattered down upon the roof. It was a long while before I returned to sleep.

The next morning proved no better than the day before. The sky still glared the color of a festering bruise, and the thunder and lightning were incessant, yet no rain fell upon the land. Slowly the villagers emerged from their homes. The business of the day could wait no longer, yet it was with haste they darted from one building to another, not wanting to be out in the sinister, stagnant air for any length of time.

Despite the ominous clouds overhead, I determined to visit Eliendor that day. Yet as I saddled Avencloe for the trip into the woods, I was surprised to turn and see the old man standing in the open door of the stable. I caught my breath for a moment as I regarded him, for I could see the lore master's old donkey standing outside laden with what appeared to be traveling bags, pots and pans, and some blankets.

"Eliendor, I was just..." I began.

"Thought I would save you the trouble," the old man said as if he had read my thoughts. "'Tis not safe to venture far from home at such a time."

"Indeed, it seems my lot to remain in this village," I replied bitterly.

"I know you question your decision to remain in Bensor,

yet it was the most sensible thing to do."

"Was it?"

Eliendor's eyes softened and he touched my arm gently with an old, withered hand. "There is no sense in traipsing off to lands unknown at such a time and, although I do not doubt the prince's heart, if he loves you as he professes, then you can take comfort in the hope he will return for you someday. 'Twill be a test of love and patience for the both of you, to be sure."

The more rational side of me knew a test of our love was not without wisdom, but at that moment his words stung. "And yet it appears you are off to lands unknown," I said flippantly.

"Aye," he answered. "The storm has come and I must go."

What! Eliendor was leaving me, too? I had commented in jest, but it seemed he was serious!

"But where?" I stammered.

"I've some, er, business to tend to."

"But I've so much to tell you," I protested. "There is so much for us to discuss."

"Arwyn," Eliendor said, suddenly looking old and tired. "My work here is done. Time waits for no man, and my business is urgent."

"Yet," I began, suddenly feeling quite desperate. "I need you here. There is so much I still need to know, so many questions I still need answered."

"Did I not tell you once your questions would be answered in time?"

A single tear streamed down my face, and I said nothing.

"I do not know how the will of Omni will be played out in this land, but I do know the time for you to find the answers for yourself, as it should be, is almost upon you."

"Again, you speak in riddles," I groaned.

"It is only your fear concealing what you know in your heart. Omni alone can erase the fear inside, and in that you can take courage."

"This parting is all so sudden," I said, as tears flowed freely down my cheeks. "When shall I see you again?"

"That is not for me to foretell." Eliendor took one step forward and placed his hand gently on my arm. He looked deeply into my eyes as he had done so many times in the past, and it seemed a twinkle flashed beneath the shadow of his bushy eyebrows before he spoke again. "Do you remember all I told you about Dar Magreth?"

I nodded my head uneasily and shuddered at the mention of the name.

"She has sold herself to the Underlord and is altogether evil. Furthermore, her centuries-old vendetta against Elwei and all she held dear has been simmering for ages and has almost reached its boiling-point. Such knowledge may come in useful in the days ahead," Eliendor said gravely, and turned toward the door. "Yet do not be dismayed. You have learned well and, yes, you are up to the task before you."

"But what..." I began.

Eliendor put a finger to his lips. "Remember, your questions will be answered when the time is right."

"But...how shall I ever thank you for all you have done for me?" I said. "You have been my friend as well as my mentor these past three years, and I am indebted to you for helping me to find my purpose here."

The old lore master walked toward his waiting donkey. "Arwyn, you have yet to find your *true* purpose. But you *shall* find it, and when you accept it with your whole heart, that will be all the gratitude I require," he said as he mounted the beast.

A long and slender wooden box protruded from one of the traveling bags that hung from the donkey's back. It was the same mysterious box sitting in Eliendor's rafters for as long as I had known him. Never had he revealed its contents, and I supposed they would always remain a mystery.

"Farewell, Arwyn. May Omni guide you on the path that

lies ahead."

I stood at the door of the stable and stared, unbelieving, as the old donkey carried its master out to the road.

"Talthos, come!" Eliendor called. With a loud "caw" the black raven came streaking through the air to land on the old man's shoulder.

In shock I watched as the lore master lumbered up the road on the back of his donkey. He had given my life purpose in this alien land, and the prospect of never seeing him again made me feel empty and abandoned, as if my anchor of strength and wisdom had vanished, leaving me with nothing to keep me from drowning in the tempest. Where could Eliendor possibly be heading?

The mysterious lore master disappeared from sight up the road to the north. My eyes misted over, the pain of yet another parting too fresh and unexpected to completely accept. Wearily I closed the door to the barn and went about the task of removing Avencloe's saddle. I felt much too despondent to ride.

Numbly I opened the side door to the stable and led Avencloe to the pasture behind the house. I entered the cottage through the stable door. Loralon swept the parlor floor. She looked up and furrowed her brow immediately upon seeing my contorted expression.

"Don't tell me there's somethin' else awry!" she exclaimed as she dropped her broom to the floor. "What more could possibly befall us than this incessant thunder?"

I looked at her dully. "Eliendor is gone."

"Dead?" she cried with astonishment.

"No, he has left Baeren Ford."

"'Tis all so sudden-like," Loralon said, perplexed. "What could possess 'im to do such a thin'?"

I shrugged. "He is a man who does not readily share his business," I sighed, fighting the next wave of tears.

"Ah, ye poor dear. Already ye've suffered enough loss without another o' yer friends flyin' the coop," Loralon said as she walked over to embrace me. "Come now, ye'll always 'ave Frondamein and meself. O' that ye kin be sure."

I wanted to believe her yet could not help but think she spoke from naivete. The world was changing. It seemed nothing we clung to could ever remain the same. "Thank you," I said gently, grateful at least for the sentiment.

CHAPTER 26

"We have but one hope now, and that hope lies with the rebellion," I said gravely. "We shall all perish if it fails . . . may Omni help us!"

The dark days ticked by at a snail's pace, yet time did pass and eventually there were only two weeks left until Summer's Eve and the third anniversary of my arrival in Bensor. Yet to me there was little to celebrate. Gargalocs were commonplace, passing in and out of the village without even attempting to conceal their presence. Ever-present shadows covered the land, with only the faintest rays of sunlight penetrating through to at least give some semblance of daytime. The loud booming of thunder and flashes of lightning continued to rage, sending many in the village into fits of madness, yet not even a single drop of rain fell from the sky. People hurried from building to building, trying to carry on business as best they could while avoiding open spaces as much as possible. Gardens withered and streams ran dry.

The very clouds had formed a blanket above the earth, smothering everything beneath, choking life from the land and from its people. The village of Baeren Ford, like many places in Bensor, fell into a deep despair with no end to the darkness in sight. It was as if the darkness had been sent to break our will. And it was working.

I spoke little to anyone and found comfort in nothing. My supply of medicines had become all but depleted, and few people came in search of my services unless their maladies caused enough discomfort to warrant a trip to the edge of the village. Kiril rarely made an appearance, remaining close to the tavern, as Padimus had fallen mysteriously "ill" and needed the young man to take over.

Draigon's soldiers passed through regularly, but rarely

did they linger. Still, I kept mostly to the cottage, taking afternoon rides only to work Avencloe's muscles. Even our outings were melancholy. Riding across a gray, stagnant landscape held no joy. Quickly I would pass beneath the walls of Arnuin's Hold on my way to the high meadow. It loomed above me, suffocating me with its presence, and I felt a pain in my shoulders as if I carried an enormous weight every time I happened to glance at its walls, as they stood silent against the black sky.

Several days following Eliendor's departure, when I thought I would go mad if I had to sit and stare at the four walls of the cottage a moment longer, I grabbed a basket and walked up to the village, careful to keep to the back lanes on the way. I ducked into the butcher's shop for lack of anything better to do and had to wait for several minutes until Manyus the butcher appeared from the back room, bleary-eyed, with a strong smell of stout about him. With a grunt, he sold me a measly side of bacon and returned immediately to the back room.

Just as I put my hand on the door to leave, it swung open abruptly, and my blood turned cold when I found myself face-to-face with none other than Draigon's slimy-haired chief lieutenant, Halthrax—aside from Draigon himself, the most dangerous person I could have the misfortune of running into. Immediately he recognized me and shut the door behind him, trapping me inside the vestibule. My back was to the wall, and I felt my legs go weak as he regarded me like a cat regarding a cornered mouse.

"Your Endaran lover has cast you aside already, eh?" His gaze traveled to my bosom, and I felt his hand caress my sleeve. "Pity for one so beautiful to be thrown to the wolves—a mere plaything."

My blood turned to ice. Trapped between paralyzing horror and a strong desire to disfigure his leering gaze, I could but force myself to brush around him and through the front door—the only thing I could muster the wherewithal to do. I could feel his eyes upon me as I rushed down the road, fool that I was! How could I have disclosed my presence so readily? And for what—a stroll to the market? The entire ruse, my voyage to Galymara—had been for naught! My heart did not stop racing until well after I reached the cottage and bolted the door shut.

Every day following, at all hours of the day and night I could look out the front window and see one, sometimes two and even three gray-clad men pausing in front of Frondamein's home before continuing on. They never spoke to either Loralon or me, but I knew they could pounce at any time, now that it was common knowledge I had returned. The dagger Allynon had given me I kept strapped to my waist, and I looked for Galamir every day, certain the rebellion was close at hand. Still he did not come.

And still the gray-clad men did not pounce.

There was no solace to be found even in the midst of slumber, for my dreams continued to be plagued with the images of two great felines, one the color of midnight and the other of snow, circling about each other on a tall mountain, fangs flashing and claws bared. Their growling and teeth-gnashing caused me to wake with a start, only to hear the eerie sounds of wagon wheels creaking by on the road outside amidst the groaning thunder groaning above.

For several nights the sounds from the road continued, and it was rumored throughout the village—by some who had dared to peek outside in the middle of the night—that the creaking came from what appeared to be carriages, dozens of them, each covered with a large black canvas concealing what lay beneath. By morning, there was no sign of whatever had passed by the night before.

Like cornered hares, the villagers of Baeren Ford retreated deeply into their homes, silently awaiting the next evil to befall them. The streets were all but abandoned, even during the daytime, such as it was, except for a few brave souls who out of necessity had to step outside.

Only four days were left before First Summer, yet no celebrations were planned, nor were Loralon and I in any mood to commemorate the third anniversary of my arrival in Bensor. It was the end of the day, and we tried as best we could to carry on some semblance of normalcy amidst the gloom. Amerigo was in bed, as Loralon and I sat before the fire. Loralon occupied her hands with a pair of knitting needles and a ball of red yarn as I stared silently at the glowing embers.

"For the love o'...Blast! That's the fifth mistake I've made in as many minutes!" Loralon exclaimed as she threw her work onto the floor. "If this thunder doesna stop soon, I'll go mad!"

I was about to comment when a noise from the stable made us freeze. Avencloe whinnied loudly, and we heard the sound of the stable door slamming shut.

I rose to my feet and pulled Allynon's dagger from its sheath. "Go, get Amerigo. We shall climb through the window in your bedchamber," I whispered to Loralon as I ran to the door leading into the barn. Although it had remained locked of late, it could easily be kicked in if the desire were great enough.

Footsteps came from the other side. "Loralon, Arwyn, ye needn't be alarmed. 'Tis Frondamein."

Before I could stop her, Loralon ran to the door and unlatched the lock. The dark outline of a man appeared in the doorway. I continued to clutch the dagger until he stepped into the firelight where we could see it was indeed Frondamein.

"Frondamein, why, we weren't expectin' ye for another few days, at least!" Loralon reached to embrace her husband but stopped with a gasp, her eyes widening with horror.

It didn't take long to discover the reason. I saw in the firelight that his hands and tunic were covered with blood.

"Frondamein!"

"Not to fear, love," he said wearily. "'Tis not my blood."

"Then, whose..." Loralon's voice trailed off as Frondamein walked over to the settee and plopped down.

"Seems Festius relieved me o' me duties at the Gate." Though this should have come as happy news, Frondamein stared numbly at the wall.

"Relieved o' your duties?" Loralon said with disbelief. "Festius 'as finally seen fit to let ye off for good? Why, 'tis a miracle!" The excitement in her eyes soon disappeared as she saw the anguished look on her husband's face.

"I only wish 'twere so," he said solemnly. "Nay, I fear 'tis only an omen for ill."

I closed my eyes and felt the gathering storm closing in around me. "Draigon has no need for pretense now. He and the one he serves to the north have all but won."

"Beggin' yer pardon, Miss Arwyn," Frondamein interjected with a whisper, "but they've not won yet. E'en now, final preparations are bein' made for a rebellion two nights hence what shall take place all across the land."

Loralon's eyes grew wide at the news.

"Aye, for months now, there's been a secret alliance brewin' between men and, would ye believe, th' elves. They plan to take back our villages from the ruffians and overthrow Draigon once and for all," Frondamein whispered. "We'll muster at secret locations all about Bensor. Weapons 'ave been hidden. There's a plan what's been in the works to begin with the villages and then come together to march on Maldimire."

"And I suppose ye'll be right there in the thick of it," Loralon said as the elation of her husband's homecoming gave way to fear.

"Aye, I must."

"I won't let ye take part in such a thin'," Loralon exclaimed, as she stomped her foot. "'Tis much too dangerous! Why, ye're lucky to have left the Gate alive, as it is."

"Loralon, me darlin', this is our only 'ope for freedom from Draigon, and I canna sit back whilst others risk their lives for us all." Frondamein pulled his wife closer still and kissed her tenderly on the forehead. He grew silent, his hollow eyes staring blankly at the fire. "They took me sword," he said at last.

"What need does a farmer 'ave of a sword leastwise?" Loralon shrugged uncomfortably, trying to lighten the mood, but I could tell she was concerned with Frondamein's apprehension. I was, too.

"They took me sword, but they'd not found this..." Frondamein reached a hand down into his boot and withdrew a dagger caked with dried blood, which he held dispassionately in his hand.

"Frondamein...what on earth?" I said.

Frondamein lowered his eyes to the floor in shame. "On me way 'ome, I stopped at the river to give me hairse a drink when I came upon a Gargaloc a-sleepin' on the bank," he began, his voice shaking with emotion. "'E didna hear me approach, nor were there others about and...as I saw 'im lyin' there, I could feel a rage growin' in me heart...and so...I saw me chance to be rid of one, at least." He stopped speaking for a moment and gave a gasp as if choking for air. "I killed 'im! In cold blood, I killed 'im!" There was no sense of gloating in Frondamein's eyes—only a look of horror.

"And that's not the wairst of it," he continued with a gasp. "When I struck 'im, 'e looked at me afore 'e died. . . and in 'is eyes there was fear, and...oh, 'is eyes, 'ow they convicted me...guilty!" He sobbed. "Guilty I am, no better than the poor, wretched creature I killed in cold blood, pitiable pawn of far greater fiends than 'e. This blood on me hands, e'en though it be washed off, 'tis a stain I'll carry with me forever!"

Loralon and I looked at each other helplessly. Nothing we could say would take away Frondamein's anguish. No matter what one thought of Gargalocs, whether they were men or beasts, Frondamein had killed out of hatred and spite and would now be haunted by the memory for the rest of his life.

Tenderly Loralon sat down beside Frondamein on the settee and put her arms around him. "There, there, love, I still see naught but a good man when I look at ye."

"Would that I could as well, but when I look into me heart, I see nothin' but darkness."

"Then ye musn't look to it," Loralon said as she took his chin and guided his eyes to meet hers. "Look to yer wife instead, the one what loves ye."

Frondamein nodded slowly, his eyes still red with emotion. "Aye."

My own heart was heavy and full of emotion. Everything was unraveling, from the village, to the country, to the people I loved. And I felt absolutely helpless to do anything to stop it.

Another awful thought occurred to me. "Frondamein," I interrupted. I could understand the gravity of his personal crisis, and my heart ached for him, but there were other matters needing to be addressed.

"Aye."

"When did you say the rebellion is to take place?"

"Two days hence, on the Eve o' Summer."

"Galamir!" I exclaimed. "What has become of him? He promised to come for us before the rebellion and bring us to safety." Several weeks had passed since he left. I suddenly felt sick to my stomach.

"There still be time for 'im to show," Frondamein offered, but I knew better. Galamir would have come for us by now.

"I...I should go with you," I said quietly. "Perhaps my bow and arrow could be of some use."

"Perhaps yer arrows *will* come in 'andy, though ye'll need save 'em to protect me family, whom ye swore ye'd look after, did ye not?" Frondamein implored. "Nay, the battlefield's no place for a woman!"

My sense of duty getting the best of me, I bowed my head in submission. "I accept your decision, if only for the sake of protecting Loralon and Amerigo."

"Verra well, then," Frondamein said glumly. "Miss Arwyn, relieved I am ye've retairned safely from the northern forest. 'Tis not the time for a woman...nay, for anyone to be travelin' about, and I'm just as 'appy Loralon'll not suffer th' uncertainty o' the next few days alone."

"'Tis only by the goodness of 'er 'eart she's still with us," Loralon said, "and not off to Endara to wed a prince."

"Loralon, perhaps now is not the time..." I began.

Frondamein cocked his head at me curiously. "A prince, ye say?"

"Met 'im in the forest, she did," Loralon explained. She did not do well with strong emotion, and I was quite sure she was glad for the diversion from the heavy mood of the past minutes. "He's returned 'ome for a bit until 'is father the king dies. Then he'll retairn to Bensor to claim 'is bride."

Frondamein sighed. "'Tis not surprisin' ye'd be marryin' a prince. But why ye didna go with 'im while ye had the chance is somethin' I canna understand...though grateful I am ye're still 'ere," he said, shaking his head. "P'rhaps ye kin tell me o' yer adventures as we sup tomorrow night. As for now, all I desire is to crawl into bed with me wife by me side."

"I'll see to Haseloth," I said, in a hurry to be alone outside with my thoughts, and to conceal the sting of once again being reminded of what I had forsaken—all in the name of duty.

"And after that, I suggest ye get some rest. We'll all need it for the days ahead," Frondamein offered. He headed into his bedchamber, but suddenly he turned again to face us. His eyes were solemn and appeared those of an old man. "And not a waird to anyone o' the plan. These days ye canna know them ye can trust and them what means to stab ye in the back."

The next morning Frondamein disappeared before I woke up and was gone for the better part of the day. Loralon and I went about our chores as best we could, trying to preoccupy ourselves until Frondamein returned. Loralon's joy upon her husband's dismissal from the Gate was short-lived as the full weight of the situation began to sink in. I watched as she went about her duties with little enthusiasm, sweeping the same spot on the floor for a long while as she stared listlessly out the front window.

My own mood was grave as I thought upon those I loved—Frondamein, Loralon, Eliendor; all my friends in Baeren Ford, the dwarves, the elves of Isgilith . . . and dear Galamir. What in the world had become of him? What would become of us all?

And then I thought of Allynon. In vain I tried to picture his face in my mind, but all I saw was an image shrouded in shadows—such had been my thoughts of late. The pain in my shoulders I fought with warm compresses, yet it seemed to worsen daily despite efforts to keep it at bay.

My chores done, I had nothing better to do than to lie up in my loft, where I found myself staring out the window above the rooftops toward Arnuin's Hold. Ominous it looked against the dark sky, yet something about it held my gaze. For a moment my mind returned to that day, nearly two years before, when Eliendor bestowed upon me the Gifts of Old in the midst of the Circle of Omni within its walls. In that moment I had stepped into the presence of the divine—and came out forever changed.

I bolted upright in bed, knowing I *must* make my way there that morning. No matter how foreboding that bastion and its secrets seemed, within its walls resided solace, perhaps even the remedy to my malaise. It was worth the risk to make my way there.

"I shall return shortly," I quipped to Loralon, reaching for my cloak.

"But where...?" Hardly had she uttered the words from her sewing loom when I disappeared out to door to the privy behind the house, where I hoisted myself up the waist-high retaining wall at the base of the hill out back and then up and over the hill, keeping out of sight of the main road. After traversing the dried-up creek on the north side of the house, I quickly made my way to a small lane behind a row of cottages and eventually to the usually bustling village center, now oddly quiet. Pulling my cloak tightly about my head, I skirted across the road and up the grassy hill to the base of the Hold. With every step I took deeper into the ruins, I was aware my shoulders throbbed as if they bore a great burden.

At last, I stumbled through the high walls sheltering the ancient Circle of Omni and made my way to its edge, desperate for something, *anything* that would give me hope and comfort. I stared at the stone circle and ran my hand along the weathered runes etched in its surface: "*The thirsty shall be quenched, the hungry shall be nourished, the weary given rest.*" How odd I had never taken the time to read those words before.

Taking a deep breath, I stepped across the low stone into the center of the Circle, where I waited breathlessly, half expecting some great drama to unfold as it had that Summer's Eve nearly two years before. But without Eliendor there, I had no idea what to expect, if anything.

For several minutes I waited.

Nothing—just the maddening boom of thunder.

I collapsed in the middle of the Circle. After days of restraint, the floodgates opened and a deluge of tears washed over me, tears I had held back ever since that afternoon when Allynon's ship sailed into the west. With great, convulsive sobs my body shook, the sound of them drowned out only by the incessant rumbling overhead. Had I been a fool to let him go without me? I felt so alone without him, without Galamir, without Eliendor. For everyone else I had to be so strong, but in those three I found my strength—but they were all gone.

And I was afraid.

"Help me." My voice was little more than a whimper. "Please."

There were no mystical visions, no dramatic insights—only the sound of my weeping and the feel of the cold, hard stone I had slumped onto.

For a long while I lay there, grateful at least for the chance to release my pent-up emotion. The tears came to an end and there seemed an intermittent break in the rumbling as quiet descended for a fleeting moment. I lifted my head from its resting place on the Circle, and in my mind I glimpsed a memory. The window into my previous life had grown to the point it was like looking down a tunnel through the opening into the dwarves' cave. And through the opening I saw a scarred hand reaching out to me—a strong hand it was, and behind it emitted a brilliant white light.

"Remember!" Inago had insisted. Would that I could! How it frustrated me when only small pieces of the puzzle that was my previous existence filtered through to my conscious mind! And yet there was tremendous comfort in that simple vision.

They will mount on wings like eagles, they will run and not be weary, they will walk and not faint.

My shoulders still felt heavy, around me the storm still raged, but in that moment, my visit to the Circle was enough—enough to give me the strength to stand up, grit my teeth, and walk back down to the village to face the tempest.

Late that afternoon Frondamein returned from Ingmar's home, where an organizational meeting had been held in secret with a few key men in town whom Ingmar chose to lead in the rebellion.

"The rebellion 'as already begun," Frondamein announced with a whisper. "E'en now, rebels as far north as Mindlemir are on the march, buildin' in strength and numbers afore they arrive in Baeren Ford tomorrow night.

We'll be there to meet 'em, we will! By then we'll 'ave the numbers to attack and o'ertake th' enemy's fortress what lies just south. From there, we continue the march to Maldimire and in three days time, muster with forces from the east and west o' Guilden to storm the Palace o' Lords."

"Then go and be done with it!" Loralon exclaimed, stomping her foot, eyes burning with anger. "And I hope ye're the one to finish 'im off, what for all 'e's done to us these past years."

"I've no doubt there'll be many a victim of Draigon's who'd line up for the chance to bring about his demise," Frondamein replied with a shudder.

Throughout the evening, I noticed Frondamein holding tightly to Amerigo and appearing misty-eyed as he listened politely to the account of my time with the elves. Even news of Maerta and Fergil did little to lift his spirits. My own words rang hollow in my ears, as if they were but an exercise to pass the time while we awaited our fate.

"I'm sorry 'tis not under better circumstances we celebrate the end o' yer third year in Bensor, but glad I am ye come to us three years ago," Frondamein said as he raised a glass to his lips and drained the last sip of wine from the last bottle from the cupboard. "Ye've saved us from disaster on more than one occasion, and we'll fore'er be grateful to ye."

"Hear! Hear!" Loralon agreed as she raised her glass.

My own eyes misted over as I looked at Frondamein, not knowing if after that night we would ever share a meal together again, still not able to shake the sense something about the rebellion was not quite right, that whatever zeal we had leading up to it had been sucked as dry as the parched creek outside. "It is I who should be grateful. Not only did you take a stranger into your home when I was all alone in the world, but you gave me a family in the absence of my own. I love…I love each of you dearly…" My voice trailed off. So overcome with emotion was I, tears of sorrow streamed down my face and it was a moment before I could speak again. "If...if ever there was more I could do to make it up to you, I would, though I know not if I should dare to hope."

"I suppose there's always 'ope, if nothin' else," said Frondamein, but I could see even as he spoke he was trying desperately to conceal doubt, as if he felt it, too. "Now let us all get some rest, for we don't know the trials we shall face come the morrow."

The next morning dawned dark and silent, as if the sky itself was holding its breath. Even after many days of constant thunder, the silence brought no comfort, for with it came the scent of death. Not even the smallest hint of a breeze blew across the land. In the stagnant, suffocating air it seemed the very leaves hanging dully on the trees trembled at some impending doom. All around the cottage of Frondamein a hush fell, silent as the grave.

Besides the time it took to take care of the animals, Frondamein, Loralon, and I remained locked inside the small cottage. The hours ticked by slowly as we awaited the coming of the revolt that night. Frondamein held Amerigo in his arms the better part of the day, refusing to put the little boy down even as he managed to choke down a few bites of food.

The lad must have sensed something was very wrong. He took to bouts of crying as he clung to his father's chest. Loralon went about the house in a daze, tidying many times over spots she had cleaned earlier. I remained in my loft, coming down every now and then for a bite to eat and to look after Avencloe. I had not ridden for several days, nor did I have any desire to do so. All I wished was to retreat to my bed where I would sleep and stare for hours at the stone around my neck, until at last, fed up with the lack of any purposeful activity, I took it from around my neck to give it a good polish. Yet at that moment Loralon called me downstairs to help with dinner, and I left the precious jewel on my bed, with the intent to return to it after dinner.

As the last bit of gray slipped into the inky black of night, Frondamein gathered his family together in the parlor. With tears in his eyes he placed his hand onto my shoulder. "Such a thin' o' beauty should ne'er be subject to such sadness and despair," he said as he looked at me mournfully. "Take care of 'em. Take 'em to someplace safe should I...should I..." Frondamein became too choked up to continue.

Overcome with emotion, I put my arms around him for a fleeting moment. "May the grace of Omni go with you now," I whispered tearfully into his ear. "When all is done, look for us in the dwarves' cave in the wood. That is where we shall go if we must flee."

"Nay!" Loralon protested. "We shan't leave until we know yer fate and the fate o' the village!"

Frondamein looked his wife squarely in the eyes. "I go to await our reinforcements from the north and gather our weapons from the shoemaker's cellar where they've been hidden all this time. From there, I'll march on to Maldimire and 'elp take back the city. There'll be them what remain in Baeren Ford to keep it secure, for no doubt many from the rebellion'll sweep through on their way south, but such may drive the enemy south as well. If there be any sign o' trouble, ye *must* go to the cave. Promise me that!"

With eyes full of tears, Loralon nodded slowly. "Aye, but only if need be."

Frondamein's eyes softened with a look of remorse. "I canna take back what I did, but I can 'elp make it so me son'll ne'er be driven to such madness that would make 'im less a man, as now I am, a man forever stained with guilt." Frondamein stroked his son's cheek. "If I don't make it back...tell 'im I died tryin' to save 'is innocence."

Frondamein embraced his wife and son for several moments, tenderly kissing each before he turned to the front door. "See the door remains locked. There'll be many a rebel what'll pass this way—and p'rhaps some o' th' enemy attemptin' to escape the snare. Do not open it unless ye know 'tis me on th' other side." With that, he disappeared into the night.

I bolted the door behind him and went to place my arms around the weeping Loralon and her son, who had begun to cry with bewilderment the moment his father vanished through the front door. It was a long while before he calmed down, and even then he would have nothing to do with his crib, insistent on remaining in Loralon's arms as if he knew something dreadful was happening.

It was useless to even consider going to bed. Nervously Loralon sat in the rocking chair before the fire, holding tightly to Amerigo, as I peered from behind the drawn curtains at the road outside. For a long while all remained quiet except for some occasional dark figures running along the road, but otherwise the south side of the village was silent.

After a while, I heard the sound of shouting from across the lake, and I saw the glow of torchlight in the direction of the village. The light seemed to move slowly to the south. With it came the din of loud, angry voices, along with the sound of metal clanging against metal. It grew louder and louder. Had the fighting already started? The enemy forced south into the waiting trap?

I knew the battle would pass right by the cottage as they began the march to Maldimire, followed in waves by even more rebels coming down from the north, and I wondered if I should indeed take Loralon and Amerigo to the dwarves' cave with all haste.

An orange glow appeared over the tops of the buildings in the distance. It grew brighter by the minute, until I could see flames shooting into the sky. What could have been set alight to create such a blaze? Overhead thunder boomed so loudly it sent a tremor through the cottage. I winced and covered my ears, and Loralon let out a small, startled shriek, which set Amerigo to crying once more. I ran over and knelt beside Loralon to help calm him. For a long moment we huddled together before the fire in an effort to gain what little comfort we could in the midst of the deafening storm outside.

We raised our heads when someone pounded on the front door and a voice shouted outside. I ran and peered out the window and could see in a flash of lightning Frondamein had returned, less than two hours after he had left. Confused at how quickly he had returned, I ran and unlatched the door.

Frondamein burst through and slammed it shut, latching it securely behind him. Loralon bolted upright and both of us could see his face was white as a ghost.

"The entire rebellion..." he said breathlessly, "the Alliance...it has been for naught."

CHAPTER 27

"All is lost!" I moaned in despair as tears fell from my closed eyelids. "What a fool I was to think I could have played a hand in bringing about Draigon's downfall. Why did I not leave with Allynon when I had the chance? And here I am, all alone and lost in this world once more."

"You have the power to end this," Dr. Susan said. "All you have to do is say the word and I will bring you back into the present."

But something urged me to press forward. It was the same something that had always been inside me, urging me to continue, even when I couldn't see the way before me.

—————

"Like sheep among a pack of wolves we were, trapped in our own snare," Frondamein continued. "They were there, just a-waitin' for us, ready to pounce, and barely did I escape their clutches when we were ambushed. Omni has abandoned us for sairtain."

I could but stand there, numb, listening as the words fell like stones from Frondamein's lips. Both Loralon and I stared at him in disbelief as our last shred of hope vanished into the stifling air inside the cottage.

"What is more," Frondamein continued, "a rider from the north broke through the enemy's blockade on 'is way to warn us it's 'appenin' all about the land—the revolt's gone awry. E'en the secret 'eadquarters o' the Alliance 'as been raided and all the leaders arrested."

"Galamir!" I cried.

"Aye, I'm afraid ye shouldna hope for yer friend, nor any of us for that matter." Frondamein walked hastily to his bedchamber.

"But how?" Loralon demanded as she followed him through the door.

"Draigon no doubt got wind o' th' operation, though with

thin's as watertight as they've been, I don't see 'ow."
Frondamein knelt before an old trunk sitting at the end of his
bed and began to feverishly rummage through it, scattering
the contents about the room.

"What are ye doin'?" Loralon asked with alarm.

"The only thin' what kin be done," he said, as he pulled a
worn piece of parchment from the trunk and unrolled it on
the bed. On it was an old map of Bensor. "Our only 'ope is
to enlist th' aid o' King Hobarth o' Caldemia, though I fear
'twill come too late."

"And just 'ow do ye expect to do that, what with
Draigon's army all about and the borders bein' watched?
And why not go west to Endismere? 'Tis much closer,"
Loralon said, alarm growing in her voice.

"Aye, but the ferry across the River Iona 'as no doubt
been closed and what's more, e'en if I were to cross it, the
capital city lies still two hundred miles to the west.
Caldemia's capital city o' Lindenhall is but forty miles from
the border, and I remember well in the days o' me youth
King Hobarth was a friend to Bensor, afore Draigon came to
power." Frondamein held the map down on the bed with
both hands and examined it carefully. "The ferry south o'
Lake Gildaris 'as been closed, and I've no 'ope o' crossin'
the Silvendell at Stone Harbour. The only other bridge lies
east o' Maldimire on a desolate stretch o' the Emraldein
Road. 'Twill be a miracle to get past Maldimire, but 'tis the
only way."

"But that road goes straight to Carona!" Loralon cried, as
panic overtook her.

"Nay, close it goes, but see 'ow a road forks off to the
north through Fernwood," Frondamein said, as he traced the
route with his finger. "'Twill take me a week at the least to
make it to Caldemia, and who knows 'ow long to muster an
army, should the king be willin', but now 'tis our only hope."

"You must take Avencloe," I said decisively. "You shall
cut your time in half. He will be upon the enemy before they

are even aware of his coming." I had been standing in the doorway, staring quietly at the map as I listened to Frondamein. How could it have come to this? Even I held little hope such a desperate plan could work—or work in time.

"Aye, but the beast will carry none but you," said Frondamein.

"I will see he submits to you," I said. "He must."

"'Tis a longshot at the verra least. We kin only but pray for a miracle." With tears in his eyes Frondamein turned on his knees and grabbed his wife's hand. "Ye must leave quickly, and the three o' ye need to get yerselves to a safe place, away from the village. Miss Arwyn," Frondamein said, turning to me with terror in his eyes, "they were lookin' for ye—th' 'elven witch,' I heard 'em say—expected ye'd be leadin' the battle."

"Me?" I exclaimed with a shudder.

"'Twas Kiril who stepped forward…asked 'em if they'd let th' others go free if 'e told 'em yer whereabouts…"

Kiril, betray me? I felt like I'd been punched in the gut.

"Told 'em he'd seen you escape to th' east on foot, toward Farnmoor, disguised as a man."

Why, Kiril was buying us time to escape!

"Omni help 'im when they discover 'e lied!" Frondamein exclaimed. "But when they don't find ye there, they're sure to come a-lookin' 'ere."

As panic set it, Frondamein had one more warning: "And there's some sort o' devilry at work with th' enemy. They've brought in several dozen carts what they've fashioned into cages."

"What need 'ave they for cages?" Loralon asked with dread in her eyes.

"They're for the rebels, no doubt," Frondamein answered hesitantly. "And yet…there seemed to be women and children amongst those captured."

A chill traveled down my spine. "We shall flee to the

dwarves' cave and there wait out the storm until you return to Bensor with reinforcements," I said.

"Aye," said Frondamein. "Now go! Make haste afore th' enemy comes upon us!"

The cottage became a flurry of activity. I made certain to secure Allynon's dagger on my waist, glad to be wearing my most comfortable traveling clothes—my riding gown and leggings—if I was going to have to go and hide out in a cave for a while. Nervously, I saddled and harnessed Avencloe, all the while hearing a commotion up the road toward the Blue Willow that made my heart pound. Loralon rushed into the stable with a sack full of stale bread, some puny apples, and a flask of water I tied to the saddle as I had during my travels.

"You must fly tonight as never before," I said urgently, as I looked Avencloe in the eyes. "Pray carry Frondamein with you. It is our only hope—*you* are our only hope, and you *must* do this—while I remain behind."

Avencloe shook his head violently and neighed as if he had understood everything I had said. Anxiously he pawed at the ground, and I knew he was ready to be free of his confinement and out on the road, but there was still much to be done inside. As I ran into the cottage, I passed my bow and quiver of arrows hanging next to the door inside the barn and for a split-second thought to strap them on. Yet I knew they would be much too cumbersome inside the cottage. I could just as easily grab them on the way out.

I found Frondamein and Loralon hurrying about, gathering blankets and what little food could be easily taken by sack into the woods. A frightened Amerigo stood crying in the middle of the parlor as the adults in his life ran to and fro in an obvious state of turmoil.

I was about to help Loralon throw a few pots into a pillowcase when, to my horror, I realized the jewel Allynon had given me was missing from around my neck. In an instant I remembered having removed it earlier and placed it upon my bed. Immediately I climbed the ladder and felt at once relieved to see the aquamarine jewel lying on my quilt. Quickly I threw it around my neck, letting it fall under the neckline of my dress as I grabbed the handkerchief Rohana had given to me, and stuffed it into my corset.

There was a great commotion of shouting voices out on the lawn, followed by the sickening sound of someone trying to kick in the front door. We were too late! The enemy was upon us!

I gasped, blew out the candle next to my bed, and crouched in the darkness behind the chimney. I peered down into the parlor in time to see the front door splinter into the room. Loralon let out a shriek, holding tightly to Amerigo, as Frondamein stepped protectively in front of them both.

Several pairs of feet stomped into the parlor. "'Tis me ye want. Let the women and child go!" Frondamein pleaded.

I cringed as I listened from up above. They would know there was another, as if I wasn't already trapped like a mouse.

"Where's th' elven wench? We know she's 'ere!" I immediately recognized Halthrax's husky voice.

I could hear a shuffling noise, and Loralon screamed.

"Argh! This one packs a wallop in 'er foot! I'll wager she broke me kneecap!"

"Ne'er ye mind about her. It's th' elf the master wants!"

My heart pounded in my chest. I would be discovered soon enough. In desperation, I dove forward and grabbed the top of the ladder, pulling it with all my might.

"Grab that ladder!" yelled Halthrax, holding a struggling Frondamein with an arm wrapped around his neck. A burly Gargaloc lumbered up to the entrance to the loft and gave a mighty jump, barely missing the bottom of the ladder. A third soldier, who had been holding Loralon and Amerigo, came to his aid.

"You stupid beast!" Halthrax yelled at the Gargaloc. "Come, we shall smoke her out!"

I shuddered at the thought of being trapped as smoke and flames consumed the roof. Is this how I would die? Or should I give myself up?

Then, in a flash, I saw a vision. It was a memory of three years before when I stood in the loft for the very first time, watching as Frondamein pulled the trunk through to the hayloft on the other side of the small door. He had never sealed it!

In an instant I tugged at the bureau that concealed the hidden opening and pulled it to block the entrance to the loft. Easily, the door behind swung open, and I crawled through the small space, sending a pile of hay plummeting to the floor of the barn below.

I heard several thuds on the roof above me and a crackling sound as the tinderbox of dried river reeds on the roof began to burn—right next to the secret opening where I had stuffed Allynon's pouch full of gold—but there was no time to retrieve it. Down below, the animals moved about nervously. Desperately I climbed down the ladder and onto Avencloe's back. Voices came from inside. The door into the house swung open.

"*Atheron methuel! Atheron methuel!*" I yelled, using the Gifts. At those words every door and window in the barn flew open as if some great explosion had gone off inside. The animals were loosed, and all made a mass exodus through the open doors.

"There she is!" came a voice from the door. "Grab her!"

I slapped Avencloe's reins against him, and he bolted out the stable opening. Before I reached the front gate, I turned in horror to see one of Draigon's soldiers deliver a blow to the struggling Frondamein. Loralon wept and clutched a screaming Amerigo as a man in gray led her to a caged wagon. Frondamein's head pivoted in agony, yet with blurred eyes he looked in the direction of the road. Only a faint glimmer of light remained in them, yet when he saw me sitting there, I could tell he recognized me, and in his eyes a flame grew.

With whatever strength was left in him, Frondamein raised slightly to his feet and drew in a deep breath. "Ride!" he yelled. "Ride to Caldemia! Ride to your freedom!"

At that same instant I heard a din of voices, all yelling in my direction so loudly that Frondamein's voice became muffled in a sea of noise. All at once there were men upon me, attempting to subdue Avencloe and to claim me for their master. I pulled the dagger from underneath my belt and slashed an assailant in the face, sending him reeling, crying out in pain, and giving pause to the others.

With one last agonized glance at Frondamein, I pivoted Avencloe to the road. Past the front gate a small regiment blocked the way. In their midst stood a black carriage. The carriage door flew open and out came Draigon himself. He had been waiting for me.

I looked around frantically, yet even from the north his troops were closing in. I was trapped.

"Come now, Arwyn," he said cunningly, "you did not *really* think you could oust me, did you? Surely you have not become so enamored of this town's superstitions that you suffer from the delusion you are somehow more than a mere peasant."

My brow furrowed. I wondered what on earth he was babbling about, while at the same time my eyes searched for an escape route.

Draigon stepped down from his carriage and began to walk slowly toward me, his wooden leg causing him to limp slightly. "I know where you're going, and I know what awaits you there."

What! Was he mad?

"Believe me, you would be better off giving yourself up to me now than to foolishly travel down a road leading to certain death."

Avencloe shrank back as the man in the black cape approached. From behind I felt two hands wrap around my waist and attempt to pull me from my mount. I turned and saw it was Halthrax who groped me. With one blow, I stabbed behind his collarbone. Eyes bulging, like a stone he slumped to the ground with the dagger still protruding from the base of his neck.

Draigon shook with fury. "Trap her, you idiots! She must not get away!"

There was nothing left for me to do but flee.

"Hold tight!"

There were so many soldiers, I did not see how I could possibly get by. I leaned forward and closed my eyes as I whispered into Avencloe's ear. He reared beneath me, and I was certain the enemy would take the opportunity to overpower us both. I was completely unarmed, and I knew I would need a miracle.

I heard shouts of astonishment and tentatively opened my eyes to find myself staring down the open road. A rain of arrows whirred past and into the darkness beyond as Draigon's wild yelling faded away behind me. Turning to look back at Baeren Ford, I saw fires billowing from the rooftops in the village, silhouetting at least a half dozen riders in hot pursuit. It was only a matter of seconds until their yelling voices receded in the distance.

This was still no time to let down my guard. There remained many dangers ahead, and I could not tell how long Avencloe, with all his ethereal power, would hold out.

All along the way I passed homes, raided and burned and their inhabitants carted away unmercifully in the evil black cages. But why? Where could they possibly be going? That would be a question to ponder later. For the time being, I had to remain alert in order to dodge groups of Ashkars who went about their wicked task as I came upon them. I then darted away before they even had a chance to draw a weapon. There must have been hundreds, thousands perhaps: all working together like some well-refined machine of war. Whatever Draigon's plan, it was working.

Up ahead there were dozens of the caged wagons. I had come to the walled clearing I had passed weeks before on my way to Maldimire. Its purpose was now clear—to house the vehicles of the enemy until the time came to spring the trap. And all in conjunction with the rebellion.

At the entrance to the structure there was a bottleneck of wagons. Quickly Avencloe tore off along the edge of the wasteland. Like a ghost he moved through the stumps with ease, as men ran about with torches on the road above, their gruff voices barking orders.

A group of caged Bensorians approached from the south, no doubt the first of many, and a way had to be cleared for their trek to the north. Fortunately the soldiers were much too immersed in the task of dispersing the wagons to notice the silent fugitive dashing by them a short distance away.

Once I was certain we were well clear of the area, I urged Avencloe onto the road where he took off at a full gallop once more. For many miles the scene was much the same. Inhabitants of small hamlets, who had been sleeping peacefully, were suddenly and quite forcefully roused out of bed, most still in their nightclothes. Avencloe came down upon them and their captors, like a mighty wind out of the north, and passed away into the night.

For several hours I rode southward until I came to a wide-open field with a stream running through it. I pulled back on the reins, knowing the time was well past for Avencloe to have a rest, and yet the mysterious horse's breathing seemed not the least bit labored. I even felt of his neck, and it was not at all wet from perspiration. Surely he could not keep going at such a pace, and yet I desperately needed to get past Maldimire at the very least.

I urged Avencloe down an embankment to the water's edge where I dismounted and took a drink from my flask. The stream was running quite low, but at least the water was cold and wet. As Avencloe drank his fill, I sat upon a rock and splashed water onto my face. The events of the night seemed all too unreal, and I still could not quite believe what was happening. I realized my heart had not stopped pounding ever since the moment when Frondamein burst through the door to the cottage with news the Alliance had been compromised.

Could Draigon have somehow infiltrated the headquarters with a spy? Coerced someone within under threat of mutilation or death? *Or*—and the thought sent a tremor to my core—could someone within the Alliance have willingly betrayed it? I shook my head, unable to believe anyone working within that cavernous place could ever do something so despicable.

Barely had I paused to think when Avencloe lifted his head at the sound of wagon wheels upon the road. Cautiously I inched my way up the bank and peered out from behind a tall stand of grass. A large group of wagons was slowly heading north, far too many for me to simply slip by.

I slid back down the bank into the streambed and grabbed Avencloe's reins, leading him quickly under the shelter of the bridge. It seemed like an eternity before the wagons made their way to our hiding place. I listened to the echo of them creaking inches above my head, and the sound of weeping and moaning from the dazed Bensorians trapped inside made my stomach wrench. If any of the guards took a notion to come down to the stream for a drink, I would certainly be discovered.

And I had no means of defense. Allynon's dagger had been lost during the scuffle back in Baeren Ford, and I had been much too frantic to grab my bow and quiver on the way out. My gaze darted from one side of the bridge to the other as I crouched on Avencloe's back.

An angry shout came from inside one of the cages. As the wagon approached, the voices became clearer. "What is the meanin' o' this outrage!" a man yelled at his captors.

"Aye, what do ye mean, takin' us from our beds in the middle o' the night? We're not a one of us criminals, yet we're bein' treated as such!" said another.

A chorus of enraged voices rose from several of the wagons, and I could hear the captives shaking the bars of their cages in desperation, but to no avail.

"Quiet!" demanded one of the guards, and I winced at the crack of a whip and someone crying out in pain.

"Ye'll discover yer fate soon enough!" another guard jeered.

Mournful tears fell down my cheeks as I listened to the sound of people crying in bewilderment and misery as they rode by slowly in their prison cells. These were all common people, like me, who had been caught up in the whims of an evil tyrant. And for what purpose were they all being carted off to the north?

For a while longer I waited tensely as the procession passed. It seemed the last of the carts had crossed over. Then two guards halted on the bridge.

"Good slaves they'll make. Hearty ones there are in the bunch."

"Aye, but not for long, not after *she* gets ahold of 'em." One of the guards laughed.

"A year, I'll give the lot of 'em, in the mountains of Ashkaroth. Most won't survive the winter."

"She'll need longer than that to build 'er city, she will, and to tear down the wall. Why, 'twill take a century to do that!"

"Ah, but there's plenty more where these came from, and with the roads to Elwindor secure, them what live to th' east'll not get wind of it 'til we cart 'em off, too. Once Guilden's ours, 'twill be easy to expand Ashkaroth's borders, 'specially with the wall down."

"Aye, Arnuin's Wall indeed! I curse the name! Seems now it's no more than a garden fence, 'specially as we've 'ad 'elp on this side by the likes o' them renegades and their chief."

"Him what expects he'll rule by 'er side," the guard

laughed. "Nay, she'll share 'er throne with no one."

"She's been a patient one all these years, she has, waitin' for all the players to be put into place until the right time to pounce."

"Aye, and ruthless. Do ye see the looks in their eyes? Not a one of 'em saw it comin'. Like rabbits in a snare they are."

"And about to be skinned, boiled, and served up for dinner."

The two guards laughed so hard, I felt repulsed. So that was the self-styled queen of Ashkaroth, Dar Magreth's game? To empty Bensor of its people and make them slaves in her mountains, thereby expanding her own rule into Bensor and perhaps beyond?

I remembered how Eliendor had told me long ago the evil sorceress to the north wanted more than anything to destroy the land of Elwei and all Elwei had loved and nurtured. My heart sank as I remembered the ominous words spoken by the lore master as we stood in Arnuin's Hold that starry night so long ago and realized they had now come to pass.

"Me throat's parched. Now we've come to a decent stream, I'll 'ave meself a drink."

"Aye. We've at least two days afore we make the Gate, more if ye consider the hundreds o' carts in our way. Go and take a break—ye kin catch up in a bit."

My mind jolted back into the present. I listened intently to the rustling brush on the west side of the bridge. A dark figure appeared at the water's edge. He looked up in time to see Avencloe bolt from under the bridge to the east.

"One's got away!" I could hear him yell, as he darted up the embankment, an arm waving in our direction. Yet hardly did the other guard have time to respond. We were gone. Avencloe took off at breakneck speed to the south, refreshed from the short respite at the stream. It seemed, by his boundless energy, he had merely taken a trot down the lane since leaving Baeren Ford hours before.

The miles melted away as I raced to the south, though the

hours crept by at a snail's pace. The Baeren Ford Road had become the corridor between Maldimire and Ashkaroth, and I guessed a trail of tears stained its expanse from the sea all the way to the Guildenmoor Gate, where thousands would enter into bondage.

About an hour after the eerie gray light of the morning sun began to filter through the dark clouds, I approached the city on the sea. At least two miles north of Maldimire, I looked to the southern horizon and saw a red glow against the black sky. With a sense of dread I drew closer. At last only the wide plain lay between me and the city walls. I slowed Avencloe to a trot, aghast at the sight before me. With horror I gazed at the city on the hill, for the entire section east of the palace was alight with flames that leapt into the nightlike sky.

In my mind I saw the image of another city in another time, twin monoliths set ablaze like torches against a brilliant blue sky before crumbling to the ground. The sight before me was no less horrifying. Why would Draigon destroy that which was his own? If an easterly wind picked up, the cinders could consume the heart of the city, palace and all. As it was, a weak breeze blew in from the southwest. I hoped it would be enough to keep the flames contained.

I remembered walking the meandering streets of the city at the time of the census. The census, I thought humorlessly, as understanding began to creep into consciousness. For tax purposes, indeed! The only purpose the census served was to provide a way to seize slaves with precision. And to think we all played right into Draigon's hand!

Below me on the plain, hundreds of the caged wagons moved north in the darkness, like a herd of grazing cattle. With a shudder I realized I had been spotted by several soldiers who sat upon horses on the road before me as they surveyed the progress on the plain. They shouted, and with a cry I kicked Avencloe, easily breaking through the ranks, as startled soldiers scrambled to block my path and stop my progress with their deadly arrows. Avencloe and I tore across the plain until the city of Maldimire, and our pursuers faded away behind us.

Gasping for breath, I wondered how much more of this endless running I could take. One mistake and all could be lost.

In a matter of minutes we at last came upon the Emraldein Road. The territory was completely novel, and I found it quite unsettling to be traveling in unfamiliar territory on such an important task. I simply could not miss the bridge across the Silvendell. It was my only hope of getting across the great river too deep and wide to ford or jump. Surely it would be guarded closely, yet I hoped it would be the last major obstacle before the border of Caldemia.

For a long while I knew nothing more to do than to follow the road as it paralleled the river to my right, flowing in a steady northeastern direction. I kept my eye to the river, and on beyond I could see distant flames from small fishing villages that hugged the coast to the south. Along the way I passed pockets of the enemy, all slowly moving carts laden with moaning prisoners to the north.

Nearly three hours passed before I spotted the bridge over the Silvendell. The river cut through a narrow but deep gorge at that point, and the bridge lay high above the water. As I had guessed, a number of armed guards stood at both ends of the bridge, bathed in torchlight. Draigon had successfully cut off virtually all access to Elwindor, from the Andains all the way south along the line of the Silvendell to Maldimire. Would the people of Elwindor even know of the atrocity going on in their own country, until it was too late?

Not if I could help it!

With eyes aflame, like a demon from the underworld, Avencloe bore down upon the guards at the bridge, using the darkness of the enemy to appear ostensibly out of nowhere. Overtaken by complete surprise, the guards scattered before his thundering hooves for fear of being trampled. Before they even had the opportunity to give chase, the demon horse disappeared into the darkness.

A desolate land of windswept grass stretched out before me. I was utterly alone, and I knew it would be unlikely for me to meet anyone else along this barren stretch of road.

For the first time since my flight began almost twelve hours before, my heart stopped pounding, and I loosened my grip on the reins. My hands cramped. Though time was still of the essence, I slowed Avencloe's pace. I did not wish to press my luck with such a noble animal. Already he had far outrun what could be realistically expected from a mere horse, though a mere horse he was not. Despite the grueling pace he pressed onward—as if he had been born for this very moment.

Finding myself alone and out of immediate danger, the full weight of the day's revelations came crashing down upon me, and I began to sob inconsolably. I thought of my beloved country at last caught under the spell of the evil one to the north, and I grieved for its people and the beautiful land that would be decimated under her cruel hand. And all for a long-ago grudge with the elven maiden Elwei that had simmered through the ages.

But mostly I was haunted by the memory of Frondamein, Loralon, and Amerigo's faces the last time I laid eyes on them. So full of terror they had been. And now, I knew I would never see them again. What fate would befall them in the mountains of Ashkaroth, I dared not imagine. It was too awful.

And then I thought of Allynon. Why, oh why did I not go with him when I had the chance? In all likelihood I would never see him again. What a fool I was to think I could make a difference in this doomed land! Even if my quest succeeded and I made it before the king of Caldemia, my efforts would come too late to save anyone.

With a heavy heart I wept bitterly for a long while, for friends and loved ones who would be lost forever, for a dying land, and for the spirit within me that would never again be the same.

Somewhere in the gloom of the never-ending night, I was overcome with exhaustion. I knew I was still many miles from the road that veered north into Fernwood—and I trembled at the thought of missing it. Letting Avencloe slow to a walk and a nibble at the grass on the side of the road, I lay forward on his back, wrapping the reins firmly around my wrists.

And then I heard something akin to a lullaby inside my head. Was it a comforting tune bubbling up from my memory? Or was I under some spell? Whatever it was, I could not keep my eyes open a moment longer. As I lay there draped across Avencloe's back, my mind filled with images of the people I loved, and at some point I dreamt of men's voices yelling but, strangely, the sound came from far beneath me, as if my soul had left my body and now hovered somewhere between heaven and earth. And then I thought I heard Talthos cawing. And the image of two bushy eyebrows. What an odd thing!

CHAPTER 28

"I have seen this place before...I have visited it in my darkest dreams."

Something was different. No longer did I hear the sound of Avencloe's hooves thunderously thudding against the dusty road, only the sound of slow, echoing *clip-clops* on cobblestones. Dully, I opened my eyes. I had ventured into an alien landscape of twisting vines and gnarled, sprawling trees growing from the most unlikely of cracks and crevices, virtually swallowing a row of buildings that lined a silent road.

All at once, the events, which had begun a little before midnight the night before, came flooding back, and with them, overwhelming despair. I had become hopelessly lost on my quest to Caldemia.

Surrounding me was a deathly silent world enshrined in an ever-encroaching tomb of green foliage. Yet the very air hung tense and suffocating, as if the earth held its breath, waiting for some unknown fate to befall it. Not a leaf moved. I startled at a faint stirring in the shadows. A tiny lizard moved cautiously from under a pile of leaves and scurried across the road.

The silence was dreadful, even worse than the horrid thunder and lightning of the previous weeks. Yet at that moment, nothing seemed more dreadful than being all alone in such an accursed place.

I glanced behind me, down the road from whence I had apparently come to a bridge spanning a narrow river. Through a slight gap in the buildings I could see the water emptied into an unnaturally quiet sea. At the far side of the river was a once-grand, column-lined plaza, now covered with many years of decaying muck.

A tremor of fear shot through me. Though the wiser part

of me did not wish to linger in that place a moment longer, something akin to curiosity urged me onward. Slowly I nudged Avencloe to follow the curve of the road as it sloped gently upward, under archways and next to ancient walls covered in a proliferation of green.

We came to a trickle of water that surfaced from some underground spring. Avencloe stopped to lap what he could of the clear water, and I was suddenly aware of my own parched throat. With a cautious glance at my surroundings, I slid down to the ground where I cupped my hand and lapped the water. How cold it was—and surprisingly refreshing— but not enough for a horse.

As I drank enough to satisfy, I happened to look up and see a curious piece of rotting yellowish-orange fruit on the ground a few feet from the spring. Up above dangled more of the same fruit on the boughs of a sprawling tree. I led Avencloe to the tree and climbed atop his back where I could easily reach up and pluck the fruits from the branches. With my fingernails I ripped into meaty flesh. Then I bit into its satisfying sweetness, not caring as juice ran down my chin. Such a meal was far better than stale bread and the few small apples I carried in my sack, which I knew had to be saved for the remainder of the journey.

Ah, the journey, I thought miserably. Every moment I lingered meant it would be longer before I reached our help, yet the fruit trees, probably planted by someone ages ago, had provided a brief but unexpected pleasure. For a while longer I remained, eating the tropical sweetness until my hunger was satisfied.

I decided to pick a few more pieces for the road and then be on my way. I did not wish to rouse anything from the shadows here.

I could only guess I had come from the direction of the bridge, but otherwise I was hopelessly lost. The sea was to the south. I reasoned that if it remained generally to my left, I would eventually find the way back to the road leading into

Fernwood. Perhaps it was closer than I thought. Certainly Avencloe, with the uncanny way he always sensed danger and kept me from it, would not have taken me too far into places that should never be disturbed…certainly not.

I spied through another archway yet another trickling spring. This one emptied into an ornate basin. Cautiously I coaxed Avencloe up onto the landing and over to the fount where I dismounted once more and washed my sticky hands in the cool water. He took in several long draughts from the more substantial basin.

Fifty paces or so before me stood a huge iron gate inside a high, imposing wall. The gate was ajar. Though I could not yet see what lay beyond, my eyes were drawn above the wall to dark spires that pierced the blackened sky like spears. A stench of rotting carcasses so foul came from the gate I thought I would be ill.

Suddenly I remembered. This was the place I had seen in my vision long, long ago, standing in Arnuin's Hold, with Eliendor. It was the vision that had haunted me deep inside all this time.

And the bridge. It was not over a river at all. This was an island—the island—the most accursed place I could possibly imagine. The last place I ever wished to be!

My nightmares had become my reality. Terror gripped my heart as it had when first I saw the image of the dark tower in my mind.

My quest for nourishment forgotten, I frantically mounted Avencloe and urged him to make a dash for the bridge. He neighed wildly and struggled against me. Confounded by his sudden belligerence, in a panic I slapped the reins against his neck and tried with all my might to turn his head, all the while fearing what evil our commotion would awaken.

An unearthly cry arose. It drained the blood from my head. An unintended scream escaped my own lips, as at last Avencloe made a dash for the bridge. Yet in an instant a dark shadow was upon us. It screeched high overhead and followed us above the treetops. In terror I glanced through the limbs and barely made out the outline of a huge winged beast. It disappeared.

Up ahead lay the bridge. Somehow, if we could only reach the other side, Avencloe could speed us to safety. It was the only hope I had left.

How foolish I had been to believe, even for an instant, such a place was the mere product of myth and legend—that the beast guarding it was something out of a fairy tale! If my rational mind had ever doubted, I now knew all Frondamein had told me about the accursed castle was true.

I remembered Frondamein's account of men being ripped to shreds by the beast—back when he was forced to accompany Draigon on the ill-fated quest that left the dictator without a leg. What a pity for my life to end here, alone, in such a desolate place and in such a gruesome manner.

Frondamein had been in this place and lived to tell of it. If he could escape, I could not give up, desperate though I was. But there was little hope I would live to see another day.

I had almost reached the bridge. A ghastly stench fell upon us like a cloud, and I came face-to-face with something akin to a giant winged werewolf bearing a long tail that swept behind it like a whip. The great winged fiend swooped down and landed upon the road before us, dashing all hope of escape. It stood erect on two muscular rear legs the thickness of ceiling rafters. Its huge, arched feet ended in three ravaging claws that jabbed into the ground. Giant, bat-like wings spanned the width of the bridge, barring our only means of escape. The beast regarded us with gleaming red eyes, and sharp fangs dripped with the anticipation of fresh meat. Its long, razor-like claws could easily choke a horse the size of Avencloe.

Barely was I able to keep my seat as Avencloe reared in terror. We were trapped. I wildly pulled back on Avencloe's reins until he turned and bolted in the direction of the castle walls. There was nowhere to go, nowhere but straight through the iron gate.

But what then? If I could only make it to the castle, I could take cover there—that is, *if* I found a way in.

Desperately, I glanced behind me, but the beast was nowhere to be seen. Yet I could feel the stirring of putrid air above us. The thing was there, readying to pounce at any moment, and I doubted even Avencloe could outrun it.

"Run!" I shouted urgently as I lowered my head against an onslaught from above.

In a blur, Avencloe dashed through the castle gates and up a long, tree-lined avenue as my heart pounded in my ears. I could only see what lay straight ahead, an ominous fortress rising from the earth like a sarcophagus, a place where countless lives had met their fate over the course of its long, bloody history. It reeked of death and despair. If I went inside its walls, there would be little hope of ever coming out.

A great, long wail came from the sky as Avencloe approached the castle entrance. Effortlessly the great horse bounded up a staircase that led off to the right and then onto a landing. The beast descended with a shriek. Avencloe veered out of the way just in time. The winged creature reeled into a tower, sending a shower of brick and mortar onto the landing along with its grotesque body. For a moment it shook its head, clawing at an ear, giving Avencloe enough time to follow yet another set of stairs up to a circular landing that overlooked the front entrance of the castle.

Weakened not in the least, the beast shook itself and glared at us with its red eyes. In a bound, it alighted on the porch before us. Avencloe reared, neighing in terror, sending me toppling onto the stone landing. Stunned for a moment, I staggered to my feet. The beast came toward me. Behind me a semicircle of archways marked the entrance to a dark cavernous room.

I fled through the nearest archway, daring to look back, in time to see the red fire of rage glow in its eyes as it struggled in vain to fit through the narrow opening between the columns.

My beloved horse neighed once more. "Avencloe!" I screamed. There was no way to coax him into safety, for the beast stood between him and the entrance. In horror I watched. The red eyes fastened on Avencloe, who appeared no more than a foal next to the beast's hulking shape.

In the darkness and confusion, I tripped over something, and sprawled upon the floor with a cry. I landed on my side against cold, hard marble. With a groan, I looked toward the entrance. I saw neither the beast nor Avencloe. Somewhere in the distance I thought I heard the high-pitched sound of Avencloe's whinny, followed by the bone-chilling wail of the monster.

I held my breath, not knowing which way to turn, until something overhead caught my attention. I looked up. The ceiling was inlaid with once-beautiful stained glass, made opaque by ages of wind and rain. I could barely make out the hazy impression of a dark shadow passing above.

For a moment all was silent.

I rose to my feet and looked again at the columns and the outside. An indiscernible sound came from above. I raised my eyes to the ceiling of the great hall. Once more, through the grime, I thought I saw not one, but two shadowy figures pass overhead, one after the other.

Barely did I have time to consider this when a shower of broken glass shattered the tomblike silence. I shielded myself as best I could as the beast plunged through the glass ceiling, wings flapping violently, and landed on the floor.

With rage in its blood-filled eyes it regarded me, its cornered prey. Slowly, almost in a teasing manner, it lurched forward. I backed away, shaking uncontrollably. I could only imagine what would happen. Without warning, I fell against something in my path. It splintered under my weight with a *crack* that echoed throughout the room.

A white skull bumped down the step I had tripped over. Wildly I struggled to shove the skeleton I had broken aside, and found myself crawling up a staircase as the beast beat its wings, showering me with dust, glass, and the putrid smell of death. Its head drew back. Its breath was hot on my cheek, when in the darkened gloom my eyes detected a blade, burnished and sharp. I reached for it and held it aloft.

To my astonishment, for a split second the beast hesitated. Then with a roar that shook everything in the room, it rushed upon me with a fury that turned my blood cold.

The beast grabbed for me with its outstretched claws. I ducked and swung with all my might, a diagonal stroke across the beast's midsection. Blood spurted, splattering my gown. With a look akin to surprise, the beast teetered for a moment and then slumped to the ground. Its breath whispered across the stone.

Trembling from head to toe, I stood looking down upon my fallen foe, lifeless at my feet. Then, roaring into my consciousness, came awareness of the cold, hard steel I gripped in my hand. I raised the piece of forged metal. An unmistakable emerald encrusted the hilt.

That which had saved my life would inevitably end it, for none save the heir of Elwei could touch the Veritana Sword and live.

I let out a shriek and cast the sword aside, the echo of its fall reverberating throughout the castle as I dropped to the marble floor, waiting for the coldness of death to take me.

For a long moment I lay there, waiting, when the movement of a slight breeze stirred against my cheek. From somewhere up above, a ray of sunlight penetrated the dark clouds. It streamed through the hole in the ceiling to reveal a wondrous hall, adorned in green and gold. Like one waking from a night of restless sleep, I lifted my head and felt the light bathe me in warmth. How long had it been since I had seen the light of the sun?

I stared around me. I lay at the bottom of a short flight of stairs that led to an empty throne. Before me, only a few feet away, was the sword. The Sword. The Veritana.

Slowly I pulled myself to the place where it lay. With shaking hand, I fearfully reached for its hilt. Suddenly it bounded into my grasp, as metal to a magnet. Laboring to breathe, I watched in wonder. Bright light emanated from within the emerald, brighter and brighter, until the hilt of the sword felt warm in my hand. Still death did not come.

I was Elwei's heir?

"How can this be? It…it just can't be!" Stunned, I could but gasp in amazement.

The echo of Eliendor's words resounded in my mind. *From the shadow of Arnuin's Hold.* Why, he had known it was I who would fulfill the prophecy all along—as I knew, deep in my heart, though I had wished it were not so.

Choked with emotion, I felt as though I would collapse. Yet now, of what consequence would it be? Would anyone ever know?

I grieved as the image of burning villages and people being forced into Draigon's loathsome cages came to mind. I thought of Frondamein, Loralon, Amerigo and all my other friends, carried off through the Guildenmoor Gate to a foreign land for a life of slavery.

Once more I looked at the yellow light burning within the green emerald encrusted in the Sword's hilt, and suddenly there grew inside me a mounting determination of purpose that obliterated all sense of despair.

I could feel Elwei's pleasure.

It was for this reason—despite the temptation and uncertainty that had plotted to lure me away—I had remained in Bensor. Valdir had conjured nothing aboard Allynon's ship to keep me here—it was my own body revolting against the transgression of abandoning the place where I truly belonged.

I *was* Elwei's heir!

"Nay," I said at last, "it is for this moment Eliendor has prepared me, for this moment I have been called, and I shall not turn away from it."

I knelt before the throne of Bensor, holding the Sword of Emraldein up before me. "Elwei, I do not yet know why you have chosen me for such a task, but I now ask for your spirit to flow through this sword into me—and for the light of Omni to guide my path—as I do now what must be done."

I opened my eyes. Before me the sharp blade of the Veritana gleamed in the light streaming down from above, and it filled me with awe. The hilt felt smooth and secure in my grasp. After all, it had been made for Elwei—and for her heir—me.

Suddenly the light dimmed. All I could see was a pair of flaming red eyes reflected in the blade and the sensation of hot breath upon my shoulder.

In an instant, I sprang to my feet and spun. With one decisive blow, the head of the revived beast tumbled to the floor. Barely had I time to move away before the beast's body collapsed where I had been standing. Breathlessly I watched as it twitched violently before at last growing still.

From close by came a loud neighing. I looked toward the grand opening to the throne room. Avencloe stood there, his golden mane shimmering against his snow-white hide. He bobbed his mighty head up and down and stamped the ground, excited, as if urging me to ride to my destiny.

I hailed him with sword lifted high. "Bensor cannot await its true ruler a moment longer!"

I paused to grab the head of the beast by a clump of long, mangy black hair. I ran to Avencloe and quickly emptied the sack of food and thrust the disembodied head inside.

Avencloe threw up his head at the smell of the beast's blood and began to back nervously. "Be still. I only ask you to carry this burden for a short while," I said. "It shall be a sign that the curse of Emraldein has indeed ended." With that, I tied the bulky sack to the rear of Avencloe's saddle.

I felt a flame flickering in my eyes and in my spirit as I mounted. "Fly now, Avencloe, as never you have before!"

***

"I am breathless as Avencloe takes off down the front steps of the castle and down the road beyond the front gate. In a matter of moments we pass over the bridge to the island and fly beyond the bounds of the ancient city, into the jungle. Destiny drives him . . . it drives us both."

Somewhere between the boundaries of this world and the other, I heard the sound of sniffling, close by. I waited for a moment, yet no words were forthcoming. My mind once again raced back, to a moment in which I felt a power growing inside me as never before.

"All thought of Caldemia is forgotten," I continued. "Nay, there is but one place I must go. And when I arrive . . . somehow I will find a way to save my people."

END OF BOOK TWO

Coming soon:

Book Three of THE SOULTREKKER CHRONICLES
The dramatic conclusion to *The Soultrekker Chronicles* unfolds as Arwyn confronts Draigon for a final showdown, only to discover there are even more sinister foes she must now face. Amidst rumors of a traitor, temptation that challenges her devotion to Allynon, and crumbling alliances with her closest confidants, Arwyn realizes her greatest enemy lies only a heartbeat away.

ABOUT THE AUTHOR

Photo credit: Sherri Hanley

Mary E. Calvert is a former psychotherapist whose thirteen years of practice at a psychiatric hospital for adolescents prepared her to weave psychological complexity into her characters. Currently a stay-at-home mom to three sons, her *other* creative endeavor involves scrapbooking her family's adventures, notably their sojourns in Atlanta, Denver, Italy and currently the Midwest.